IMMORTAL DARK

SHERMON KODI

To everyone wallowing in darkness
You are not alone

CHAPTER 1

THE JOB IS SIMPLE.

Enter the room unseen. Wait for Ajjan to distract the mark—a foreign dignitary from the south. Then acquire her handbag and deliver it to the other side of town.

No blood. No trace.

My employer was very specific about that last bit. It's common protocol in my line of work, along with an understanding that pay will be docked by half if I'm spotted. If there's blood, I might not get paid at all. My mark must never know I was here. Personally, I thought I'd outgrown grabbing purses in the night. But it's an easy job, and I can use the money.

The red night moon casts the world in crimson light as I pull myself onto the third-story balcony of a slummy brothel in the west end. The window is webbed with ice, obscuring my view inside—I can only make out pale blotches of yellow light. There doesn't seem to be any movement, but I can't be sure the room is empty. I just have to hope the Blackbones did their job and set everything up.

I give the windowpane a shove, but it doesn't budge. Damn. The thing hasn't been opened in months, and it's frozen shut. For a common thief, a frozen window stymies a job. But I'm no common thief.

I take out my trapper tone pipe, a metal cylinder with a single reed, tuned to one specific note. The reflective surface catches light from the lanterns below, illuminating my name inscribed along the side in big bold letters: *BEXIS*. It was a gift from my deadbeat father right before he abandoned me. It's the last thing I have from him, and if it weren't so damn useful, I'd have tossed it years ago.

I bring the pipe to my lips and blow. The note is inaudible, like a dog whistle, too high for the human ear to hear. But the vibration weaves through the air and seeps into my skin, where it sparks like flint on steel, and a sonorous ember catches deep in my chest. Resonance hums through my body. The ambient darkness around me shimmers with feathered lines of silver that only I can see.

A burst of power shudders through me, and I hold it within my realm of focus, like cupping a candle against a sea wind.

This is resonance trapping—the first step in performing harmonic magic. Mine is the harmony of shadow. Sparking the ember is the easy part. Trapping it is more difficult, but *holding* it once it's been trapped? Well, that's like riding an angry wolverine. If I'm not careful, I might lose control, and people could get hurt. It's been months since that's happened, but there's always a chance the resonance will lash out, sending me into an episode of uncontrollable power.

Resonance quivers through my veins. I reach my hand to the glass, willing the vibration into my fingertips, and the shadows obey. Tendrils of silver swirl across my wrist and through my palm. I touch the window-pane, and the shadows run through it, seeping like oil into the hinges.

The window squeals as ice crumbles around the edges.

I shift my awareness to the space above my head. Resonance purrs in my chest as I weave gossamer strands of silver around me like a cloak. This is my greatest trick. So long as I can hold the resonance and have enough ambient shadow to work with, I can conceal myself from prying eyes. But I can't maintain it for long; already, I can feel my energy beginning to drain as heaviness settles behind my eyes.

Best be quick now.

I heave the window open and squeeze inside.

Warmth greets me as I drop to the floor and close the window behind me. The room is quiet, but muffled voices bleed through the walls. The adjacent rooms are occupied. There's a door to my left. The only other entrance is the window I just came through. A large bed in the middle of the room is covered in red satin sheets and big fluffy pillows. An old armoire stands against the wall opposite the bed with a stack of linens piled inside. Oil lanterns on the walls cast the room in soft yellow light. It looks like any old room you'd find in a brothel on the west end. Clean, but not necessarily nice. The scent of myrrh on the pillows doesn't quite mask the musk that's seeped into the carpet.

Footsteps thump in the hall outside, drawing nearer.

I jump into the armoire, pulling the cabinet drawers nearly closed but leaving them open a hair as I crouch amid the stack of linens. I release my trap and the resonance fades, making me visible once again. Relief floods through me like cold water as the tension in my muscles bleeds away. From this position, peeking through the crack, I have a clear view of the bed and the entrance.

The bedroom doors swing open as the matron enters with a swish of her scarlet robes. She's young with an impish face and silver beads braided into her red hair. Her name escapes me, but I recognize her. The Blackbones don't own this brothel, but they employ people all over the city to arrange setups like this.

"Here we are, Madam Vogul." The matron sweeps her gaze to the window and purses her lips. "This room will be yours for the night."

An older woman—probably mid-thirties—pauses in the doorway. She's tall and wears a black brocade dress embroidered with purple flowers down the bodice. A black shawl covers her shoulders, and she has dark gloves that reach her elbows. Long black hair falls down her back.

Vogul frowns. "Is this it? I was expecting something a bit... fancier."

The matron bows her head. "The luxury suites are booked in advance."

"I *did* book in advance."

"Yes," the matron explains, her tone apologetic but firm. "But you didn't book a luxury suite. You booked this room."

"I see." Vogul crosses the room and places her bag at the foot of the bed. A spark of recognition runs through me. The bag looks exactly as described: black leather with red straps and gold buckles shaped like dragon heads.

Target acquired.

Vogul turns to the matron, hands on her hips. "Could you please bring me a candle?"

"Of course. Is there anything else I can get you? Wine? Or perhaps something stronger?"

"Wine would be lovely."

"I'll have something brought up with your escort." The matron smiles sweetly as she curtsies. "We hope you enjoy your stay."

Vogul watches the matron stroll down the hall, then turns her attention to the room. She has brooding eyes of deep emerald, and her wide cheekbones are sprinkled with gold glitter.

I almost feel bad for her. She's defenseless, and it takes discipline to keep still in my hiding place. No blood, no trace is a pain in the butt. This would be much easier if I could pop out and show her my knife—not to hurt her, of course, just to frighten her—then I could grab the bag and be out of here in ten seconds. Job finished. Instead, we have to do a whole dance in the shadows.

Someone knocks at the door, and Ajjan stands in the threshold wearing nothing but briefs.

I have to suppress a laugh. Oh, this is marvelous.

Ajjan is a member of the Blackbones, which makes him a work acquaintance, but he's around my age, and we've always been friendly. He'd mentioned that he would play an active role tonight, but this is more than I could have hoped for. His long black hair is tied in a ponytail. He carries a silver tray with two glasses, a lone black candle, and a decanter of wine. His abdomen and shoulders are covered with oil. The yellow lamplight caresses his lean body. A sense of glee flutters in my belly as a smile breaks on my lips. I'll have to remember to tell him he makes a good whore.

"Hello." Vogul wrings her hands. "Um. You can put the wine on the table if you like."

"Yes, Madam." Ajjan enters the room.

The dignitary settles on the bed and folds her hands in her lap. "So, what is your name then?"

Ajjan places the tray on the nightstand. "You may call me whatever you wish."

"Alright." She crosses her legs and squares her shoulders. "Have you lived here long?"

Ajjan pours a glass of wine. "In the Dancing Lilly?"

"In the city." She gestures to the window. "Coppejj is a fascinating place. Although, it's a little cold… and dark."

"Yes, that's Coppejj. Cold and dark." Ajjan hands her the glass. "You don't get used to it."

Vogul shrugs. "I'll be back in the sun before long."

"What brings you this far north?"

She swirls the wine and takes a sniff. "I came here to find resonance trappers. Coppejj is home to the last Aevem on the continent. I want to meet him."

I perk up at this. The Aevem is the only Khatori in the city—a traditionally trained trapper who's undergone years of strict education to refine his abilities. There might be others like me, self-trained amateurs who keep their abilities secret, but Khatori are rare. Why would this foreign dignitary be searching for trappers?

Ajjan nods, as if impressed. "You must be important."

"Depends who you ask." Vogul stands and places a hand on Ajjan's shoulder, something about her demeanor shifting. She seems less nervous, less uncertain of herself. "Have you ever met one?"

Ajjan snorts. "A Khatori?"

"Forget those stuffy wizards." She smirks. "How about an amateur trapper? Someone who appears normal but has a knack for the supernatural."

"Don't think so," Ajjan says.

I squirm in my hiding spot. This conversation has taken an unexpected turn. Of course, Ajjan knows what I am. But I'm grateful he's keeping it to himself. The less people know about me, the better.

"We'll see." She runs a hand down his abdomen. "I'm ready. Let's get on with it."

"Oh—" Ajjan laughs. "Right. Let me show you to the bathhouse. It's right down the hall—"

"No." She drains the glass of wine. "Get on the bed."

I purse my lips. This isn't working out quite how I'd hoped.

"Our baths are world-class," Ajjan insists. "The water is already hot—"

"Do you think I smell?" Vogul crosses her arms, sticking out her bottom lip. "Is that what you're saying, No-name?"

"No, I—" He catches himself. "Of course not."

"Good." She points to the bed.

The standard procedure is for the client to bathe before engaging in promiscuous activity. Ajjan needs to be firmer and say it's a policy, but instead, he's climbing on the bed.

I pinch the bridge of my nose. *Bleeding stars, this is a mess.*

Ajjan spares a furtive glance in my direction. Is that apprehension I see? Or perhaps embarrassment? Either way, he sprawls on the bed with his hands behind his head. "Is this alright?"

"Perfect." Vogul lets her dress fall to her feet. Underneath, she's wearing a diaphanous white shift. She kneels on the edge of the bed and holds the black candle to her bosom. "Would you like to know a secret?"

"I love secrets," Ajjan says.

She wrinkles her nose. "Once I've told you, you can't tell anyone else. Okay?"

"Of course. I'm no one, remember?"

Vogul leans close to him and drops her voice, so I have to strain to hear. "I'm on a special mission. And you can help me." She holds her palm above the candle. Faint red lines bloom to life between her fingers, and a yellow flame catches on the wick.

My jaw drops. *She's* a trapper! And a skilled one at that. She didn't need a tone pipe to spark resonance. This dignitary is much more dangerous than she first appeared. I lean forward, curiosity getting the better of me. She's not using shadows; instead, she's harmonizing with something in the room.

Ajjan stares at the candle, his eyes wide. "How did you—?"

"Shh..." Vogul tilts her face to the ceiling, and red lines form around her waist, a current of ruby threads that wriggle in the air like tentacles. "Can you sense it?" she asks. "Coming to life within you, turning in your blood?" The vibration crackles across Ajjan's skin, casting him in a net.

Dread coils in my gut. I can't help him without revealing my presence, and if I do that, I don't get paid. But Ajjan doesn't seem to be in pain, at least not yet. I have to hope she's just playing with him.

"Hezha's light." Ajjan stares at the ceiling and goes limp, his head falling flat on the pillow. "W-what are those things?"

"You see them." Vogul places the candle on the nightstand. "Good. Let them in. Don't try to keep them out." The candle flickers and goes out. Strands of smoke spiral into the air.

"P-please." Ajjan arches his back and lets out a strange wheeze. "Make them stop!"

I sit still, transfixed. Horrified. My heart batters against my sternum. There's no protocol for this.

Vogul places her palms on Ajjan's sternum and glares at the ceiling, her eyes searching, as if taking note of constellations that only she can see. "Ajjan, you little liar," she says, "you do know a trapper. Tell me about the young woman with dark hair and blue eyes. Where is she now?"

"Bexis!" Ajjan croaks. "Make them stop!"

I can't watch this. Like it or not, Ajjan is my friend, and I have to do something. I blow into my tone pipe. Resonance flares in my chest as I ensconce myself once more in shadow.

So much for no blood, no trace.

I throw open the armoire doors and hurl my knife through the air with resonance-enhanced precision.

Vogul reacts to the sound and ducks, causing my blade to miss its mark and glance her shoulder. A splash of blood hits the wall as she calls out in surprise. I press the attack, leaping across the room, then crashing my knee into her stomach while I unsheathe my last knife. Vogul lets out a whoosh of air and staggers backward.

I shove her against the wall and hold my knife to her throat.

"Don't move a muscle," I hiss.

"Bexis, I presume." Vogul recovers and grins. Her face is splattered with blood, and streaks of red run down her right arm, dripping onto the floor. The cut was deeper than I thought. "A Shadow Dancer. Don't see that every day."

I grit my teeth as my resonance kicks. I force it into submission.

"Oh, you're not good at this." Vogul licks her black lips. "Why don't you drop your trap before you lose control? Besides, I'd like to see who I'm talking to."

My resonance bucks again, and a cold sweat breaks out on the back of my neck. She's right, I realize with dismay. An episode is incoming.

"Come now," Vogul whispers, her emerald eyes blazing. "We don't need things to get ugly."

My mind spins as adrenaline courses through my veins. I need to drop my trap, but I can't. Not until I save Ajjan. He's still lying on the bed with red resonance wrapped around him. I put as much steel in my voice as I can. "Let him go. Right now!"

Vogul rolls her eyes. "Alright. Have it your way."

A low drone erupts with a flash of blinding red. Before I can react, the knife is wrenched from my hand, and a fist slams into my throat. I double over, wheezing. My legs are kicked out from under me. My back hits the floor and my lungs seize. Red streaks rush over my legs and arms like vines, binding me in place.

Crap. I had every advantage, and Vogul apprehended me like I was nothing. I struggle to rise, but it's no use. My cloak of shadows winks out, but my trap continues to burn like starfire.

"There you are." Vogul bends over me, her dark hair falling over her shoulders. "Release your trap, girl, before you hurt yourself."

"I can't!" I grit my teeth as pain radiates through my limbs. Panic seizes my throat. There's nothing I can do now but let the episode run its course.

Ajjan stirs on the bed and breaks into a coughing fit.

Vogul clicks her tongue. "I'll make this quick then. My name is Kandra Vogul, and you're going to remember this night for the rest of your life."

"What do you want?" I stammer.

Vogul touches my cheek. "It doesn't matter what I want. It only matters what He wants. And He wants you." She holds out her hand, and a fiery vortex swirls above her palm. "This is going to hurt."

"No!" I gasp. "Please—"

Vogul grasps my right forearm and directs the fire into my flesh.

Blinding pain rips through me. Lights flash in my vision. It feels like molten pliers are searing into me. I scream as the skin on my forearm blackens and a symbol emerges on my flesh: a crescent moon and a snake.

Vogul stares at my wrist with genuine surprise. "Entaru's sigil," she whispers. "I've finally found you."

My breathing runs ragged as I try to tear my wrist from her grip, but it's no use. "What did you do to me?"

"You are marked." She pats my cheek and stands. "I'll be seeing you again very soon." Red lines flicker across her skin, and her form dissolves into smoke. Her emerald eyes are the last to fade as she disappears.

I whimper and clutch my wrist as pain shoots up my arm. My resonance is leaking now, causing the floor around my knees to char and turn black.

"Bexis!" Ajjan kneels beside me. He places his hands on my back. "What's happening?"

"Don't touch me," I shout. "I'm having an episode!"

"What can I do?"

Before I can respond, raw vibrational energy surges through my veins. The storm breaks free. An explosion of power rushes through my head and emanates outward in a ring of destruction.

When I come to, I'm curled on the floor as shockwaves of pain radiate from my forearm. I cough and rise into a seated position, blinking rapidly. The room is full of dust and smoke. Alarmed shouts bleed through the adjacent rooms, and footsteps crash in the hall outside as people flood down the stairs, trying to escape.

"Ajjan?" I rasp.

The walls are scorched black, the floor cracked and broken. The bed has been thrown across the room, its sheets burned and smoldering.

A cold knot of dread twists in my stomach. I did this. This is my fault. I lost control.

"Ajjan!" My voice is hoarse. I ignore my screaming muscles and crawl on my hands and knees. Blood drips down my wrist, and I leave bloody handprints as I force myself forward.

Not again.

Please.

Not again.

I find him propped against the far wall, blood oozing from his lips.

"Ajjan!" I sit on my knees and cup his cheeks with my hands. "Don't be dead. Please, don't be dead."

He moans. "I'm not dead."

Relief rushes through me. "Oh, thank the Saints." I press my forehead into the wall as tears fill my eyes.

He's alive. I didn't kill him.

Ajjan laughs weakly. "Are you crying?"

"I'm not crying, asshole." My cheeks flush as I wipe my eyes.

"That's sweet. I didn't think you cared."

"I don't."

His arms are burned, but he's otherwise unscathed. "Next time we do this," he says with a cough, "I'll be the one hiding in the shadows with a knife and you can be the one covered in oil on the bed."

I snort. Some of the tension releases from my shoulders. "I thought you were a good whore."

"Of course I was good. I was *too* good."

"You're an idiot." I hold my breath as another wave of pain lances up my arm. I grimace as I peel back my sleeve. It's still there. A crescent moon and a snake branded onto my forearm.

Entaru's sigil.

"Bleeding stars." A shiver runs down my spine. "What did she do to me?"

"Hey, check it out." Ajjan holds up a bag with red leather straps and dragonhead buckles. "At least we got what we came for."

I frown. "She just left her bag?"

"Apparently, it wasn't that important to her." Ajjan shrugs. "Zhira will be pleased."

"Silver linings." It's hard to get excited about the bag, especially since I'm unlikely to be paid after this fiasco. I pull my sleeve over the mark. I'll have to sort that out later. "Let's get out of here."

"Wonderful idea." Ajjan pulls me to my feet. "Let me find my clothes first."

CHAPTER 2

YEARS AGO, THE DRIFTWOOD PALACE WAS ONE OF COPPEJJ'S MOST illustrious theaters. Playwrights and poets and the city's most distinguished musicians used to play here while old men in suits drank cocktails and smoked cigars with their wallets out for all to see. Now, the marquee is torn, and the stage room is boarded up. The walls don't retain much heat, but the building serves just fine as the Blackbones' headquarters.

Two hours after leaving the brothel, I enter Zhira's office on the second floor. Ajjan is already seated on a stool in the corner, wearing a cotton black cloak and gray trousers, his ponytail resting over his right shoulder. He gives me a reassuring smile, but his eyes are dark and hollow.

He doesn't look so good.

"Nice of you to join us." Zhira, the Blackbones' leader, sits in a plush leather chair with her fingers laced on her stomach and her steel-toed boots crossed on the desk. She's a thin woman, tall and wiry, with feathered black hair and a sharp angular face that has always reminded me of a raven. Her eyes are black and brimming with sharp cunning. She gestures to the empty chair across from her. "Have a seat, Bexis."

"I'm fine standing." I cross my arms. I've done lots of jobs for Zhira over the years. The familiarity might give some a false sense of security, but I'm no fool. Zhira is one of the most dangerous people in Coppejj—a cutthroat gangster with a seat on the City Council. Her position in the city government is a terrifying juxtaposition with her influence in the world of organized crime: If Zhira wants me dead, there won't be a safe place to sleep from the Slags to the Burrows.

Zhira sighs and removes her boots from the desk. She fixes me with that sharp black stare that turns men's insides to jelly. It takes everything I have not to look away. "The matron told me you made quite a mess. The job required discretion. What the stars happened?"

I purse my lips. I'm walking a fine line here. Zhira values strength; if I want to maintain my position in her confidence, I need to stand up for myself. But she also won't tolerate disrespect, so I choose my words carefully. "The dignitary, Kandra Vogul, is a resonance trapper. That would have been nice to know before we set up the grab."

Zhira frowns. It's the only indication that she's surprised by this revelation. She leans back in her chair. "Vogul is a trapper. Are you sure?"

"Yes." I keep my voice level. "She put Ajjan into a trance, made him give away my position, then disarmed me like I was nothing. She was like a lynx playing with her prey."

"It's true." Ajjan runs a gloved hand along his forehead. Somehow, he's even paler than before. "We never stood a chance."

"I'm aware of your stance, Ajjan," Zhira says. "Right now, I'm talking to Bexis. I'll deal with you later." Ajjan stares at his feet, chastened.

What's happening here? There's so much tension in the room I can taste it.

"Bexis." Zhira opens a drawer in her desk. She takes out a small notebook and writes a note with a quill pen. "Tell me more about Vogul. Do you think she's a Khatori?"

"I don't think so," I say. The Khatori are trappers with immense power and skill. For thousands of years, they have held positions of authority and leadership in the world, but their numbers have dwindled recently. There are three orders of Khatori trappers—Aevem, Yawji, and Olezhi—and each order specializes in a certain type of resonance, but none of them are known for reading minds.

"So, what then?" Zhira asks. "She's just a talented amateur, like yourself?"

"It's possible." Trapping is a diverse art, and resonance can manifest in thousands of different abilities. Where the powers of particular Khatori orders are predictable—all Aevem wield light, and all Olezhi are great fighters—the abilities of amateurs are more difficult to predict.

"That's not helpful." Zhira places the pen on the table.

"Who is she?" I ask, my curiosity getting the better of me. I'm not supposed to ask questions, but the new mark on my forearm makes this personal. The pain has receded to a dull ache, but it's still fresh on my mind. I need to discover what it means and why Vogul gave it to me, but I don't want Zhira to know about it, otherwise she'll find a way to leverage it against me.

Zhira purses her lips as if weighing how much she wants to tell me. "Ostensibly, Vogul is a foreign emissary from Shezhi. But my contacts there have never heard of her. It's as if she's popped out of the ground. She has the ear of the Magistrate and half of my colleagues on the City Council. I can't figure out how she's done that, but stars, if she's a trapper with some talent for mental persuasion, that could explain it. Is she as strong as Aevem Juzu?"

I shrug. Juzu Khinvo is the last Khatori in the country. He's an Aevem who has assumed an ornamental role in Coppejjian society, a celebrity of sorts, highly visible during public events. Everyone has seen him summon lightning and orbs of radiance that illuminate an entire city block. "I don't know," I say. "But she's strong. Ajjan and I are lucky to be alive."

"That does raise some interesting questions." Zhira scribbles more notes in her journal. "If Vogul disarmed you both so easily, then why *are* you alive?" She lifts the handbag and places it on the desk. "And why do you have this?"

Because she doesn't care about the handbag. She was there for me. My forearm still aches but I ignore it. "I had another episode," I admit. The words are bitter on my tongue. "She escaped before I destroyed the room."

Zhira sighs, disappointment written across her brow. "I had hoped you would have learned more control by now."

I bite my tongue, shame curling in my gut. Usually, young trappers progress as they age, but I've been stuck in the same place for years. If anything, holding the resonance has grown more difficult, and these episodes have made it impossible to practice or experiment. It's endlessly frustrating, but what can I do? I don't know what I'm doing, and I don't have anyone to teach me.

When I don't respond, Zhira clicks her tongue and leans forward. "Well, let's see what you two brought me." She unfastens the dragonhead buckles and turns the bag upside down on the desk, then organizes the items that spill out. Three human skulls in a small pile. A coin purse. Some kind of dagger in a leather sheath. She leans back in her chair and inhales deeply.

Ajjan stares at the skulls, his eyes wide, but he doesn't say anything. He doesn't have to. I share his sentiment. *What kind of person carries skulls in their handbag?*

Zhira picks up the dagger with both hands as if holding a precious gemstone. Her eyes light up and a smile plays on her lips. "I can't believe it. It's here."

I glance at Ajjan. He shrugs.

"This, my young friends," Zhira says as she unsheathes the dagger, "is nedozul glass." The hilt is black with a ruby pommel, but the blade is glowing jade. It gives off a garish green light. A sense of dread shudders through me as Zhira holds it up, her eyes deadly serious.

"Is it valuable?" I ask.

Zhira's eyes dance with mirth. "They say a cut from a nedozul dagger will imbibe the victim with visions of demons for the rest of their life." She slides the blade carefully into its sheath. "Just stories, of course, but yes. This will fetch a grand price on the black market. Enough to purchase a small city."

I don't mention that Vogul conveniently left the purse behind. It seems strange that Vogul would forget about something so valuable. But rich people rarely make sense. Who would pay so much for an antique dagger? It doesn't even look sharp. I cross my arms. "So you got your prize. That means I made good on my end of the bargain. Let's talk payment."

Zhira snorts. "No blood. No trace. Those were the rules. You were spotted, *and* you drew blood. You also destroyed half a brothel. That kind of negligence could be forgiven if you were a Blackbone. But you're not one of us. You're lucky I don't slap you with a bill."

Anger flares in my chest, but I keep it contained, my expression neutral. Zhira responds to boldness and confidence, so I need to make my case without appearing to grovel and without causing undue offense. "If you'd told me she was a resonance trapper, we would have done things differently."

Zhira opens her mouth, but I cut her off.

"It was an impossible job. Either you knew she was a trapper—and intended for me to die—or you didn't know and put my life in danger." I clear my throat, my heart racing. Here goes nothing. "So actually, I think you owe me double."

A thin smile curls on Zhira's lips. "Double?"

Ajjan stares at me, horrified. He silently mouths the words: *What are you doing?*

"Yes," I say, ignoring him. I'm committed now. "Or I'm taking my business elsewhere. There are other gangs in Coppejj. Other mob bosses that would literally *kill* to obtain my services." I hold my chin high. It's not an empty threat, and Zhira knows it.

"Ajjan," Zhira says. "Leave us."

Ajjan stands stiffly, smoothing the front of his cloak. He gives me a worried look as he leaves the room and closes the door behind him. Ajjan is a Blackbone, so he has no choice but to do as he's told, while I have more freedom. One benefit of being freelance is that I have the right to barter and test the market.

Silence settles in the office. Zhira drums her fingers on the desk, weighing her words. "How long have we known each other, Bexis?"

"Five years?"

"When my boys brought you to me, you were a scrawny little thing. Skin and bones and beaten to a pulp. You'd been stealing from the Blackbones' coffers. Do you remember?"

Of course I remember. That had been a few months after my father left. I was twelve years old and had just started using my talents to survive on the streets. A black market vendor had offered me a small fortune for a series of jobs stealing jewels from the safe hidden under the Driftwood Palace. Everything seemed to be going well for my first few runs, but then I got cocky. My resonance crapped out, and I found myself in a room full of thugs who jumped me and beat me to within an inch of my life. They proffered me to Zhira, begging for permission to execute me.

"You were a viper," Zhira says. "You made my boys look like fools. For months, they thought they were dealing with a master thief, when you were only a little girl. They wanted me to cut off your hands and hang you by your feet until you bled out. But you weren't afraid. Do you remember what you said to me?"

I frown. The memory of that day is branded into my mind. "I told you to let me work for you."

"That's right." Zhira places her palms on the desk. "I spared your life and let you pay off your debt, and then I gave you your freedom. Awful generous of me, wouldn't you say?"

"I guess."

"Now, after everything we've been through, you're going to throw it away—for what, a couple of silver pieces?"

I sit on the offered chair, using the momentary distraction to gather my thoughts. My response needs to project strength, but without being too confrontational. "It's not about silver pieces," I say. "It's about trust. You sent me into a lion's den with my head up my ass."

"You're a thief." Zhira shakes her head. "That's the cost of doing business. You have to expect the unexpected. It's not my fault you met your match. Maybe if you'd practiced your skills, made some progress with your trapping, this wouldn't have happened."

I ignore the jab. "I can't work with someone I don't trust."

Zhira laughs. "Name one person in this Saints-forsaken world that you trust unequivocally with your life."

I bite my tongue. Zhira is right. I have no one. Trust is for the weak—my father taught me that.

"That's what I thought," Zhira says. "You want someone to hold your hand and make sure the big bad world isn't going to hurt you? You want to be pampered like a baby?"

I clench my hands into fists. "No, that's not what I meant."

Zhira opens another drawer in her desk and takes out a thick piece of parchment. "You want to talk about trust? I got this from the Magistrate's office this morning, signed with his own seal. You might be interested in what it says."

I eye the paper, a tremor of apprehension twisting in my belly. "What is it?"

Zhira frowns. "Resonance trapping is hereby outlawed in the city of Coppejj—"

"What?" I say, unsure if Zhira is messing with me.

"—Anyone with knowledge of persons with trapping ability," Zhira continues, "is directed to report to the Magistrate's office. Anyone who harbors or aids such an individual or fails to abide by the law will be sentenced to *death*." She stares at me, gauging my reaction.

I try and fail to keep my expression stoic. This is a blatant reversal of Coppejjian tradition. Historically, resonance trapping has been celebrated. Even if people don't think they need Khatori, the notion that the Magistrate would outlaw the practice seems too absurd to be real. There are so few of us left. Aevem Juzu is the last Khatori in a thousand miles. There can't be more than a handful of amateurs roaming the streets—and we tend to be discreet. I've never even met an amateur trapper until Vogul. "Why would they do this?"

"It wasn't brought before the City Council, and if it was, I wouldn't have voted for it." Zhira sighs, laying the paper on the desk. "The Magistrate has leveraged his executive power to force it through. This was solely his decision."

"But what's the point?" I ask. "He wouldn't do this without a specific goal in mind."

"It's a purge and a power grab." Zhira steeples her hands on the desk. "I told you Vogul is in court. Well, the Magistrate hasn't been himself since she showed up. He keeps to himself, and he's become surly and distant. I think this ordinance is a desperate play to put Aevem Juzu behind bars."

I scoff. "They can't arrest Juzu."

"Oh?" Zhira raises an eyebrow. "That's exactly what they're trying to do. A warrant was issued late last night. Although apparently, he's disappeared. Vanished without a trace."

Bleeding stars. This makes no sense.

Zhira leans back in her chair. "It's a dangerous time for people like you, all alone in the world."

She has a point; maybe I should lay low for a while. Nobody knows where I live, and I don't have any friends or family in the city. Still, it's best to exercise caution.

"It's time for you to reconsider my offer."

My stomach churns. *Not this again.*

Zhira stands, smoothing the front of her tunic. She approaches the window behind the desk, her hands clasped behind her back. The red moon cuts through the sky like a scythe. "No sentinel would dare touch a Blackbone, trapper or not. Take the Bones and join us."

Zhira has been trying to recruit me for years, and I've always rebuffed her. Despite the many supposed benefits to joining the Blackbones, there are drawbacks too. For starters, I'd have to participate in the bone taking ceremony—a walkabout through the crypts below the city. If I pass the ceremony, I'd swear my loyalty to Zhira for the rest of my life. I wouldn't be able to leave Coppejj or barter for better pay. I'd be like Ajjan, chastened by a word and subject to Zhira's temper. I don't know what my future holds, but I'm too young to limit my options.

"I work alone. I always have, and I always will."

Zhira turns. "You said it yourself. You don't have one person in the whole world who's in your corner. That's no way to live. Take the Bones, and you'll have an army at your side. We are the world's largest syndicate. We have charters in six of the ten great cities. I have more money than entire nations." She spreads her hands. "You'd have our protection, and you could rise in the ranks to a position of leadership. I could use someone with your skillset and your gumption. In a few years, you could run this place."

"The Driftwood?" I wrinkle my nose. "It's a little dusty for my taste."

"Power. Prestige. Respect. You could help me run this city. With your talent and my backing, nothing would stand in your way. We could even get you a seat on the City Council."

I roll my eyes. "What makes you think I'd want that?"

"Alright, then what *do* you want?" Zhira runs her fingers through her raven hair. "What is your great vision for your future?"

The question takes me off guard. I've been surviving on the streets for five years, making ends meet, keeping myself fed with some coins in my pocket. I'm not a weak little girl anymore, and soon, I'll have enough experience to go my own way. If I can ever master my resonance, I'd make serious money on the black market. The demand for someone like me in full control of her powers will never go away. And with how rare trappers are these days, I can set my prices, take on high-profile jobs and travel anywhere in the world. But I'm not quite there yet.

"What I want," I say, "is none of your business."

Zhira wrinkles her nose. "Unless you want to be a Slag rat for the rest of your life, working crap jobs for pennies, you have to think about these things. If you take the Bones, you can have anything you want—Safety? Jewels? Fancy clothes?" She gives me a penetrating glare. "Family?"

I wince. One thing I learned when my father left me is that people let you down. If you want to survive, the only person you can depend on is yourself. You get what you can take. Anything else is weakness.

Zhira nods to the door. "You and Ajjan get along."

A horrible suspicion creeps into my mind. Did she tell Ajjan to befriend me to convince me to join? It's just like Zhira to leverage any connection I have to get me to do what she wants. I can't allow myself to be manipulated like that. She doesn't want me to take the Bones because she cares about me; she wants to use me.

"Enough of this." I rise to my feet, preparing to take my leave. "Are you going to pay me or not?"

Zhira holds up her palms. "I'm willing to be patient, but someday, my generosity will run out, and when that happens, you'll have to make a choice. Join us, or try your luck in the streets." She picks up a bag of coins and tosses it to me. "Double."

I catch it in midair, give it a shake, then stuff it in my pocket. Pride blooms in my chest. This worked out better than I could have hoped. The money will hold me over for a few weeks while I figure out my next play. "I'll keep that in mind."

Zhira collapses in her chair. "You understand that the rules have changed, right? The sentinels will be looking for you, and then there's Vogul. She's a threat."

"What's your point?"

"I have a bad feeling, Bexis. My instincts are screaming in my gut, telling me not to let you leave the Driftwood. Why don't you stay here tonight? Lay low for a while."

I narrow my eyes. Everything Zhira offers comes with strings attached. If I give her an inch, she'll take a mile. "No thanks. And don't have me followed."

"Fine." Zhira picks up the nedozul blade and stashes it in a drawer. "Go on then. Don't say I didn't warn you."

I hesitate at the door. I don't trust Zhira's intentions, but she's treated me fairly, and she did me a favor by telling me about the new ordinance. My situation is perilous—with the sentinels and Vogul... and I still don't know what the mark on my forearm means. "Thank you," I say. "I appreciate the offer, but I can take care of myself."

Zhira waves me off and turns her attention back to her journal, writing furiously with her quill pen. "I'll let you know if I have any more jobs for you."

I nod and take my leave. Despite my own assurances, a cold tremor cuts through my bones as I close the door behind me.

CHAPTER 3

IT STARTS TO SNOW AS I LEAVE THE DRIFTWOOD AND HEAD DOWN THE hill toward Oldtown. This vantage offers a unique view of the city: a sprawling mass of canals and steepled roofs, the cobbled streets illuminated with blue and yellow streetlights that wink through the morning fog. Soon, these quiet streets will be overrun with horse-drawn carriages, and the markets will be flooded with the tantalizing scent of freshly baked bread as a hundred thousand people start their day.

A salt breeze cuts through my cloak as the sun's light brightens the skyline above the Shadow Sea, making the clouds bloom like pink orchids. Coppejj sits on the northernmost coast of the northernmost country on the continent. It snows every day, all year long, and the sun never rises all the way. But in the mornings, we get these little dawns, where fingertips of sunshine bleed into the sky, teasing us with shadows of daylight for a few moments before fading back to darkness. Then the silver day moon will rise, standing vigil over the city until dusk, when the red night moon takes its place.

I stuff my hands in my pockets. Exhaustion creeps behind my eyes, but sleep won't be possible for a few hours, and I don't want to go home yet. The mark on my forearm is a dull ache that sets my teeth on edge.

Entaru's sigil.

I don't know what it means or what I'm going to do about it, but it doesn't seem to be an immediate threat, so it can wait. I can still make my meeting with Mo and the Rovers, but I don't want to show up empty-handed. I give my pocket a reassuring pat. The extra coin will buy plenty of cinnamon bread. The Rovers are going to be glad they waited.

I start down the walk when a voice calls out: "Bexis, wait up!" and Ajjan trots up to me, his breath pluming in the morning light. "Stars, you're faster than you look."

"Now's not the best time," I say. "I'm heading to the market—"

"That's fine. I'll walk with you."

I groan internally but don't protest.

Ajjan walks down the sidewalk beside me. He doesn't say anything at first, just takes a swig from a metal flask. He holds it out to me. I wave him away. Liquor destroyed my father from the inside out. Even the smell of the stuff makes my stomach churn.

"What do you want?" I ask.

He wipes his lips and stashes the flask in his black wool coat. "How do you do it?"

I cock my head. "Do what?"

"We almost died last night, and you're acting like it didn't affect you."

In truth, the encounter with Vogul has left me feeling deeply disturbed, but I'm not about to open up to Ajjan about my feelings. "It's not the first time," I say. "And it won't be the last."

"I wish I had your stomach." Ajjan presses his lips into a line. "Since the brothel, every time I close my eyes, I see these *things* looking back at me."

Anxiety bubbles through my belly. "What kind of *things*?"

"I don't know what they are." He stares at his boots, his voice growing soft. "When Vogul blew out that candle, it was like something came to life inside me. I saw creatures with fangs and red eyes moving around in my head. They kept saying the same thing over and over again."

I frown, remembering how I'd watched Vogul's resonance twist into his chest and invade his mind as she straddled him on the bed. "What did they say?"

He lifts his gaze to me, his hazel eyes lined with shadows of fear. "They said your name. They hunted through my mind for any trace of you. It's like she set hounds loose in my head, and there was nothing I could do about it."

A shiver runs down my spine. I've never heard of resonance being used like this. If I hadn't seen it with my own eyes, I wouldn't believe it was possible. Vogul is dangerous, and I suspect the only way I'll discover the meaning of this mark is to find out more about her. While I don't have any leads, there are ways to obtain information in the Slags. That's a problem for later though.

Ajjan takes out his flask again. This time, his hands tremble as he takes a drink.

He's afraid, I think. And why shouldn't he be? Still, it upsets me to see, and my instinct is to comfort. Ajjan isn't a trapper. He's a grunt in a glorified street gang that just came face-to-face with a demon he doesn't understand.

"Don't let her get to you," I say. "It was only a spell, an illusion meant to frighten you."

Ajjan glances at me. A dusting of fresh snow covers the top of his head. "You're saying it's not real? Are you sure?"

No. I'm not sure at all. Frankly, his story scares the crap out of me. But I can't say that. What Ajjan needs is reassurance, not panic. "Definitely," I tell him. "Go home and sleep it off. You'll feel better when you wake up."

"You're probably right." Ajjan runs his palm down his cheek. "Thanks."

We cross under a wooden archway and enter the Oldtown market. Yellow lanterns line the pedestrian walkway and flute music pipes down the alleys. Early risers traverse the streets to start their day.

They wear coats and gloves and wool hats stuffed over their heads. The smell of sweet bread swirls in the air, making my mouth water.

There's a scuffle, and someone shouts. I step aside as a pair of sentinels rush by in black plate armor with fur-lined surcoats, swords swinging on their hips. The presence of sentinels in the market feels like a weight pressing against my stomach. Zhira's news echoes in my mind.

Resonance trapping is now illegal. It's a strange law that affects almost no one. But it complicates things if the sentinels are hunting people like me. I'll have to be more careful who I let into my confidence. All it takes is one person ratting me out and I'll find myself on the wrong end of a manhunt.

Even then, they'll have to catch me first.

"Come on," I say to Ajjan. "I need to find a baker."

We stop at a street vendor. I order six cinnamon cakes, four loaves of sourdough, and three blocks of salt cheese.

"Hezha's fire." Ajjan raises an eyebrow. "Hungry?"

"It's not for me."

"You hosting a dinner party you didn't tell me about?"

I roll my eyes. "Shut up."

A bard sits on the curb across the street. He looks about my age and wears a blue cloak, the hood pulled over his head. He plays a bone flute. The notes dance from his fingers and weave through the air. A crowd gathers around him, tossing coins into a tin cup at his feet.

Ajjan watches him too. "He's talented."

"Yeah, he is." I bite my bottom lip. Something about the bard gives me pause. I could swear I've seen him before, but I can't put my finger on it. When the baker comes back with my items, I give him seven copper coins and take the bag.

"So, listen," Ajjan says as we rejoin the pedestrian traffic on the walkway. "I'm gonna lay my cards on the table. Bones to barrel, okay?"

The muscles in my shoulders tense. Whatever he says next is the real reason he joined me. "Go ahead."

He takes me by the shoulders, so we're stopped on the sidewalk, then takes a deep breath. "I'm finished with the Blackbones. I'm leaving."

"What?" I wasn't expecting that. I lick my lips, trying to wrap my head around what that means. "The Bones are for life, Ajjan. Zhira won't let you leave. She'll kill you."

"I don't care," he says. "I'm sick of this life. I'm sick of this place. Every day, I wake up and pray I don't find myself with a blade in my belly when the night moon rises. And for what? So Zhira can stack her coffers and extend the reach of her influence? Tonight was the final card." He rubs the back of his neck.

"The final card?" I ask. "We've been in dangerous situations hundreds of times. What was different about last night?"

Ajjan presses his lips into a thin line. "I'm going to die someday. I know that. But before then, I want to live. And when my time does come, I want it to have meant something. I don't want to die just because Zhira wanted a fancy knife to add to her collection."

I hitch a breath. All the signs were there—the circles under his eyes, the haunted looks, the trembling hands and excessive drinking. I thought he was reacting to what Vogul had done to him, but there's more under the surface.

"So, what do you think?" he says, his eyes expectant.

I smooth the front of my coat, collecting my thoughts. It's crazy for him to flee—Zhira will chase him to the ends of the earth—but I can't blame him either. I've thought of leaving more times than I can count. But Coppejj is all I know, and I've carved a living for myself here. Plus, there's no guarantee that anything will be better some-where else. "Where are you going to go?" I ask.

"South." His hazel eyes flash with anticipation. "Emceni."

Emceni. An island nation on the southern tip of the continent, known for sunny beaches and long seasons of tropical rain. I snort. "That's thousands of miles from here."

"The further away, the better. I've saved up some money. I have a connection with the captain of a freighter bound down that way. Once I get there, I'll find myself a place to live."

"And then what? Join a southern gang and start the whole thing over?"

"I'll figure it out." He's watching me closely, gauging my reaction. "Fisherman's wharf. Two days." He presses a piece of paper into my hand.

It's a ticket for a chartered lodging bound south. I frown. "What's this?"

Ajjan's gaze is full of hope and determination. "You're private. I respect that. But we make a good team. We should stick together."

"You want me to go with you?" I laugh, unsure what else to do. The situation is so absurd, it can't be serious. "You've lost your mind."

"Why not?" Ajjan insists, a touch defensive. "What's keeping you here?"

I search for words. Trapping is my greatest asset, but I don't have enough control yet to command top value on the market—the latest episode in the brothel is evidence of that. If I go to a strange place now, I'll be limited in the kind of work I can take on. There are good reasons why this is a terrible idea, but the allure of leaving this place is strong. I have no family. No friends. Resonance trapping is illegal in the city, and Vogul is a threat. Lately, it seems like Coppejj is out to get me. Maybe Ajjan is right. This is my opportunity to get out.

"I don't know." Doubt clouds my thoughts, but I have to admit, it makes sense in a crazy, stupid way. "It's pretty sudden."

"That's not a no." Ajjan grins. "The timing is right, and you know it. The longer you stay here, the more likely you'll stay forever."

"Alright," I say, resigned. "I'll think about it."

"You won't regret this." He squeezes my shoulder affectionately. "Make whatever arrangements you need to, but keep it quiet. Zhira can't catch wind of this or we're both dead."

"Don't worry." Deserting on Blackbone oaths is the most heinous crime a member of the gang can commit. If Zhira discovers our intentions, she'll close the harbors until she roots Ajjan out and burns him alive. "I know how to be discreet."

"Excellent," he says. "I'm gonna hit the sack. You watch yourself, okay? I'll see you soon."

I shake my head as he fades into the crowd. This is crazy, a childish fantasy. What do I expect is going to happen? Ajjan and I are going to sail halfway around the world and live in a hut on a beach eating coconuts and bananas? But stars, what if we can make it? My instinct is to crush the ticket into a ball and toss it on the ground. But instead, I tuck it safely in my jacket pocket.

Dawn is fading. The horizon darkens to twilight, and the day moon resumes its silver crawl through the star-studded sky. I'm already late. If I don't hurry, Mo will think I forgot about her.

As I continue down the block, the bag of sweet bread slung over my back, my steps are lighter than they've been in weeks, like a huge weight has been lifted from my heart.

* * *

Mo is a young girl, ten or eleven years old, who runs a gang of orphans in the Slags that call themselves the Rovers. We have an arrangement: They do small jobs for me—nothing major, just little recon assignments—and I pay them with sacks of food every few days. Street kids are surprisingly efficient spies, even the little ones. Nobody looks twice at a rat.

I leave the shattered sidewalk two blocks before my apartment and take a short detour. On an abandoned block, sandwiched between two dilapidated apartment buildings, sits an old temple pagoda with slanted roofs and a small courtyard in the back. Denizens of the Slags call it the Rat Shack, but it used to be a shrine devoted to Ujjek, Saint of the Red Moon. The temple has fallen into disuse, the grounds claimed by dust and vermin. Nobody's prayed in the holy chamber for years, and it's been Mo's preferred meeting spot for months now.

I ascend the steps and pass under the pagoda. I pause out of habit by the crimson altar on the crumbling dais. It's carved to resemble the petals of a large rose. Above the altar is a metal filigree backboard depicting an embossed carving of the shadow moon—a circular orb surrounded by beams of light. Although the walls are covered in dust and slime, the carving is still beautiful.

Each of the three Saints—Orran, Hezha, and Ujjek—form the basis of the three major religious sects of Sainthood: the Orrethics, Hezhani, and Ujjarum. The shadow moon is a holy symbol in each of the sects. Supposedly, anyone born while the shadow moon graces the sky will have the potential to become a trapper. It is the source of all resonance magic. But it hasn't risen since the day I was born, seventeen years ago. It's the longest resonance drought in recorded history, and no one knows when it will end.

The sight of this altar always sends a shiver down my spine. What would it be like to gaze into the sky and see the shadow moon, a blue specter roaming through the dark, adding a touch of the true divine that we mortals cannot hope to understand? Someday, I hope it comes back, otherwise, trappers will die out and the world will forget we existed.

I pass through the chamber and exit into the dark courtyard—the remnants of a stone garden, fenced in by the broken brick walls of the adjacent housing complex.

"Mo?" I call out. It doesn't look like anyone's here, but the Rovers are excellent at hiding, and the darkness is nearly complete. "Sorry, I'm late."

Silence.

As the seconds tick by, anxiety creeps into my guts. Two weeks ago, I gave the Rovers an assignment to tail the Aevem and note his movements. I guess I thought it would be a safe starter job. The Aevem is harmless, and the little ones need to practice their skills if they're going to survive on the streets. But I had no idea the Aevem was being hunted by sentinels. I chew my bottom lip as tension mounts in my jaw. If anything happened to those kids, I'll never forgive myself.

"Bexis?" A shadow moves at the end of the alley, and Mo inches forward. "That you?"

Relief washes over me. "Yes. Of course."

Mo creeps closer. She has sandy-blonde hair that she keeps tied in a bushy tail and wears a grimy black cloak. Her face is so dirty it's almost black, but her eyes are sharp blue. When she's close enough, she straightens, placing her hands on her hips and looking me up and down. "What happened, coppe? You look terrible."

Like any proper crew boss, Mo is well-versed in Coppejjian street slang, and she's got all the sass of a greased-up weasel. I suck my teeth. "You're one to talk."

"I live on the street. What's your excuse?" She pinches her nose, a coy smirk on her face. "You smell like sweaty boots and wet dog."

"Must be the company I keep." I smile and use my foot to nudge the bag of food on the ground. The bread is still warm, and I can smell it through the sack. Mo's eyes grow wide. She squats on her haunches and rummages through it. "Did you get everything?"

I tap my foot on the stone. "You can count it if you want."

She peers over her shoulder and sticks two fingers in her mouth, giving off a shrill whistle. "Ay, Rovers!" she shouts. "Time to eat."

Shadows move at the end of the alley, and the Rovers emerge. There are six of them, all between the ages of four and ten. I don't know their names. Mo is fiercely protective, so I don't ask. They gather around Mo and me like a pack of mangy wolves, their eyes big and hungry. Even after all this time, they still don't trust me.

Smart kids.

Mo distributes the food, making sure everyone gets an equal share. I watch with my arms crossed. The Rovers look better than they have in weeks. When I first found them, they were hollow-eyed and practically feral. Now they have some color, and their cheeks have filled out. I notice each of the kids carries a strange cloth doll made of black and white fabric stitched to resemble skeletons.

I feel a tug on my pant leg. A little boy stares up at me with green eyes as big as saucers, thumb jammed in his mouth.

"Hello." I crouch to look him in the eye. "You alright?"

He holds up his doll, extending it out to me.

I smile and take it. It's an odd thing, sewn with black cotton and white strips, stuffed with hay. "This is cute," I say. "Is this your friend?"

The boy sucks his thumb.

"Okay." I try to hand the doll back, but the boy pulls out another doll, hugging it to his chest. He points at the doll in my hands, then at me.

"This is for me?" I ask.

He nods, then turns and joins the others. When he receives his share of bread, he stuffs it into his mouth.

I hold the doll, confused. I suppose I should be touched, but what am I going to do with a little cloth doll?

"The Toymaker," Mo says by way of explanation. She's finished distributing the food. "She gave them all dolls."

I frown. "The Toymaker?"

"You know. The crazy lady who makes toys for orphans." Mo shrugs. "She's got a workshop that moves all over the city. Likes to sell *jalpe* on the wharves too. Pit wanted you to have a doll."

Pit must be the little boy. "I've never heard of the Toymaker," I say. "What do I do with it?"

"Whatever people do with dolls, I guess." Mo squints up at me. "Put it in your pocket, coppe."

One by one, the Rovers merge back into the shadows. The boy named Pit waves at me as he leaves. I wave back, then tuck the doll in my coat pocket.

Mo stays behind. She stuffs a cinnamon cake in her mouth, then closes her eyes, savoring the taste. "Sweet hez, coppe. Good stuff."

I shake my head. Children shouldn't talk like sailors. But I guess you stop being a child when you start running your own crew. "Any news?"

"Yeah." Mo wipes her mouth with her sleeve. "Bad news. The Aevem is gone. Two days ago, he goes into his apartment in the Burrows, and he never comes out. His place gets raided by sentinels, but they never find him."

I sigh. "Yeah. That's what I was afraid of."

"What's this all about anyway?" Mo takes another bite of cinnamon cake. "Why have us follow the Aevem?"

I cross my arms. The truth is, I've been asking myself the same question all week. I suppose because he's the only Khatori in the city.

If anyone might be able to help me control my resonance, it would be him. But I never gathered the courage to approach him. Why would I? He's an investigator who works for the Magistrate, while I'm a thief doing jobs for thugs and criminals. The Aevem is more likely to arrest me than to help me.

"Well?" Mo asks, narrowing her eyes. "Aevem's full rezzy. Dangerous nabbing a guy like that."

"I wasn't going to nab him. It's null anyway. The Magistrate put a warrant out for the Aevem's arrest."

Mo frowns, disappointment plain on her face. "Will he be back for the Solstice Festival?"

Aevem Juzu's lightworks displays are the headlining attraction of the festival. People come from hundreds of miles to see him perform his resonance, using the night sky as a canvas for dazzling illuminations of animals and explosions of color. The festival won't be the same without him. "I don't think so. It looks like Juzu has gone underground."

"The Magistrate is an asshat." Mo kicks a rock. "So if the Aevem is gone, does that mean there are no more Khatori in the north?"

The thought hadn't occurred to me, but she's right. "I guess so. But there must be some in other parts of the world."

"Are you worried?" Mo asks. "Without Khatori, who will keep the demons away?"

I laugh. The Khatori orders are steeped in antiquated legend and mystique. Because they're so powerful, people assume they fight evil spirits regularly, but I've never witnessed any evil that didn't come from human beings. "There's no such thing as demons."

Mo gives me an inquisitive look. "You of all people should know better than that."

"What do you mean?"

She gestures to the sky. "The shadow moon is a doorway to the spirit world. And you were born under it. That's why you're a trapper."

It's amazing, the stories people conjure up about things they don't understand. "Mo," I say. "I'm a trapper. I've never seen a demon. Never even heard of one except in songs. They aren't real."

She scoffs and tosses the last of the bread in her mouth. "Whatever you say, coppe. You got more work for us?"

"I'll think of something." I stuff my hands in my pockets. With the new ordinance, it could be dangerous for Mo to be associated with me, but it should be safe to keep these clandestine meetings going for a little while longer. "Tomorrow, same place, same time."

"See you soon." Mo smiles sweetly as she retreats into the shadows. "Maybe you take a bath, eh? You smell like skat."

I shake my head. *Snooty little brat.*

My apartment is only two blocks down the road. Snow falls from the black sky, and flakes melt on my cheeks. There are no streetlights in this area—no sentinels or pedestrian traffic either, for which I'm grateful. The exhaustion behind my eyes has finally spread throughout my body, and the urge to collapse on my cot is over-whelming.

As I cross the street to my apartment and stand before my stoop, an icy chill creeps beneath my skin, and my exhaustion is forgotten.

My front door is open, and a pair of bloody bare footprints lead down my stoop and onto the street.

CHAPTER 4

I LIVE ON THE SECOND FLOOR OF A RED-BRICK APARTMENT COMPLEX ON a quiet street deep in the Slags. It's nothing special, just a small hovel with a kitchenette, a bedroom, and a closet to store my things. I chose it for its discreet location in a relatively safe part of town. The entrance to the neighboring first-floor apartment is in the alley, but my front door is on the street, with a small cement stoop that leads to a rickety stairway.

The bloody footprints run straight down the stairs and onto the street, staining the snow a deep crimson.

Tendrils of fear snake down my spine as I crouch, leaning my back against the brick wall. The street and the alley are empty. There's no noise or commotion from the neighboring apartments. Most of the windows are dark, but a few are lit with the amber glow of oil lamps. I don't seem to be in immediate danger.

Keep your head. Think it through. Someone's kicked in the front door—the jamb is splintered, and the doorknob hangs at a wrong angle. It's impossible to tell how many entered. No prints lead into the apartment, which means the break-in occurred before it started snowing—at least an hour ago. The prints that lead down the steps and onto the sidewalk are fresh. They head east toward the bridge and back into town. The blood indicates some kind of violence took place inside.

I can't imagine Vogul kicking down my front door. But the sentinels? Yes, I can see the sentinels doing this. It seems unlikely that a soldier could have lost his boots during an altercation, but the alternative is a barefoot murderer running through the streets of Coppejj in the middle of winter. Frostbite would set in quickly in these temperatures.

Every instinct tells me to walk away—to head down the street and forget I ever had an apartment. I can use the silver Zhira gave me to buy a room in the Burrows and disappear. But I can't hide forever. I need to know if this was caused by the sentinels or something else. And to find answers, I have to go inside. But the last thing I want to do is climb those stairs.

I could scale the wall in the alley to my second-story bedroom window and use resonance to open the lock quietly, but the thought of trapping right now fills me with sickening dread. If I lose control while clinging to the wall, I could plummet to my death. So that leaves the stairs.

"Bleeding stars," I mutter under my breath. I unsheathe my knife and hold it in an underhand grip as I step around the bloody footprints and ascend the steps slowly, one at a time.

The stairs creak as they carry my weight, setting my teeth on edge. Damn this old building. If anyone *is* up there, they'll know I'm coming. My ears strain to pick up any sound from the landing above, but it's quiet. I try to convince myself that's a good thing.

At the top, I swing open the foyer door. The smell hits me. Blood and human waste. My stomach twists in revulsion, and I have to pause to steel myself. There's definitely a body up here. But that makes no sense: Why would the sentinels break into my house and kill each other? I have a bad feeling about this.

I creep into the kitchenette, my muscles ready to spring to action and my senses finely attuned to the silence. The room is dark. The only light comes from the moonglow leaking through a small window on the wall. Even so, I spot obvious signs of a struggle. My table has been smashed and thrown against the wall. My plates are shattered on the floor. The cabinets look like they've been battered with a hammer. And there are streaks of blood on the floor, as if someone has dragged a body from the kitchen to the bedroom.

I drop to my knees and run my hands along the floor. My fingers come away dry. Whatever happened here took place hours ago. I grit my teeth and poke my head into the bedroom. It's much darker in here, but I can make out the shape of two sentinels arranged side by side on the floor.

The smell is beyond horrible, but dead people can't hurt me. I try breathing through my mouth as I enter the room, but that only makes things worse. My stomach churns as I crouch on the ground. The sentinels wear full plate armor with helm and cuirass. They're young men, both staring sightlessly at the ceiling, their mouths twisted in expressions of horror and pain.

A bubble of panic rises in my chest, along with a voice in my head that screams for me to leave this place and never come back. But I must understand what happened first. The key to staying safe is knowing the nature of the threat.

The steel cuirass of the first soldier has been split cleanly down the middle. I've never seen a wound like this. What kind of weapon can cut straight through steel armor? The second soldier's helm has been caved in as if struck with a mace. Their sword sheaths are empty, and I don't see any spears or halberds. Whoever killed them took their weapons before leaving.

I sit back on my haunches, puzzled. It's reasonable to assume the sentinels came looking for me, which means the government knows who I am. But that doesn't tell me who killed these men, or whose footprints lead down my stairs into the snow.

Zhira? It's the only explanation that makes any sense. She's been so persistent about me needing someone to watch my back. She could have easily had my apartment watched. Stars, with the resources at her disposal, she could have set up this entire thing. Paid the sentinels to show up, and then paid an assassin to kill them. But would she really go through all that trouble?

The sentinels have nothing on them. No ordinance. No papers. Nothing to indicate who sent them here. And the killer left no trace beyond the bloody footprints. This makes no bleeding sense! I growl in frustration. When the bodies are discovered, it will look like I did this. Then the manhunt will truly begin.

Only one thing is certain. I can't stay here. Not tonight. Not ever again.

I grab a tote bag from under my bed and start throwing things inside: socks, briefs, shirts, a sweater, and trousers. I'll have to be careful moving forward, operate under a fake name. Once I start moving, the emotions begin to settle. Ajjan's offer stands on the tip of my mind. I just have to lay low for two days, and then I can leave this place. Until then, I need somewhere to stay.

Ajjan has an apartment in the Flats on the other side of town, a complex owned by the Blackbones. That won't work. Until I can rule out Zhira as a suspect, I need to keep my distance from the gang. I jiggle my pouch of coins. I can use an alias and rent a room in the rich part of town. And once I've collected myself, I'll reach out to Ajjan quietly.

I hoist my bag over my shoulder.

As I enter the kitchenette, a loud creak makes my blood run cold—someone's coming up the stairwell. Hezha's fire! I hurry back into the bedroom and close the door softly as footsteps echo from the foyer. I clutch the tone pipe in my fist and try to breathe as quietly as I can.

"Oh damn," a man's voice says. "You smell that?"

"Saints!" A second man coughs. "This is bad, Mel. Maybe we should come back with a phaser."

"Yeah, right. They're going to trust *you* with a phaser."

What the stars is a phaser? Blood crashes through my ears. I hear the metal scrape of a blade pulled from a sheath.

"The blood trails lead to the bedroom."

Bleeding stars! I dash to the window, fumble with the lock, and wrench it open. Frigid air rushes in, blasting me in the face. The footsteps draw near, and the doorknob starts to turn as I climb onto the sill and pull myself onto the outside wall. I hug the icy brick and the wind whips through my cloak. The door opens, and I can hear the voices through the window.

"Is that—"

"Yep. What kind of witch does Phekru have us chasing?"

Phekru? The name doesn't mean anything to me, but I stash it away for later.

"Look at those wounds. Can a trapper do that?"

"Maybe. Whatever she is, she's gone. The window is open—"

I'm too exposed here. All they have to do is poke their heads through the window and they'll see me. I force myself to move, hauling myself upward, not daring to look down. Thankfully, there are plenty of handholds on the cracked wall. I reach the lip of the roof and heave myself onto the flat landing. I roll onto my back and gasp for breath. The snow has stopped, and there's a hole in the clouds where a small pocket of stars winks against the black sky.

That was far too close. I should have known better than to linger. There's no question now. The sentinels are after me. Someone named Phekru is in charge. Voices rise from the room below, but they're too far away for me to make out any words.

Milky moonlight floods the snow-covered roof. From up here, I should be able to see when the sentinels leave. Then I'll make my way down to the street, cut through the Hollow, and cross the bridge—

A shadow moves along the rooftop. A boy sits on the edge of the roof several feet away.

I vault to my feet, my hand reaching reflexively for my knife. Was he there the whole time? I squint in the darkness. "Hello?" I say, perplexed. "Who's there?"

He has his back to me, legs dangling over the edge of the roof. His black hair blows softly in the wind. My boots crunch in the snow as I step closer. Anxiety coils in my belly like a snake.

"Hey," I hiss, trying to keep quiet. "What in the bleeding stars are you doing up here?"

Nothing. He may as well be a statue. Fear traces icy fingers down my spine, causing my hands to shake. I wish I could see his face. I inch closer.

"What's wrong with you?"

The boy shivers. He turns his head slowly until half of his face is revealed to me, doused in moonlight. I don't recognize him. His voice is so small, so quiet, I can barely hear him. "Come closer, Bexis."

"What?" I freeze in place, gooseflesh breaking out on my arms. "How do you know my name?"

His neck snaps as his head twists all the way around. Two coal-red eyes burn into my soul. I lurch backward in shock and stumble to the ground. The boy's lips peel back, exposing bared teeth. Tendrils of shadow reach from his face like tentacles, and his skin starts to blow away like ash. Paralyzing fear cuts through my chest, making it hard to breathe. I grip the handle of the knife so hard my knuckles turn white. I don't know what that thing is, but it's not a boy.

"Come closer!" the creature croaks, its voice morphing into an inhuman rasp. "Come closer!" It rises in the air, floating like a phantom. Its bones pop and crack as its spine contorts. The child-like arms turn black and twist at wrong angles as they elongate. The fingers morph into razor-sharp talons, and skeleton wings rip from the phantom's back. Steaming black viscera splashes onto the snow. The creature opens its wolf-like jaw and shrieks, revealing dripping white fangs.

Searing pain tears through my wrist. The mark feels like it's on fire. But I'm experiencing this like it's happening to someone else—to a body that's not my own. All I can do is stare into those fiery red eyes while blood crashes through my head. The phantom swings for my throat.

I fling myself backward, narrowly avoiding being decapitated. I fall to the ground, my bottom landing in the snow. The tone pipe is back in my hand before I even think of it. I blow, and the resonance tears through me, too quickly to catch. It slips through my grasp and bleeds into the cold night. The phantom screams at the moon and pumps its skeleton wings, rising higher into the air.

"Hezha's fire!" My hands tremble, and my legs quake. I can't fight this thing. I can't escape. But I can give a little hell before I die. I grit my teeth and brandish my knife.

The phantom strikes. I leap back, but not quick enough. The talons slice into the shoulder of my knife hand and rake down the back of my arm. Blood gushes down my biceps and abdomen, seeping between my fingers. I expect to feel pain, but there's only a cold numbness that spreads into my bones. I drop the knife in the snow and sink to my knees.

This is it. This is how I'm going to die.

The phantom roars and rears its claws for the killing strike. A blinding light crackles around me. I blink in confusion as warmth bleeds into my arms, and with it, a shield of light forms between me and the phantom. A wave of dizziness makes me swoon. Every ounce of breath has been squeezed from my lungs. My arms go limp, and I collapse in the snow. I can hear the pumping of wings as the phantom takes flight. Its silhouette fades against the silver moon until I can't keep my eyes open any longer.

As I drift into unconsciousness, I imagine strong arms lifting me from the ground. They cradle me against the warmth of a beating heart. I hold onto that sound for as long as I can, but exhaustion overtakes me, and my world goes silent as I slip into darkness.

CHAPTER 5

WHEN I WAKE, I HEAR VOICES NEARBY. I KEEP MY EYES FIRMLY SHUT AND pretend to still be asleep.

"Someone brought her to us." A woman's voice comes from my right. Her tone is gentle but lined with authority. "Just left her bleeding on the stoop like an animal, the poor thing."

"She'll survive." The second voice belongs to a man. "That's what matters."

"Well, you don't have to be so smug about it," the woman says.

"I've earned it, Siras. Now let me have a smoke."

"Not in the ward. You behave yourself, or I'll put you back in the basement. I mean it!"

The basement? I don't recognize either of the voices, but the air is warm and smells of juniper. My head rests on a pillow. And I'm wearing some kind of frock with no pants. Someone changed my clothes. Sheets are pulled up to my navel, covering my bare feet and legs. My tone pipe, I realize with dismay, is gone.

Memories rise in the dark of my mind—red lupine eyes and demon wings. A shapeshifting phantom with talons that tore through my shoulder. Blood soaking through my cloak. My pulse quickens. By all rights, I should be dead. How am I still alive? *Stay calm,* I tell myself. *Collect information.*

"We're running short on time," the man murmurs. "Captain Phekru and his sentinel goons will catch wind of this soon. We shouldn't be here when they do."

My breath hitches. *Phekru.* The sentinels also mentioned that name in my apartment. I can assume these people aren't working for the Magistrate. But that doesn't mean I'm safe.

"She's slept all day and night. I've done everything I can to keep it quiet," the woman says. "We should still have some time—" I feel a light pressure on the side of the bed. "I think she's awake. Young lady, can you hear me?" My heart skips a beat. There's no point in pretending anymore. I hold my breath and open my eyes.

A woman with shoulder-length black hair and deep blue eyes peers down at me, her face shrouded in shadow. She wears a gray robe adorned with teal blue triangles on her collar—vestments that mark her as a luminary of the Orrethic Church. A silver crown rests on her brow.

My throat tickles as I work moisture into my mouth. "Who are you?"

"I am High Radiant Siras Shelju."

High Radiant. My eyes widen. This woman is the highest-ranking member of the Coppejjian branch of the Orrethics—one of the most influential people in the city.

Siras touches the back of her hand to my forehead. "A bit warm, but nothing to fear. We'll give the *yras* root a chance to settle before you take a second dose."

I sit up on my pillows, trying to gather my bearings, but my head swims. The room is dark, and my vision blurs, but I make out dim blue light coming from the wall sconces. "What is this place?"

"The Sanctum, of course."

Ah. I should have figured. The Sanctum is the largest church structure in the city, a temple that doubles as a community center and infirmary. Each of the ten great cities has an Orrethic Sanctum. But that doesn't explain how I got here. The last thing I remember was being attacked on the roof by that beast with eyes of fire. And now, somehow, I've traveled halfway across the city.

"Who brought me here?" I ask

"Perhaps you have a guardian angel." The second voice makes me jump. Siras steps aside, revealing a tall man dressed in a collared blue shirt and a black waistcoat with silver buttons. He's thin and angular, with a black fedora tilted over his shaggy gray hair. A pair of dark spectacles sits on his nose, framing vibrant silver eyes. The intensity of his gaze freezes my blood.

Juzu Khinvo, the Aevem. I'd recognize him anywhere. But he's supposed to be missing.

Juzu holds an umbrella with a metal hook handle, which he uses like a cane. "What happened to you out there?"

"Uh." I try to clear my thoughts. His presence has thrown me off. "I don't... I'm not—"

"Juzu!" Siras scolds. "This isn't the time for an interrogation. Give her a minute."

The Aevem rolls his eyes and adjusts the lapels of his vest. "My apologies, Your Radiance. I need a smoke is all. Settle my nerves."

"You are a plague." Siras sighs and turns to me. "How is your shoulder? Do you feel any tingling? Any pain?"

"My shoulder?" I try to flex my elbow, but hiss as white heat lances up my neck.

"Easy!" Siras wags a finger. "Don't rip those stitches. Give the medicine time to work. When you're ready, take this—" She gestures to a small bowl on the nightstand full of yellow powder. *Yras* root. Bitter as stars and used to make a powerful healing tonic.

I groan and throw my head back against the pillow. *Yras* is fast-acting, but painful to endure. Like it or not, I should listen to Siras. If I have some time before Phekru and the sentinels return for me, I should take advantage of it. Once I'm healed, I can get out of here and figure out what comes next.

"Where are my clothes?" I ask.

Siras blinks. "Burned, I should think."

Burned? A tremor of panic shoots down my spine. Ajjan's ticket was in my jacket pocket. And I only have the one tone pipe. If it's gone, I won't be able to trap until I get another one—and it's not like they grow on trees. I won't be able to protect myself or do any work. My whole life is tied to that stupid pipe. "You *burned* my things?"

"They were soaked in blood."

I push myself up. "But those were my things! I need them—"

"Shush." Siras places a hand on my uninjured shoulder and gently pushes me back down. "I don't know where you grew up, young lady, but this is the Sanctum of the Orrethic Church. We do not steal, we do not lie, and we certainly don't take advantage of those who come to us for aid." She nods to the foot of the bed. "Your belongings—minus the blood-soaked clothes—are here. And your knives and weapons will be returned when you leave. Are you hungry?"

"No." Even as I say it, my stomach growls embarrassingly.

Siras gives me a satisfied smile. "I'll have something brought up. In the meantime"—she stands, addressing the Aevem—"she's all yours, Juzu. But try not to be too... you know."

"Polite?" Juzu guesses.

Siras frowns. "Overbearing. The girl needs rest."

"I'm not overbearing," he says. "I'm pragmatic." The Aevem's eyes dart to the corner of the room. I follow his gaze, but there's nothing there.

"Yes, well." Siras pats Juzu on the shoulder. "Be pragmatic in a calm and reasonable way, please."

The Aevem watches Siras leave the room, then presses his lips into a thin line. He turns his silver gaze to me and rests on the stool by the bed. He gestures to the bowl of *yras* root. "You're not going to use *all* of this, are you?"

His question takes me by surprise. "What?"

"Thanks." He extracts a briarwood pipe from his coat pocket and packs it with *yras* powder.

I raise an eyebrow. "I don't think you can smoke that."

"What are you, my mother?" He strikes a match. "Don't tell Siras."

This isn't what I was expecting. Every time I've seen Juzu in public, he's been the picture of propriety: clean-cut, well-mannered, easy smile. Up close, he seems a bit rougher around the edges: bags under his eyes, splotches of dust on his vest. Still, I have so many questions for him.

"Is it true you can't lie?" I ask.

He takes a drag from the pipe and exhales. Yellow smoke curls over his lip. "Unfortunately, yes. I can never lie."

"How do I know you're not lying about not lying?" I sit up against the pillows.

He snorts. "Truth is the most important of the Virtues—the Code of the Aevem Order. If I start telling lies, I'd violate my oaths, and then I wouldn't be of any use to anyone."

Interesting. "So your resonance stops working if you lie? I lie all the time, and it's never stopped me."

Juzu quirks an eyebrow. "Is that so?"

I open my mouth to retort, but those silver eyes penetrate straight through me. Something tells me he knows I'm lying.

"I had hoped we'd have an occasion to meet before this." Juzu rests his elbows on his knees. "But hope is of little consequence these days."

"You know who I am?" A pang of anxiety flutters in my belly. How many people know about me?

He inclines his head. "You're Bexis. You grew up in the Slags and make your living working contracts with Zhira and her Blackbones. Although you're a talented thief, you struggle with resonance. Some of your earnings are spent to coerce the most adorable little orphans to follow me around the city." He gives me a discerning look. "But I suppose that's mostly a charity, which is commendable. Means there's some hope for you."

My mouth falls open. I thought I was being clever keeping an eye on him, but he's been watching me too. It's disconcerting to be so exposed. "Why do you know all that?"

"I'm an Aevem." Juzu rises to his feet. He's built like a scarecrow: lanky, long, and insubstantial. He clasps his hands behind his back and paces the room. "Part of my job is to keep Coppejj safe from supernatural phenomena—ghouls and spirits and demons—things that most people cannot see or touch."

I frown. If I'd heard this a few hours ago, I'd have told him demons weren't real, but after my encounter with the phantom on the rooftop, I've revised that belief. Maybe I didn't give the Aevem enough credit. I'd often imagined what it would be like to meet him, but I never thought he'd be so disarming and unapologetically direct.

"So," I say, changing the subject. "You've been hiding in the basement of the Sanctum?"

Juzu continues pacing. He takes off his spectacles and rubs his eyes. "The enemy has infiltrated the highest levels of the city government. They hold the Magistrate, the city watch, and half the City Council. The Orrethics are an independent religious organization, so the Sanctum is off limits to the sentinels' searches, but that won't last. Siras has done her best to keep things quiet, but the Magistrate has rats everywhere. It's only a matter of time before Phekru knocks down the front door. As such—and I cannot emphasize this enough—you are in terrible danger."

"Right," I say, trying to wrap my head around this. I already knew I was in danger and that the sentinels were chasing me, but hearing *him* say it adds a level of severity to the situation. That thing that attacked me on the roof—it seemed connected to my mark, which means this was Vogul's plan all along. A shiver runs down my spine. "Who is the enemy, exactly?"

"Kandra Vogul is the easy answer," Juzu says. "This all started when she came to court. I fear she's just a pawn in a greater plot, but I don't know what they're planning. So far, she has succeeded in poisoning the Magistrate's mind and using his executive power to make resonance trapping illegal, which is patently absurd. When the capital hears about this, the ordinance will be reversed, but that will take months."

"If it's going to be reversed, then why bother doing it?" I ask. "If Vogul wanted to remove you as Aevem, why not just attack you?"

"She's smart, Bexis. If she attacked me, I'd have the right to defend myself. But she knows I'm bound by the Virtues to uphold order. By turning the institutions I'm sworn to protect against me, she has effectively cut me out. I can't take action against the Magistrate or the sentinels unless they intend to do me or others harm. But the sentinels are nothing compared to the creature that hunts you."

My blood runs cold. "What do you know about that?"

"I have pursued Vogul's demon for three weeks now—a spirit of shadow, a shapeshifting menace that stalks the streets of our derelict city." Juzu sighs, giving me an apologetic look. "You bear a beastmark on your right forearm. I saw it when you came in."

Beastmark.

I clutch my bandaged arm to my chest. "Do you know what it means?"

Juzu pushes his spectacles up on the bridge of his nose. "It hasn't made the papers—the Magistrate's office has made certain of that—but bodies have been coming into the mortuary for weeks now. The only thing that ties them together is similar marks that appear on the mutilated corpses." He raises his eyebrows. "Do you understand what I'm saying?"

Bleeding stars. A jolt of pain runs up my arm, as if the mark can hear us and resents being spoken of. Ajjan's offer stands out in my mind. If I can survive for a little while longer, I can board a ship and leave all of this behind, assuming he'll still take me. "So what should I do? Run?"

"You don't understand." Juzu grimaces. "You are *marked.* Even if you run to the end of the world, this spirit will follow. You cannot escape it. You must face it head-on. And I can help you, but I need your help in return."

My breath catches in my throat. "Help you how?"

His gaze flicks to the wall behind me. "I need a ward. Someone to pick up the slack and share the burden. And if need be, someone who can carry on after I'm gone."

My heart skips a beat. "You want me to be the next Aevem of Coppejj?" The idea is so baffling it borders upon the absurd. Aevem are sorcerers of light and truth. I'm a thief whose only useful trick is bending shadows. "Is that possible?"

"Of course. If you embrace the Virtues—truth, forgiveness, and duty—you will begin to see the light in the world, and your resonance will stabilize and change. But let's not get ahead of ourselves. It takes years to become an Aevem. All I want from you is your commitment to learn and live by the Virtues."

I frown. Bending shadows is part of who I am. It's difficult to imagine a world in which I give that up to wield light. "But why me?" I ask. "There must be someone more qualified to be your ward."

"There isn't," Juzu says firmly. "Trappers are increasingly rare, and you're not just any trapper. You're a good person, and you have a strong foundation of courage and strength. You have all the makings of a powerful Khatori, but you need someone to show you the way."

His words send a strange sense of pride bubbling to the surface, but it's quashed by a stronger wave of doubt. "You don't know me," I say. "You have the wrong girl."

"I don't think so." Juzu touches a finger to his chin. "I can promise my earnest tutelage and protection. I can promise to teach you about resonance. Additionally, I can help you with your episodes."

A tickle of excitement drips down my spine. I shouldn't be surprised that Juzu knows about my episodes. He seems to know everything about me. A hunger gnaws inside of me. If he can really help me get rid of my episodes, everything would change. There's no telling what I could be or who I could become. I lick my lips. "What's the catch?"

"It's not a burden to take lightly," he says. "To live by the Virtues is to live with one foot in shadow and one in the light. You will have power, but you will also have responsibility. The rest of your life will be inhabited by discipline and demons." He takes a deep drag from his pipe. "But other than that, no strings attached."

Hmm. That doesn't sound great. I'd have to give up my whole life, my work as a thief, my freedom. It wouldn't be so different from joining the Blackbones, but at least there are better perks. "What happens if I say no?"

"You are free to make your own choices. I will not pressure you one way or the other." He rises to his feet and takes off his fedora cap, revealing a mass of curly frazzled hair. "Take some time to gather your thoughts. The luminaries will take care of you, and no matter your decision, you will be free to leave."

I rub my arms and sit up, unsure of how to process everything that's happened. "Why should I trust you?"

"You're used to distrusting everyone." He reaches into his pocket and tosses something onto the bed. "That's a habit we'll have to break."

My tone pipe. I snatch it up. The cold metal is a reassuring weight in my palm.

"If you want to run," Juzu says, "run. I won't stop you, and I won't follow you." He stops by the door and peers back at me. "But look inside yourself and think of the future you want, Bexis. If it's any future at all, be wary of the road you choose. There is no going back."

CHAPTER 6

AFTER THE AEVEM LEAVES, AN INITIATE BRINGS ME A STEAMING BOWL OF stew and a glass of water. She can't be more than fifteen years old. She wears the traditional vestments of a New Dawn—a pale yellow cassock and a white vest embroidered with a visage of the full moon on the left lapel. She places the bowl on the table beside me.

"Smells good," I say. She nods, a shy smile on her lips, but she doesn't speak.

Right. New Dawn initiates take a vow of silence for a year before they are accepted into the church. What a strange life that must be. Why would anyone sacrifice and suffer so much to become an Orrethic? Are people so desperate to belong to something?

I take the bowl in my lap. It looks like carrots and beef and some kind of dark green vegetable. "Thanks."

She gives me an awkward curtsy and leaves the room.

After I've finished eating, a warmth settles in my belly, then spreads up my chest and into my shoulders. I take the rest of the *yras* —the bit that Juzu didn't smoke—with the water. The bitter powder makes me gag, but I force it down anyway and lie back down on the bed.

My body is a mass of aches and bruises, but the initial dizziness I felt upon waking has receded. I sit up and try to stretch my shoulders. My back feels like it has been beaten with a large stick. But the *yras* is working. The flesh on my arm has already started to mend, and the bruises on my ribs are nearly gone.

I never thought I'd find myself in the Sanctum being treated by Orrethic luminaries, but I know I'm lucky to be here. It still doesn't make sense: one minute I'm lying in the snow, my arm torn open, and the next I'm in an infirmary halfway across the city.

My bag is at the foot of the bed, just like Siras said. The strange cloth doll sits beside it, its button eyes catching in the light from the blue sconce lanterns on the wall. My skin prickles at the sight. Such a strange thing. The luminaries must have found it in my jacket pocket, but it doesn't have a drop of blood on it. Curious.

My shoulder aches as I ease out of the blue infirmary gown and pull on an extra pair of trousers and a baggy wool sweater. I find Ajjan's ticket in the bottom of my bag, with only a few drops of blood staining the edges. I smooth it out, breathing a sigh of relief, and tuck it into my pants pocket next to my tone pipe before I lay back on the bed, staring up at the ceiling. Finally, I have a moment to think.

The sentinels want to arrest me, Vogul is a threat to everyone in the city, and a shadow demon wants to murder me because of this damned mark. I can't run, and I can't fight. So what are my options?

Aevem Juzu wants me to be his ward.

It's a dream come true, only now that it's happened, the idea fills me with a strange mix of emotions. Reluctance, because I'm used to operating alone, answering to myself, setting my own rules. Being a ward means accepting the role of a student. I'd have to do what I'm told, practice, study, and be accountable. And what kind of a teacher would Juzu be? He might be an addict, like my father, and while jalpe isn't as destructive as alcohol, I'm still wary of trusting people like that. I'd always assumed the Aevem's role was more ornamental than practical. But the responsibilities he faces are clearly taking a toll. I don't know if that's something I'm prepared to take on. But...

The prospect of getting rid of my episodes and learning about resonance makes me feel lighter than air. It's exciting and new. Juzu might be the only man alive who can teach me about trapping, how to control it and how to keep the power from spilling out and hurting people. Plus, he's a professional demon hunter—and it's hard to deny the existence of demons after my encounter with the phantom.

I go to the window and try to distract myself by gazing at the courtyard below. It will be dawn again soon. The night moon is a red shadow on the horizon. Somehow, I've been sleeping in the Sanctum all day and deep into the night. Fat snowflakes spiral in the lamplight and settle on the marble fountain. A statue of Orran, the Savior, stands amid the snow, his arms outstretched to the sky. A stone dove is perched on his shoulder.

The White Keep stands across the hill, a towering fortress of pale stone lined with fortified crenelated walls, the ramparts silhouetted against the dark waters of the Shadow Sea. The Keep is the seat of Coppejjian government, where the Magistrate and his City Council live and run the city. Zhira is probably there right now, wearing her officious blue councillor robes and trying to keep the Council from collapsing under Vogul's calculated political assaults. A pang of worry runs through me as I wonder where Ajjan is right now. Which is silly, because he's not a trapper, and he's not in any danger, so why should I worry about him? Still, I'd like to see him. At the very least, he'd listen as I complained about everything that's happened since we parted. The thought brings a smile to my lips.

Pedestrians pass through the courtyard. A bard sits on the steps of Orran's statue, playing a bone flute. Somber notes waft up to the window. His trousers are dirty and torn, and he wears a heavy blue cloak with a hood pulled over his head. A sense of certainty grows in my gut. It's the same man I saw in the market yesterday morning. But that's a ridiculous thought. There are hundreds of bards in Coppejj. The odds that I'd see the same one in such disparate parts of the city are next to nil. But my instincts still tell me it's him.

The bone flute glows in the blue light from the lamppost. His fingers dance over the holes as the muffled notes waver and dive. It's beautiful, even from this distance. A few early risers amble through the courtyard, tossing coins in a tin cup as they pass. I lean my elbows on the windowsill and press my nose against the glass, captivated.

The bard pauses, letting the instrument rest in his lap, then turns his face into the light. A swarm of butterflies flutters through my stomach. His eyes are icy blue, almost white. He's about my age, young with hard cheekbones and a square jawline. A breeze rustles through his hood as his gaze locks on mine. He waves, a smile breaking across his lips, then he picks up his flute and plays. A tinkling melody swirls in the air behind me.

I spin around, my heart in my throat. The room is empty—a bed, a nightstand, and a stool. The walls are bare except for the wall lanterns emitting a soft blue light. I can hear muffled voices from the hall outside, but otherwise, it's silent. I narrow my eyes. A strange feeling settles in my gut.

I turn back to the window, gazing down at the courtyard. The bard is gone. His tin cup, his flute, everything has vanished. It's as if he never existed. I blink, trying to clear my vision. Perhaps I'm going crazy, or the *yras* has other side effects. But it seemed so real…

"You should be dead." The voice sends an icy tremor down my spine.

I spin again, pressing my back into the wall. The bard reclines on my cot, legs crossed, his ratty cloak dusted with snow that's already begun to melt. He removes his hood, revealing shaggy black hair that falls over his shoulders and frigid blue eyes that dance with youthful vigor. But beneath his cloak, he wears boiled leather armor studded with iron.

Bleeding stars. This is no bard.

Anxiety spikes in my chest. Instinctively, I reach for the knife at my waist but grab air. I have no weapons except for my tone pipe. I pull it out of my pocket and prepare to blow.

The bard clicks his tongue. "I wouldn't do that if I were you."

I freeze. "Why not?" My body aches, but adrenaline courses through my veins. I shift away from the wall, so I have space to move if he attacks.

Dimples form on his cheeks as he smirks. "I have no interest in hurting you. But I will if you threaten me."

He's a trapper. There's no other way he could have gotten in here. The realization raises the hairs on the back of my neck. I inch toward the door. Perhaps I can stall for time. Get a signal to Juzu or Siras. "What do you want?" I ask.

"I just want to talk." He props his hands on the mattress and pushes himself up. "I have some questions, and I need honest answers from you."

I swallow the lump in my throat. Another couple inches and I can make a break for the door.

"Stop." He holds up a finger. "Be still. If you try anything, this will end badly for you. And that's not what I want."

I purse my lips. He hasn't moved from his position by the bed, and despite his smiles, his face holds no trace of friendliness. His features are sharp and striking. He's built like a warrior, but nothing about his posture is threatening. Even his tone is measured and calm. But the last time I encountered a mysterious trapper, I ended up flat on my back with a mark branded on my forearm. I will not underestimate this intruder.

I take a deep breath, willing my pulse to slow. "What do you want to know?"

He nods, seemingly satisfied. "Let's start with introductions. What's your name?"

I clench my hands into fists. "Bexis."

"Hi, Bexis. My name is Xaleo. So far, so good, right?" He holds up his palms in a placating gesture. "Now, you recently spoke to a foreign dignitary in a brothel. Do you remember?"

He's been following me. I cock my head in surprise. "Kandra Vogul. Of course I remember."

"Not everyone who encounters her does." His voice is cool. "She gave you a mark, didn't she?"

I press my lips into a line. My instinct is to lie. I don't owe anything to this trespasser. But his gaze locks on my right forearm and the bandage that gives me away. "Why are you asking questions you already know the answer to?" I ask.

"I'm sorry," Xaleo says. "Did she tell you why?"

The question catches me off guard. "What is this, an inquisition? Go ask her yourself."

Xaleo's eyes flash, and he crosses his arms. "Did she say anything to you? Anything that might give some clue into her intentions?"

"She wants to kill me. I think that's bleeding obvious."

Xaleo takes a step forward. "Think, Bexis. Please. Did she say anything else?"

I lick my lips, incredulous. But I take a breath and think back to that night. Everything is a blur. My pulse quickens. "She said the mark was Entaru's sigil."

"Entaru?" Xaleo asks.

"I've never heard the name. Does it mean anything to you?"

"I don't think so." Xaleo takes a step forward, his bare feet silent on the marble floor.

My blood runs cold. "It was you!" I stammer. "*You* killed the sentinels in my apartment."

"I did." He steps closer to me, the scent of wet wool and smoke wafting through the space between us. "I wanted to talk to you. And the sentinels were *very* rude. They attacked me." He's a full two heads taller than me and must be twice my weight.

I take an involuntary step back.

Xaleo pauses. "I said I'm not going to hurt you. Are you frightened?"

My heart hammers against my ribcage, and my palms are slick with sweat. "No."

"You're right to be afraid." He continues to move closer. "But you don't have to fear me, Bexis. I'm not the one who's hunting you." My back hits the wall. I have nowhere else to go.

He is so close now, only inches from my face. "May I?" He takes my wrist, gently peeling back the bandage. My breath hitches at his touch, but I don't pull away. Xaleo stares at the mark, eyebrows raised. "A black moon and a serpent. This mark is unique. What does it mean?"

"I don't know." I pull my arm away from him. "Who are you, and why are you following me?"

Xaleo steps back, putting space between us. "Vogul has done this before in other places. She's hurt people dear to me. I'm going to make sure she pays for the damage she's done."

For the first time, the tension in my muscles relaxes. If it's Vogul he's after, maybe we're on the same side. Besides, he killed the sentinels. He was at my apartment...

"You're the one who brought me here," I whisper. "You fought off the phantom."

A spark twinkles in his eye. "When I arrived, the phantom was fleeing. You'd fended it off all on your own. I could have pursued the creature, but you were losing blood fast. I made a decision. For what it's worth, I'm glad that you're alive."

My mind races. My memories of the attack are muddled, but I know the phantom overpowered me easily. My knife was useless, and my feeble attempt to trap resonance failed. "I didn't fight the phantom," I say. "I didn't do anything."

Xaleo narrows his eyes. "I saw a shield of white light. It formed around you. When the creature attacked, the light repelled it. I assumed you'd used resonance."

"No," I say. "I didn't."

He purses his lips. Maybe he thinks I'm lying. "You're alive, that's what matters. But for how much longer? The phantom *will* attack again. Do you have a plan?"

"Not really. Aevem Juzu wants me to be his ward."

Genuine surprise flickers across Xaleo's face. "The Aevem is here?"

Crap. I shouldn't have said that, but it's too late now. "He says he can keep me safe."

"That's probably true. He's the last Khatori left in this part of the world," Xaleo says. "But you should be careful."

"Why?" I ask, my curiosity piquing.

He presses his lips into a line. "All I know is what I heard. Years ago, Juzu went on a covert mission for the Magistrate. He showed up in the outskirts of Shezhi, and he did horrible things there. He hurt people."

I frown. Even if this is true, it's only half of the story. "What was he doing in Shezhi?"

Xaleo shakes his head. "All I know is that Juzu Khinvo is not the kind of person to be taken lightly."

"And why should I trust you?" I clench my hands into fists, feeling strangely defensive. "Juzu has been in the public eye for as long as I can remember. The only thing I know about you is that you're a murderer."

"And I saved your life," Xaleo reminds me, his tone softening. "If he makes a vow, the Aevem will protect you. Just be careful, that's all I'm saying. Don't let him turn you into something that you're not."

"Why are you pretending to care about me?" I say. A seed of doubt has taken root in my mind. What does this stranger know about the Aevem that I don't?

"Look. We want the same thing." His bright blue eyes pierce straight through me. "I'm going to stop Kandra Vogul. But in order to do that, I need you to keep your mouth shut. Don't tell anyone I was here, especially the Aevem."

"Why should I?" I jut out my chin. "For all I know, you could be working with Vogul."

Xaleo continues in a measured voice. "I revealed myself to you because you're the only person I know who has survived the phantom's attack, but even this was a risk. If Vogul finds out I'm here, she'll kill me." He gestures to the mark on my wrist. "In return, I think I can find out the origin of your beastmark."

I hitch a breath. This would be a great first step in figuring out what the stars is going on around here. "Alright," I say. "If you find out what this mark means, I'll keep your secret."

"Deal." His smile falters. "Someone's coming."

There's a soft knock on the door. I turn, my heart stuttering. "How did you know?"

But he's gone. Vanished into thin air. Damnit.

I gaze around the room helplessly. Vogul pulled the same trick in the brothel. I have to learn how to do that.

Siras cracks open the door and pokes her head into the room. "Are you alright, Bexis?"

"Yeah." I let my hands fall to my sides, exhaustion creeping back into my muscles. "Yeah, I'm fine."

"I'm glad to see you up." Siras enters the room and frowns. "Did Juzu smoke in here?"

"Yeah," I say, glancing toward the window. Xaleo isn't in the courtyard. "He told me not to tell you."

"Insufferable man." Siras sidles up to me and opens the window, letting cold air rush in. She touches my elbow. "How is your shoulder feeling?"

I move my arm from side to side, surprised at how much better it feels. The flesh has almost completely healed. "Pretty good."

Siras beams. "The Savior smiles upon you. If you're able, we can visit the inner sanctum."

I suck my teeth. "You're not going to make me pray, are you?"

"Only if you feel so inspired." She laughs. "Aevem Juzu wants to show you something. Grab your things. Take them with you."

I spare a final glance out the window. Xaleo is an enigma. I'm not sure if he's an ally or another problem that I'll have to deal with. Uncertainty creeps into my guts. Something tells me I'll see him again.

"Alright." I sling my pack over my shoulders. "Let's go."

CHAPTER 7

SIRAS LEADS ME DOWN A WHITE CORRIDOR LIT WITH YELLOW SCONCE lanterns. The scent of herbs lingers in the stale air—a sour smell that brings to mind luminaries and prayer sticks. The halls of the infirmary ward are mostly quiet, but nurses and New Dawn initiates pass by, bowing politely to the High Radiant and keeping their distance from me. I can't blame them for that; despite Mo's insistence, I haven't yet had the opportunity to bathe.

"You don't like it here much, do you?" Siras asks. She's donned a gold dress with a low cut neckline, revealing a silver feather pendant that shimmers against her chest.

I shrug. Being in the Sanctum brings contradictory emotions. On one hand, I detest the Orrethics: They wear self-righteousness and piety like a badge of honor, but it's a mask to hide the overt hypocrisy of their order. While they sit here in their grand cathedrals, preaching about charity and light, kids like Mo and her Rovers are eating trash and sleeping in crates by the docks. But on the other hand, they saved my life and aren't asking for anything in return. Somehow, I have to square those two ideas, but resentment and gratitude are tough to mix, like oil and water.

"My father was a luminary," I say by way of explanation.

"Really?" Siras raises an eyebrow. "Who was he?"

"Lum Carro." The name tastes bitter on my tongue. My father was a priest and a drunk. After my mother died, he became a shadow of himself, and that's what he raised me to be.

Siras frowns. "I don't know that name."

"I'm not surprised," I say. "He spent most of his time at bars or sick in bed. And then one night, he didn't come home."

"And that's why you hate luminaries." The High Radiant's voice is steeped in compassion. "I'm so sorry that happened to you, Bexis."

"I'm not," I say with a huff. My life with Lum Carro was full of darkness and secrecy. He kept me locked in his crappy apartment. I wasn't allowed to play with other children on the block or make friends. Every night, he'd read me scripture and lecture me on the dangers of resonance trapping. He taught me to fear myself and to fear the world. And yet, like a fool, I loved him, trusted him, relied on him for everything. I won't make that mistake again.

"I would never presume to speak for your father," Siras says, "but as for luminaries, wearing a cassock doesn't make you a saint. In the end, we're just people with flaws and wounds and dreams. But under the ideals of Orran, we strive to be better than we are. That's all it means to be a luminary. You accept your faults, and you strive to fix them."

"Well," I say. "Some people try harder than others."

The High Radiant nods. "Most people want to do good, but it's hard. To make the world better, one must be willing to suffer. People like that are the real heroes." She scoffs. "I suppose that's why I put up with Juzu."

"You think he's a hero?"

"Absolutely," she says without hesitation. "He's a stubborn old mule, but don't let that fool you. He plays an integral role in the world, and he suffers greatly for it. While the Magistrate worries over condemnations from the king and the Council bickers over tariffs, Juzu lives up to the ideals of the Saints. He protects those who need it most, and he doesn't do it for glory or accolades or power."

I bite my bottom lip. In my experience, when something sounds too good to be true, it usually isn't true. Nobody is *that* good. "Then why does he do it?"

"You'll have to ask him." We reach a wide set of rosewood doors under a limestone arch. Siras turns to face me, smoothing the front of her dress. "You're going to be alright, Bexis. There are few people in this world I truly trust, and Juzu is one of them. If he says something, he means it."

The High Radiant isn't what I expected. There's an energy about her, a genuine earnestness that's oddly alluring. Despite my reservations about Orrethics and luminaries in general, I find myself liking Siras. "Thanks," I say.

She smiles warmly. "You can wait inside. Juzu will be a moment."

I push through the doors. A waft of cool air greets me as I step into a large rectangular chamber lined with marble columns and wooden pews arranged in concentric circles around a central altar. Hundreds of white candles line the perimeter of the room. Red moonlight cuts through the stained glass windows. There's an energy about this place, austere and sacred. Under Orran's steeples, I could almost believe the Saints are real, that they listen to our prayers and care about our mortal toils. Almost.

I walk down the central aisle, my footsteps soft on the red runner. Upon the altar, there are three rows of three candles, the flames wavering in the still air.

"One candle for each of the phantom's victims." The Aevem's voice makes me jump. He stands by the door. The candlelight reflects off his dark spectacles, and his fedora sits at an angle on his shaggy head. He rests his hands on the hook handle of his umbrella. "Each of them bearing a different mark on their forearms. The first candle was lit almost three weeks ago."

So this is why he brought me here—to witness my inevitable fate. Unless I can find a way to escape, I will become another candle on the altar. A shiver runs the length of my spine as I examine the first candle in the row. A bouquet of fresh snow lilies sits in a vase beside it.

"A boy from the merchant quarter," Juzu says, following my gaze.

"A scion of a wealthy house. His mother visits every morning wearing a veil of grief." The candles dance as if a breeze circles through the chamber. Juzu crosses the room and tucks his umbrella under his arm. His jaw tightens. "The luminaries will keep this vigil, adding candles, until the killings stop."

Seeing them arranged like this drives the point home: I am in danger, but this problem is bigger than me. "Were they all trappers?"

"I believe they were," he says.

"But you don't know?"

"The Magistrate has records of every child born under the shadow moon, but he's shut me out."

So that's how the sentinels knew where I lived. "What makes you think they're all trappers?"

"Trappers are born under the shadow moon, which last rose seventeen years ago. Each of the victims appeared to be the same age." He sighs and takes out his pipe. "I think it's a reasonable assumption."

"So it's a purge." Dread curls in my belly. "The ordinance and the marks. Vogul wants to kill every trapper in the city. But why?"

Juzu strikes a match and inhales, then breathes out a plume of thick yellow smoke. The floral scent of jalpe stings my nostrils. "I don't know what she's planning, but Kandra Vogul is like no one I've encountered before. She's a trapper, but her resonance is twisted and evil. Somehow, she's harnessed dark harmony to summon a monster from the demon realm. Perhaps she seeks to destroy resonance trappers because they pose a threat to her. Or perhaps she needs them to feed the beast. Either way, we must stop her."

I can't tear my eyes away from the candles. For so long, I've felt alone, when there were nine other resonance trappers my age living in the city this whole time. And now they're dead. "How many of us are left?"

"Not many," Juzu says, his face a mask of pain. "The last victim was found almost six days ago. I fear we may be the last resonance trappers in the city, aside from Vogul herself."

Juzu doesn't know about Xaleo. I'm still not sure what to make of the young trapper. He's dangerous; the sentinel's corpses attest to that, which isn't in itself a bad thing. In this world, you have to be dangerous if you want to survive. He saved my life, but that alone isn't reason enough to trust him. I find it hard to imagine Aevem Juzu killing someone in cold blood. But Xaleo's cautions have sowed a seed of doubt in my mind. I shouldn't trust anyone. Not until I have more information. So for now, Xaleo's secret is safe with me.

"I wanted you to see this"—Juzu gestures to the altar—"so you would understand the danger that you face. This beast will not stop until you are dead."

This is the moment of truth. Do I accept Juzu's offer to become his ward, or do I try to hide for one more day until there's an opening to flee? There are still so many things I don't know. I pick at the bandage on my wrist. The mark has started to itch. "If I become your ward, you'll teach me about resonance, how to control it, how to use it?"

"Of course." Juzu turns his silver eyes to me. I catch a glimpse of his grief, his fatigue. The pressure that rests on his shoulders must be immense. "Should you accept, I will teach you the Virtues, and if you are diligent, you may become the next Aevem of Coppejj. You will become a Khatori."

An idea begins to take shape. I want to learn how to use my powers more than anything. If training to become the next Aevem is the only way to do that, then I have no choice but to accept. And Juzu's protection is a bonus. But in truth, I'm not sure I want to become the next Aevem of Coppejj. I certainly don't want to spend the rest of my life fighting demons. Life is hard enough as it is. But there's no reason I can't stay with Juzu now, take advantage of his protection, and if things aren't working out, I can leave with Ajjan tomorrow morning and head for Emceni.

A searing pain jolts up my wrist. I hiss and clutch the mark.

"What is it?" Juzu asks, his tone urgent. "What's wrong?"

I grimace. "It's nothing."

"It's the mark, isn't it?" He holds out his hand. "Show me."

"No, really. It's fine." The muscles in my hand spasm. The pain is nearly blinding.

"Bexis." Juzu's silver gaze pierces through my pain. "If you're to be my ward, you must learn to trust me."

I grit my teeth. Trust him? Bleeding stars! This might be harder than I thought. "It doesn't hurt that bad—"

"And you must *never* lie!" Juzu waves a finger in the air. "Not to me. Not to yourself. Not to anyone. Never again."

Never? What kind of insanity is this? A bead of sweat runs down my cheek. What's the worst that could happen? I hold up my arm.

"Thank you." Juzu takes my wrist with gentle hands and lifts it to the light. The bandage is wet with fresh blood. He unwraps it carefully and tosses the soiled fabric on the floor. We take a simultaneous inhalation of breath. The flesh on my arm outlining the serpent and crescent moon has transformed into an ugly black wound with bubbly yellow blisters, oozing blood as if the burning I feel is real—

"That's gross," Juzu whispers.

"You're the one who wanted to see it!" Sweat breaks out on my forehead. "I thought the *yras* was supposed to help this."

"*Yras* is a powerful tool for physical healing, but the mark is not a physical wound."

"Really?" I hiss. "It feels pretty physical to me!"

Juzu nods softly. "I'm going to help you now. Try to relax, okay?"

"How?" Anxiety rumbles in my belly. "What are you going to do?"

He places his palm over the wound. I try to pull away, but he holds tight. "Try to stay still—"

White light emanates from his palm, filling my arm with warmth. My vision erupts in a kaleidoscope of colors, and when it fades, I'm standing in a market full of people.

I see Juzu as a younger man, his hair curly and black and wavering in the wind. He carries a young girl in his arms as he weaves through the crowd on the banks of the wharf. The girl has dark hair and red cheeks. She giggles at something Juzu says and raises her arms to the sky. A wave of love washes over me, and it fills me up from head to toe. It is the most amazing thing I've ever felt.

The scene before me bleeds to darkness, and I am standing once more in the Sanctum chamber before the altar. The blisters on my forearm have faded, and the flesh has sealed and mended over. The symbol is stark black against the paleness of my skin, but the pain is gone.

"There." Juzu releases me. "That wasn't so bad, was it?"

"I... How...?" I flex my fingers. "Was that harmonic magic? I didn't know it could be used that way."

"Of course."

I close my eyes, trying to hold onto the vision that came to me. "I saw you in a market. But younger."

"The Solstice Festival fifteen years ago," Juzu says. "Strong emotions produce strong harmony. Memories are terrific stores of emotions. That was a happy day. Before everything went wrong." He trails off, lost in his thoughts.

"Was that your daughter?" I didn't know he had one.

"No. My sister's kid. Her name was Dhaima." He casts his eyes downward and touches his cheek.

I shouldn't pry, but I can't help myself. "What happened to her?"

His lips twitch. His eyes shift from me to the nearest candle. "It's the memory I use most often for healing work."

Somehow, seeing this vision and feeling his love for that child makes me trust Juzu more. He might be rough around the edges, but there's a warmth in him that I can't deny. I don't think I've ever loved anyone as much as he loved that little girl.

"So," Juzu says, stirring me from my thoughts. "You accept?"

I cross my arms. This could go wrong in about a hundred different ways. Can I even go a day without lying? I have my doubts, but there's no harm in trying. At least this way, I'll get to learn about resonance. And if it doesn't work out, I'll try something else.

"Yes," I say. "I accept."

"Good." Juzu nods. "I vow to prepare you for the darkness ahead, and I vow to protect you with my life."

I shrug. "Okay. If you say so."

"This is serious."

"Seems serious." I smile.

Juzu narrows his silver eyes. "You're going to be trouble for me, aren't you?"

The door to the chamber bursts open. Siras stands in the doorway. "Juzu." She gasps, breathing heavily. "They're here!"

Juzu sighs. "Well, it was only a matter of time."

A pang of anxiety ripples through me. "Who's here?"

"Captain Phekru," Juzu says, "and his sentinel goons. It's time for us to leave."

"Quick." Siras dashes down the aisle between the pews. "Follow me. There's a door—" She pulls up short and glares at Juzu. "Did you *smoke* in here?"

"Focus, Siras," Juzu says, snapping his fingers. "Secret door. Saving our lives."

"Damnable man." Siras pushes against the wall, revealing a dark tunnel. "This will lead you to the street."

"Appreciate it," Juzu says. "Sorry about all the smoke."

Siras scoffs. "Just get to the bottom of this. And don't get yourself killed, okay?" She thrusts the sheathed knives the luminaries had confiscated from me into my arms. "Remember, Bexis, don't lose hope. If you need anything, come find me. I'll help you however I can."

Before I can respond, Juzu pulls me into the tunnel.

"Good luck!" Siras whispers as she closes the door, enveloping us in darkness.

As the silence settles around us, my heart begins to slow. "So, what now?"

"We're going to see an old friend in the Hollow. I think she might be able to help us." Juzu lights a match and then a cigarette. "But first, we'll have to give the sentinels the slip."

"Haven't we already done that?" I ask.

"Phekru is like a bloodhound. Once he catches the scent, he'll chase us to the ends of the world. So be quick." Juzu starts down the tunnel. It's so dark I can barely make out his form as he inches along the wall.

I pause to let the moment sink in. For better or worse, I am the Aevem's ward. Despite the soldiers pursuing us and the threat of

Vogul and the phantom hanging over my head, a thrill of excitement courses through my veins. For the first time in my life, I'm moving forward.

"What are you doing?" Juzu hisses. "Don't stand there like a rock. We need to move!"

"I'm right behind you." I take a deep breath and follow Juzu into the darkness.

CHAPTER 8

My lungs burn in the frigid air as I run, my boots struggling for purchase on the icy walkways. The sentinels spotted us two blocks from the Sanctum and chased us north toward the Hollow and the Slags.

"Stop!" The sentinels' metal boots crash on the pavement fifty yards behind us. "Submit at once!"

"Don't stop running." Juzu holds his hat on his head as he leads us up a dark alley, his umbrella tucked under his arm.

"I wasn't going to," I huff. Despite their heavy gear, the sentinels continue to gain on us. The *yras* healed my shoulder, and Juzu healed my wrist, but the rest of my body is still riddled with aches and pains. We take a left at the end of the alley onto an open thoroughfare.

"We're almost there!" He gestures ahead to the arched entryway into the Red Tree Market. Orange oil lamps line the park promenade that runs perpendicular to the market street, with a crowd of people funneling in and out the front gate. Now I understand why Juzu led us this way. If we can't lose them in the streets, we can lose them in the crowd.

We dive into the throng of moving bodies that carries us along like an ocean current. The scent of fried squid balls and roasted eel swirls in clouds of steam and smoke. The streets are lit with paper lanterns of all different colors, which decorate the shop fronts and restaurants.

I make myself small to squeeze through the crowd as Juzu pulls me along by the sleeve of my jacket like a fish he's angled on a hook. Within minutes, we've ridden the stream of people several hundred yards from the entrance, and the cries from the sentinels have blended in with the din of the market.

Juzu slows, his silver eyes scanning faces in the crowd. "Stay close. We'll head toward the east exit. From there, we can slip the guards."

"Why are we running?" I rasp. Sweat drips down my back. "You're a great Khatori sorcerer, right? Why don't you trap? Get them off our tails."

"Phekru would not pursue me like this unless he brought along a phaser," he explains.

I remember the term from the sentinels in my apartment. "What's a phaser?"

We dodge a troupe of dancers, and Juzu grunts as someone elbows him in the gut. "It's a weapon used by non-trappers to track and nullify harmonic magic." He pauses to adjust his coat. "If it gets us in a disharmonic snare, we're cooked."

I frown. "So, no trapping?"

"Precisely." He gazes behind us, where the sentinels have gotten held up at the front gate, throwing elbows and making a scene and slowly clearing a path through the crowd. It's only a matter of time before they spot us again.

"Bexis?"

I blink as Ajjan emerges from the crowd, arms spread and a drunken smile on his face. He wears a black wool jacket and a scarlet scarf. His black ponytail is draped around his shoulder. "Hezha's fire! Why are you all sweaty?"

"Uh." I'm so surprised to see him I don't know what to say. "What are you doing here?"

"What's it look like?" He raises a mug of beer. "I'm drinking away the demons in my head."

"Excuse me." Juzu taps the ground with his umbrella. "As fascinating as that sounds, we don't have time for this."

Ajjan's smile falters. "Aevem Juzu? But—the ordinance—I thought you disappeared."

"Yes," Juzu says. "And we need to disappear again. Quickly."

I'm impressed by the speed with which Ajjan's demeanor snaps from relaxed cheer to officious competence as he spots the sentinels a hundred paces behind us.

"We need to hide," I tell him. "Can you help us?"

By now, a small circle has formed around us, as other people notice Juzu too—between his black fedora, dark spectacles, and wild mess of gray hair, he's not exactly inconspicuous. Excited mutters of "It's him!" and "The Aevem!" rise around us. A moment of dread passes through me. The penalty for aiding a resonance trapper is death. Surely, one of these people will turn against us. But to my surprise, they look at Juzu with admiration.

A man wearing the common clothing of a mid-level merchant—tan trousers and a gray jacket with a tattered scarf—steps forward. He bows to Juzu, then glares at the sentinels. "Those bastards won't take you if there's anything we can do about it. How can I help?"

Juzu holds up his hands. "I can't put you in that position—"

"Shut up!" Ajjan snaps. He points to the man. "Divert the sentinels. Buy us any time you can. I'll take them to Red Square and find them a place to hide."

The man nods, his jaw set, and he pushes his way through the throng to intercept the sentinels. About six others follow.

Ajjan takes my hand. "I know a place you can hide, but we have to hurry."

Red Square is a small public park, about fifty square feet, surrounded by shops and stalls. In the middle, there's a garden area and a marble statue of Orran the Savior. It's a popular destination for tourists and families because of the view of the clocktower to the north and the White Keep high on the hill, its parapets glowing in the distance with pale blue light.

Ajjan leads us to a fruit stand on the periphery of the square with rows of crates and large baskets containing lemons and pink apples.

"This is one of the Blackbones' shell stands. Hide under here." Ajjan indicates a crawl space beneath the stall obscured by baskets and crates.

Juzu tucks his umbrella under his shoulder and places a hand on Ajjan's shoulder. "Thank you."

"The people are on your side." Ajjan glances over his shoulder. "I'll try to draw them away." He gives me a soft smile and fades back into the crowd.

Juzu grins at me and falls to his hands and knees. "I like him."

"Yeah, me too." I grimace as my palms hit the icy stone. The ground is filthy and cold and wet. The knees of my trousers soak up spilled beer and puddle water, and the chill seeps into my bones. I hold my breath and crawl beneath the stand. The table covers our heads, and the fruit baskets shield us from the sides. Lying on our stomachs, we have a clear view of the square. We won't be easy to spot.

The sentinels burst through the crowd, decked out in polished black plate armor and sabers on their belts—I can see at least ten of them from this position. Three sentinels sprint past, just like Juzu hoped. But the others linger behind.

One soldier in particular stands out. He's shorter than the others, has a slimmer build, and wears a scarlet surcoat over a black chest plate with a sigil of a white bear. He has a bulbous nose, a scar that runs from his ear to his neck, and shoulder-length black hair. The crowd parts before him.

"The captain of the guard," Juzu whispers. "Jordy Phekru."

My breath catches in my throat. This is the man the sentinels mentioned in my apartment, the one in charge of finding me. For some reason, I imagined the captain of the guard would be physically imposing and brutish. But Phekru's demeanor is calm and cold. His beady black eyes scan the crowd with calculating perception. About fifty people have gathered around the square, surrounding the sentinels.

Most are half drunk, eyes glazed from jalpe smoke and a night of revelry. Some of the faces are wary and concerned, while others are hardened into truculent scowls. The sentinels aren't popular right now. It seems the Magistrate's ordinance wasn't well received by the people.

"Good evening," Phekru says, smoothing his hair, then prowling into the crowd like a lynx. His voice is like ice water. "I apologize for the disruption, but we have pursued a dangerous fugitive into this market. We're looking for a man and a teenage girl."

The crowd stares at him in silence. My heart slams against my sternum.

Phekru strolls forward, his hands held up to show he means no harm. He reaches into his surcoat pocket and takes out a silver ball, proffering it in his palm. The ball starts to glow and hover in the air, darting from position to position as it pulses with soft light that shifts from white to red.

Juzu curses. "It knows we're in the area, but it can't pinpoint our exact location."

My gaze is drawn to the ball. It doesn't look threatening at all. It's actually kind of pretty, like a child's plaything.

"They're here," Phekru says, his voice carrying through the square. He gazes around the crowd. "You all know the new ordinance. Anyone who harbors enemies of the state will see the gallows. Tell me where they are, and you can all go back to enjoying your evening."

More faces in the crowd harden, but others swallow nervously. A voice breaks the silence, and Ajjan steps forward. "You're looking for the Aevem, aren't you?"

Phekru cocks his head, resting his hand on the pommel of his blade. "Yes."

"What the stars is he doing?" I whisper, my heart racing.

"Trying to be a hero." Juzu shakes his head. "I think he loves you."

"We're just friends," I hiss, but Juzu silences me with a finger to his lips. I clench my hands into fists.

"We saw him run through here." Ajjan points up the street toward the eastern exit. "They went that way." Rumblings of assent rise from the crowd. Some nod and others fold their arms across their chests.

"Is that so?" Phekru steps closer. His boots are black iron with gruesome spikes on the toes. He shifts his attention beyond Ajjan. "I'll give a hundred thousand pieces to the person who tells me where they are."

A murmur runs through the crowd. My heart stutters. A hundred thousand pieces is a fortune, enough to change someone's life forever. How many people saw us crawl under here? It would only take one person to speak out and our covers would be blown. Juzu presses his lips into a thin white line, indicating that he's thinking the same thing.

When no one steps forward, Phekru clicks his tongue. "Really? No one?"

"I told you. They're not here." Ajjan puts his hands on his hips. "You're wasting time—"

"Phasers do *not* lie." Phekru's voice is a cold whisper. "Which means you are compliant in aiding a criminal of the state." He smirks. "I could have you executed for treason where you stand." Taking their captain's cue, two sentinels snatch Ajjan's arms. He resists as the others draw their swords.

Bleeding stars! My muscles tense, and Juzu places a hand on my shoulder, keeping me in place. But my instinct is to move, to act. I can't let anything bad happen to Ajjan.

"You can't hang all of us." Ajjan clenches his jaw.

Phekru addresses the crowd. "Treason will no longer be tolerated in the city of Coppejj. The Magistrate has given me full authority to deal with rats how I see fit." He takes out a knife and holds it to Ajjan's throat. "Aevem Juzu Khinvo, will you stand by as others pay for your crimes?"

"What do we do?" I hiss.

"I have to turn myself in," Juzu says.

"Aren't you going to fight?" My stomach drops. If anything happens to Ajjan, I'll never live with myself. But without Juzu, I'm right back where I started. The phantom is still out there, and I need the Aevem's protection now more than ever.

"There's nothing I can do." He frowns. "You stay here. There's no reason for you to get caught too. I'll see what I can do for your friend."

Phekru's eyes swivel across the crowd. Angry faces glare back at him, but no one moves. "Well?" he shouts. "What's it going to be?"

"Bleed this," I mutter. If it were only Juzu, I might be able to sit tight, but Ajjan has exposed himself, and there's no way they'll let him walk after this. He's in direct opposition to the ordinance. They'll kill him whether Juzu gives himself up or not. I only have one card to play. Phaser be damned.

Before I can convince myself otherwise, I wrench my tone pipe out of my pocket, bring it to my lips, and blow.

"No!" Juzu slaps my hand, but it's too late. The vibration rattles through me, and I open myself up to it, embracing the resonance as it bursts to life, ready to cradle it in my mind's eye. But something goes wrong. Instead of a steady hum, the vibration splinters, shattering into a million pieces that bounce and ricochet in my mind. I gasp from the shock as a blast of white heat streaks through my veins. I whimper and pull my arms across my chest.

"Breathe, Bexis." Juzu's hands are on my shoulders, and he cradles me in his lap. His electric eyes glare down at me with open despair. "Try to stay calm."

"W-what's happening?" My body trembles and my arms are numb. The wrongness fills me from head to toe. I'm too hot and too cold at the same time. A painful discomfort sears through my bones, and I cannot let it go.

"What you're experiencing is *dis*harmony. I told you. You can't trap with a phaser nearby." The silver ball pulses with deep red light and chirps frantically as it darts toward us, disappearing from view above the table.

"There you are." Phekru grins, removing the knife from Ajjan's throat. "Come on out, Juzu. I know you're under there."

Pain ratchets up my neck. "I'm s-sorry," I stammer. "M-make it stop."

Juzu pats me on the shoulder and sighs. "Hold tight. I'll see what I can do."

I watch through the opening in the baskets as Juzu crawls out from our hiding place. Despair clutches at my throat and my chest heaves.

If the phaser is keeping him from trapping, is Juzu going to fight Phekru and six guards with an umbrella? I curse myself for a fool.

Juzu dusts off his trousers as he makes his way into the square.

"Good of you to show." Phekru rolls his shoulders. The phaser darts around Juzu's head, then returns to Phekru. Each pulse of red light sends a sick tremor through my veins.

Juzu stops about ten paces from the sentinels and leans casually on his umbrella. "Phekru," he says. "Let them all go, turn off the phaser, and I'll come quietly."

"The phaser is the only thing keeping you from tearing us apart." Phekru raises his arms with an unctuous grin. "But I have no quarrel with the good people of Red Tree." He turns to the crowd. "It's time for you all to go home. Count yourselves lucky we don't press charges and arrest the lot of you."

No one moves. The people glare at him, their mouths pressed into tight lines.

The sentinels brace their weapons, flashing cold steel in the lamplight. Phekru's grin melts as he turns to Juzu. "Tell them to leave, or this will be a slaughter."

Juzu raises his palms in a gesture of supplication. "Listen, everyone. I thank you for your efforts. But you need to go home now." There's a touch of steel in his voice. "Nobody needs to die tonight."

His last words seem to resonate as the crowd begins to disperse. It's clear they don't want to leave the Aevem alone with Phekru and the sentinels, but the threat of death is enough to send them on their way. I don't blame them.

My teeth chatter. I wrap my arms across my knees. I don't know how much longer I can stand this feeling. But I can't just sit here either. I scoot forward, but it's like my limbs are trapped in molasses.

When the square empties, a tense silence settles across the street. The lamps around the empty stalls give off a yellow glow, and the wind whips at Juzu's fedora. He adjusts the collar of his waistcoat, tucking his umbrella into his armpit. "I submit," he says, offering his wrists. "You win."

I watch in horror as Phekru closes the space between them and punches Juzu in the face with a gauntleted fist. The Aevem's head rocks back with a sickening snap; he stumbles backward, collapsing on the ground.

My jaw hangs open. The unnecessary use of violence shocks me so badly I jolt upright. Why would Phekru do that? He's already won.

"Not so strong without your magic, are you?" Phekru snarls. He barks at the other guards. "Find the girl."

"No!" Ajjan shouts, straining against the sentinel who still holds him. "Stop this!"

Crap! I curl on my side and grit my teeth. Shame twists around my guts. I'm Juzu's ward. I'm supposed to help him, but I can't even run as the sentinels kick over the fruit baskets, sending apples rolling across the ground. They haul me out and drag me across the square, dropping me in a pile at Phekru's feet.

My hands shake as I glare at Phekru, willing strength that I don't have into my muscles. I've fought too long and too hard to make a name for myself in this Saints-forsaken town to be taken out so easily. I need to fight, to do something. But when I try to rise, a spasm of disharmony works through my spine, and I crumple back onto the cold ground.

The captain of the guard observes me with interest. "And you must be Bexis." He crouches on his haunches and grabs my right wrist. I try to pull away, but his grip is like an iron vise. He tears the bandage from my wrist, revealing the black serpent and moon beastmark. Phekru purses his lips. "Yes, you're the one." His eyes flit from me to Ajjan. "Who is he to you?"

"N-no one!" I stammer.

"Leave her alone." Juzu moves into a fighting stance, his umbrella raised like a sword.

"Aevem." Phekru turns to face Juzu, squaring his shoulders. "Now that we have her, we don't need you anymore." He flicks his wrist, gesturing to his men. "Kill him."

Six sentinels attack as one, their blades swinging for Juzu's head. My heart leaps into my throat as the Aevem ducks and kicks the legs of one guard while using his umbrella to hook the heel of another. His momentum springs him upward as both sentinels fall flat on their backs. Juzu releases a roar of triumph as he weaves around deadly blows like a dancer, striking with his umbrella. Phekru stands, his mouth set in a frown. All of the sentinels are preoccupied with Juzu now as he moves with impossible grace to disarm one soldier, then sends another careening into a wine stand, smashing a casket and spilling summer red into the street.

Phekru draws his sword. "Enough of this," he says. The two remaining sentinels break off, nursing minor wounds. Juzu breathes heavily, but he's light on his feet. He swings his umbrella in a figure eight pattern, his silver eyes crackling with menacing fury. Phekru swings wide, and Juzu ducks, but the captain expects this and counters with a left uppercut. Juzu flies back and hits the ground. Phekru pounces, kicking him hard in the stomach. Juzu moans. His face is a sheet of blood.

Despair curls in my gut. I can't do anything. I wasn't Juzu's ward for an hour before the whole thing came crashing down.

"Now, Aevem," Phekru says. "You die." He raises his sword in the air.

"Hey!" Ajjan yells. In the confusion of the melee, the sentinels had released him. He holds the phaser in his fist.

Phekru's face turns the color of sour milk. "What do you think you're doing with that?"

"Step away from the Aevem," Ajjan says. "Or I'll destroy it."

Phekru raises a palm, inching forward. "You know I can't do that—"

"Stop!" Ajjan shouts. "Don't come any closer."

Phekru growls and lunges, streaking across the square with incredible speed. Ajjan yelps and smashes the phaser on the ground. Sparks fly into the air as relief floods through me. I gasp for breath as the strange wrongness dissolves. Phekru crashes into Ajjan, and they fall into a heap. Then the square explodes in a ring of white power.

I shield my face as the wind tears at my skin and my hair whips my back. Electricity fizzles across the ground. Juzu rises to his feet, lightning forking from his fingers. It slams into Phekru's abdomen. The captain screams as he flies across the square, his black armor steaming. Ajjan scrambles backward, rushing to my side.

White light crackles across Juzu's arms. He hoists his umbrella over his shoulder and grins, looking maniacal with his bloodstained face and glowing silver eyes. With full access to his resonance, the sentinels don't stand a chance against him.

The sentinels gather by Phekru, helping their captain to his feet. He shrugs them off, his face a mask of twisted fury. "This isn't over, Juzu. We'll be back."

In answer, Juzu summons a beam of light from his palm that shoots toward Phekru. It explodes in the air, creating a rain of sizzling sparks. The captain and his guards sprint down the street and disappear from sight.

Juzu straightens the lapels of his jacket. His face is a swollen bloody mess. He takes out his pipe, lights a match, and inhales. "Are you alright, Bexis?"

"I'm fine," I say, shame coiling in my chest. Ajjan helps me to my feet, but my knees buckle, and he has to support my weight, bracing a shoulder under my arm.

"That was quick thinking," Juzu says to Ajjan, breathing out a plume of yellow smoke. He crouches next to the remnants of the phaser and picks up what appears to be a small iridescent bead. "Saints know, I despise these things."

Ajjan shrugs. "It was nothing."

"It wasn't nothing." Juzu pockets the bead and stands. "I'm in your debt. If there's anything I can do for you—"

"There isn't." Ajjan smiles weakly. "Bexis has saved my life more times than I can count, so I'm just paying her back in kind. Plus, it was real nice seeing those assholes get what's coming to them."

"All the same." Juzu smiles, gesturing to a side alley. "We need to keep moving."

Frustration swells in my chest. I made a fool of myself. Far from proving that I know what I'm doing, I only reinforced Juzu's impression that I'm a child who needs to be looked after. That's not how I wanted to begin this relationship, but there's nothing I can do now but move forward.

"Ajjan," I say. "Phekru knows your face. You're not safe out here. You should come with us."

Juzu quirks an eyebrow, but he nods. "She's right. Now that the sentinels know you have a connection to Bexis, they'll seek you out."

Ajjan glances from me to Juzu. "I can't," he says. "All of the council members are being held under guard in their offices in the White Keep. Zhira is losing her mind. The Blackbones are going to break her out." But the words he's not saying echo in my head. *If Zhira is in the keep, this is the perfect time to try to escape.* "I don't know what you guys have planned, but maybe try to steer clear of the sentinels from now on."

"Sage advice," Juzu says, "but breaking into the White Keep won't be easy."

"We'll manage." Ajjan squeezes my shoulder. "Fisherman's Wharf?"

I nod. A small indication that our plan is still on. The ship leaves for Emceni tomorrow morning. I have a full day and night to make my final decision.

"Good." He waves as he turns away. "I'm glad you're both okay."

Juzu bends at the waist and picks up a leather glove that someone's left on the street. He nods and stashes it in his pocket. "This should do nicely."

"What's that for?" I take an unsteady step forward.

Juzu holds my arm as he leads me into an alley. "Come along, Bexis. And try to keep an open mind."

CHAPTER 9

DAWN HAS COME AND GONE.

The silver moon hangs overhead as Juzu and I cut through a maze of empty back alleys and deserted streets, turning off every thoroughfare and doing circles through the slums. It doesn't take long before I'm disoriented and lost. We must still be in the Hollow, but I don't recognize these neighborhoods, and the buildings have an abandoned look to them—as if no one has lived in this section of the city for a decade or more. No paper lanterns or streetlights. No people on the sidewalks. There's not even trash in the gutters.

I've recovered from the dizzying effects of the phaser's disharmonic snare, but a deep exhaustion has settled into my bones. Every step sends an achy throb through the bottoms of my feet, and the mark on my wrist tingles. I'd love nothing more than to sit on the curb and rest my eyes, but the Aevem won't relax his pace. "Do you know where we're going?" I ask for the third time in the last hour.

"I told you." Juzu steps off the curb and turns down another alley. "I'll know when we get there."

"But we're going in circles!" I point to an abandoned storefront with a cracked front window. "We walked by that shop ten minutes ago."

He scratches his head. "Are you sure?"

"We're lost." I stop short of the alley. There's a bench on the side of the street, and I plop down. I know the phantom is still out there and could come out at any moment, but I'm so tired I don't care. "Just give me a minute."

Juzu stuffs his hands in his pockets and sighs. "You'll feel better soon. And for what it's worth, you're right. We *are* lost. But that's the only way to get where we're going."

I rub my temples. "What are you talking about?"

"I'm taking you to see a Dreamspeaker." Juzu's silver eyes glow in the darkness, muted by his shaded round spectacles. "A practitioner of old magic who deals almost exclusively with the spirit worlds. She's a bit mad, if you ask me, but she's a repository of information on the subject of demons and ghosts." He puffs at his pipe, sending smoky clouds floating down the street. "I think she can help you get to the root of your episodes. We can't have you exploding every time you need to trap resonance. You'll never learn anything that way."

I perk up. This is the reason I agreed to be Juzu's ward in the first place. The prospect of being able to trap without fear of losing control and hurting people sends a tremor of excitement down my spine. After sleeping so long, I only have one day now until the ship leaves for Emceni. That isn't much time. I know I won't be able to master my resonance by then, but every bit will make a difference. "How will a Dreamspeaker help me with my episodes?"

"We're going to wake up your *wolsai*."

I lean back against the bench and place my hands in my lap. "My what?"

"Hmm." Juzu glances around at the empty street. His eyes flicker to a space above my head, then he nods. "How much do you know about trapping, Bexis?"

How do I answer that? I've been trapping for almost seven years, but I still don't know much about how or why it happens. I'm accomplished enough with my abilities to have made a decent living for myself on the streets. Zhira knows my value enough to want me to join the Blackbones, which means I must be doing something right. I jut out my chin. "Enough to get by."

Juzu chuckles. "Fair enough, but do you know how someone becomes a trapper?"

It's a well-known fact that only children born under the shadow moon can be trappers. The Orrethic texts claim the moon is a portal to a realm of demons. No one but the luminaries actually believes that garbage.

"It has something to do with the shadow moon," I say.

"Correct." Juzu taps ashes from his pipe onto the sidewalk. "The shadow moon is a gateway to a spirit world called Nhammock, which is home to all manner of beings: ghosts, wraiths, demons, angels, and everything in between."

I furrow my brow. Mo told me this exact theory only yesterday, and I all but laughed at her. "I thought that was a story the Orrethics made up."

"I assure you, it's true," Juzu says. "Wolsai are spirits that live in Nhammock. They have a strong affinity for humans. When the shadow moon rises, and the gateway is open, wolsai pour into the mortal world and bond with newborn human souls. That's why any child born under the shadow moon will have the ability to trap resonance. It's the human-wolsai bond that makes harmonic magic possible."

Doubt washes over me, but Juzu's tone is serious and sober. "So, wait," I say, failing to keep the incredulity out of my voice. "You're saying I can trap resonance because my soul is bonded with a *demon?*"

"Wolsai are not demons," Juzu corrects. "They are friendly spirits that hunger for connection and synchronicity with their human companions."

"Still." I shiver. The idea that I'm sharing my body with some kind of spirit feels wrong. "You're saying my body has two souls, like I'm possessed?"

"You're not possessed. Your thoughts are your own, and your body is yours. Think of it like a symbiotic relationship in nature. Wolsai cannot exist in the mortal world without a human to bond with, and humans benefit from the relationship with resonance and power."

"I don't know." Doubt wriggles through my gut. "Wouldn't I know if I had a spirit bonded to my soul?"

"Yours hasn't woken up yet." Juzu packs more jalpe into his pipe. He frowns at his empty bag and stashes it back in his pocket before striking a match. "At least, not all the way. Which is why you have to use a pipe to catch resonance. When it wakes up, you'll have far more access to your abilities."

"What happens then? I'll have a sentient being in my body waiting for me to trap?"

"Not quite," Juzu explains. "The wolsai is tethered to you, but it is not bound by you. My wolsai, Olppeo, likes to eavesdrop on people. He finds it endlessly entertaining. Like right now"—he waves a hand, gesturing across the street—"Olppeo is floating above those buildings there, vigilant, just in case the phantom decides to drop by."

I follow his gaze, but there's nothing there. Suddenly, it clicks. "When you stare off into space like you're seeing things that aren't there—"

"Yes," he confirms. "It's Olppeo."

My jaw drops. "Are you messing with me?"

"I can't lie," he says. "Remember?"

"Can I see Olppeo?"

Juzu grins. "He's an introvert, I'm afraid. And it takes a considerable amount of energy to materialize in the physical plane. Someday, you'll meet him, but not now."

I frown, leaning back on the bench. It starts to snow lightly. Tiny cold prickles melt against my cheeks. "Okay, so let's assume this is all true," I say. "How does it work? What does the wolsai do that makes trapping possible?"

"I'll give you the basics, but we should keep moving." He reaches out a hand. I take it and let him haul me to my feet. Together, we cross the street and enter an alley.

Juzu takes a drag from his pipe and exhales a plume of yellow smoke. "It's helpful to think of this in musical terms," he says. "There are two components to a human-wolsai pairing. Each one is like a musical note that vibrates at its own unique frequency. The human note—what we call internal resonance—is the foundation. It sets the key. If the internal resonance is strong and pure, the wolsai will harmonize. This synergetic energy results in power that we can harness to perform harmonic magic."

I consider how this applies to my issues with trapping, how the resonance has always resisted and fought against me. "So the reason I have episodes is because I have an issue with my internal resonance, and my wolsai has trouble harmonizing with it?"

"Yes and no." Juzu grins. "Your episodes happen because your bond with your wolsai has been obstructed. Once we awaken your wolsai, holding resonance should be much easier, but your internal resonance will dictate what kinds of powers you have and how strong your abilities will grow."

"How does internal resonance get obstructed? How do I change it?" I ask as we emerge from the alley into an empty thoroughfare. The snow has picked up, absorbing the sound. It's like we're not even in the city anymore; we've stepped into an alternate world.

"A human soul is a complicated thing. Everything you do, every thought that runs through your head, and every emotion that you feel contributes to your internal resonance. Negativity obstructs. Anger, hate, distrust, grief. The only way to change it is to change who you are. That's why the Khatori orders each have a set of codes. The Aevem code is called the Virtues—truth, forgiveness, and duty—by living according to those tenets, I tune my internal resonance to a frequency that Olppeo likes to harmonize. It's what allows me to heal and to conjure light. It's what makes me an Aevem."

That's why he can't lie. Doing so would disrupt his internal resonance, and his wolsai wouldn't be able to harmonize with him the same way. I brace my back against the icy wind that snakes up my sleeves. "What determines the types of powers a trapper has—internal resonance or the wolsai that's bonded with us?"

"Both," Juzu says. "The most formidable trappers understand that internal resonance is a balancing act, being true to themselves in a way that also makes them resonate strongly enough for their wolsai to harmonize."

We stop at a corner and take a right turn, heading into a dark abandoned lot. Juzu's eyes flick skyward, and I assume he's watching Olppeo up there, scouting ahead. I imagine him looking like a small spirit—a fairy or a ghost. But that's silly. I have no idea what wolsai look like. "This is a lot to wrap my head around."

"It's alright." Juzu places a hand on my shoulder. "It will become clearer as you gain more experience. For now, it's enough to understand that your actions affect your resonance, which affects your abilities and strength. To be a trapper is to recognize that everything you do matters. Every decision has consequences, even if you don't see how in the moment." As we enter the lot, Juzu turns and spreads his arms. "Look. We're here!"

I stop. We're standing in front of a dead end. The lot is empty except for a pair of trashcans that have been pushed conspicuously under a lone lamppost. The light is out, and all the buildings are dark and deserted. There aren't even footprints in the snow. Nobody's been back here in days.

I can't help but feel disappointed. After all this walking, I was expecting to end up somewhere warm. But now we're in the middle of nowhere, and I have no idea how we got here or how to get back. "Where are we exactly?"

"You're in for a treat." Juzu swings his umbrella around his wrist and makes for the trashcans. "Welcome to Shytar's workshop."

I stand on the curb with my shoulders hunched against the cold. "Juzu, there's nothing here. No workshop. No speaker. This was a waste of time."

He leans on the trashcan and bashes his fist against the lid. "Keep an open mind. Shytar is one of the wisest and most powerful Dreamspeakers in all of Coppejj."

A voice comes from inside the trashcan. "Who is it?"

My heart skips a beat. There's someone *in* there.

"Wake up, Shy." Juzu removes the lid. "I need your help."

"Juzu?" A middle-aged woman with short black hair and layers of baggy clothes pokes out of the trashcan. She has red cheeks and a round face with large brown eyes that she rubs with her knuckles. "Hezha's fire, you went through that bag already?"

"What?" His gaze flicks to me. "No, I—"

"It's alright. I got you." Shytar yawns and crosses her arms. "How much do you need?"

"No, Shy. I'm not here for that—"

"Are you kidding me?" I'm unable to contain my disbelief. "You brought us to your drug dealer? That's why we're out here? So you can buy more jalpe?"

"Ju." Shytar narrows her eyes, scanning me up and down. She jams a thumb in my direction. "Who's the square?"

"Everyone, calm down." Juzu rubs his forehead. "Shytar, this is my new ward, Bexis. She's alright, I think. I'm not here for jalpe. But we do need your help."

"You're not here for jalpe, and you need my help," Shytar repeats. She sucks her teeth. "That can't be good."

"It's not," Juzu says. "Can we come in?"

My anger is muted only slightly by my confusion. I had expected a Dreamspeaker would have a holy or spiritual disposition, but Shytar resembles one of the destitutes that live under the bridge in the Slags. And she apparently sleeps in trash cans.

Shytar purses her lips to the side. "Are you hot?"

"Yes," Juzu says. "The sentinels are searching for us right now. And we're also being pursued by a shadow demon."

"Oh, right. That one you mentioned last week?"

Juzu nods.

"Alright. Fine." Shytar grasps the edges of the trashcan and heaves herself out. She's covered in a layer of dust and muck. She takes two steps, then starts stomping her foot on the cobblestones beneath the snow.

I pull on Juzu's sleeve. "I'm not climbing in that trashcan with you."

"Don't worry. The workshop isn't in the trashcan. Everything is okay."

"It's not okay," I tell him. "I can't believe you went through all this to meet with your drug dealer. I thought we were trying to save people. Find the phantom—"

"I wasn't lying!" His silver eyes burn with conviction. "Shytar really is a wise and powerful Dreamspeaker. She just happens to also be my drug dealer."

"Convenient." I cross my arms.

"Yes, it is." He adjusts his fedora at a tilt on his head. "Sometimes life works out."

"Bleeding flower blossoms!" Shytar shouts, digging in the snow. "I can never remember which stone—" A loud groan rises through the ground. The cobblestones start to shiver.

My heart quickens as the ground starts to tremble. "It's a quake," I shout. "We need to find cover!"

"Just relax," Juzu says. "Watch and learn."

The stones beneath the trashcan slide sideways, revealing a circular door in the ground with a brass loop handle. The shaking subsides and the alley falls into silence once again.

My eyes open wide. A hidden door in the middle of an abandoned cul-de-sac? I bite my bottom lip. The world is, indeed, more complex than I thought. What kind of magic is this? It's not resonance trapping, or at least, not any kind I've heard of. Maybe Juzu is right, and there's more to Shytar than meets the eye.

"Well, here it is." Shytar places her hands on her hips and inspects the door. Crusts of dried mud flake off her jacket and fall onto the snow.

"Well done!" Juzu says. Together, they heave the door open as I remain standing on the curb. I swear, ever since I agreed to be Juzu's ward, it's like the world has gone strange. Nothing is normal anymore. I kind of love it.

"Hey, square," Shytar calls to me. "You coming?"

CHAPTER 10

"MAKE YOURSELF AT HOME," SHYTAR GRUMBLES AS SHE IGNITES A handheld lantern and shoves past me, leading us through a dark subterranean hallway. "But for the love of the Saints, don't touch anything."

"Sure." I wrinkle my nose as a soft trash scent leaks from Shytar's jacket into the space between us. My instincts tell me not to follow the crazy lady into the dark basement, but my instincts also told me to ignore Juzu's warnings and trap next to a phaser. Still, truth is a Virtue, so if he says Shytar can help me smooth over my resonance issues, I'll take him at his word.

Shytar sets the lantern on a table and claps her hands; a series of yellow lamps bloom to life along the walls and ceiling, illuminating a large rectangular chamber with long wooden workbenches arranged in three rows. A pile of refuse sits in the far corner—rags and burlap sacks full of cotton and bags of buttons and needles and thread. Another work station contains various cuts of wood and buckets of tools: hammers, chisels, and saws. And then, closest to me, there's a painting station with tubes of dye and brushes of every size. Shelves line the walls, holding rows of dolls and dollhouses, stuffed animals, puppets, kites, masks, drums, and wooden horses.

I stand in the doorway, my bewilderment mingled with awe. I don't know what I expected, but this certainly wasn't it. "What is this place?"

"This is my home." Shytar pulls off her many layers of jackets and shirts as if they were a single coat and tosses them in the corner. She is now wearing a black tank top and trousers with black leather boots. Her arms are pale and covered with intricate black tattoos that spiral up her neck. Gold rings adorn her long fingers, and a gold chain necklace hangs around her neck. The transformation is stunning—one moment, Shytar looked like a bum from the Hollow, but in the next, she could pass as a gangster from the east side.

"If this is your home," I say, moving into the room, taking care not to bump into anything. "Then why do you sleep in trash cans?"

She gives me a toothy smile. "A side effect of the magic. When Juzu triggered the workshop to materialize in the lot, the spirits sent me to meet him. Personally, I wouldn't have picked a trash can. But the spirits have their sense of humor."

"What spirits?" I ask. "Are they here now?"

Shytar scoffs. "Spirits are everywhere all the time. Most people can't see them or hear them."

"But you can?"

She touches her nose. "That's why I'm a Dreamspeaker."

I purse my lips, resolving to keep my expression neutral, and turn my attention to the workshop. A long marionette dragon hangs from the ceiling, its wooden teeth bared in a menacing grin. "So," I say, "you make toys?"

Shytar narrows her large brown eyes. "Sure do."

"Why?" I ask. "Is it a front for your drug operation?"

"Oh no. It's the other way around." She crosses her arms. "I sell drugs so no one will suspect I make toys."

I jump as a spark of recognition runs through me. Mo told me about the crazy lady who makes toys for orphans. "You're the Toymaker!"

"Brilliant deduction!" Juzu leans against one of the benches and runs his fingers along the parapets of a toy castle. "What gave it away?"

I scowl and rummage through my pack. "You make dolls for orphans," I say, taking out the skeleton doll. "The youngest boy in Mo's gang gave me this."

Shytar's posture softens as her eyes fall on the doll. "You know Mo?"

"She's a friend of mine. Every time I get paid, I bring the Rovers a bag of sweetbread."

"I see." Shytar's face continues to soften. She stands beside me and sighs. Her eyes glisten in the yellow lamplight. "These are Kolej dolls. They're protective talismans, designed to ward off foul spirits—the Saints know there are enough of *those* wandering the streets these days. I give them to kids on the street because they deserve to have someone looking out for them."

I frown, holding the doll with two hands. Its black-button eyes stare back at me. "When the phantom attacked me on the roof, it disarmed me like I was nothing. I tried to trap but couldn't hold onto resonance. I was saved by a shield of white light that I couldn't explain."

Shytar raises an eyebrow at Juzu. "The same creature you've been hunting?"

"Yes." Juzu strokes his chin. "Bexis, you didn't mention this earlier."

"You didn't ask," I say, "and I didn't know if it was important."

"Fascinating." Shytar takes the doll from me. "For a Kolej talisman to work, it must be given with the intention of protecting the receiver. Each time it is given, its strength is increased. The boy who gave this to you wanted you to be safe."

Juzu clicks his tongue. "I've never heard of a Kolej doll creating a shield that powerful."

Shytar shrugs. "It was a damn good doll. Thank you very much. The charm should be depleted now, but if you give it back to the boy who gave it to you, it will work doubly strong for him."

"Why don't you give it to him for me?" I ask. The last thing I want is to bring danger to Mo and the Rovers. "When all this is over, I'm going to buy them a hundred cinnamon cakes, but until then, I should keep my distance."

Shytar weighs my words, nods, and tucks the doll into her pocket. "Suit yourself."

"Now then." Juzu leans his umbrella against a bench and pulls out his pipe. "My inquisitive young ward here is dealing with a nasty block, and we need to get to the bottom of it sooner rather than later."

"Ah." Shytar pushes away from the bench and crosses her arms. "You want a Calling."

"Yes." Juzu reaches into his pocket and takes out a dirty leather glove. He holds it up to the light and places it on the workbench. "I believe this should suffice as payment?"

Shytar lets out a squeal of excitement and takes out a small golden loupe. She bends over the dirty glove to examine it more closely. I quirk an eyebrow. Shytar is, by far, one of the strangest people I've ever met.

"Hmm. Where did you find this?" she asks.

"Red Tree Market." Juzu examines his nails with practiced nonchalance.

"In a bin?"

"On the street. Someone discarded it."

I remember Juzu picking it up. It seems like an ordinary thing, just a piece of trash. If there's something special about it, I can't see what it is. Judging by the piles of refuse in the corner, she must use garbage as raw materials to make her toys.

Shytar twists her mouth, then nods. "We have a deal." She places the glove in her pocket and begins rummaging through her drawers, taking out a mortar and pestle and bags of herbs. "One Calling, coming right up."

I lean against the bench, trying to settle my nerves. "What's a Calling?"

Juzu sits on the table beside me, dangling his legs like a child. "A Calling is a ritual designed to bring you to the Aoz, a parallel dimension constructed by your mind."

"A parallel dimension," I repeat. "And this will let me speak to my wolsai?"

"Precisely," Juzu says. "The connection between trapper and wolsai forms over time, as you build your internal resonance and the wolsai learns how to harmonize, but in some cases, the bond stalls, and it requires a little push to get things moving again."

The prospect of traveling to another dimension and meeting a foreign spirit fills me with a strange mix of apprehension and excitement. Until a half hour ago, I'd never heard of a wolsai, and now I'm about to meet one face-to-face. "What are wolsai like?" I ask.

Juzu places his hands in his lap. "They're all different. They have names and personalities, strengths and weaknesses. Some are elusive and shy, while others are bold and exuberant."

"Some of them can be quite clever," Shytar mutters as she crushes herbs with a pestle in one hand and lights a row of candles with the other. "But I've also met some wolsai that were simple-minded. The only thing they all have in common is that they like synchronicity, and they abhor friction."

Well, that doesn't narrow it down at all. I'm still not sure whether it's wise to trust Shytar. "And this ceremony, the Calling," I say, "is it safe?"

"Of course." Juzu smiles. "Shytar is the best of the best. And I'll be here with you the whole time. We won't let anything bad happen to you."

"That's reassuring." I take a breath, willing the tension in my shoulders to relent.

"If you want to wake up your wolsai," Juzu says, seeming to sense my reluctance, "this is the fastest way. Otherwise, the process could take months or years, and we don't have that kind of time. The phantom could come for us at any moment, and we need to be prepared."

I bite my bottom lip. He's right, of course. The ship to Emceni leaves tomorrow morning. If this ceremony can resolve my trapping issues quickly, it'll be worth the risk. "Alright," I say, a steely resolve settling in my bones. For better or worse, I'm going through with this. "What do I have to do?"

Shytar clears a space on the table. "Lie down here, Bexis."

I climb onto the table, feeling a bit like a doll about to be painted under the lights, and lie on my back, gazing up at the ceiling.

"Good." Shytar hands me a bowl of brown liquid. "Drink this."

I frown. It smells like dirt. "What is it?"

"Ground herbs and fungus. To help you open your mind."

Hmm. I take a sip. The flavor of dried mushrooms makes me gag. "Oh Saints, that is foul."

"Don't spill it!" Shytar says. "Drink as much as you can."

I take two more sips, grimace, and hold up the bowl. "Is that enough?"

Shytar shrugs. "It'll do."

"Don't be such a baby." Juzu takes the bowl from me and drains the rest. "It doesn't taste *that* bad."

"Hey!" Shytar snatches the bowl from Juzu. "You're a plague! Has anyone ever told you that?"

"Yes, as a matter of fact." Juzu burps softly. "Several people. I'm beginning to think it's true."

I shake my head. At least he's consistent.

"Bexis," Shytar says. "In a few moments, you're going to feel a bit disoriented. That's the fungus doing its work—nothing to worry about. I'm going to guide you safely to the Aoz. When you get there, your wolsai will be waiting for you."

I lie back on the table. A warmth begins to spread across my chest. I wipe my palms on my thighs. "So what do I say?"

"Make sure you get a name," Juzu says. "That's very important for strengthening your bond. And if you think of it, ask about the beastmark."

I raise an eyebrow. "You think my wolsai will know about that?"

"It's possible. Remember, the beastmark is not a wound of the flesh. It's a physical manifestation of something that Vogul did to your spirit." Juzu leans back. "Which means your wolsai has also been marked and may have information you aren't aware of."

"Enough," Shytar interrupts. She holds her palms above my forehead. "It's time. Close your eyes, Bexis."

I clasp my hands on my belly, trying to keep my breathing steady. My throat tingles. A tightness is growing in my shoulders.

"Listen to the sound of my voice." Shytar's cadence is like sunshine, yellow and warm. "Breathe deeply and allow an image to come to you. When it does, hold it in your mind."

At first, I don't see anything—just the black behind my eyelids. Then, shapes begin to form in the darkness—triangles and circles that wriggle through my internal vision. I inhale sharply as they bounce and dance and twist, pulsing with varicolored light—blues and oranges and pinks. As I breathe, the shapes coalesce into a kaleidoscope of colors that explode against my eyelids.

"Whoa," I breathe. My stomach does a flip. I turn my head as a cold sweat breaks out on my neck. The sensation is like I'm being torn from my body, yanked straight out of my skin. I clench my teeth and prepare to dig in.

"You're doing great, Bexis." Shytar's voice distorts and rolls like waves on the beach of the wharf. "Allow the feeling to take you. Don't fight it."

I give in to the sensation. The colors bleed into a swirling mass of light. A burst of energy erupts from my chest, crawling out of my throat. I try to scream, but my airway is blocked. *I can't breathe*, I think, terror flooding through my veins like a gushing stream. *I'm going to die.*

A tsunami of power rolls over me with a sudden *whoosh* of exhilaration.

And then nothing.

CHAPTER 11

I LIE ON MY BACK WITH MY EYES SQUEEZED SHUT. MY HEART RACES. THE sudden calm is so unexpected my stomach is still spinning. Bile creeps up my throat, and I have to clench my hands into fists to keep my fingers from shaking. That's the last time I drink any fungus water I'm given by a Dreamspeaker.

"Shytar?" I stammer. "What happened?"

When she doesn't respond, I open my eyes, expecting to see the workshop, the lights, and Juzu's silver eyes peering down at me with a wry smirk. Instead, I'm greeted by a black sky splashed with swirls of galactic dust and thousands of enormous stars—a cosmic tapestry of celestial lights and nebulae.

Bleeding stars! I'm on the flat stone surface of a platform suspended in the infinite void that sparkles around me. The platform is shaped like a long rectangle, extending about fifty yards to my left and another fifty to my right. Before me is a sheer drop. I lean forward to peer over the edge, but below is the same as above—stars and dashes of dust that glow in brilliant greens, golds, and blues. Behind me, the edge of the platform is adorned with rows of doors. There is no wall between the doors, only empty space. Each of them appears to have different shapes, colors, and sizes. Some look like regular doors one might find attached to a house, while others are shaped like triangles, hexagons, and trapezoids; some are pink and painted with white flowers, while others are stained glass or solid steel.

Alright, I tell myself, rising to my feet. *What now?* This is the Aoz, a parallel universe created by my mind. My goal here is simple: Find my wolsai and get to the root of my episodes. But there's no one here, and there's no way off the platform. Am I supposed to walk through one of the doors? Which one? I shake the tension out of my hands and face the row of doors.

After a quick count, I estimate the number to be about a hundred. There's no way to know where they'll lead me. I pace the length of the platform, trying to determine a methodology for choosing one of them. If the Aoz is a manifestation of my mind, then it would stand to reason that these doors are memories… or thoughts buried in my subconscious. I pause by a metal door with long steel stakes protruding through it. Streaks of what looks like dried blood hang from the handle. I swallow a lump in my throat. *Maybe not that one.*

I keep moving, unsure what I'm looking for. Tension mounts as my uncertainty grows. What if I can't find the right one? What if I go back to the workshop without awakening my wolsai and this whole ceremony was a waste of time?

The next door in the row makes me freeze. I would recognize it anywhere—chipped white paint with tinges of yellow around the corners, two cracks that run parallel from the top to the bottom, and a rusted copper handle. It's the front door to my father's old apartment in the Slags, the place he raised me after my mother's death.

Not this one, I plead. But my feet remain planted, and the certainty is something I cannot explain or rationalize. I need to walk through this door. I need to face what's on the other side. I take a deep breath, anxiety churning in my stomach like seafoam.

I swing the door open. Once inside, I'm greeted by the familiar darkness of the apartment I haven't seen for seven years. Dusty wooden floorboards. Two windows on the eastern side, both cracked but letting in weak strands of milky moonlight. The walls are slanted, the paint peeling, but there's a stove in the corner that lets off waves of radiant heat. As I creep forward, the stench of black mold and woodsmoke swirls into a mnemonic cloud that brings tears to my eyes. I bleeding hate this place.

Soft whimpering rises from a huddled form in the corner. It's a girl, no more than four or five years old. She sits with her back pressed against the wall, her knees drawn up to her chest. Her black hair falls around her shoulders, hiding her face, and her clothing is little more than tattered rags. Her skin, where it's exposed, is smudged with dirt and grime. My cheeks prickle at the sight—the squalor is worse than I remember. It's hard for me to gaze upon the younger version of myself and accept that I once lived like this.

"It's your fault." Lum Carro's voice, slurred and dangerous, sends a tremor of fear through my spine. He wears black trousers and a leather jerkin, both threadbare and filthy. His face is covered with a long gray beard, and his features are drawn, his eyes sunken with drunken grief. The floorboards creak as he paces the room, clutching a bottle of liquor in his fist. "You murdered her."

"No!" the girl cries. "I didn't mean to—"

Lum Carro's voice booms. "Your own mother! Dead." He unscrews the cap and, draining half the bottle, lets the liquor dribble into his beard and spill down his chest.

I stand between them, horror and guilt spreading through my limbs like ice. I've often thought back on my life with Lum Carro, revisiting the shame of my unforgivable sin, but I'd forgotten how bad things were, how horrible my life was before I learned some basic control over my resonance.

The girl buries her face in her hands. "Please. I didn't—I wasn't—"

"That's enough!" Carro wobbles on his feet. "I'll do what I should have done at the start. I'll finish this." He pours the rest of the bottle down his throat and gasps, blinking bleary red eyes, then holds the bottle by the stem and smashes it on the furnace. Glass shatters and pieces fall to the floor. Lum Carro holds a jagged remnant like a knife and rushes at the girl. She screams as he snatches her by the scruff of her neck and brings the glass to her throat.

"Stop it!" I shout. "Let her go!" But my words have no effect. I'm not here. It's just a memory. I can't change what has already happened.

"I'm sorry!" The girl sobs hysterically, her eyes filled with terror, tears streaking down her face. "I'm sorry. I'm sorry. I'm sorry!"

"What kind of demon are you?" Lum Carro's words are so thick I can hardly understand him now. The liquor is weighing him down.

"I'm not!" the girl sobs. "I'm your daughter."

"My daughter?" Lum Carro's muscles tense as a war seems to play out in his mind. His eyes narrow, and he drops the glass. Then he collapses on the floor and begins to sob. "I can't do it," he whimpers. "Lord, have mercy. I'm not strong enough."

The girl scampers away from him and huddles in the corner.

Lum Carro gazes at the ceiling, his face covered with tears and snot. "My daughter. My fault. I'm going to help you, Bexis. I promise you that. I'm going to fix you."

The girl wipes her cheeks and crawls on her hands and knees, picking her way through the broken glass. She rests her head in his lap. "Thank you," she whispers. "Thank you, Daddy."

My lip curls in disgust. I can't take any more of this. These are memories that I'd buried long ago. Things I've refused to acknowledge or think about in years. This was just the beginning of a war Lum Carro played on my sanity, teaching me to hate myself.

I stand before him, fists clenched. "You never fixed me. You broke me. Over and over again. The best thing you ever did was leave."

Lum Carro's eyes snap open with a sudden sober clarity. He glares at me, his mouth twisted in a malicious sneer. "Is that what you think?"

He's speaking to me. I'm so shocked, it takes me a moment to recover. The memory is over, or... has it taken on a life of its own? "You were evil." I gesture to the emaciated younger version of myself. "I was just a little girl. I needed love and guidance. What happened with Mom was an accident. I didn't know what I was doing."

"So I should have just forgiven you, is that it?" Lum Carro's words no longer slur. He pushes the little girl off his lap. She doesn't stir, and he rises to his feet. His breath is heavy with booze as he leans into me, poking his finger into my chest. "You were dangerous. A child with the power to kill and no self-control. You are a murderer. A monster. I should have put you out of your misery. But I was weak."

I recoil, transported back into the shell of a five-year-old girl. "I loved her too!" I shout. "You don't think I feel guilty? You don't think I feel shame?"

"Not enough." Lum Carro leans close, his beard scratching my cheek. The stench of booze is overwhelming. "I hope you suffer with it for the rest of your life. I hope it eats you alive, consuming your soul from the inside out—"

"No!" Anger explodes in my chest. I shove him hard, and his body slams against the wall and crumples. His eyes pop open, his face erupting in panic. Sweat streams down his face as his terror-stricken gaze locks on me. He lets out a piteous moan that rises until it's a scream. His skin sags and turns to dust. Muscle, sinew, and tendon melt away until there's nothing left but a pristine white skeleton slumped against the wall.

Blood thunders through my ears. What did I do? The skeleton grins up at me, the empty eye sockets somehow gloating. *See? You are a murderer. A monster!* But no. That's not fair. All I did was push him. I didn't mean to kill him.

The girl stands and moves to my side. Her face is concealed behind a mass of tangled dark hair. She points to the far side of the room, where a steel door has appeared. "You must go on."

Part of me wants to hug her, to tell her that everything is going to be alright. How many times in my life did I need to hear those words? But the girl isn't real. And neither was Lum Carro. This is all in my head.

I bite my bottom lip. "What will I find on the other side of that door?"

"You must go on," the girl repeats. Her eyes stare vacantly at nothing. I nod slowly. This memory is over. The Aoz needs me to keep moving.

"Alright," I say, putting steel into my heart. I push open the next door and step into a circular chamber with stone walls and a stone

floor. The ceiling is open, and the universe winks down at me—
constellations of stars and galaxies and planets in swirls of color. In
the center of the room is an altar—a raised platform of mortared
black brick.

My footsteps echo as I approach the altar. I've never been in this
room before, which means it's not a memory. This is new. On the
altar is a square trough of dirt. A simple kitchen knife sits next to it. A
piece of paper rests before it with the inscription: *Bleed.*

I frown. The meaning is clear, although the implication is disturbing. But if none of this is real, what's a little blood? I pick up the knife
and slice into the tip of my ring finger. I hiss as pain shoots through
me. This place might be in my head, but the pain is very real. Blood
pools and drips into the soil.

The room begins to shake, and an omniscient hum fills the air as a
stone obelisk rises from the dirt. It's about three feet tall and a foot in
diameter. A ball of shadowy light glows on the top, hovering in
the air.

"Holy crap." The voice makes me jump. "It worked!"

I blink. *What in the Hezha's fire is happening?* "What worked?" I ask.

"I'm awake." The ball of light flickers as it speaks.

"Yeah." I take a step forward. This is it. This must be my wolsai.
"Who are you?"

"Hm," the ball says. "That's a good question. I can't remember."

There's something distinctly childlike about the voice. "You can't
remember?"

"Give me a minute. I've only just woken up."

"Well, do you have a name?"

The ball seems to consider this. "My friends call me Urru. I think.
But it's hazy."

"Urru," I repeat. "I like that name."

The ball flickers. "It's a bit stuffy in here. Do you mind if we
change this up?"

"What do you mean—"

The room erupts in a fountain of black and silver light. I don't
have time to blink before the stone room dissolves. I find myself in a

field of green grass, dotted with patches of yellow dandelions that extend for miles. The sky is pure baby blue, and the sun hangs in the middle of the sky. My jaw drops, and I shield my eyes from the brightness. I've often marveled at the little dawns in Coppejj, but after living my entire life in perpetual night, I never dreamed the sun could be so powerful.

"That's better." Urru has transformed into a young girl, about ten years old. She has black hair, dark eyes, and she wears a white dress that contrasts with her dark skin.

My jaw hangs open. "Is this what you look like?"

Urru shakes her head. "I don't look like anything. I'm not a person. I'm a wolsai." She looks off to the left, where storm clouds have gathered. "Ah, I was worried about that."

"About what?"

"The *shaji*," Urru explains. "It's here, and it's not happy that I'm awake."

"What's a shaji?"

Urru gestures to the storm clouds. "The spirit that's bonded to us. I've seen its like in Nhammock—a piece of the Immortal Dark. It wants to consume us, corrupt our energy, and destroy us. But we must not let that happen."

She's talking about the phantom, I realize. "How can I fight it?"

Urru loops her arm through mine, and we walk together through the green field, the sunshine blasting down on us. "That's why I'm here. There's a message I'm supposed to relay to you. This shaji is just the first. There will be others, and you are the only one who can stop them."

"Me?" I say. "What am I supposed to do?"

"Here, hold on. Let me see." Urru detaches herself from me and smooths the front of her dress. "It'll be a while before all of my memories come back to me, but I should be able to—" She takes a deep breath and closes her eyes, holding both her palms to the sides of her head. A circle of light flashes around her. When she opens her eyes, they are burning bright purple and pink. Urru holds out her hand. A small trickle of fire dances in her palm. "Daughter of Shadow." The voice emanates from all around us, no longer Urru's voice, but a whisper that cuts through the air. "The Flame of Khamonji is yours to wield. Unite the blood of the Saints. Where the moons meet the sea and the stars bleed into dusk, the Aevem's light will falter, and the Bard's heart will burn. That will be your final test."

The light fades, and Urru shakes her head. Her eyes return to their normal dark brown, and she steadies herself on my arm. "Phew. Did you get all that?"

"I don't understand." Frustration swells in my chest. "What does it mean?"

"I told you." Urru sighs. "I don't remember who I am. All I can do is relay the message. You're the one who has to decipher what it means."

"But it doesn't make any sense," I say. "What is the Flame of Khamonji?"

Urru shrugs. "Stars if I know."

Lightning forks across the sky, followed by a deafening boom of thunder. The light of the sun dims as rain falls, causing my skin to prickle as it's struck with tiny cold droplets.

"What do you know about the beastmark?" I ask, desperate for information. "How do I get rid of it?"

"The only way to remove the mark is to kill the shaji," Urru says. "I know that much."

"How do I do that?"

"Ask the Aevem." Urru puts a hand on my shoulder. "Courage, Bexis. You have everything you need to succeed. Your sacrifice is your greatest gift. Use it. And remember, you are never alone. Call my name when you walk in the shadows. I will be there."

Before I can respond, a deafening crash splits the sky. The ground shakes as red lightning slashes through the storm clouds. It's pitch black now. I can barely see Urru's outline, and the air has grown tense and vapid.

"Time for you to go," Urru says. "Before he finds us." She begins to dissolve into golden sand that blows away in the wind.

"Wait!" I shout, clinging to her shoulders, as if I can hold her in place. I still have so many questions. "Come back!" But it's no use. In seconds, Urru is gone.

My heart races as torrents of wind whip at my hair. The sky turns black, and a shrill hum pierces through my mind. I clench my jaw as tendrils of yellow fire explode in the sky, casting long shadows on the field. The grasses smolder as swirls of black smoke congeal into a mass before me. Red lupine eyes blink from the depths of that darkness. Flames crackle and spit red heat. I retreat, intending to run, but a wall of interlaced bones rises from the ground and blocks my escape.

"Shytar!" I shout. "Get me out of here!" A blood-curdling shriek echoes through the din as the shaji takes shape—a hulking mass of twisted spines and writhing black shadow. Skeletal wings spread twenty feet across as the beast drops to all fours, its gray lips peeling back to reveal a wicked set of hooked yellow fangs.

All I can do is scream as white fire scalds my forearm and the shaji sinks its razor talons into my throat.

CHAPTER 12

THE AURORA BOREALIS LIGHTS UP THE SKY LIKE A FIREWORKS DISPLAY. Pedestrian traffic bustles up the promenade as flute music bops between the stalls and stands. I step around a couple as they dance in the square, arms wrapped around each other. They're encircled by a crowd of onlookers that sip cups of wine and beer. Paper lanterns float in the air while waves crash on the pier below.

I'm back at the Solstice Festival. This is Juzu's memory from fifteen years ago—the one he uses for healing. I touch my neck where the shaji's fangs sank into my flesh. There's no wound, no pain, but also, only one reason for me to be here. Anxiety swirls in my gut. The shaji must have done some damage.

A young Juzu emerges from the crowd. His hair is curly and black, and his face bearded. He's very handsome. He's also a head taller than anyone else. He clutches his niece's hand as they stroll down the street.

"Candy apple!" Dhaima hops up and down, clapping her mittened hands. She turns rosy cheeks up to Juzu, a grin plastered across her face. She can't be more than three years old. "*Please*, Uncle Ju?"

"Hmm. I don't know." Juzu feigns deep thought. His eyes narrow under his dark spectacles. The crowd flows around them as he runs a hand down his beard. "You'll rot your teeth."

"I don't care!" Dhaima pulls on his sleeve. "Who needs teeth?"

"Oh?" A woman approaches. She has black hair tied in a bun on the top of her head and wears a fur-lined jacket. She touches Juzu's arm in greeting and beams at Dhaima, resting a hand on her head. "You want to eat soup for the rest of your life?"

This must be Juzu's sister—Dhaima's mother. They have the same nose and shape to their mouths, but her eyes are blue. A flutter of curiosity runs through me.

I follow at a distance as they cross the promenade. No one in the crowd notices me. It's like I'm a spirit haunting the ghost of a dream.

"I like soup." Dhaima skips, barely containing her excitement. "Candy apple!"

Juzu's sister touches her finger to her chin in a gesture that reminds me of Juzu. "I don't know, Dhai..."

"Addy, let the girl have a candy apple." Juzu gives Dhaima a wink. "She'll grow new teeth."

"You're going to spoil her rotten!" Addy rests her hands on her hips, but a smile touches her eyes.

"Then she'll remember me fondly," Juzu says, a hint of sadness in his voice.

"Don't talk like that," Addy whispers. She scoops Dhaima into her arms and bops her nose with an index finger, arousing a flurry of giggles. "Okay. Your uncle is buying."

"Candy apples all around!" Juzu kisses his sister's forehead as Dhaima squeals in delight.

A current of love radiates from the top of my head and drips like oil down to my toes; its warmth awakens every muscle and bone in my body. I breathe it in like steam as the world around me shatters.

—

"Bexis!"

I'm wrenched from the vision and thrown back into my body. It's as bad as being tossed into a pond of icy water. I gasp from the shock.

Someone slaps my cheeks softly as I blink, waiting for my eyes to adjust to the light.

"Bleeding stars," I stammer. "What happened?"

Juzu peers down at me with that discomforting silver gaze. Having just seen the young version of him, it's clear how much he's aged in the subsequent years—his hair has gone gray, and his skin is sallow and wrinkled. He looks so damn tired as he rubs his eyes and leans back. "Thank the Saints," he says. "You're alright."

Shytar looms to my left, her eyes wide with concern. My back aches, and the right sleeve of my sweater is soaked with blood. *My blood.*

"What happened?" I ask.

"The beastmark," Juzu says. "I acted as fast as I could, but you're a bleeder." He places his palm on my forehead.

"Get off me." I swat his hand away and push myself up, swinging my legs over the side of the table. The room spins. One of my sleeves is rolled back and soaked. The metallic tang of blood hits the back of my throat, making my stomach twist. The beastmark doesn't hurt anymore, but the moon and serpent symbol is pristine black against my pale skin. I know it's not entirely fair, but I can't help feeling betrayed. "I thought you said it was safe in the Aoz."

"It is safe." Shytar uses a rag to wipe up blood that's spilled on the table. "I've never seen anything like this. It shouldn't be possible."

"What did you see?" Juzu sits beside me, his forehead wrinkled with worry.

"It was the phantom," I murmur, flexing my right hand. "It attacked me."

Juzu stares at the blood, the guilt plain on his face. "Bexis, I'm sorry. If I had known the beast could hurt you there, I never would have agreed to this—"

"I believe you." I relax my jaw as the room stops spinning. Juzu can't lie, which means he really thought it was safe. Still, it's a good reminder that even someone who can't lie should be treated with skepticism. "You couldn't have known. Besides, I don't know if this has anything to do with being in the Aoz. The same thing happened with the mark in the Sanctum."

Juzu presses his lips in a line. "This was worse than that. The beastmark opened up like a fountain. If I hadn't been here, you'd be dead right now."

Shytar throws the bloody rag in a garbage receptacle and crosses her tattooed arms. "The Aoz is not some vacation hideout for ghouls and demons. It's a spiritual manifestation of your mind. Creatures *cannot* just inhabit your mind without you knowing!"

"My wolsai said it was bonded to us," I say. "Using me as a tether to the mortal world. So it's a part of me now." A shiver runs down my spine as the realization settles in my bones; I can't get on a ship and sail to Emceni and expect things to get better. The whole plan to run with Ajjan has been rendered moot. Juzu told me this, but I hadn't truly believed it until now.

"So these instances where the beastmark flares up aren't random." Juzu removes his spectacles and rubs his eyes. "It's the phantom attacking or trying to influence your spirit."

"Looks like it." I frown. "But does that mean it can attack me whenever it wants through the Aoz?"

"If it could, you'd be dead already." Juzu takes out his pipe and starts loading it with jalpe. "It sounds like you managed to awaken and speak with your wolsai. What else did you discover?"

I tell them about my interaction with Urru, steering clear of the confrontation with Lum Carro—I'm still not sure how to process that, and it's no one's business but mine. When I get to the part about Urru's prophecy, Shytar takes out a quill pen and jots down notes while Juzu stares at the ceiling, puffing his pipe and sending spirals of floral smoke into the air. Once I've finished, I wash with soap and water and change into fresh clothes while Shytar makes tea and serves a small platter of roasted nuts.

"The ceremony was a success," Juzu proclaims after we've reconvened around the workbench. "Urru is awake, and that means your episodes should be diminished, if not gone entirely. And we can begin working on your resonance trapping in earnest."

This should make me happy—clearing up my episodes was the whole purpose of this exercise—but after everything I saw, it seems somehow secondary. Urru's message was urgent and opened a whole new mystery that needs to be solved. "Is it normal for a wolsai to give a prophecy like that?" I ask.

"No." Shytar fiddles with a bracelet on her wrist. "But you said the prophecy didn't come from her. That the voice was separate."

I nod. "It was like the Aoz itself was speaking. Urru was just the messenger."

"But where did the message come from?" Juzu wonders aloud.

"I don't know." Shytar presses a finger into her forehead. "The message would have to come from Nhammock—or a being that lives there—which could only happen if Bexis is connected through the shadow moon…"

"Not likely." Juzu clasps his hands behind his back and paces the room. "The shadow moon hasn't risen in seventeen years. No, there must be something else. Something we're not seeing."

I bite my bottom lip. None of this makes sense to me. "What is the Flame of Khamonji?" I ask.

"I have no idea." Wrinkles form on Juzu's forehead as he furrows his brow. "Shy?"

"Sorry." Shytar hands Juzu a mug of tea. Her face is pale in the yellow lantern light. "I don't know anything about Khamonji."

"Hmm." Juzu places his mug on the table and puffs his pipe. "If Shy hasn't heard of it, then we're dealing with something quite obscure. We'll file that away for later. Let's start with something a bit more solid."

"Like what?" I press my fingertips into my temples. The whole interaction with Urru was a blur of confusion.

"The Aevem's light will falter, and the Bard's heart will burn. That will be your final test." He shakes his head. "I'm clearly the Aevem. We can agree on that at least."

"But why is your light faltering?" I ask, remembering Xaleo's warning about Juzu's actions in Shezhi. According to Juzu's explanation of resonance, if he does anything to violate the Virtues, his powers would be diminished. Could Urru's message refer to Juzu breaking the code?

Juzu shrugs. "The wording is a bit concerning. But I'm more interested in who this bard is and why his heart is burning."

I press my lips into a line. Despite all our conversations about the Virtues and truth, I still haven't told Juzu about Xaleo, and I'm not sure if I should. Urru thinks the bard is a part of this, which means it might be important to tell Juzu. But I promised Xaleo I would keep his presence a secret. In return, he's supposed to be finding out the origins of the beastmark.

"Perhaps the bard is a metaphor," Shytar says, rousing me from my thoughts. "For resonance or for a trapper."

Juzu blinks at me. "Do you think Vogul could be the bard? It's quite difficult to imagine her singing, but I suppose you never know..."

I sigh, guilt wrestling through my guts. I never used to think twice about lying or keeping secrets, but now it's causing a heaviness in my shoulders. "I think the prophecy is too vague to be helpful and we should focus on what Urru told us about the phantom," I say, changing the subject. "She said it's called a shaji. And that the only way to remove the beastmark is to kill it. That's what we should be focused on."

A silence settles over the workshop. Juzu stops his pacing and frowns at me. "A shaji—Are you sure that's what she said?"

I nod. "She told me she recognized it from Nhammock."

"The Immortal Dark," Shytar whispers. "But that's not possible. The shaji were banished to the Shadow Realms thousands of years ago. If this creature is a shaji, it can't enter the mortal world."

"Unless it has a tether, like Bexis," Juzu says. "That must be the purpose of the beastmark. The creature is half-here and half-not, which explains why it's so difficult to find."

The prospect of being a proxy for some evil spirit sends a tremor down my spine. "What is the Shadow Realm?" I ask.

"It's a prison for ancient demons." Shytar purses her lips, her face drawn. "A permanent dwelling for horrors that mankind hopes never to face. A world of darkness and terror."

"The shaji cannot be killed in the mortal world," Juzu explains. "Unless we tear out its roots, it will always come back. The only way to kill it is to face it in the Shadow Realm."

Shytar shakes her head. "That's crazy, Juzu, even for you. The Shadow Realm is no place for mortals. Some of the creatures that live there have no name, no beginning, and no end."

I set my tea mug on the table. "Shytar, if I *don't* go there, I'll die. The only way to remove the beastmark is to kill the shaji, and if the only way to do that is to face it in the Shadow Realm, then that's what we need to do."

"Bexis is right." Juzu places a hand on Shytar's shoulder. "I don't like it either. It's risky, but if the shaji finds a way to cross fully into the mortal world, imagine the harm it could do. Right now, it's vulnerable in the Shadow Realm, but once it passes into the mortal world it becomes all but invincible. Please, Shy. You know more about this stuff than anyone. Where is the nearest gate to the Shadow Realm?"

Shytar takes a deep breath and runs a hand through her dark hair, making the bracelets on her wrist jangle. "Are you sure this is what you want to do?"

"Yes," I say, anticipation mounting. "Please."

She closes her eyes. "The lighthouse on Deadman's Wharf. That's where you'll find the gate."

Deadman's Wharf. The wharf on the northernmost point of the city has been abandoned and condemned for years—after a fire left hundreds dead. Since then, the whole area has been presumed haunted. No one goes out there.

"But going there is pointless unless you can open it." Shytar opens her eyes. "And the only way to do that is with nedozul."

Juzu frowns. "Soulbound steel?"

"Yes," Shytar confirms. "Nedozul acts as a key. Without it, the prison doors stay locked. I don't suppose you have any lying around?"

Juzu's conviction crumbles. He crosses his arms and leans against the workbench. "No. I don't."

"I know where to find some," I say, my breath catching in my throat.

Shytar narrows her eyes. "You do?"

"Zhira has a blade made of nedozul, glowing green glass. She had me steal it from Vogul…"

"But?" Juzu cocks his head. "What's wrong?"

"Vogul left it behind. It's like she wanted us to have it."

"You think it might be a trap?"

"It seems odd that Vogul would leave behind the key to the Shadow Realm," I say. "Unless she wanted us to use it."

"Or perhaps she wanted Zhira to have it," Shytar says. "Nedozul is a tool for terrible evil. It can be used to manipulate minds and inflict human beings with powerful demons."

Juzu nods. "Zhira is the last holdout on the City Council. Perhaps Vogul is planning something else."

"It's possible," I admit, rising to my feet, "but I guess it doesn't matter. We need to get the nedozul from Zhira and use it to open the gate. Then we can find the phantom in the Shadow Realm and kill it." I realize how ridiculous all this sounds as soon as the words leave my lips. Even if we get to the Shadow Realm, what then? How will we kill the shaji?

"When you put it that way, it all sounds quite simple," Juzu says, echoing my thoughts. "Once we deal with the shaji and remove the beastmark, we can turn our attention to Vogul and expunging her influence from the Magistrate and the City Council." He turns his silver gaze to me. "How hard will it be to get the nedozul from Zhira?"

"That depends. We might have to trade for it. That's the Blackbone way."

"Trade." Juzu gazes around the workshop. "I don't suppose she'll take payment in the form of toys?"

"No," I say. "She likes gold. Or jewels. Or favors. That kind of thing."

"I'm short on jewels and gold." He pats his pockets. "And we don't have time to trade favors. Any chance she would just *give* us the nedozul? Perhaps if we ask politely…"

"Zhira would never give something so valuable away for free. But future arrangements can be made. Or we can steal it if we have to."

Juzu rubs his cheeks. "Then we must go see Councillor Zhira."

"Ajjan said she's under guard in the White Keep," I say. "We'll have to break in to see her."

"Very well," Juzu says. "There are hidden ways into the Keep. But we should wait for nightfall. Which gives us several hours." He jumps to his feet. "Are you hungry, Bexis?"

"What?" The question catches me off guard. "How can you think of food right now?"

"I know someone who might be able to tell us about the Khamonji Flame." Juzu places his fedora over his shaggy gray hair and adjusts the lapels of his coat. "And he just happens to make the most fabulous noodle stew in all of Coppejj."

CHAPTER 13

THE HEZHANI MONASTERY TAKES UP TWO CITY BLOCKS ON THE EASTERN bay, overlooking the black waters of the Shadow Sea. A grand central temple is erected in the middle of the grounds—two golden towers with layered pagoda rooftops surrounded by gardens and cobbled walking paths. Opposite the temple sits a housing structure for the monks and trainees, an L-shaped three-story building with a sprawling courtyard full of stone statues and frozen fountains. The whole complex is surrounded by a six-foot wooden fence.

Juzu and I crouch in a thicket of manicured boxwood bushes that overlook the monastery entrance—a single arch of two wooden posts with a crossbeam resting on top. Two incongruous willow trees grow on either side of the arch, their bright yellow foliage crusted in a layer of ice. Blue streetlights illuminate the quiet road that runs between our hiding place and the entrance. Four sentinels stand guard before the arch, their spears unwavering in the ocean breeze that sweeps in from the coast.

"You want to hide in there and eat noodles?" I whisper. "Isn't this where they train sentinels?" I've already spent too much energy running from sentinels today. The last thing I need is another prolonged chase through the city.

"We need a place to rest while we wait for nightfall." Juzu takes out his pipe.

"Don't use that here," I hiss. "They'll smell it."

"Oh. Right." Juzu frowns and puts the pipe back in his pocket. "The monastery does serve as a combat academy for the city watch, but after graduation, recruits take oaths to serve the country, and forswear all allegiance to Hezha or Sainthood. Thus, sentinels are not allowed on the grounds without an invitation."

"There's four of them watching the entrance right now," I say, frustration mounting.

"The street belongs to the public," Juzu explains, his voice calm and reasonable. "They can stand guard outside the complex. But they can't go inside without Grandmaster Olaik's say-so. As long as we can get inside without being spotted, we'll be safe."

"And what makes you think Phekru will honor that agreement? He's already infiltrated the Sanctum. What's to stop him from raiding this place and slaughtering everyone inside?"

Juzu snorts. "The Hezhani monks aren't as helpless as Orrethic luminaries. The sentinels may train here for a few months, but the Hezhani devote their entire lives to the study of martial combat. Phekru knows he can't overpower the monks with brute force." Juzu wipes his nose. "This is the safest place in the city."

It still seems like an unnecessary risk. The silver moon is a crescent that's descended through the sky. In a couple hours, the red moon will rise, signaling the fall of night, and that's when we'll break into the White Keep on the other side of town. "Why don't we just go to the keep and wait there until night?"

Juzu frowns. "We're not going to hide in the snow all afternoon like a pair of indolent squirrels. I'm hungry, and you've been through three near-death experiences in a short period of time. We need to rest."

"I'm fine," I say, gritting my teeth.

Juzu clicks his tongue. "Liar."

I grimace. In truth, my body aches, and I'm weak from exhaustion and blood loss. I would like nothing more than to sprawl on a mattress and sleep until next week. This honesty thing is going to be more difficult than I thought.

I sigh. "I'm tired, but it's nothing I can't handle. The phantom is still out there."

"All the more reason to have a roof over our heads, rather than waiting out in the open."

I grunt in the affirmative. "How do we get inside?" The monastery seems quiet, but I can hear the monks training in the courtyard. The winter chill bites at my cheeks, and I turn my back to the wind as it cuts through my jacket.

"Looks like these are the only guards." Juzu rubs his hands together. "Take out your tone pipe."

A worm of anxiety wrestles through me. "You think that's a good idea?"

"We'll need the shadows to cross the road."

"But what if I have another episode?"

Juzu's silver eyes flash in the darkness, shining through his circular dark spectacles. "The Calling was successful, despite all the drama and blood. You went to the Aoz, and Urru awoke, which means you should have established a connection. We need to know if it worked," Juzu says. "Go on."

I sigh and take out my tone pipe, rubbing my finger along the inscription. The last time I trapped, I blew up a brothel and almost killed Ajjan. A mistake like that here, now, could have devastating consequences.

"You'll be fine." Juzu rests a hand on my shoulder. "I'm right here."

"That's comforting," I say with a hint of sarcasm, but despite my attempt to brush it off, it *is* comforting. I've never had someone guide me through this process before. For the first time in my short trapper career, I'm not alone.

I take a deep breath to steady my nerves, bring the pipe to my lips, and blow. The vibration trembles through the air and seeps into my skin. Resonance sparks to life, and I catch it with ease, reveling in the steady warm hum that circulates through my veins. My fatigue and exhaustion bleed into a vibrant buzz that awakens every sinew and bone in my body. The world sharpens as the darkness comes into focus.

"Whoa," I say. The sensation is both familiar and incredibly foreign. In the past, the resonance had a sharp edge to it, an unpredictable truculence like I was hugging a mountain lion that was just as likely to bite me as it was to lick my hand. But now, the vibration is smooth and calm like the contented purr of a drowsy house cat.

Juzu observes me, his silver eyes narrowed. "How does it feel?"

"Good," I say, surprised. "*Really* good."

"Excellent. Later, we'll try it without the pipe. But for now, try cloaking yourself in shadow."

I bring my attention to the space above my head. A small bead of light blooms in the air as gossamer strands extend to my shoulders and envelope me in a tight vortex. Exhilaration floods through me. This is the first time I've held resonance without the sickening dread that I might lose control. This is the first time it feels natural, like it's meant to be.

"Well done." Juzu spreads his arms. "Now give me a cloak of shadows, and let's get going."

I frown. "I don't know how to do that."

"You've never concealed someone other than yourself?"

"No." The thought had never occurred to me. "I've never tried."

"It's alright," Juzu says. "First, gather shadow resonance into your palm."

I hold up my hand, willing the vibration into my fingertips. Tendrils of silver swirl over my wrist. The energy flows so effortlessly, it makes my heart flutter. A ball of pale light forms on my index finger.

"Good," Juzu whispers. "Now, transfer it to me."

I pause, uncertain. "I thought you only wielded light."

He nods. "I cannot summon shadows like you, but once you give me the resonance, I can manipulate it just fine." He holds out his hand.

I touch my index finger to Juzu's palm, and the silver strands transfer from me to him. Juzu beams as he weaves the resonance around himself. I've never seen another trapper use a shadow cloak before. It's like Juzu's skin and clothes are embossed in a web that shimmers across his skin.

"Great job, Bexis," Juzu claps me on the shoulder. "I'm proud of you."

"Thanks." Heat rushes to my cheeks. I can't remember anyone saying those words to me before. My father certainly never did, and Zhira isn't one to dole out praise.

"Let's go." Juzu dusts snow from his jacket before creeping beyond the bush line. We stand in the open by the road. The sentinels are across from us. If not for the shadows, we'd be spotted.

Juzu raises a hand, and I freeze. Soundlessly, he points at his feet and our footprints in the snow. I understand his meaning: Our boots leave evidence of our presence. Even though the sentinels can't see us, they might see our footprints or hear the crunch of ice beneath our feet. A knot of worry forms in my chest. We'll have to go farther down the road to put enough distance between us and the guards.

Without saying anything, Juzu extends his pointer finger, touching it to his shadow cloak, and extracts a bead of resonance. He bends over and touches it to his boots, where pools of silver circle his feet, then he does the same to mine. He straightens, gesturing to his boots as he takes exaggerated steps.

The threads spread across the footprints in his wake, concealing them from prying eyes, and the shadows muffle the sound of the snow crunching. I've never thought to do that before, but it's genius. This is the first time I've trapped with Juzu, and I've already learned two new tricks to add to my arsenal.

We cross the street, our feet as silent as the night itself. We pass the sentinels and follow the wooden gate up a snowy hill for several minutes.

Juzu gestures to the fence. "This is far enough." He clasps his hands together and gives me a wordless gesture. I nod and plant my boot on his hands as he boosts me up and over the fence. I land on the other side. A moment of worry runs through me, as I'm not sure how to help Juzu get over, but he leaps into the air, curling his body into a tight front flip, and lands in a noiseless crouch.

"Showoff," I mutter.

He adjusts his fedora and allows his resonance to fade. "We're safe now."

Reluctantly, I follow suit. It's easier than it used to be, but it still takes focus and energy to hold resonance. As the resonance fades and the abundance of energy bleeds from my muscles, the fatigue comes back. My shoulders slump.

"You did well." Juzu rests a hand on my shoulder. "Welcome to the Temple of the Sun."

We're in a snowy grove with a small fountain and a statue of a woman dressed in full plate armor and a feathered helm. One hand rests on the pommel of a stone saber, the other raised before her in a gesture of supplication. Hezha—the Warrior Saint. A sense of awe fills me. In stark contrast to the Orrethics, the Hezhani are minimalists. They have no grand cathedral, no stained glass windows or altars. But the austerity and power are unmistakable. The simple garden of manicured bushes and spruce trees emanates a strange sense of purpose.

Juzu straightens the lapels of his coat. "Alright, let's go see Olaik and get some spicy noodles—"

Dark figures emerge from the shadows, men and women wearing heavy yellow robes and carrying weapons—staffs and knives and wooden truncheons. Hezhani monks have us surrounded. I fall into a fighting stance, my hand on the hilt of my knife.

"You dare trespass in the Grove of Solitude?" A tall rotund monk steps forward. He has a long black beard braided with gold beads and he wears a yellow brocaded coat with a black sash across his waist. "Aevem Juzu Khinvo."

"Hello, Olaik." Juzu leans on his umbrella. "How did you know we were here?"

"I am the grandmaster of this temple. I have my ways." Heavy cords of muscle stand out on his neck as he stares imperiously at Juzu and unsheathes a long curved saber. The metal sings as he points it at Juzu's throat, the steel blade reflecting moonlight like a mirror. "I didn't think you'd have the balls to show your face here again. Not after last time."

Juzu rubs his chin, making a show of looking around. "Is this about the money? Because I can assure you—"

"Money!" Grandmaster Olaik booms. "You're standing in the burial ground of my ancestors. Trespassing on holy soil. What gives you the right to sully our sacred places?"

I blink. What the stars is going on here? "Juzu," I hiss. "I thought you said Olaik was your friend."

Juzu shakes his head. "I assure you, Bexis. Olaik and I are very close."

"Enough!" Olaik bellows, his voice laden with icy chill. The hairs on the back of my neck stand on end. "We require penance from the both of you. Immediately. Or you will die."

Juzu frowns. "What kind of penance?"

"Your ears." Olaik proffers his hand. "That is the price you must pay."

"*What?*" I stammer. "You can't be serious."

"Oh?" Olaik raises his dark eyebrows as if seeing me for the first time. "Alternatively, you may fight each other to the death on the training ground. Blood will suffice, but Hezha is growing impatient. Choose quickly!"

My heart thuds against my sternum, my gaze shifting from Juzu, with his muscles tensed and umbrella at the ready, to Olaik, who is tightening his grip on his sword.

A moment passes, and the tension thickens to bursting. Then the old monk smiles. "You should see your faces."

"Damnit." Juzu scowls. "Is this even a sacred grove?"

"Nah." Olaik giggles, sliding his sword into its sheath. He embraces Juzu with the warmth of a long-lost friend. "It's just a garden."

I rest my hands on my hips. "Are you finished messing around?"

"Your ears!" Olaik guffaws. "Who would want those dusty old things?"

"I would," Juzu says. "I use them almost every day—"

"Stop being silly," Olaik shouts. "Come inside!"

CHAPTER 14

WARMTH WASHES OVER ME AS WE ENTER THE COMMUNAL HALL, A VAST chamber in the housing structure with a vaulted roof and two roaring fires in matching brick hearths on opposite ends of the room. Torches line the walls and the railing of the second-floor balcony. A stage has been erected in the middle of the hall, and rectangular dining tables are arranged around it. The room is full of about fifty men and women of all ages, all wearing the same yellow robes, eating and drinking with smiles on their faces.

"Welcome to Hezha's Hall." Master Olaik claps Juzu on the back. "You must be hungry. Find yourselves a seat. I'll see what I can scrounge up from the kitchen."

"Thank you." Juzu watches Olaik saunter out of the room, then raises an eyebrow at me, gesturing to the hall. "Told you it would work out."

I roll my eyes. "Don't gloat. We need to find out what Olaik knows about the Khamonji Flame, and then we need to leave."

"Sweet stars, Bexis." Juzu shakes his head. "We're safer here than on the streets."

"The phantom is a shapeshifter," I remind him, thinking back to the first night I encountered it, how it assumed the form of a boy to lure me in. "It could be any one of these people."

Juzu sighs. "It can take a person's shape, sure. But I don't think it can mimic someone's speech or personality. If we see a hooded figure sitting alone in a corner of the room, then we can worry. Until then, lighten up. We'll talk to Olaik when he comes back with our food. Then we'll retreat to our rooms."

I follow Juzu to an empty section at one of the tables along the periphery of the room. None of the monks have noticed our entrance. Most of them are preoccupied with a heated discussion by the stage with lots of hand-wringing and shouting. I take note of every face, searching for anyone who doesn't belong, and I'm surprised to see such a variety of people here. Coppejj is mostly northerners, with a dash of Xappemese and Zhippekan blood mixed in. The result is a homogenous blend of dark-haired, blue-eyed Coppejjians. But the monks are much more varied—there's a pair of blond-haired Southerners, with shades of violet in their eyes; a man from the Omenos Isles with eyes as black as pitch; and at least three members of the mountain tribes of Bhejjos, with characteristic bushy red beards and wild untamed hair.

Juzu follows my gaze. "People come from all over the world to train here. It's one of the few parts of Coppejj that draws in foreigners, and it's what makes the temple such a remarkable place."

I spot a huddled figure sitting among the others, a hood pulled over his head, not speaking to anyone. I narrow my eyes, but if it were the phantom, someone would have surely noticed.

"Would you please stop scowling at everyone?" Juzu sounds exasperated. "The phantom is not here. Olppeo would tell me if it was."

Right. I forgot about Juzu's wolsai. I take a deep breath, forcing myself to relax. Juzu is probably right. "I'm sorry. I'm just tense." I nod to the monks by the stage. "What's happening there?"

"They're placing bets on the evening's test," Juzu says with a chuckle. "Hezhani monks have a reputation for being uptight disciplinarians, but they're all degenerates."

"That's why you owe Olaik money?"

"Oh, that's crap. He's not getting anything from me."

"Hmm." I'd suspect he was lying but unlike me, Juzu takes the Virtues seriously. "What kind of tests do they do?"

"Just friendly competitions," he explains. "They have them every night to keep everyone sharp. Sometimes they're used as initiation ceremonies—"

"Here we are!" Olaik booms as he places a tray on the table containing three bowls of noodle soup, a stack of cups, and a flagon of golden wine. He places a bowl of noodles and tofu in front of me. The aroma of spicy broth makes my stomach gurgle. I pick up the spoon and take a bite. Pepper burns my tongue as salty peanut flavor explodes in my mouth. I close my eyes in pleasure as the melody of sensation spreads warmth through my shoulders and down to my toes.

"Good, huh?" Juzu slurps a spoonful.

I have to admit, Juzu was right. This was worth it.

"Wonderful!" Olaik sits next to me on the bench. "They're about to begin."

I follow his gaze to the stage where two monks climb onto the dais. One is the young southern girl. She's about my age, and her long blonde hair is tied in a tight bun. She removes her yellow robe, revealing a white sleeveless tunic that covers a wiry muscular frame. Her opponent is the lone figure I noticed a moment ago. I watch with interest as he positions himself on the far side of the dais and removes his hood.

Shaggy black hair and icy blue eyes.

I drop my spoon on the table and broth goes down the wrong pipe. I start coughing, heat rushing to my cheeks as the spice burns my throat and brings tears to my eyes.

"Whoa there, champ." Juzu pats my back. "Chew your soup."

"I'm fine!" I shake my head, trying to clear my throat. "It's a little spicier than I expected."

What in the bleeding stars is he doing here? Xaleo wears a sleeveless Hezhani tunic and tan trousers with a black sash around his midsection. He swings his muscular arms in circles as he warms up.

Olaik snorts. "Looks like your ward has spotted our newest novice." He gestures to the stage, where a third monk begins to tie Xaleo's hands behind his back with thick cords of rope. "I don't blame her. He's quite a striking figure, and those eyes have a hypnotic quality to them."

I scoff, picking up my spoon. "It wasn't that," I say, aware of the lie as it leaves my lips. I groan internally. I'm never going to be Aevem material. I hunch my shoulders and continue eating. "Forget it."

"Who is he?" Juzu pours himself a cup of wine. "I don't think I've seen him before."

"His name is Xal." Olaik wipes his mouth. "He came to us from the Shezhi Isles a few weeks ago. He's an elusive one, likes to keep to himself. But he's a damn fine musician, and he fights like a pit bull. Tonight, he has a chance to become a true initiate." He raises a finger in the air. A topaz ring on his index finger catches in the light. "*If* he can pass his test."

My head spins. So this is where Xaleo has been hiding from Vogul. He's training with the Hezhani monks, sharpening his fighting skills. From Olaik's introduction, it doesn't sound like they know he's a trapper. He's probably masquerading as a normal initiate and keeping a low profile. What will he do when he spots me? Will he approach me? Pretend that he doesn't know me? Anxiety spikes in my chest as I watch him from the corner of my eye, not wanting Olaik or Juzu to see my interest.

Xaleo and his opponent are alone on the stage now, both of their hands bound behind their backs. Grandmaster Olaik rises to his feet. The entire hall settles into a hushed silence. All eyes draw toward us. I take the spoon out of my mouth, heat rising to my cheeks as everyone stares in my direction.

I can feel Xaleo's icy gaze on me, and a flicker of genuine surprise sparks in his eyes for a moment before his face returns to its unreadable mask. My pulse quickens. I've caught him off guard. It gives me a strong sense of pleasure that the shoe is on the other foot. When he entered my room in the Sanctum, I was surprised and shaken, but this time, I discovered something about him that he didn't intend for me to know. Now it's his turn to feel exposed and vulnerable.

Olaik brings his hands together. "Brothers. Sisters. Before we begin, I want to introduce our guests, here to bear witness to the evening's initiation. Please welcome Aevem Juzu Khinvo and his young ward, Bexis. They are friends of the Saints, and so we offer them sanctuary from the cold night."

Murmurs of assent rumble through the room. Many of the monks nod and place a fist on their chests in salute. Even Xaleo bows his head in respect. Juzu raises his cup in acknowledgment. Olaik gestures to the stage. "Xal of the Shezhi Isles. Tonight, you have the opportunity to walk among us as an initiate, taking one step closer to the rank of venerable monk. The game is *alcai* and the rules are simple. Last one standing wins!"

The monks cheer and raise their glasses as the participants bow to the grandmaster and turn to face each other. Olaik plops in his seat. He gives Juzu and I each a discerning look. "I know we have things to discuss. But this is important. A grandmaster must be present for his students. Enjoy the show, then we'll step into my office."

"Of course," Juzu says.

The combatants on stage bow to each other and sink into fighting stances—legs spread, hips forward, knees bent at right angles. Then Xaleo leaps into the air, contorting his body as he spins and lands a brutal kick into his opponent's abdomen. The young woman doesn't even attempt to evade the attack but absorbs the full force of the blow, her face twisted in concentration. She slides backward across the dais but maintains her balance. My jaw drops as the crowd erupts in applause. A kick like that would have shattered my sternum.

Xaleo barely has time to react as his opponent dips into a crouch and her leg shoots out in a spinning sweep aimed at his ankle. He lifts his foot so the sweep misses, and attempts to counter, but his opponent continues her spin, switching legs as she jumps and lands a ferocious spin hook kick on Xaleo's chest. He stumbles back, his jaw clenched in pain but somehow stays on his feet.

I gasp, mesmerized by both of the participants' control and

balance. Either one of those strikes would have sent me sprawling onto the dais. I've heard stories of the martial prowess of the Hezhani monks, but this exceeds my expectations. No wonder Xaleo wanted to train here. It's obvious to me that he's holding back his resonance, trying to pass off as an ordinary person. Otherwise, he'd win this fight easily. Still, I find myself on the edge of my seat, rooting for him to win.

Olaik chuckles. "Sister Fadi is a tough opponent for Xaleo. He's going to have to do better than that to beat her."

Both participants trade blows for nearly five minutes—jumping and weaving and leaping and spinning, landing kick after kick until they're both breathing heavily, coated in sweat, their shoulders slumped in exhaustion. My soup has gone cold as the whole room watches in tense silence.

Xaleo's shaggy hair is slicked to the side of his face, his mouth set in a line of determination. He shouts as he drives a front kick square in his opponent's stomach; once again, she absorbs the impact and counters with a quick kick to his planted knee. Xaleo recovers, but he's off balance. Everyone in the room holds their breath as he leaves an opening. Fadi shifts her weight and brings her leg up in a crescent kick landing square on Xaleo's chest.

The impact echoes through the hall. The entire room inhales. My heart skips, expecting to see Xaleo flung backward. Instead of toppling over, he absorbs the blow. It's as if Fadi has kicked a tree trunk. Her eyes open in surprise. Xaleo is still not on the ground.

Quick as a viper, he takes advantage of her precarious balance and sweeps her planted foot. She crashes to the ground and for several beats, the hall is shrouded in silence. Then the room explodes in uproarious applause. The monks jump onto the stage and envelope Xaleo, removing his binds and clapping him on the back. He beams and accepts congratulations from everyone. I clap with the rest of them. Everyone in the room is smiling except for Grandmaster Olaik.

"What's wrong?" I ask. "Aren't you happy?"

Olaik stirs himself from his thoughts. "Xal did well. I'll congratulate him later." He stands and gestures to a hallway. "Let's retire to my office."

* * *

"When I read the ordinance, I nearly crapped myself." Olaik leads us into a small minimalist office on the second floor. The walls are bare, and the three of us sit on the wooden floor, huddled around a circular table with an empty teapot in the middle. We can still hear the celebration below, but the office is private and quiet. Olaik puckers his lips. "The Khatori orders were started by the Saints, and this law is an affront to all who worship them."

"Believe it or not," Juzu says, "that ordinance is the least of our worries."

"Oh?" Olaik cocks his head in surprise. "I assumed you were here to avoid the sentinels."

"We are." Juzu adjusts his fedora on his head. "But there's something else, a dark spirit in the city that's actively hunting my ward here."

Olaik blinks at Juzu, then turns his gaze to me. "Forgive me for saying so, but you're just a child. What does a demon want with you?"

"I've been marked." I roll up my sleeve and show him my forearm. "A trapper gave me this, and ever since, the phantom has been after me."

Olaik leans forward to get a better look. He opens his mouth, reaching out and touching the beastmark with his fingertips. "Well, I'll be damned," he whispers. "It's the sigil of Entaru. The Daughter of Shadow."

"You recognize it!" Excitement shoots through my veins. If Olaik can tell me anything about the mark, our trip to the monastery will have been worth the risk. "Do you know what it means?"

Olaik leans back on his cushion. He brings his hands together and fiddles with the yellow topaz ring on his right index finger, pulling at it as he nods. "I understand its historical context," Olaik says. "But I'm afraid I don't know why it would find itself on your arm."

I sigh, frustration rising in my chest. "Who is Entaru?"

"Ah." Olaik's eyes glimmer with excitement. He reaches to the bookcase by the wall and extracts a dusty tome. "The story of Entaru is the story of the Immortal Dark and the founding of the Khatori orders. It's a story of power and politics and betrayal, of the rise of the Orrethics and their desire to wipe all memory of her from the records."

"We are short on time," Juzu warns. "Perhaps we could get the abridged version?"

"Of course." Olaik places the book on the table. "Thousands of years ago, an ancient civilization discovered the spirit realm of Nhammock and made contact with spirits called shaji that live there. The shaji are immensely powerful and malevolent, derived from the Immortal Dark. These ancient people were deceived by the shaji into opening a rift between the mortal world and Nhammock, and through it, they came." Olaik opens to a certain page and flips the tome, showing Juzu and me an ink rendering of a massive portal and the dark spirits pouring out.

My breath catches in my throat. The shaji are amorphous blobs with dark eyes and rows of fangs. They look vaguely like the phantom, although the likeness isn't exact; they certainly don't have spines or skeleton wings.

Olaik continues: "The shaji king, Rhazaran, led his armies of shaji warriors to enslave humankind. For seventeen years Rhazaran ruled unchallenged, until the wolsai—the natural enemies of the shaji—came to our aid."

He flips another page, this time showing an image of the shadow moon, a glowing orb with spirits descending from the heavens. "Resonance trappers were born," he says. "The first to rise to prominence are the names that everyone knows."

"The Saints," I say. "Orran, Hezha, and Ujjek."

"Yes," Olaik confirms. "But the strongest and most important Saint has been buried in the sands of history. Her name was Entaru. She brought the others together, and she founded the Khatori orders. She led the rebellion war against the shaji armies. But the Immortal Dark cannot be destroyed."

"Then how did she defeat them?" I ask.

"With a magic sword." Olaik leans his elbows on the table and twists the topaz ring on his finger. "As the story goes, an unknown sorcerer forged for Entaru a weapon unlike any the world had seen."

"The Flame of Khamonji," I say, dread circling in my gut.

"Yes!" Olaik agrees. "The Flame is what Entaru used to banish Rhazaran to the Shadow Realms and save humankind. But the weapon was too volatile for a mortal to wield. It corrupted her, tainted her soul, and turned her into a monster. In the end, Entaru died horribly, but her sacrifice saved everyone."

I frown, trying to absorb everything Olaik said. The beastmark is the sigil of a lost Saint. And Urru said the Flame was mine to wield. But why would my wolsai tell me to wield a weapon so powerful it could banish the Immortal Dark and corrupt my soul?

"The Flame," Juzu says, rousing me from my thoughts. "Where is it now?"

"Ha!" Olaik shakes his head. "Lost. After the war ended, all records of Khamonji fell out of mention. The Orrethics destroyed almost all of the primary sources, so we don't have much to go off. Some say it is buried beneath the great shrine in Shezhi or forged into the walls of the largest church of the three Saints in Emceni. Others say it was destroyed along with Entaru when she died. But all we have left is legends."

"Why would the Orrethics want to destroy records of Entaru?" I ask.

"Orran himself never claimed to be the Savior of the world," Olaik says. "But after his death, his followers wanted power and influence. They wrote Entaru out of history and presented Orran as the chosen champion of humankind. It's hard to argue with their results. Today, the Orrethics are the largest, richest, most influential sect in the world, and that didn't happen by accident. But it's a lie. Which is why it's so important for people like me to remember—"

There's a knock, and Xaleo stands in the doorway, his hands clasped behind his back. A chill runs down my spine, but he doesn't look in my direction.

"Apologies, Grandmaster." Xaleo bows his head. "Fadi said you wanted to see me?"

Olaik purses his lips as his gaze shifts from Xaleo to Juzu and me. "I'm sorry to cut this short, but I have duties I must fulfill. If you have more questions, we can talk in the morning."

"This has been wonderful, my friend." Juzu shakes the grandmaster's hand. "Thank you for your hospitality."

"You are always welcome here," Olaik says. "Find Fadi, and she'll show you both to your rooms."

I rise to my feet, my knees aching from sitting on the floor. Juzu places a hand on Xaleo's shoulder. "Congratulations, young man. That was quite a display."

Xaleo nods his head respectfully. "From you, Aevem Juzu, that means a lot."

Juzu smiles and gestures for me to follow. Xaleo doesn't make eye contact with me, but as I pass, his fingers reach into my pants pocket. It's almost imperceptible, but my senses are honed from years of pickpocketing.

I force myself to maintain a neutral expression as I follow Juzu into the hall. He leads us to the stairwell and sighs. "Well, we got some answers, but nothing that helps us immediately."

"No," I agree. Olaik's story was instructive. It's good that we know the origins of the beastmark, but it's still a mystery that is yet to be unspooled. I rub my eyes and stifle a yawn.

"You look exhausted," Juzu says, his voice laden with concern. "You wait here, I'll go find Fadi. We can rest for a few hours before we storm the White Keep."

"Alright," I say, my heart in my throat. When he's gone, I reach into my pocket and find a tiny ball of paper. I peel it apart and read the message inscribed on the bottom.

· · ·

Tonight.
   Meet me in the courtyard.

CHAPTER 15

AN EVENING WIND BLOWS ACROSS THE COURTYARD OUTSIDE THE MAIN hall, sending snakes of dusty snow across the cobbled walking path. I nuzzle my chin in my scarf and step into the cold. The silver moon has vanished into the eastern horizon, and the ghost of the red moon floats in the north. In a few hours, Juzu and I will break into the White Keep.

A part of me wanted to ignore Xaleo's message. After I was shown to my room—a cozy little dormitory with a cushy mattress and soft down pillows— it took all my willpower not to collapse onto the bed in a deep stupor. But until a few hours ago, I wasn't sure I'd ever see Xaleo again. Back in the Sanctum, he promised to discover the origins of Entaru's sigil for me, but Olaik revealed it first. Still, Urru's prophecy said he was important—*The Bard's heart will burn*—so like it or not, I have to see what he wants.

I climbed into bed and listened through the paper-thin walls until Juzu's movements quieted in the adjacent room and the noise from the mess hall died down. Then I slipped out of bed and carried my boots as I padded down the hall, my tone pipe at the ready—but there was no need to worry. The monks don't keep a watch, and no one expected me to sneak out.

There's a garden in the middle of the courtyard, a partition of boxwood bushes manicured into different shapes—circles and cones and rectangles—along with winter willows and spruce trees. The scent of pine and hemlock hangs on the breeze.

A shadowy figure sits on a stone bench by the garden. At first, I think it's a monk, and my instinct is to retreat. No one told me I couldn't leave my room, but I don't think Olaik would be pleased to find me sneaking around in the night. As I draw nearer, I recognize the shape of Xaleo's shoulders, the way he slumps his elbows on his knees.

I slip across the courtyard as quietly as I can. The grand hall rises to my left and right, with balconies and windows. This isn't exactly a private spot. Anyone could see us from the inside. Perhaps Xaleo doesn't care. Would Juzu be upset if he found me here? He'd probably give me another lecture about truth and honesty, but I haven't lied. I just didn't tell him the truth. Big difference.

Xaleo stands as I approach. He's exchanged his yellow robes for a blue cloak over a leather doublet with dark trousers and black boots. His hood is pulled over his shaggy black hair, but his icy blue eyes shine through the dark as his lips curl into a tight smile. "I wasn't sure if you were going to show."

"I had to wait until Juzu fell asleep," I say. "And the monks here drink an awful lot."

"When I first came here, I was expecting a community of austere assassins." Xaleo snorts. "They're formidable, don't get me wrong. The Hezhani monks are the best fighters in the world—but they're also people. They have vices and weaknesses just like everyone else." He gestures to the cobbled walking path that disappears through a dense spruce orchard. "Walk with me?"

"What's down there?" I ask, wary. The path will hide us from anyone observing from the hall, which a moment ago seemed like a good thing, but I still don't trust Xaleo. Do I want to be alone with him where no one can see us?

Xaleo seems to sense my hesitation. Dimples form on his cheeks as he smirks. "There's an altar to Hezha in the middle of the orchard. It's one of my favorite spots in the monastery—a secluded space for meditation and reflection."

I have my tone pipe in my pocket and my knife on my belt. If Xaleo wanted to hurt me, he would have done so in the Sanctum when I was unarmed and defenseless. I steady my heart and match his step as we slip between the spruce trees.

"This was the last place I expected to find you," I say. "What are you doing here?"

"Training." Xaleo stuffs his hands in his trousers pockets. "And trying to keep a low profile. The monastery is private and off-limits to anyone without an invitation. This is the ideal place to collect information and remain undetected."

I remember what Juzu said about the monastery being the last safe place in the city. "Does Olaik know you're a trapper?"

"He has his suspicions, but he can't prove anything."

"If he does, will you be thrown out?"

Xaleo shrugs. "I won't be here much longer."

"Why?" I ask. "What are you planning?"

We come to a small circular clearing with a willow tree growing in the middle, its icy leaves descending around us. At the foot of the tree is a small black obelisk with a white carving of a radiant sun and three moons. A circular stone bench wraps around the willow. We're surrounded by a dense thicket of spruce trees, completely alone and isolated from the world.

"Don't take this the wrong way." Xaleo sits on the bench. "But the less you know about my plans, the better."

"You don't trust me?" I can't keep the incredulity from my voice. "I've kept my end of the bargain, by the way. Juzu thinks he and I are the last trappers in Coppejj."

"I know." Xaleo leans his elbows on his knees. "I saw his face in the hall. You did everything I asked."

I remain standing and cross my arms. "And for what? Olaik already told me about the sigil of Entaru."

"I figured that's why you came." Xaleo presses his lips into a line. "So he told you about the lost Saint?"

"He told us a story about an army of evil spirits and a magic sword that defeated them." I hold up my arm where the serpent and moon beastmark contrasts with my pale skin. "But he didn't tell me anything that can explain the connection between me and Entaru and the shaji. He also didn't explain why *this* mark is on *my* arm."

Xaleo sits silently, observing me with those brilliant blue eyes. "I don't know what the connection is with Entaru, but I can tell you what I know about Vogul. Perhaps that would suffice as payment for keeping my secret?"

Vogul has been a mystery to me since the moment I met her—a puppet master pulling strings and influencing every facet of my life. And I know next to nothing about her. Anything Xaleo tells me could be invaluable as we move into the White Keep. I sit next to him on the bench. "That would be a good place to start."

"I was born in a small village outside Shezhi," Xaleo says. "It's not the kind of place anyone's heard of. There were only about fifty people, a community of farmers and traders that was unremarkable in every way. But that small village was gifted two trappers the last time the shadow moon graced the sky. Me and my neighbor, a girl named Ceirsa." He shakes his head, sending his shaggy hair wavering in the cold. "Ceirsa was a resonance prodigy. At the age of twelve, she could do things that shocked the elders. Things no one had heard of before."

"What kinds of things?" I ask, my curiosity piquing.

"She could move the earth below our feet. She could bring dying crops back to life. I once saw her levitate in the air as if she were weightless." He smiles at the memory.

"What happened?" I ask.

His smile fades. "The elders believed she was destined for great things but would never realize her true potential unless she was trained by a Khatori. So they sent word to Aevem Juzu. Three weeks later, Vogul showed up instead."

Xaleo's voice tightens. "She came with soldiers and told us she was a Khatori. That she was sent in Juzu's place to test Ceirsa."

My heart sinks. "But instead, she gave her a mark?"

"First, the mark. Then Ceirsa was visited by a dark spirit." Xaleo shudders. "She was terrified, but we didn't have time to figure out what was happening. That night, Vogul's soldiers slaughtered the entire village. Men, women, children." He closes his eyes. "I can still hear them screaming. Smell the blood that spilled onto the soil and hay."

He falls silent, trapped in the memory. His breathing quickens, and his muscles tense. This can't be easy for him to tell me, and his vulnerability is so human and raw. Although our stories are different, I can feel the war within him, and I see myself in his need to be understood and heard, but also the paralyzing fear that he is not worthy of it. The air around us seems to shrink, and I'm overcome by a desperate need to comfort him.

Tentatively, I take his hand. A spark jolts between us.

He flinches but doesn't pull away. Those icy blue eyes find me, and he nods, a gesture of gratitude and recognition. "I wasn't strong enough to save them," he whispers. "My parents. My sister. All of my friends. Everything I ever knew was gone."

My heart aches. I struggle to keep my voice from cracking. "And Ceirsa?"

Xaleo hangs his head. "When I couldn't save my parents, I was in a daze. But I heard Ceirsa in the town green, shouting and screaming. I ran to her. She was tied to a post, her tunic torn, and a green dagger stabbed into her sternum."

A shiver runs down my spine. "Nedozul."

"I tried to untie her. She wept and screamed at me to stop. Told me to run. Told me to leave her, but I didn't listen. I cut the ropes, and she slumped into me. I tried to carry her, but I was shaking so much I could barely stand—"

"You were just a kid," I say. "It wasn't your fault."

He steels himself. "Then Vogul was there. Ceirsa tried to fight, but Vogul was too strong. The nedozul brightened, and then the whole square went dark with black mist. Ceirsa collapsed, and shadows exploded around her, and I watched as she transformed into smoke and talons." He shakes his head. "The phantom was born that night. I think Ceirsa was its first tether."

My mind spins. I could not imagine seeing someone I loved cut down like this. His story is too terrible, too horrifying. I clear my throat, forcing myself to speak. "And you escaped?"

"I was a coward." His voice is thick with contempt. "I hid and did nothing while my friend was torn to pieces."

"That's why you're hunting Vogul, to get revenge?"

"To stop her." His eyes blaze with a cold fury that takes my breath away. "What she's doing is wrong. It's evil. Ceirsa was innocent and pure, kind and gentle and beautiful. Vogul turned her into a blood-thirsty beast. I will not rest until I make things right. No matter how long it takes, I will be the one who puts an end to her."

The horrible creature that attacked me twice used to be a twelve-year-old girl. The thought sends a tremor of horror through my skin.

Xaleo shakes his head. "I've tailed her for five years, and in all that time I've never seen Vogul use the nedozul like that again. The phantom feeds on the victims she marks. Resonance trappers seem to give it some kind of sustenance. But Ceirsa is the only one she transformed into a monster." He runs a finger along my forearm. His touch sends a bolt of electricity across my skin and warmth rises to my cheeks. "I'm worried she sees something in you—the same thing she saw in Ceirsa all those years ago."

A chilling thought. "But that doesn't make sense. Vogul had me incapacitated when she gave me the mark. She could have used the nedozul right there."

"No." Xaleo sighs. "These things happen in phases, Bexis."

"What do you mean?"

"First, Vogul gives her victim the mark. Then there's a visitation. If the trapper survives, she can move on to the nedozul phase. At least, I think that's how it works."

I bite my bottom lip. "Did Ceirsa have this mark?" I ask. "Entaru's sigil?"

"No," Xaleo says. "They're all different. Hers was a dragon and a lotus flower. I tried to find any mention of it in Olaik's books, but he keeps his library locked, and it's difficult to get in there, even for me."

"So you don't know what it means?"

"The dragon is a symbol often associated with the shaji king," Xaleo says. "The last great war was called the War of the Dragon and the Serpent. But I don't know what the beastmark is, or why different marks show up on different people." Xaleo throws up his hands. "In all this time, I've learned so little."

"Hmm." Xaleo opened himself up and told me something personal. I'm not foolish enough to think that means I can trust him, but if Urru says he's a part of this, then I have to believe her. "We know how to lay Ceirsa to rest," I say. "But to do it, we have to face the shaji in the Shadow Realm. It's the only place where it can be killed."

Xaleo narrows his eyes. "How are you going to do that?"

"We're going to break into the White Keep and retrieve a nedozul dagger from Councillor Zhira. Then we'll use it to open the gate to the Shadow Realm. Once we're inside, Juzu says he knows what to do. And with the phantom gone, Vogul will be vulnerable. You can make your move."

Xaleo licks his lips. "Are you sure that will work?"

"Not at all, but the only other option is to wait for it to kill me."

"I don't like the idea of you holding nedozul. It's dangerous," Xaleo whispers. "You should stay away from it."

I purse my lips. Why does everyone think I need to be protected? "We don't have a choice."

Xaleo shakes his head. "What if Vogul catches you with it? What if she uses it on you the same way she used it on Ceirsa? You could become a tether for another shaji monster. If I'm right, you're exactly what she's been waiting for. By going for the nedozul, you could be playing right into her hands."

A trickle of doubt washes over me. Maybe he's right. Vogul did seem pleased when she saw Entaru's sigil on my arm. And if the spell works in phases, that explains why Vogul didn't stab me with nedozul in the brothel. I cross my arms and lean back on the bench. "Do you have a better idea?"

Xaleo turns his gaze to the willow tree, brooding and silent.

"It's a risk," I press. "I know that. Juzu knows it. But it's our only chance."

"Fine." Red moonlight spills through the trees and hits his face. "I can help you. The White Keep is impenetrable. The sentinels are all over the place, and they have phasers lining the entryways. You won't get in without a distraction."

The mention of phasers makes me shiver. "What do you have in mind?"

His mouth tightens. "Leave that to me. When the clock tower strikes two—that's when the guard changes—I'll draw them into the eastern quarter. That'll give you a chance to get inside."

"What will you do if the phasers catch you?"

Xaleo scoffs. "They won't."

"How can you be so sure?"

"It's about time we start trusting each other."

I inhale sharply. "Does that mean I can tell Juzu who you are?"

His expression darkens. "Not yet."

Frustration swells in my chest. "You think he sent Vogul to your village—that's why you don't trust him. But don't you think it's more likely the elder's message was intercepted?"

Xaleo rises to his feet. "You've proven that I can trust you." His gaze is like blue fire. "But I don't trust him."

"But why?" I insist. "It's not his fault Vogul came to your village."

Xaleo's jaw tenses. "I'll help you. But Juzu doesn't need to know that I'm involved. Got it?"

I sigh. I've already kept his secret for this long, what's a few more hours? "Fine. But if you want to help us in the Shadow Realm, you'll have to tell Juzu who you are."

Xaleo turns his face to the sky. "It's getting late, Bexis. You should go back to your room." He walks down the cobbled path. "Remember what I said."

"When the clock tower strikes two," I repeat. "That's when we'll make our move."

CHAPTER 16

THE WHITE KEEP IS THE BEATING HEART OF COPPEJJ—A FORMIDABLE tower surrounded by a sprawling stone fortress. The perimeter boasts three levels of crenulated walls arranged in concentric circles: the highest stands two hundred feet tall. Black lampposts adorn the ramparts, splashing the stone walls with blue and yellow light. On the eastern and western flanks, two monolithic buttressed watchtowers pierce the sky. Against the dim light of the red moon, I can make out the thin silhouettes of sentinels keeping watch over the sea.

Juzu and I lay on our bellies in a terraced orchard in the grounds outside the Keep. The Shadow Sea roars to our left and the White Keep rises before us. Anxiety is a knot in my stomach. Hundreds of sentinels man the walls, and Xaleo's warnings of phasers sink in my gut like a dead weight.

"Did you sleep at all?" Juzu asks, his face lined with concern.

"Like a baby," I lie. When Juzu's mouth tightens in a disapproving line, I sigh. "I'll be fine."

"This is going to be dangerous. Maybe you should sit this one out—"

"Stop worrying and tell me the plan. How do we get in?"

For a moment, it seems like he might argue, but then he shifts his attention to the keep. "Soon, the guard will change." Juzu points at the parapets. "We'll strike out just before that happens—guards are least alert at the end of their shift—then we'll cross the grounds using your shadows as concealment. There's a hidden passage to the catacombs beneath the keep."

I prop myself up on my elbows. "Catacombs?"

"A burial ground for the old kings and royals. We won't be going to the actual crypts. The keep has a system of tunnels that lead to and from every major room. They were constructed so the royal families could escape if the keep was overrun by invading armies."

"Okay." Xaleo said he would create a distraction to lure away the guards any minute now. I'm still not sure what to make of him, but if he pulls through here, that'll go a long way toward trusting him in the future. The fact that I have to keep his presence a secret from Juzu frustrates me. But there's nothing I can do about that now. "So we get into the tunnels. Can we follow them all the way to Zhira's office?"

"No." Juzu takes out his pipe and pokes it between his lips. Even unlit, he seems calmed by its presence. "But we should be able to get close. The tunnels will take us to the Judicial Ward."

"That's near the throne room," I say. "Right in the middle of everything."

Juzu nods. "The heart of the beast."

"And we're going to stroll in like we own the place? What about the phasers?"

"Oh—that reminds me..." Juzu pinches his pipe between his lips and pats his pockets, searching for something. He reaches into the lapel of his jacket and extracts a small iridescent stone that shimmers in the red moonlight.

My breath catches. "What is that?"

"This is a *Vadan* pearl—I took it from the phaser your friend Ajjan destroyed for us. It's made of an alloy of metals mined north of here. When combined with its sister component, it creates a disruption field of disharmony. But in isolation, it does quite the opposite. Keep this on you when you trap, and the phasers won't be able to track you or inhibit your resonance." He places the pearl in my palm.

It's heavier than I expected, and it's warm despite the frigid cold. "Are you sure it'll work?"

"Positive." Juzu runs a hand through his gray tangle of hair. "Phekru gave us a key to the castle."

A thrill shoots through me. Suddenly, this plan doesn't seem so crazy. "But only one of us can trap at a time?"

"We'll need to share the pearl to take advantage of each of our abilities at the right time. If we're going to pull this off, we'll need teamwork and trust. Needless to say, do not trap for any reason unless you have the pearl in your possession."

My cheeks flush. "I learned my lesson." The last thing I want is to be caught in another disharmonic snare. The mere thought sends a tremor down my spine.

A commotion draws our attention back to the parapets. "Something is happening," Juzu whispers. Despite the distance, we can hear orders being shouted and sentinels leaving their posts. The seaward flank is exposed. *Xaleo!* A burst of excitement courses through my chest. He came through.

"Time to go!" Juzu hisses. "Remember, our first priority is to retrieve the nedozul, but if anything goes wrong, I want you to take the pearl and run. Don't stand and fight. Get yourself to safety." I roll my eyes and take out my tone pipe.

We streak across the grounds like wraiths, resonance concealing our footsteps in webs of silver. When we reach the stone wall, Juzu gestures for me to stop. My heart races. I haven't felt the thrill of a job since Ajjan and I were at the brothel, but this time the stakes are higher than ever.

Juzu places his hands on the wall. "It should be right here."

I frown. There's nothing but sheer stone. "I thought you said there was a secret door. What are you—?"

Dark blue light spreads from Juzu's palm and seeps into the stone, where resonance lines trace an intricate filigreed circle in the wall. Juzu adjusts his fedora. "It's a harmonic doorway. Only a trapper can open it." He pushes inward, and the wall moves out of the way, revealing a dark tunnel. I've seen all kinds of crazy crap the past couple days, but I still marvel at the simplicity of it. Every time I'd broken into the keep, I had to circumvent guards and time my positions with careful precision. Of course, I'd never worried about phasers before, and the keep hadn't been under such heavy guard. But if I'd known about the harmonic door, my life would have been much easier.

Juzu starts down the steps. "You can drop your trap in here and save your strength. Hand me the pearl, and I'll give us a light."

I do as he tells me, relief flooding through my veins. Resonance is easier to hold than it used to be, but it's still draining, and I'm glad for the opportunity to catch my breath. A light blooms from the tip of Juzu's umbrella, illuminating a damp stone corridor that leads into the depths below the keep.

Juzu purses his lips. "Stay close to me. We'll be out of here in no time."

For thirty minutes, we creep down passage after passage. Juzu seems to navigate the dark by smell alone, pausing to sniff at each intersection, making hand gestures, and muttering under his breath. At first, the tunnel descends, and I worry we're going to end up in the catacombs after all, but it turns into a set of stairs and rises quickly. Soon, my thighs are burning, and sweat coats my back.

Juzu stops and stuffs his umbrella under his arm. His silver eyes glow in the dark, half obscured by his spectacles. "We're here."

There's nothing about this location that stands out. The tunnel wall is solid. Everything else is black. "Another harmonic door?" I ask.

Juzu taps his umbrella against the wall. A trickle of gold light traces the outline of a doorway in the stone. "Now"—Juzu points to the ceiling—"the council chambers are right above us."

I close my eyes, creating a mental map of the keep. Normally, when I need to see Zhira, we meet in the Driftwood, but I've broken into the palace plenty of times. Usually, I enter through the seaside portcullis and scale the flank. From there, I have easy access to the floor that holds the council chambers, where it's plenty dark and I can use my resonance to hide.

"This isn't a great entry point," I say. "The throne floor is well-lit, and there will be sentinels crawling all over the place."

Juzu places a hand on my shoulder. "No. We won't be able to use shadow on this floor. However, we have light, and that's just as good. If we can get to the stairwell, about a hundred yards from this door-way, we'll be in the clear. I'll give you the pearl, and it'll be a straight shot to Zhira's office."

It's a risky plan, but it might be crazy enough to work. "Let's hope she's still there."

Juzu nods. "If not, we'll have to reconvene and make a new plan. Until then, follow my lead, and do exactly as I tell you."

"Alright." I take a deep breath. "I trust you."

In the faint light, I can see Juzu pressing his ear to the wall. He squints in concentration. "I don't hear anyone. Come on."

He steps straight through the wall. I follow, my heart skipping through my chest.

It's so bright that I'm temporarily blinded. I blink, trying to get my eyes to adjust to the light. We stand in a grand hallway with arched ceilings and columnar pillars that extend a hundred yards in either direction.

"Welcome to the Judicial Ward," Juzu whispers.

"Which way?" I twist my head from side to side, hand on the hilt of my knife. Plodding footsteps echo to our right.

"Shh!" Juzu touches my shoulder. "Someone's coming."

My stomach lurches. It didn't take long for this plan to blow up in our faces. We're exposed, and there isn't an ounce of shadow for concealment. "Which way?" I ask again, desperate for direction.

"Remember, follow my lead." Juzu twirls his umbrella in a figure eight and erupts in a shower of golden light. Warmth radiates across my body, dripping from my head to my toes. The sensation is similar to the healings, except there's no memory associated this time.

When the light fades, Juzu wears a full sentinel uniform—black armor and helm with a dark surcoat that covers his shoulders. His umbrella has transformed into a spear, which he holds upright. *Light resonance*, I realize. *It's an illusion.*

My clothes have changed too. I'm wearing armor—I mean, not *actually*. I'm still wearing my cloak and sweater and cotton trousers. The touch of soft fabric on my skin hasn't changed, but it *looks* like I'm wearing metal armor across my chest and iron bracers on my forearms.

A sentinel stalks toward us, his polished black armor reflecting light like a mirror. A sergeant's badge is pinned to his lapel. He spots us and begins to slow.

Juzu snaps to attention, feet together, spine straight, and right hand raised to his chest. "Sir!"

I follow suit, snapping off a sloppy salute, doing my best to mimic Juzu's motions.

The sergeant frowns at me. He opens his mouth as if he might say something, then shakes his head and continues down the hall without stopping.

"That was close." Juzu breathes a sigh of relief. "Saints, that was the worst salute I've ever seen."

"I've never done it before!" I say.

"We'll work on it." He grabs my elbow and pulls me in the opposite direction.

"This is awesome!" I pat my chest plate. It wavers in the air like mist. There's even a scimitar on my waist, but when I reach for the handle, my hand passes straight through it. "When are you going to teach me how to do this?"

"When you learn to stop lying through your teeth," Juzu whispers.

Ah, right. "So, never?"

"Let's focus on the task at hand. The staircase is just ahead—"

We turn the corner, and my stomach drops. A crowd of sentinels is standing guard on the stairway. Juzu extends an arm across my chest, pulling me back. "There's too many of them."

"The disguises will work, won't they?"

"It's too risky. We'd have to get close. If they discover the ruse, we'll be surrounded." Juzu frowns. "We'll have to think of something else."

"No way!" The only reason we've gotten this far is because Xaleo created a distraction on the other side of the keep. If we let this opportunity slip away, we might not get another one. "We're too close to turn back now."

"We need to be smart," Juzu says. "I can't risk your safety."

"If we don't get the nedozul, I'm dead." I shake my head, my resolve hardening into steel. A plan takes shape in my head. "If you can draw the guards away from the stairwell, I can get to the second floor. From there, I can make it to Zhira's office easily."

"We'd have to separate." Juzu pinches the bridge of his nose. "It's too dangerous—"

"Stop coddling me," I hiss, frustration bubbling into my throat. "You said we needed teamwork. Trust. This is how we do it."

Juzu relents. "I'll draw the sentinels and the phasers away from you. But you need to keep the pearl." He holds it out.

"You need it," I say. "I'm not a child. You don't have to hold my hand."

"We're not arguing about this. I'm not leaving you alone in this place without your resonance. So either take it or come with me back to the tunnels."

Reluctantly, I put the pearl in my pocket. "Where will we meet when this is over?"

Juzu adjusts the illusion-helmet on his head. "When you get the nedozul from Zhira, head to Deadman's Wharf. I'll be waiting for you."

"Got it." I peer around the corner. By my count, there must be at least nine sentinels gathered around the stairwell.

"Are you ready?" Juzu takes a deep breath.

"How are you going to—"

"TO ARMS!" Juzu screams as he dashes around the corner, his spear raised. "Intruders have broken into the keep!"

The sentinels snap to attention. "It's the Aevem, isn't it? Where is he?"

"Yes," Juzu confirms. "The Aevem is here. Follow me!"

This rouses the guards. "We're with you. Let's get this sono-fabitch!"

Juzu charges down the hall. The sentinels' boots clang as they sprint after him and disappear around the corner.

Light crackles across my arms and chest as the illusion around me fades. The black sentinel armor dissolves, revealing my cotton clothes.

Damn. I guess Juzu couldn't keep the illusion up from a distance. No problem. I can take it from here.

A jolt of excitement shoots through me as I dash down the hall, sprinting toward the stairway. But as I draw near, two sentinels come down the steps, blocking my path, their spears leaning on their shoulders. My blood freezes in my veins. The stairwell is too narrow to make it past them, and I can't use my tone pipe without shadows. The sentinels stare at me, confusion on their faces.

My heart sinks. So much for this plan. I sprint past the stairwell, continuing down the hall in the same direction Juzu led the others.

"Stop!" The steady thunk of metal boots tells me the sentinels are about ten yards behind me, giving chase.

Bleeding stars! I need to find another access to the next floor, but I don't know this part of the keep. I try to picture the floor above me and guess where the stairwells might be, but it's hard to think with sentinels barreling on my back. There are more sentinels up ahead, so I take a right turn, heading down another bright corridor.

Despair clenches my guts as sweat breaks out on my forehead. I have no idea where I am. I give up hope of finding a stairwell and instead try to find some hint of darkness so I can wield enough resonance to hide myself, but every corridor I turn down is brighter than the last.

Judging by the footsteps, there are many sentinels in pursuit now. I clutch my tone pipe in my fist and sprint down the hall, pumping my arms. I can't keep this up forever.

The hallway ends abruptly at a bare wall. I skid to a stop, my heart hammering in my chest.

"This way!" the sentinels shout from behind me.

"Hezha's fire," I whisper, desperately searching for a sliver of shadow, but there's a chandelier hanging from the ceiling, emitting steady streams of bright yellow light. I'm trapped.

I put my back to the wall, my heart thumping so hard it hurts. This is it. My knees tremble as I draw my knife with one hand and clutch my useless tone pipe with the other. I don't stand a chance against a squadron of armored soldiers.

But I'm not going down without a fight.

CHAPTER 17

THE SENTINELS GATHER AT THE END OF THE HALL, THEIR CHESTS heaving and faces coated in sweat. One guard steps forward, his spear leveled. Its curved tip shines in the light of the chandeliers. "You're surrounded." He swallows. "We don't want to hurt you."

It's the sergeant that passed by me and Juzu in the hall—I recognize the lapel on his surcoat and his narrow dark eyes. Not only does he not recognize me, but he's afraid of me. Of course, they know I'm a trapper, but they don't know I need ambient shadows to trap, which means I have leverage.

Sweat drips down my back as I draw myself up, squaring my shoulders. "Take one more step and every single one of you will die." I speak with a sneer, putting as much icy steel in my voice as I can. The trick, in moments like this, is to project confidence. "Leave now, and you'll get to see your families when the day moon rises."

The guards glance at each other, a silent conversation passing between them. Is this a risk they're willing to take?

I've bought myself a few precious seconds. Blood thunders through my ears as I search for a way out. Six armored soldiers stand before me. Without resonance, there's little hope I can survive a head-to-head confrontation—and even if I somehow escape, my only recourse would be to flee down the hall, where more sentinels would find me. If I want to survive, I need to kill these lights. The chandelier above us hangs on a chain, supported by a single bearing. If I hit it just right...

"Fall in," the sergeant shouts, tearing my mind back to the guards. They assume formation, adding their spears to his, the deadly steel pointed at my belly. The tight phalanx inches forward. "Reinforcements will be here shortly," the sergeant says through gritted teeth. "Surrender, or we'll take you by force."

"Phekru wants me alive." I muster an easy smile, but adrenaline courses through my veins. My muscles scream to attack, fight, run, *do* something. There is no room for error here. "If you kill me, you may as well cut your throats."

"Enough!" the sergeant barks. "Drop your weapons now!"

"Alright." I hold out my palms in a gesture of supplication. I bend my knees and lower myself to the ground. Then, at the last moment, I hurl the knife with a flick of my wrist.

The sudden movement catches the sentinels off guard, causing them to flinch. The blade sails over their heads, whistling as it spins through the air. Seven pairs of eyes follow its trajectory. Horror blooms on the sentinel's faces as the blade strikes the bearing with a resounding *clink*.

The knife bounces off, and the chandelier swings dangerously. The sentinels spread out, crashing against the walls, but the bearing doesn't give.

It didn't work.

Despair is an iron weight in my belly. I'm out of options. I can either die here or submit to Phekru and Vogul.

The sergeant places his hands on his hips, his mouth twisted in annoyance. "Real clever."

"I can still turn you into dust," I say.

"I don't think so." He watches me as one might watch a deadly snake. "I think you know there are phasers in the keep, and if you trap, you're as good as dead."

"I guess there's only one way to find out," I say.

He snorts, but I can see my words had an effect. "Maru," he hisses, grabbing one of his men by the shoulder. "Go get Phekru. We'll hold her here as long as we can—"

There's a metallic *ping*, and sparks fly as something strikes the chandelier. I blink in surprise. The ping is followed by a soft snap as the bearing breaks and the chandelier crashes over the sentinel's heads. The crystal shatters into thousands of shards that spread across the floor. In a flash, pandemonium erupts in the hall.

Guards scream. Oil spills on the floor. A few small fires break out. The air is tinged with smoke and the acrid scent of burning carpet fiber. The hallway is plunged into beautiful darkness.

I ignore the mayhem and use my tone pipe. The spark ignites in my chest as I reach for the shadows and wrap them around myself. It's not dark enough to disappear completely, but the extra energy is a welcome advantage. Electric power courses through my muscles, lending strength and speed to my movements.

The sergeant breaks free and drives his spear at me. I dodge and slam my fist under his chin. His teeth snap together as he collapses on the ground with a thud. A second sentinel is on top of me. He's lost his spear, so he grabs my wrist. I don't try to pull away. Instead, I yank his index finger backward until I feel a pop. The guard howls, and his grip loosens. I tear free and jam my palm into his nose. He staggers backward as blood pours down his face. I need to find my knife if I want to put up a fight.

Behind me, I hear the clang of steel on steel. Confusion rises in the back of my mind. Are they fighting each other? Or perhaps Juzu has come back for me. Someone definitely broke the bearing on the chandelier. The sentinel with the bloody nose lunges again, trying to tackle me to the ground. I punch him in the throat, a soft spot in his armor, as hard as I can. His eyes pop open as he gasps and falls to the ground.

I spin around, expecting to see Juzu dispatching the remaining guards, but instead, blood splashes against my cheek, coating the wall beside me. Reinforcements have arrived, just like the sergeant promised. At least ten sentinels are engaged in combat with a hooded figure who dances between them, swinging a curved silver blade and painting the walls red.

Xaleo.

My eyes can't track his movements. He dips under the spearpoint of one guard, then dances backward to avoid the sword thrust of another. A whoosh of air cuts through the room as he leaps five feet, spinning and cutting with his sword like a tornado of death. Four sentinels lie dead or dying on the ground. Those who remain flee, abandoning their weapons and disappearing down the hall.

Xaleo stands among the carnage, his sword dripping red in the light of a small fire at his feet. His icy blue eyes hold me like a vise. Something about that gaze makes my heart skip a beat, like I've been shot through with lightning.

"Clever idea, breaking the chandelier." He clicks his tongue and wipes the blood from his sword before sliding it into his sheath. "Too bad it didn't work."

"Bleeding stars," I say, feeling numb and cold. I knew Xaleo was a killer, but seeing him in action was like watching a panther tear apart a nest of rabbits. His expression holds no joy, no revelry, just cold predatory pragmatism.

My mouth opens, but I don't know what to say. "You killed them."

"Not all of them." Xaleo stoops and picks up my knife. "You told them how it was. They could have lived if they'd let you go. But they chose death."

I take the knife in trembling hands. I can hear shouts and cries of alarm in the distance. My heart drops. This isn't over yet.

"Come on." Xaleo takes my hand and leads me away from the carnage. "I know a place where the sentinels won't find us."

His touch is soft and his grip strangely reassuring even though I can feel the stickiness of blood between our fingers. I allow him to lead me down the hall. My trap vanishes as we leave the comfort of the ambient shadow and exhaustion overwhelms me. It takes a few steps to get my feet moving, but once I do, I start to snap out of my shock. *I'm alive.* That's the most important thing.

Xaleo pulls up to a wide double door. He takes a pin from his pocket and starts working the lock.

"Where are we?" I ask, still in a daze. I'm not sure how we got here or which way will lead to the council chambers.

"Somewhere safe." Xaleo licks his lip as the lock clicks and the door swings open. We slip inside. He eases the door shut and holds up a finger as he presses his ear to the wall. Metallic footsteps thunder in the hall outside. He waits five breaths, then steps away. "We're safe. For a few minutes at least."

"What are you doing here?" I ask. "I thought you were just going to make a distraction."

"I did." He cocks his head. "But I had a feeling you might need my help."

I force myself to take a calming breath. After meeting Xaleo in the courtyard, I'd almost forgotten what he did to the sentinels in my apartment. He's not like me at all. He's a killer. But still, he did save my life. Again. "I appreciate what you did," I say. "But I don't need your kind of help."

Xaleo takes a step forward. "My *kind* of help?"

"You can't kill everyone who stands in your way—"

"Don't get all high and mighty." Xaleo crosses his muscular arms. "You think you're going to waltz in here with fairy powder and butterfly kisses and wish the bad people away?"

"No," I huff. "I don't think that. But—"

"Wake up, Bexis. These people killed my entire village. They murdered my family. Ten soldiers just tried to butcher you. It was us or them, and in that situation, it's always going to be us." His eyes brim with furious intensity.

His sheer arrogance makes me grit my teeth, but I hold my tongue, because despite the horror of seeing men cut down like that, Xaleo is right. They forced our hands. There was no other way out of that situation. "I'm sorry." I will my muscles to unclench. "You saved me. Thank you."

Xaleo observes me coolly. "Come. I want to show you something."

As he turns, I realize we're in a large bed chamber. The walls are baby blue, and the windows have drawn purple curtains with gold trim. There's an armoire on the far wall and an oak four-poster bed with diaphanous white linens.

Xaleo moves the shawl aside and peers at the form curled beneath the sheets.

An old man lies in the bed, his eyes open and staring sightlessly at the ceiling. He resembles a skeleton with skin stretched over the bones. His eyes are sunken pits of black and blue. The satin sheets are pulled up to his collarbone, which juts from his chest. Most of his hair has fallen out, and all that remains are thin wispy strands of white that fall over his shoulders.

"Xaleo," I whisper. "Who is that?"

"You don't recognize him?" He peels back the sheets, revealing a bright green stone embedded in the man's sternum. Green light ebbs with a soft glow that pulses like a heartbeat to a soundless rhythm. *Another nedozul dagger.*

My blood runs cold. I observe the man's face more closely and finally see the resemblance to the person he used to be. "Magistrate Kappe Quaijj, ruler of Coppejj."

"Yes," Xaleo confirms. "Or what's left of him."

I can't tear my eyes from the green glass in his chest. "What have they done to him?"

"The same thing they did to Ceirsa." Xaleo's jaw tightens. "The same thing they'll do to you if they get the chance."

"I thought nedozul would turn him into a phantom."

"Quaijj isn't a resonance trapper, so he can't tether a shaji. Still, the nedozul has corrupted his soul, and it's allowed Vogul to control him like a puppet. He hardly looks human, which means he's outlived his usefulness. Soon, he'll be dead."

"We have to stop this," I say. "We have to help him."

Xaleo shakes his head. "It's too late for that—"

"We have to try!" I elbow him aside and trace the nedozul with my fingertips. The glass is warm to the touch. Maybe I don't need to barter with Zhira at all. "What happens if we take it out?"

"It's fused with his bones. You can't take it out. His fate was sealed the moment they put the nedozul into his flesh."

I shudder. Looking upon this frail creature is too horrible... too real.

"Now you understand who we're dealing with," Xaleo says, his voice cold. "The Magistrate doesn't have free will, but the sentinels outside do. Captain Phekru and all of his soldiers are complicit with everything that's happened here."

"Phekru is complicit, but I don't think the rest of them know—"

"Open your eyes, Bexis." Xaleo spreads his arms. "This is a coup. The Magistrate is dying. The City Council is being held in their offices against their will. Even if Phekru is the only one who knows about the nedozul, every soldier who follows his orders is complicit in treason. Those soldiers are not innocent doe-eyed lambs caught in a bad situation. They're treasonous murderers."

He's right. No one could look at the Magistrate and see anything but a prisoner. The man is a shell of a human being, an empty husk. If the sentinels choose to follow Phekru's orders, hunting trappers, attempting to kill Juzu and capture me, they do so of their own free will.

"There's really nothing we can do to help him?" I ask, my voice coming out cracked and weak.

"There is one thing." Xaleo unsheathes a knife from his belt. "We can end his suffering and make sure Vogul can never use him again."

Of course, the answer is death. I had no idea how dangerous nedozul truly was. And the fact that I'm here to retrieve a fresh blade sends a tremor down my spine. But Xaleo is right. If we can't take the nedozul out, the least we can do is end the man's suffering. "Okay," I stammer. "Do it."

Xaleo leans over the Magistrate, bringing the blade near the man's throat.

"Please," the Magistrate murmurs.

My heart freezes. Xaleo recoils, nearly dropping the blade.

The Magistrate blinks, his eyes searching blindly. He seems to work some moisture into his mouth. His voice is a barely intelligible croak—something between a wheeze and a whisper. "Have you come for me... at last?"

My jaw drops. He's awake, and at least somewhat coherent. "Magistrate?"

The old man turns his head, his eyes wide with terror. "Who are you?"

"We're friends." Xaleo places a hand on the Magistrate's shoulder. "We're here to help you."

"Friends." The Magistrate's gaze locks on the knife in Xaleo's hand. He runs a sandpaper tongue over chapped lips. His gaze shifts from Xaleo to me, and his expression freezes. "You? You can't be here."

I hitch a breath. "I'm sorry?"

"You recognize her?" Xaleo asks.

"Daughter of Shadow." The Magistrate squeezes his eyes shut and rocks his head softly from side to side.

I clench my hands into fists. "Why does everyone keep calling me that?"

The Magistrate groans. "You can't—you can't be here!"

"Magistrate," Xaleo says. "Please, calm down—"

"Kill me!" He starts choking, a soft guttural sound. "It's coming!"

I watch in terror as the Magistrate's eyes go slack and burn with bright green light. His features elongate in the shadows. "What's happening to him?" I ask.

"I don't know, but we should do as he says." Xaleo goes to drive his knife into the Magistrate's chest, but an emaciated hand snatches his wrist, preventing the steel from puncturing flesh.

The Magistrate lifts his head, his lips peeling back in an inhuman sneer. His eyes burn with green fury. The nedozul pulses with garish power. "Come closer, Bexis." The Magistrate wheezes. "Come closer, now. You're almost there—"

"Bexis!" Xaleo grimaces and falls to his knees, the Magistrate's grip crushing his forearm. "Kill him!"

The Magistrate cackles. His face is no longer his own, twisted in shadows that dance like flames upon his skin. "You can't kill me. I am the stars that bleed into dusk. I am the ocean that meets the dawn."

His neck snaps as he lifts himself from the bed. "I am the Immortal Dark!"

"Run!" Xaleo says, his voice infused with terror and pain.

This, more than anything, rouses me from my shock. I unsheathe my dagger and plunge it into the Magistrate's throat. No blood spills from the wound. Smoke hisses and bubbles as the Magistrate flails and screams, his eyes burning from green to pewter until they gloss over with inky blackness. His grip lessens, and Xaleo wrenches away, clutching his arm to his chest. The Magistrate thrusts his head back on his pillows and goes limp. The nedozul dagger crumbles into ash.

My heart beats so hard it feels like I might pass out. "Bleeding stars," I stammer. "What *was* that?"

Xaleo cradles his arm. "I don't know. But we have to leave now."

"I can't leave without Zhira's nedozul," I say. "Help me get to the next floor."

"There are too many of them out there." Xaleo paces the room. "Phekru and Vogul know we're here. The longer we stay, the harder it will be to escape."

I shake my head. "It's my only chance to get rid of the beastmark. I need that nedozul."

Xaleo flexes his wrist and considers my words. "Alright, but you have to be quick. There's a staircase around the corner that will lead you to the council chambers."

"Come with me," I say. "We can make it together."

"No. I'll draw them away and give you an opening."

"We already tried that, and it didn't work." The last thing I want now is to go back out there on my own. "Please, come with me."

"This is the only way." He lifts his hood over his dark shaggy hair and gives me a reassuring grin. "You'll only have one opportunity. Don't mess this up."

Before I can raise another objection, Xaleo slips out of the door, leaving me alone with the Magistrate's corpse.

CHAPTER 18

SEVEN COUNCILLORS SIT ON THE CITY COUNCIL. EACH OF THEM HAS A plush office with a library, fireplace, and study. Each office is at the end of a private hallway in the Council Residency Ward—since councillors need peace and quiet to conduct their affairs. So in contrast to the opulence of the floor below, the lanterns here emit soft blue rays of light over ashy gray walls. It's sober and austere, and the absence of ostentatious chandeliers means there's plenty of ambient dark to fuel my resonance as I sneak down the long hallways, ensconced in a comforting wreath of shadows.

Finally, I'm in my element, but my mind is scattered and chaotic, like I'm being torn in ten different directions at once. I worry for Juzu and Xaleo, and the Magistrate's possession is a horrifying specter that now lives on the fringes of my consciousness. But I force myself to focus on the present. Failure is not a luxury I can afford.

I turn the final corner to Zhira's office and freeze. A sentinel stands at attention outside her door. He wears full plate and is armed with a spear. I grunt in frustration. Under normal circumstances, I would lie in wait, keep track of the patrols and the guard changes, and be tactical when I make my move. Unfortunately, I need to press the issue, and that means initiating a confrontation with another armed guard, which, strictly speaking, is not smart. If he spots me and makes a sound, this whole plan falls apart. At least this time, I have the advantage of full resonance.

I pad down the corridor, my heart raging in my chest. I push my back to the wall beside the guard, so we're facing the same direction. I spot a small pebble on the ground. *Perfect.* I scoop it up and toss it to the guard's left. As the stone clatters on the floor, the sentinel turns his head to the side.

In one fluid motion, I strike the guard's throat with the outside ridge of my left hand as I snatch the spear with the right. He lets out a startled gasp. I smack the blunt end of the spear into his jaw. He slumps against the door and sinks like a stone, unconscious. I hold my breath, keeping an eye on the end of the hall. If anyone heard the struggle, reinforcements would quickly outnumber me. After a long pause, I give Zhira's door a soft knock.

The door swings inward, and Zhira leaps back as the sentinel rolls over her feet. The leader of the Blackbones wears black trousers with a dark brown tunic inlaid with floral patterns. Her raven hair is tied in a ponytail, and her black eyes take in the scene with cold clarity. She rests her hands on her hips. "I was wondering when you'd show up."

I let my resonance fade, dropping my veil of shadow. "We need to talk."

"By all means, come in." She grabs the unconscious sentinel's arms and hauls him inside. "Quickly. There's a patrol that sweeps the floor every thirty minutes. We don't have much time before they realize no one's at the door."

Zhira's office is one of the largest in the keep. There's a massive wooden desk on one side, and a bookshelf crammed with books spans the entire wall. A hearth stands on the far end of the room with a polished marble mantle and a crackling fire. The warmth is welcome as I remove my hood and allow myself to relax. The dangerous part is over. Now I just need to convince Zhira to give me the nedozul.

She removes a handkerchief from her pocket and stuffs it in the guard's mouth, then gets to work tying up his hands and ankles with rope. "I'm going to catch stars for this."

Worry works under my skin. Perhaps I hit him too hard, but my adrenaline was up. I didn't think about his well-being. "Is he okay?"

Zhira snorts. "His jaw isn't broken, but he's not going to feel great when he wakes up, and he's going to have *lots* of questions." Zhira wipes her forehead in a gesture of immense exasperation. "Overall, I'd say he got off easy."

The office seems more lived-in than usual. There are clothes scattered on the floor and unwashed plates piled by the door. The desk is covered by piles of papers and books. "How long have you been trapped in here?" I ask.

"Too bleeding long." She circles the desk and plops into the leather chair. Usually, Zhira is one of the most put-together people I know—calm and serious and in-control. But now she appears strung out: She isn't wearing makeup, and her hair hasn't been washed in days. I can't remember seeing her so disheveled and out of sorts. She smooths the front of her tunic. "Nice of you to drop by, Bexis. I have to admit I wasn't sure if we'd see each other again."

I sit in the chair opposite Zhira. The plush fabric creaks as I sink into it. "Why wouldn't we see each other again?"

"It's a dangerous time." Zhira leans back in her chair and fixes me with her cunning black eyes, resuming some sense of her old self. "Resonance trappers are being hunted in the streets. Vogul has promised me the gallows. The Blackbones are marshaling, and soon I'll have to go into hiding."

"The gallows?" I can't contain my shock. The thought of Zhira hanging in the square is so absurd it's laughable. "Well, obviously, you're not going to let that happen."

Zhira laughs. "Is that why you're here? Is this a daring rescue mission?"

I purse my lips.

"Didn't think so." She waves a hand dismissively. "I can leave anytime I want. There's a hidden passage behind the mantle that leads to the old tunnels and the catacombs. Vogul is smart, but she's not as smart as she thinks."

I bite my lip. Juzu said there weren't tunnels to the councilmember's chambers. Since he can't lie, he must not have known about it. I could kick myself imagining the strife we could have avoided.

"So, what are you going to do?" I ask. The Blackbones have a militia that rivals the sentinels in number. Ajjan said he was mustering a force to break Zhira out of the keep. "Are you going to fight back?"

"Fight back?" Zhira releases a bark of laughter. "Vogul has every advantage. She has the sentinels, the council, and the Magistrate in her pocket. Since removing the Aevem from the keep, Vogul's position is unchallenged. Even with my army at my back, we couldn't touch her." She takes a knife and stabs it into the desk. "So, no, we're not going to fight back. We're going underground."

The small glimmer of hope withers and dies. "Then why are you still here?"

"I have a few affairs to get in order, some paperwork and orders to issue, and then I'll wait and see what Vogul wants. If we're lucky, she's someone we can work with. If not—" Zhira shrugs. "We'll cross that bridge when we get there."

"So that's it then?" I clench my hands into fists. Even if we manage to kill the shaji, we still have to take the government back from Vogul. "You're giving up?"

"Success in life is about knowing when to push and when to yield." Zhira rests her feet on the desk and polishes an apple on the front of her shirt. "So why are you here, Bexis? Looking for work?"

Bartering with Zhira is like dancing with a cobra, but I don't have the time or patience to skirt the issue. "I'm working with the Aevem. We have a plan to deal with Vogul, but we need your help."

Zhira raises an eyebrow. "The Aevem is gone, kid. Probably a thousand miles from here if he knows what's good for him."

"He's not." I place my palms on the desk. "I found him in the Sanctum. He's accepted me as his ward, and I'm training with him to become the next Aevem."

Zhira tilts her head in surprise. "Now, that is smart." She takes a bite from the apple. "Are you making progress with your episodes?"

I ignore her question. "Vogul's greatest weapon isn't the sentinels, it's a creature she's summoned from Nhammock." I expose my right

forearm and show Zhira the serpent and moon beastmark. "If we can
defeat her monster, we weaken Vogul's position, which will give us an
opening to take back the keep."

Zhira doesn't seem convinced. "Okay, so you want to fight
monsters. How does that help us with the sentinels?"

"You said it yourself, the Blackbones can handle the sentinels. Juzu
and I will deal with Vogul. Without her, we can push Phekru out and
install a new government."

"Cut off the head of the snake, and the body follows." Zhira takes
another bite of the apple and throws the rest in the corner. "I suppose
that makes sense, but what do you expect me to do? I don't know
anything about fighting demons."

"We need the nedozul blade."

Zhira nearly spits bits of apple across the desk. "You *what?*"

I cross my arms. "It's hard to explain all the details, but we need
the nedozul to kill the creature."

"Let me get this straight." Zhira strokes her chin. "You want me
to *give* you a nedozul blade worth ten million pieces? And if you lose
it, not only am I out of a fortune that could buy a city, but the
enemy gains access to a powerful weapon that could be used against
me?"

I dig in my proverbial heels. "Name your price."

"My price?" Zhira laughs. "What do you have that's worth ten
million pieces?"

I jut out my chin. "What is it worth to defeat Vogul? Now that the
Magistrate's gone, you could be the ruler of Coppejj."

"Gone?" Zhira raises an eyebrow. "Does that mean what I think it
means?"

I nod solemnly. "Quaijj is dead. If you rally the Blackbones and
crush Phekru's sentinels, you'd be the hero of the city. We could all
but assure your ascension to the Magistrate's office. Isn't that what
you want?"

Zhira reclines in her chair, a speculative calm washing over her.
"Yes. That could be useful. But it's not enough."

"What else do you need?" I ask, failing to keep the desperation from my voice. "You'd be the most powerful person in Coppejj, one of the most influential people in the country."

Zhira nods slowly, tracing her fingertips around the line of her jaw. "I've said it for years, and I'll say it again. You were born to be a Blackbone. The only thing you have that's worth a million pieces is yourself, especially if the Aevem has set you on the path to mastering your abilities." She places a palm on the table, seeming to come to a decision. "That's my price. I'll give you the nedozul with no expectation of material repayment. In return, you will vanquish this demon. Once the Blackbones take out the sentinels, you will take the Bones and join us. I will become Magistrate, and with you at my side, we will lay claim to the rubble."

Zhira's been trying to get me to take the Bones for years, and she finally has something that I need desperately enough to use as leverage. "And if I say no, you're going to let the city burn?"

Zhira shrugs. "For all I know, things will settle after the coup and Vogul's new government will be as ripe as any other for corruption and infiltration. I may lose my influence as a councillor, but my value as head of the Blackbones guarantees me a certain economic security. If it doesn't work out, we have charters in other cities. I could leave here and live a life of opulence in Shezhi. At least then I'd get to see the sunrise."

"You wouldn't—"

"The only thing that would be worth my staying here is you." She sighs. "Having a Khatori-trained trapper in my employ would boost my viability and give me the reach to expand in ways I never dreamed possible. This is how we both get what we want. Do we have a deal or not?"

I frown. Tying myself to the Blackbones all but assures that I won't be able to leave Coppejj. I'll become an indentured servant to Zhira, which will come with perks at the expense of my freedom. But right now, if I don't get the nedozul, I'll be dead—or worse, I'll wind up as a mindless hollow monster. Frustration swells in my chest. I've resisted this for five years and to capitulate now feels like failure.

"Well?" Zhira says. "What do you say?"

I don't like it, but I don't have any other choice. "You give me the nedozul. When all this is over, I'll take the Bones."

Zhira grins and holds out her hand. "On your honor?"

It makes me feel filthy but I grasp her palm in mine. "On my honor."

Zhira beams. It's the happiest I've seen her. "People like us, Bexis. We are survivors. The darkness in this city will run its course, and when the dust clears, we shall remain."

It takes all my self-discipline not to roll my eyes. "We're running out of time."

"Right." Zhira rubs her hands and steps around the desk. She peels back the carpet, revealing a small latch door in the floor. Using a long metal key, she unlocks it and extricates a black silk bundle. "Be careful with this," Zhira mutters. "Don't touch it unless you have to."

As I take it, I feel the power pulsing beneath my fingertips, a sick darkness that seeps under my skin. The power of this blade makes me sick to my stomach. In my mind's eye, I see the demon peering out at me through the Magistrate's green eyes. I take a steadying breath and slide the bundle into my pack. "I have to go," I say, "before the guards return—"

A sudden grinding of stone on stone makes me jump. Ajjan's head pokes out from a cavernous door that's opened in the wall beside the mantle. His eyes widen in surprise as he steps into the room. "Bexis?"

"Ajjan?" I stammer. "What are you doing here?"

Zhira appraises us with amusement. "Ajjan, you're right on time."

He hands her a thick sheaf of papers. "Are you ready to join us at the Driftwood?"

"Not yet." Zhira waves him off. "See Bexis out, then come on back. We have some things to discuss."

Ajjan bows his head and gestures to the tunnel in the wall. "Follow me, Bexis."

Things to discuss? A knot of worry tightens in my gut. With everything going on, could Zhira have found out about our plans to run? I don't sense any menace behind her expression, but Zhira is notoriously stoic.

She smirks as she returns to her desk chair. "Come and find me when it's done, and we'll proceed to the next phase of our plan."

I nod to indicate that I understand, then squeeze into the tunnel after Ajjan. The passage is dark but spacious. Stone steps head downward, and a railing lines the wall for balance. Ajjan leads the way. Once we're out of earshot of Zhira's office, he asks, "What was that all about?"

I groan. "I've agreed to join the Blackbones."

Ajjan freezes. It's so dark, I can't see his face, but I can practically feel his disapproval. "Why would you do that?"

"I'm sorry." I touch his shoulder. There's no easy way to say this. "But things have gotten more complicated. I have something I have to deal with before I can leave Coppejj. Otherwise, both of our lives will be in danger. Saying I'll join the Blackbones is a means to an end."

"We're supposed to leave in the morning." His words drip with disappointment. "So you're not coming with me?"

Guilt creeps into my throat, making it hard to breathe. "I don't expect you to wait for me. But I promise I'll follow as soon as I can, and I'll find you in Emceni."

Ajjan takes my hands in his. "You're a fool if you think Zhira won't hold you to your word. You're a treasure she's been coveting for years. If you run, she'll chase you to the ends of the world, and she'll find you."

"She can try," I breathe. But the same thought had occurred to me. "If it comes to that, I'll find a way. I always do."

"Have you made up your mind?" Ajjan asks.

"I have."

He gives my hand a reassuring squeeze. "Okay."

We resume our walk in silence. A weight has settled into my chest. It feels horrible to crush his hopes like this, but I did the right thing. I can't leave Coppejj until the phantom is taken care of, and now that I've made this promise to Zhira, I have to honor it... at least for a little while.

We reach a stairwell. Soft light emanates from the top. Ajjan pauses and places a hand on my elbow. "This will lead you to the surface just outside the Sanctum."

"Ajjan," I say. "You're going to be okay. If Zhira goes after you, I'll tell her that a condition of my joining will be that she lets you go. I won't let her hurt you."

"You don't have to do that." He gives me a wan smile. "Don't put yourself in danger for my sake."

A strange compulsion overtakes me. I wrap my arms around Ajjan and press my head against his chest. He's so startled, he takes a step back, but I don't let go. "Thank you for being my friend," I whisper.

He hugs me back, encircling me in warmth. "Always."

We stay like that for a moment. Me, listening to the soft thump of his heart, and him holding me tight, his arms forming a protective circle around me. Ajjan has always been kind to me and always looked out for me. I've taken him for granted, and it seems such a crime that I'm only now realizing it.

I pull away, blood rushing to my cheeks. "I'm sorry."

"It's okay." He takes my shoulders in his hands. "No matter the distance between us, I'll always be here for you. You know where to find me."

"Goodbye, Ajjan." The pain is surprising and complete. It feels like my heart is being ripped out of my chest. Before the first tear can fall down my cheek, I climb the steps to the surface and leave my only friend in the world to start a new life without me.

At least he'll be safe.

CHAPTER 19

THE LIGHTHOUSE LOOMS ON A BLUFF OVERLOOKING THE SHADOW SEA, A lonely tower of black stone that rises into the sky, topped with a dilapidated lantern room. The glass is shattered, and the lantern hasn't been lit in years. All the trading routes that ran up this side of the peninsula have been redrawn to avoid this place. Remnants of the old wharf have sunken into the frigid waters. The planks are coated in barnacles, and invasive sea moss has taken residence on every exposed surface. It smells of salt, seaweed, and rot.

An uneven path leads across the stony bluff from the pier to the lighthouse. White seafoam forms on the banks as waves crash below and dark clouds begin to form on the horizon, adorned with the fading light of the red moon. In a few hours, it will be dawn—the third morning since I met Vogul in the brothel and this whole thing started.

Juzu said he would meet me here, but I see no sign of him as I lean against the wooden railing of the old pier. My imagination starts to run wild. What if something terrible happened to him? Phekru could be torturing him in a dungeon in the White Keep, and I would have no way of knowing. Guilt crawls into my belly like a spider. Using

Juzu as a decoy was my idea. If anything happened to him, it would be my fault.

Although the nedozul is wrapped in cloth and tucked in my pack, I *feel* its presence in the back of my mind. It takes all my self-control not to hurl the evil thing into the ocean. After witnessing its power on the Magistrate, I want to be rid of it as soon as possible. If Juzu doesn't arrive soon, I'll have to face the prospect of entering the lighthouse alone.

The thought sends tremors through my skin. I don't know how to find the gate or how to open it. And even if I did get into the Shadow Realm, what then? Am I supposed to face the shaji by myself? Without Juzu, none of this works, and if something happened to him because he thought he had to protect me, the whole city would suffer the consequences. I take a breath, exhaling a funnel of vapor into the red moonlight.

"There you are." Juzu's voice makes me jump. He sidles up to me, elbows resting on the railing. "Sorry I'm late."

I breathe a sigh of relief. "Where have you been?"

"If I didn't know better," he teases, "I'd think you were coming to care for me."

"I can't do any of this without you." My last interaction with Ajjan is still fresh in my mind. I shrug. "And maybe I do care. Just a little."

"Hmm." He adjusts the lapels of his jacket. "I ran into Phekru. He sends his regards."

I frown. "Did he have a phaser?"

"Yes, several. I managed to give them the slip, but we caused a stir at the keep. They'll be coming for us." He gazes at the lighthouse. "I haven't been to Deadman's Wharf in years. This place gives me the creeps."

"Me too." I'd been staring at the lighthouse for at least fifteen minutes, marveling at the sense of dread that had settled into my bones, an icy chill that had nothing to do with the temperature outside. "I'm glad I don't have to do this alone."

"You're never alone, Bexis. I'll be with you every step of the way." Juzu turns his silver gaze to me. "Did you get it?"

"Of course." I open my pack and hand him the dagger bundled in silk.

Juzu unwraps the cloth and holds the nedozul in both hands. The hilt is black with a ruby pommel that gives off a soft red light. The black leather sheath covers the blade, but the green glow seeps from the sides. A frown deepens on Juzu's face. "I don't like this at all."

I know what he means. Ever since I got the dagger from Zhira, I've felt a terrible weight pressing on my soul—oppressive and over-bearing but difficult to pinpoint or describe. Giving the nedozul to Juzu offers some relief, but it still makes my skin crawl.

Juzu rewraps the dagger and places it in his coat pocket with a grimace. "The councillor didn't put up a fight?"

I tell him about the Magistrate and the deal I made with Zhira, but I don't mention Xaleo. It feels dirty to keep this from Juzu, but Xaleo has earned my trust. For now.

When I finish, Juzu presses his lips into a thin white line, his expression haunted. "This does answer a lot of questions. Why the Magistrate has been acting so strange. How Vogul was able to infil-trate the government." He hangs his head. "Nedozul is nasty stuff. Kappe Quaijj was a decent man—you did the right thing to end his suffering."

The act of plunging that knife into the Magistrate's throat will follow me for the rest of my life. It doesn't matter that it was the right thing to do. I shiver. "It still doesn't explain what Vogul wants or why she's doing this," I say, "but Zhira is willing to rally the Blackbones after we take out the shaji."

Juzu places his pipe between his lips. "That's good. It means we have some semblance of a plan. This deal you made with Zhira to join the Blackbones does complicate things. But we can work around it."

"So I can still be your ward, even if I join the Blackbones?"

"Of course. You and I are bound, and I will never abandon you."

His words resonate within me. I believe he means it, and it gives me a great measure of comfort. The prospect of joining the Black-bones still fills me with dread. "I can find a way out of it," I say.

"You gave her your word?"

I nod.

"Then you'll do as you said."

A pang of anxiety wrestles through me. "But I don't *want* to take the Bones. I don't want to be a gangster."

Juzu places a hand on my shoulder. "You should understand by now that your decisions affect your internal resonance. As an Aevem, if you make a promise, you have to mean it. You need to consider your words carefully, Bexis. Breaking an oath could undermine your progress."

I groan. "We probably won't survive this anyway."

"Have some faith. I have a feeling we're going to need it." He gestures to the path leading up to the lighthouse. "Let's go before Phekru catches up."

Fog rolls in from the west as we descend the slippery wooden steps and start down the path. My boots struggle to find purchase on the icy stones.

"So what happens when we find the shaji?" I ask. "How do we kill it?"

Juzu uses his umbrella as a walking stick as he navigates the rocks. "We don't unless we absolutely have to."

I furrow my brow. "But Urru said that was the only way to get rid of the beastmark."

"Yes. But after what you've told me about the Magistrate, I think the phantom may be a person infected with a nedozul blade. Probably a trapper, and probably someone who isn't even aware that they've been infected."

His conclusion confirms everything Xaleo told me. It takes all of my willpower not to tell Juzu about Ceirsa. "So you think the phantom is human—or used to be—and the nedozul allowed the shaji to possess them?"

"It would explain a lot. The infected person would be innocent, with no recollection of having committed any of the phantom's crimes, and if we talk to the host, we might discover Vogul's intentions."

"You want to subdue the shaji without killing the host." I rub my fingers along my jaw. Xaleo seemed to think the nedozul curse was irreversible. "Is that even possible?"

"Maybe not," Juzu says. "But I want to try."

A shiver runs down my spine. Our objective, if possible, just became more difficult. Thunder rumbles across the ocean. Black clouds have gathered in the sky, and a sense of cold death fills the air. The lighthouse towers before us, ominous and dark. When we get to the base of the structure, Juzu leads us up a short set of slick stairs. The front door is painted black, covered with a layer of frozen grime. No one has been here in years.

A sickening dread fills me like a chalice, and my mouth runs dry. "Bleeding stars. Do you feel that?"

"It's a dark resonance. Evil seeps from this place like ink." He adjusts his fedora, his mouth quirking into a wry smile. But he hesitates—his gaze lingering on the copper doorknob a moment too long. "Here we go..."

I bite my bottom lip. "You don't seem so sure."

He winks, masking whatever unease lies beneath, then snaps his fingers. A spark of radiance fizzles across the door, peeling back the layer of muck around the jamb and knob.

A latch pops in the lock, and the door explodes inward. I shield my eyes as blinding light erupts from within. The interior of the lighthouse is adorned with an intricate filigree of sparkling resonance, its swirls and patterns covering every inch of stone. It's so dazzlingly bright, it takes a moment for my eyes to adjust, and even then, I have to blink away tears.

"Fascinating." Juzu steps into the room, his umbrella tucked under his arm. "It's like the whole lighthouse is a resonance door."

As I enter, the designs shift and weave. Bubbles of light trace geometric patterns along the walls. The floor is meshed in a series of concentric circles that form a mandala; in the middle, there's a rendering of the serpent and crescent moon insignia. "It's Entaru's sigil," I whisper. The beastmark tingles, sending a pang of worry through my bowels.

"Entaru built the Shadow Realms," Juzu says. The resonance from the walls reflects in his dark spectacles. He runs a hand across the floor. "These are Kolej glyphs."

"Can you read them?" I ask.

"It says…" He furrows his brows. "Blood will tell."

A shiver runs down my spine. "What does that mean?"

"I'm not sure." Juzu stands upon the sigil and squats on the ground, placing his palms in the center of the crescent moon, over a small crack between the stones. "There's an opening here. Like a keyhole. I think this is where we insert the nedozul." He takes the bundle out of his pocket and unravels it on the ground.

The blade is five inches long, curved and gruesome, giving off a soft green light. Juzu's face tightens as he grips the black pommel and lowers the blade into the slot in the ground. I hold my breath, expecting the ground to shift or a doorway of light to appear out of nowhere.

But nothing happens.

Juzu scratches his forehead. "That was anticlimactic."

I rest my hands on my knees, as cold weight settles over my shoulders. "I don't understand. Shytar said nedozul was the key."

"It is." Juzu raises an eyebrow, his gaze turning toward the Kolej glyphs. "But we're missing something."

"Blood will tell." I frown as a terrible idea takes shape. "Maybe the nedozul needs blood to activate?"

"Of course." He straightens, letting the blade hang by his hip. "The things locked in the Shadow Realm are evil incarnate. The designers of this gate wouldn't want anyone to open it without incurring a cost."

"No. We don't know that." Just carrying nedozul lends an oppressive weight. The mere thought of a cut is too horrifying to consider. "We should keep thinking. Maybe there's another way—"

"We don't have time." Juzu takes a deep breath. His jaw tenses. "I will do it."

"You can't." My voice cracks as panic rises. "I can't do this without you. You're the one who knows what he's doing. You're the one who can actually fight the shaji."

"I will survive, and we will be fine." He smiles weakly. "It certainly won't be pleasant, but a small cut won't be enough to open me up to possession."

This is insane. My pulse races as I peel back my sleeve, proffering my wrist. "We can't risk you being weakened in any way. Please. Let me do it."

"I won't talk about this anymore." His voice is stern and brokers no argument. "You are my ward. I took a vow to protect you, and I'll be damned before I let anything happen to you."

"I'm not a child!" I say, aware of how childish the words make me sound. "You don't have to protect me."

"Actually, I do." He raises the dagger and, before I can protest, presses the tip of the blade into the center of his palm. Blood begins to pool, and then he flips both his hand and the dagger so the blood trickles down the blade and gathers at the hilt. Juzu groans as the green light flares stronger and stronger and the blood soaks into the nedozul.

"Juzu?" I ask. "Are you alright?"

He grimaces, his eyes squeezed shut in a rictus of pain. The dagger drops from his hand and clatters on the ground as he sways. I catch him before he falls, supporting his weight as I gently lower him to the ground.

My heart leaps into my throat. This is my worst nightmare come to life. "Please be okay," I stammer. "Please."

His silver eyes stare at the ceiling, and his mouth goes slack. Then his eyes go dark. I can feel the hairs rising on the back of my neck as Juzu begins to shake. His arms writhe and his hips twist, a white film bubbling on his lips as he convulses. I push him onto his side as panic consumes me. "Bleeding stars!" I shout. "What do I do?"

He falls still. When he opens his eyes, the silver glow has returned, albeit dimmer than before. "Don't worry," he rasps, wiping spittle from his lips. "I'm alright."

"Thank the Saints." I exhale deeply. "That was stupid."

He sits up, still a little woozy, and shakes his head, as if trying to get rid of cobwebs. "As I said, unpleasant, but I'm fine."

"You're not fine, you idiot." I put my hands on my hips, anger bubbling from my gut. "I can't fight the shaji on my own. You're the one who needs to be protected, not me."

"You still don't understand," he says. "Protecting you *is* protecting myself. That's how internal resonance works." He groans as he squats on his knees. "Besides, you don't give yourself enough credit. Even if something happens to me, you're not alone. You have friends."

I throw my hands up. "What are you talking about?"

"Siras. Olaik. Shytar. Ajjan. Any one of them would help you if you asked."

The mention of Ajjan sends a pang of hurt through my chest.

Juzu sighs. "I'm sorry I scared you, but I'm okay. Truly."

"Are you sure?" I ask. "You look a little gray. You should give yourself a healing."

"I won't be able to heal myself." He presses his lips into a firm line. "At least, not until the nedozul has worked itself out of my system."

The dagger lies on the floor, pulsing with bright green light. Juzu picks it up and jams the blade into the slot.

The weapon begins to vibrate, shuddering as cracks form on the pommel. With a hiss of escaping steam, it crumbles to ash, scattering into the air. The mandala explodes in a ring of white radiance, and then all of the resonance lines go out, plunging us into a darkness so thick I can taste it. The ground shifts as stone grinds and rumbles. The bricks move, forming two black plinths. A dark blue light glows between them.

"It's a portal." Juzu inches forward, his posture stiff. "We did it. This is the entrance to the Realm of Shadow."

My heart beats so hard it drowns out everything else. "It worked."

"Yes. The easy part is done." Juzu cocks his fedora at a confidant angle and offers another wry smile. "Now the hard part begins. Are you ready?"

I shiver, unable to answer immediately. This is the last place I want to go right now. The dark blue light feels alive. Malevolent. Like it wants to drag me into its depths and never let go. "This still seems like a terrible idea."

"Ideas never were my strong suit." Juzu tucks his umbrella beneath his arm and, with an encouraging nod, passes through the gate.

He vanishes as the darkness swallows him whole, leaving me alone in the lighthouse. The silence is alive, broken only by the thundering of my heart. Every instinct tells me to turn back while I still can. But it's much too late for that.

Juzu needs me. And I need him.

I count to three, then step into the abyss.

CHAPTER 20

I STAND IN A DARK FIELD, SURROUNDED BY DUST AND RUBBLE AND shadows.

The sky is a pool of obsidian black so deep it sparkles. There are no moons to give off light, and a splattering of crimson stars adorns the night, their long red tails streaking into the horizon, giving the impression that the stars themselves are bleeding.

"Welcome to the Shadow Realm." Juzu's voice pierces the black like a knife.

I shiver as the penetrating cold settles in my bones. As I stare into the sky full of bleeding stars, my breath runs ragged. "Is this a dream —like the Aoz—or is this real?"

"As real as the world we were born in." Juzu wipes at the dust on his shoulders and plants the point of his umbrella on the ground, allowing it to hold his weight. "Let's gather our bearings and locate our quarry."

"But... the stars. Why do they look like that?"

"Bleeding stars. I've always wondered where the saying came from." Juzu shrugs. "Focus, Bexis. We're here for a reason."

I blink, rousing myself from a daze. "Right. How do we find the shaji?"

"First, let's figure out where we are." In the pale starlight, I can make out the frown creasing the lines of his face. Visibility here is poor. I can make out amorphous sepia shadows in the distance, but I may as well be wearing a blindfold.

"It's too dark," I say. "I can't see anything."

"I can fix that." Juzu claps his hands. A flash of light nearly blinds me as a swarm of glowing blue moths spills into the air. They illuminate our surroundings—the blue light clashing with the red to create an eerie violet luminance.

Debris lies all around us: rubble, dust, and collapsed structures that have withered against the ineluctable tide of time. It's a ruin, the stone remnants of a city that existed hundreds or thousands of years ago—cracked pillars and shattered brick and plinths of stone that jut from the ground, many of them the size of horse carriages and weighing thousands of tons.

An archway to our left has survived. Although the columns are broken and big chunks of granite have crumbled, the arch itself stands firm. Beneath the dust, I can make out Entaru's sigil with floral embellishments—a serpent and moon adorned with roses and lilies. There's also writing, scrawling loopy letters embedded into the stone.

"More Kolej script?" I point to the inscription.

Juzu adjusts his spectacles and wipes his hand across the stone, agitating a small cloud of dust. "Hail Entaru," he reads, "Warden Goddess of Phalgun, City of Vigil, and the Watchers of Rhazaran."

Rhazaran. A chill creeps down my spine. "From Olaik's history?"

"The shaji king." Juzu rubs his chin. "This place is a prison. It stands to reason that this city, Phalgun, was constructed to keep Rhazaran contained."

I sweep my gaze over the silent rubble. "People live here?"

"Not for some time. Something terrible has happened—" Juzu grimaces and clutches his chest. He wavers on his feet and nearly falls.

"Whoa!" I take his arm and guide him to a boulder. He leans against it and catches his breath. Behind the dark spectacles, bags have formed under his eyes, and despite the pervasive cold, sweat beads on his forehead. "It's alright," he says. "Lost my balance for a moment."

"It's the nedozul, isn't it?" I ask.

"It must be nice to lie sometimes." Juzu takes off his fedora and runs a hand through his sweaty gray hair.

"But why would you want to lie about something like that?"

"Because I don't want you to worry." Juzu places his hat back on his head. "The nedozul is taking its toll, as I expected."

"I told you it was a bad idea!" I clench my hands into fists. "If you're too weak to fight the shaji—"

"Bexis." He holds up his palms. "I'm going to be fine. After we finish here, I'll stop by the Sanctum, say hello to Siras, eat a cinnamon cake, and everything will be fine. But we can't dally here arguing."

"Alright." Resolve steels in my heart. "But we still don't know how to find it."

Juzu grips my arm to steady himself and gestures to the arch. His swarm of moths follows his gaze, fluttering down the road to reveal a massive black ziggurat rising before us.

My breath catches in my throat. The darkness is so thick that the huge structure was almost invisible. But there it stands, a leveled pyramid that towers into the bleeding sky. The walls are sleek polished stone. The foundation looks newly refurbished, and the windows glow with soft orange light.

"Someone has been keeping that temple clean." Juzu turns his silver gaze to me. "It's the only thing in this wasteland that's not dead."

"I have a bad feeling about this."

"This place is full of bad feelings." Juzu takes a tentative step forward, using his umbrella as a crutch. "Let's take a peek through those windows."

We move at an excruciatingly slow pace. Juzu is weaker than he wants to admit, but I don't push the issue. If he says he can fight the shaji, then I believe him. We climb a flight of stairs, and he huffs from the strain, using my arm for support. "We can stop for a minute," I say.

"It's just physical," he insists. "My resonance is unaffected."

I bite my tongue. The Aevem may not be able to lie to me, but can he lie to himself? Seeing him like this hurts me. I should have been the one to take the nedozul cut. But once again, Juzu has embraced danger to protect me.

We avoid the front entrance and peek through the windows on the right side of the building. Inside, hundreds of black candles are arranged in a circle around a large wooden dais on a raised stage. Behind the stage is a chimeric statue of a beast with a horse-like face and long curved horns on its head. Its body is muscular and humanoid, its back full of jagged spines. The rest of the chamber is full of pews, arranged in straight rows divided by two aisles, each lined with a scarlet runner.

It resembles the Sanctum prayer chamber, except it's all wrong: The statues are grotesque, the symbolism dark and grisly. The black candles remind me of Vogul, which sends a tremor of fear through my gut. "This isn't a prison," I whisper. "It's a church."

"There's someone in there." Juzu presses his nose to the glass. "On the stage."

A man in a dark cloak with a hood over his head kneels at the edge of the stage, lighting candles. I can't make out any other features.

"Maybe there are survivors," I say. "Living among the rubble."

Juzu pulls away from the window. "Only one way to find out."

"Are you sure that's a good idea?"

"What else are we going to do?" He hobbles to the front entrance where a pair of massive stone doors bar our path, each carved with a sigil of a dragon and a lotus flower. Before I have time to question the strange sigil, Juzu shoves his shoulder into the door and strains. I help him and it opens with a grating creak of stone on stone.

The smell of blood all but smashes me in the face. My stomach twists as bile creeps up my throat.

"Welcome!" The hooded man spreads his arms in greeting. "I've been expecting you."

Something about that voice makes me hesitate, but Juzu continues to limp down the central aisle. His grip tightens on my arm. "You know who we are?" he asks.

"Aevem Juzu Khinvo," the man says, a note of cheer in his voice. "Last Khatori in the north. And his ward, Bexis. I am thrilled that you are here." He gestures to a table behind him laden with food: meats, cheeses, and heaping piles of oranges, pomegranates, and grapes arranged on platters. "Are you hungry?"

Juzu stops about ten paces from the man. My heart races. Something about this feels wrong. "Who are you?" I ask.

"You don't recognize me?" The man clicks his tongue and throws back his hood.

My heart stops. The years have not been kind to Lum Carro. His face is etched with lines like stone that has endured thousands of storms. Thin wisps of hair fall over his shoulders, and he curves his purple lips into a grin, revealing a row of rotten brown teeth.

"Ah." He grins. "You *do* recognize me."

Revulsion. That's the only word for the feeling that floods through me. It makes my stomach lurch and my soul recoil. The man who abandoned me five years ago stands before me like a ghost, a greasy twisted creature barely recognizable as human.

I wrinkle my nose in disgust. "I thought you were dead."

"You know this man?" Juzu asks.

"I am her father." Lum Carro hobbles forward, limping on his right side. "And very proud of her." He stops several feet away. "She's all grown up."

The stink of liquor and blood is so strong it brings tears to my eyes. "No thanks to you."

Lum Carro sneers. "I taught you everything you needed to know. That's why it was time for me to leave."

"I was a kid." I clench my hands into fists so tight my knuckles turn white. "You left me alone to starve."

"Poor baby. My life wasn't so easy beyond the Slags either." Lum Carro gestures to the statue behind us. "The Lord told me to come, and I came. He told me to wait, so I waited. But he never said anything about eating rats and cockroaches. Or wiping my ass with rocks."

I'm not sure if I want to scream, cry, run, or punch Lum Carro in his ugly face. All these years, I'd assumed he drank himself to death or drowned in the Shadow Sea, but instead, he'd been taken in by some kind of cult.

"The Shadow Realm has not been opened for hundreds of years." Juzu's grip on my arm tightens. "How did you get here?"

Lum Carro turns his attention to the Aevem. "The portal has been opened many times, but the magic that keeps the shaji locked within is iron-clad. You and I may pass through at our leisure, but the Immortal Dark cannot."

"Why are you here?" I ask.

He hobbles back to the rostrum. "Let me show you."

"I don't like this," I hiss in Juzu's ear. "It doesn't feel right."

He pats my hand. "I feel it too, but we need answers."

"MY LORD!" Lum Carro stands on the stage, his arms spread. "The night of resurrection has finally arrived!" He brandishes a long, serrated knife and slashes it across his throat.

My heart lurches, and I leap backward. Blood sprays over the rostrum. Lum Carro slumps forward and collapses on the ground.

"Hezha's fire," Juzu whispers.

Fear twists in my gut like a knife. Part of me wants to see if he can be saved, while another wants to run for the door and never look back. Instead, I stand stark still like an idiot, my mouth open. "What just happened?"

As if in answer, the windows shatter. A whoosh of frigid air blasts through the cathedral, and all the candles go out, dousing us in inky blackness. Thousands of curls of smoke rise. They coalesce into a noxious cloud at the ceiling. Tendrils of gray smog take the shape of a human skull. Black pits for eyes take us in, jaw hanging open with smoky fangs bared.

"The Daughter of Shadow has returned." The sibilant voice echoes through the cathedral. *"At last, the season of plenty has come to an end."*

"Identify yourself, demon." Juzu's voice booms through the chamber, light crackling between his fingers.

The skull blazes with fury. *"Phalgun is dead, Aevem. The wardens and the Saints have withered to dust. Your world belongs to me now."*

Juzu steps in front of me. A beam of luminance erupts from his palm, splitting the smoke in two. The skull explodes in a concentric circle that billows outward in a rush of air, whipping at my cloak.

And then silence.

The candles burst back to life, encircling us in a pale orange glow. But this time, we're not alone. The pews are no longer empty. Hundreds of shadowy figures fill every seat, their eyes burning like red coalpits. They watch us with dark faces, sitting so still they might be statues.

A commotion erupts behind us. Lum Carro's body convulses, and then he breaks out in a fit of coughs. I watch in horror as he rises to his hands and knees, his white beard covered in dark red blood. The wound in his throat has healed over, and he grins. "You see?" he rasps. "Lord Rhazaran is all-powerful."

My blood runs cold. "What is happening? What *was* that?"

"This is a trap." Juzu pushes me behind him. "Stay close."

Fear squirms beneath my skin like a snake, but my resolve is firm. If Juzu is going to fight, then so am I. The tone pipe is a reassuring weight in my fist. My other hand rests on the hilt of my knife.

"Looks like I'm late to the party." A figure emerges from the rows of dark beings and steps forward. Vogul's hair is braided and tied in a bun. She wears a black dress inlaid with gold thread depicting a dragon across the bodice. Glitter sparkles under vibrant green eyes. Her black lips curl into a wicked smile. "Hello again, Bexis."

Juzu grunts as a beam of light shoots from his palm, but Vogul spreads her arms and absorbs the light as if it's nothing. She clicks her tongue and spreads her fingers, emitting a stream of red resonance that tangles around him. Juzu shouts, and silver light gushes from him like a fountain.

It's so bright I can't see anything. He shoves me aside, and I fall to the ground. The red resonance crackles around him, but it cannot penetrate his defenses. He was right, despite the nedozul's effects, he can certainly hold his own in a fight.

I bring the tone pipe to my lips, but a boot smashes into my face. The pipe cuts my lip and skids across the floor. Stars bloom in my vision. Lum Carro stands above me, covered in his own blood. He wags a finger in the air. "We can't have any of that." Then he snaps his fingers. Green resonance crackles at his feet, encircling me with horrible garish light.

Lum Carro is a trapper. My surprise is broken only by the intense pain that erupts in my bones. I scream as I writhe on the floor in blinding agony.

"Stop!" Juzu shouts. The light around him fades as he holds up his palms. "Please, don't hurt her."

Lum Carro cackles as the green resonance recedes, leaving me twitching on the floor. The agony has disappeared, replaced with an exhaustion that transcends description. "Sorry, darling," he says. "You have no idea how long I've waited to do that."

Vogul strides up to the dais, approaching Juzu as one might approach a wounded wolf. "If you agree not to interfere, we won't kill her. If you so much as raise a finger, I'll slit her throat."

Juzu hangs his head. The bags under his eyes have grown to consume his whole face. Using resonance to fight Vogul appears to have taken the last of his strength. His words slur as he wobbles on his feet. "If you hurt her—"

"Give us your word," Vogul insists. "You must promise."

Juzu sinks to his knees, finally succumbing to exhaustion. I've never seen him so frail and weak. "I swear it."

"Good." Vogul crosses the room and smashes her boot into his gut. Juzu groans on the ground, clutching his stomach. She pulls out a knife.

"No!" I shout, tears blurring my vision. "He gave you his word!"

"Look at him." Vogul grins like a demon. "Weak. Pathetic. Killing him would be a kindness."

I struggle to rise, but Lum Carro presses his foot down on my back, pinning me in place.

Vogul leaves Juzu whimpering on the ground and crouches before me. "You are going to do exactly as we say, and you're not going to resist. If you do, I'll cut the Aevem apart, piece by piece."

My eyes burn, but I force my voice to be strong. "What do you want from me?"

She smirks. "I'm so glad you asked."

CHAPTER 21

LUM CARRO LEADS ME OUT THE REAR EXIT OF THE CATHEDRAL. I STILL can't process the fact that he's alive and in league with Vogul. I always knew he was an abusive alcoholic piece of crap—but I never took him for a heretic. It takes all of my willpower not to twist out of his grip and punch him in the face.

"Are you going to kill me?" I ask.

"Not quite." His breath stinks of whisky. As we march through the back door and plunge into the frigid dark outside, the crimson stars bleed into the black night. "This must be confusing for you," he says.

"You lied to me." The words feel hollow and puerile, but I can't help it. "You told me you were a luminary, but you worship demons. And on top of that, you're a trapper. Is there anything else I don't know?"

"Of course." He cackles. "There is so much you don't know. But none of that matters anymore. Everything is coming together just as it was always meant to."

"You don't have to do this." It feels dirty to beg, but there has to be some small strip of humanity left in him. He might hate me, but I'm still his daughter, and that should count for something. I swallow the lump in my throat. "You can still let me go."

He twists my arm, sending a wave of pain lancing up my shoulder. "And why would I do that?"

"It must be horrible to be you." I clench my jaw against the pain, anger bubbling in my chest. "You're a disgrace."

"There she is." There's a note of callous fury in his voice. "That's the insolent bitch I had to endure all those years."

"What would Mother say if she saw you now?" A familiar sense of guilt curls in my gut. I am responsible for so much pain, so much horror. It's not Lum Carro's fault he turned out the way he did, it's mine.

"That, my love, is something we'll never know."

We enter a stone courtyard with a wooden stage. Delicious waves of heat radiate from the two massive bonfires that burn at either end, their flames flickering twenty feet in the air. Coal braziers circle the perimeter, and an iron post stands in the center of the stage with a red banner bearing the sigil of the black dragon wavering in the soft breeze. Lum Carro shoves me forward.

Hundreds of people swarm the grounds; black-robed acolytes mingle with the amorphous dark figures, and at least two battalions of armored sentinels keep watch over the crowd, their spear points shimmering in the firelight.

I remember Xaleo's story, how he found his friend Ceirsa tied to a post in the middle of his village with a nedozul blade sticking from her chest. An icy fear settles over me like a shawl. He was right this whole time. Vogul left the nedozul as a trap. She wanted Juzu and me to use it to enter the Shadow Realm. We played right into her plans.

My father leads me up the steps to the stage, and I gaze upon a sea of bodies. My blood runs cold. Only now does the depth of our miscalculation set in. This is worse than anything Juzu and I had imagined. There must be hundreds of people here.

"Now you understand." Lum Carro gestures to the crowd. "This is bigger than you and me and our history. You can hate me, call me names, but you can't change the fact that *you* are at the center of it all."

"Why?" I stammer. "What is so damn special about me?"

"Honestly, I've been asking the same question for years."

Vogul comes up from behind and places a hand on Lum Carro's neck. "The hour of redemption is at hand. The Lord is very pleased with your work."

"Suak-ul-dan," Lum Carro mutters.

"Where is Juzu?" I ask.

Vogul smirks, her green eyes shimmering behind dark lashes. "Juzu is weak. The nedozul has taken a toll on his body, but his soul is strong. He'll survive, but only if you comport yourself like a good little lamb. Maybe he'll even be wise enough to dispense with his resistance, but we both know the Aevem doesn't lack conviction."

She's right. If she spares Juzu now, he'll fight for me. No matter what I become, or what I do, Juzu will never stop trying to save me. And his persistence will get him killed.

Vogul has all the leverage. She can stab me full of nedozul, and I can't do a thing about it. A growl tears through my throat. I try to wrench out of Lum Carro's grip, but he jams my arm upward. The pain brings tears to my eyes.

"Come on," he chastises. "No more of that."

"You won't get away with this," I stammer. "If you hurt him, I'll make you pay."

"I like your fire," Vogul says. "But remember to behave yourself, or we have no deal." She touches my cheek before stepping to the lectern. Silence settles over the courtyard. In the icy cold of the Shadow Realm, beneath a sky of crimson stars, the crowd watches.

"I am Kandra Vogul, Suak-ul-dan, High Priestess of the Faceless Coven." Vogul's voice slices through the night with the pious conviction of a zealot. She pauses to let her words sink in. "Two thousand years ago, a man was visited by a God. He was given an impossible task—to reverse the banishment of the Warden Saint, manifest the return of the Immortal Dark, and summon King Rhazaran from the depths of divine imprisonment. For two thousand years, we have fallen short of our Lord's wishes. But tonight, we taste victory." Vogul turns from the pulpit and gestures to me. "I give you Bexis, a worthless rat from the slums of a despot city in the desolate northern waste-lands. A thief and a coward. She has no family, no friends, no purpose except to cause pain and misery to others. She is nothing."

Her assessment isn't far from the truth, but still, it stings. Lum Carro's grip tightens on my wrist, and I bite my tongue.

Vogul turns back to her audience. "But King Rhazaran has revealed that she is the final piece of a puzzle that began five years ago on the outskirts of Shezhi. Bexis's sacrifice will bind Lord Rhazaran to the mortal world. The king shall reign!"

"The king shall reign!"

"The king shall reign!"

The crowd roars in ecstasy. Fists are raised to the sky. Drums smash over the din, and the bonfires rage as swirls of smoke float over our heads. I've witnessed disturbing things in my life, but I never understood what it meant to shake from terror until now.

"Tie her to the post!" Vogul shouts.

Two acolytes in black robes take my arm from Lum Carro and pin me to the steel pole. The dragon banner flaps above me as they strap coils of rope around my waist. A voice in my head screams for me to resist, but the horror has paralyzed me.

My arms are numb. My legs feel as if they no longer belong to me. Dimly, I'm aware of physical sensations—ropes digging into my wrists and ankles, cold steel pressing against my back, the frantic beating of my heart, and the ragged breaths squeezing from my aching lungs—but these sensations are muted, as if they're happening to someone else in some other place.

I want to shout, to scream, to cry out and curse Lum Carro, Vogul, and all the Saints that never did a damn thing to protect me. But all I can do is watch, my eyes dry in the heat of the dancing flames as my final moments unfold before me.

Vogul reaches into her jacket and takes out a shimmering nedozul dagger. The blade pulses with soft luminance. The crowd erupts in a frenzy. Vogul slices the blade down her left cheek—thick red blood trickles down her chin and drips onto the stage. The nedozul blade absorbs the blood, and the glass glows with vibrant green light.

A new wave of terror grips me, turning my knees to water. I sag against the post, heaving great gasps of air, but I can't catch my breath. I realize with dismay that despite my brave front, Vogul is right—I'm a coward.

I'm not ready to die. I don't want to turn into a murdering demon. Just once more, I want to see Xaleo, to bathe in the light of his icy blue gaze. I want to feel Ajjan's arms around me as he strokes my hair and tells me that everything is going to be okay. I want to tell Juzu that I'm grateful for everything he's done for me, that because of him, my life was finally starting to have meaning.

Vogul lifts the nedozul to the sky, tilts her head back, and screams: "Suak-ul-dan!"

In response, the bonfires turn black, their flames becoming columns of dark inferno that spill into the sky.

The crowd begins to chant:

"Suak-ul-dan!"

"Suak-ul-dan!"

A shadowy pool opens in the center of the stage. I watch in horror as a throbbing black mass rises from within. Tentacles of shadow reach toward me, dripping black viscera that steams like toxic tar. A hulking blob of putrid flesh pulses in a steady slow rhythm as black blood bubbles from cracks in the stage, forming a thick gray foam that pools around my boots. The giant heart, nearly five feet wide and three feet tall, beats to the same rhythm as the nedozul.

"My Lord." Vogul places a hand on the heart, her expression soft and reverent. "There's no need to be afraid," she coos. "The pain is only temporary." Her shoulder twists as she stabs the nedozul into the heart with a squish. Viscera sprays in a fountain as the thing recoils in agony. Vogul extracts the dagger and steps around the bleeding heart, her blazing emerald eyes fixed upon me like a raptor set on its prey. Despair clutches at my throat.

This is it. This is how I die.

The drums echo in my mind and the cheers of the crowd grow into a frenetic zenith. "Suak-ul-dan," Vogul whispers as she cuts the neck of my tunic and tears downward, exposing my sternum to the air. A blast of cold hits my chest, but sweat pours down my cheeks and pools at my throat. "When you see Him," Vogul whispers, "try not to scream."

The tip of the knife kisses my skin. I grit my teeth as tears stream down my face. The nedozul is so hot, it sears into my flesh. The pulse of the heart beats against my own, and a sickening cold floods my veins with the numb serenity of dead winter.

"Goodbye, Bexis." Vogul turns her black lips upward in a grin, bracing to plunge the nedozul deep into my chest.

And then the sky explodes.

Vogul is thrown backward into the crowd as light rains downward. The nedozul clatters onto the dais. A silver radiance shines from above, like the brightest moon I've ever seen, a beacon that cuts through the black and burns away the night. The darkness within me retreats in its wake. That light is the only thing I can see. I cling to it like a lifeline in an abyss that threatens to drown my soul.

A cry echoes across the square, and light explodes outward as a creature of white radiance slams into the dais. It walks on two legs like a man, but it has long forearms and a squat ape-like face. The beast breathes a plume of silver fire into the crowd, setting the courtyard ablaze.

"Are you alright?" Juzu pops up behind me. He has to yell into my ear to be heard over the screams.

Relief floods through me like ice water. "You're okay!" Tears well up in my eyes. "But you promised you wouldn't interfere."

"Yeah. I lied."

"You *what?*"

"What can I say?" Juzu cuts through the bonds on my wrists and ankles. "Some things are more important than perfect resonance."

The silver beast roars with such ferocity the stage quakes.

"What *is* that thing?" I ask.

"That's Olppeo," Juzu says. "He's very upset with me."

My jaw drops. "That's your wolsai?"

Juzu grips my shoulders. His face is smeared with blood and his skin withered and sallow, but his eyes are brimming with intensity.

He presses the tone pipe into my hands. "Take this." I squeeze the cold metal in my fist. "Do you remember the way back to the portal?"

I nod, my eyes wide as his meaning sinks in. "I'm not leaving you here."

"There's no time to argue about this." The sharpness in his tone cuts through my resolve. "This is bigger than we dreamed, Bexis. These people want to summon Rhazaran into the mortal world, and we must not let them succeed. You have to get out of here. Find Shytar. Tell her everything that you've seen."

The dark spirits leap onto Olppeo like gnats, their teeth digging into his side. The wolsai shrieks and twists, sending shadows flying across the courtyard.

"And what about you?" I ask, my heart thrumming in my chest.

"I'll meet you there." Juzu gives me a push. "Go now—"

"No!" Vogul raises her hands. Red resonance erupts from her fingertips. Juzu shoves me aside, lightning crackling from his palms, and fires a beam of silver resonance to meet it. The two energies clash in the middle of the courtyard. Juzu grits his teeth but holds his ground.

"Hurry!" he shouts.

Juzu and Olppeo have given me the opening I need. My first few steps are unsteady, and I wobble dangerously, but as I pick up momentum, I streak around the cathedral. The silver flames have spread with astonishing speed, and the entire ziggurat is now ensconced in a torrent of fire. Cold air and woodsmoke sear my lungs. My legs pump with exhaustion, but I don't stop.

A voice in my head screams for me to go back. Juzu saved me. Am I really going to leave him there? But he's right. Vogul needs me to complete the ceremony, so the most effective way to thwart her plan is to escape. Get back through the portal. Find Shytar.

My hopes fall as I spot a crowd of sentinels gathered around the portal. They raise their weapons and rush toward me, flashing spears and swords in the crimson light—there's no way around them.

My heart thumps like a war drum. I reach for my tone pipe and blow. Resonance sparks in my chest and burns with white heat.

Adrenaline surges through my veins, and I break into a dead sprint, streaking head-first toward my enemies.

If the sentinels are surprised to see me rushing them, they don't show it. There are about ten soldiers, but they're scattered, which is my only saving grace—if they'd stuck in a tight formation there would be no hope of breaking through.

I evade the first sentinel with a slight lateral adjustment and slip past him. The next swings his sword in a sideways slash, forcing me to duck under it, which throws me off balance. I manage to stay on my feet without losing momentum. But a third sentinel drops his weapons and slams into me with the force of a raging bull.

It's like running into a brick wall. The wind is knocked from my chest, and my shoulder pops with a horrible blinding pain. Stars dazzle my vision as I crumble to the ground. I roll onto my side, but someone grabs me from behind and lifts me to my feet. "Going somewhere?" the sentinel hisses.

I tap into my resonance and create a cloak of shadow as I twist out of his grip and jam my knife into a soft spot in his thigh. He howls and releases me. I wobble forward, but a figure doused in resonance stands before me, barring my path.

Lum Carro holds a spear with two hands. "I see you've learned a thing or two, which might work on these fools, but not on me."

I almost laugh. "You can't kill me. You need me."

He spins the spear and strikes the blunt end into my shin. My bone crunches, and pain shoots up my leg. I scream and drop my knife, falling to one knee. The rest of the sentinels have retreated to give us space.

"You always were a weak child," Lum Carro says, his voice lined with disapproval. "A sniveling little murderer."

I forget my pain and lunge. But he's too fast. He twirls the spear and brings the blunt end around in a lateral strike that hits me in the jaw. My face explodes with pain that rocks me on my feet.

"You are a monster." He strikes me again, this time on the shoulder. "You're the reason for all of my pain!"

I grit my teeth, hateful tears streaming down my face. I will myself to rise, to continue fighting, but it's over. "Why are you doing this?" I weep, ashamed of the tears but unable to stop them from flowing.

"You cause pain everywhere you go." Lum Carro sneers. "Now you have the chance to do one good thing with your life, and you can't even do *that* right."

As I lie on my back, my body screaming in agony, true despair circles in my bones. Juzu is more of a father to me than Lum Carro will ever be. Juzu cares about me. Even now he's willing to die to protect me. He's shown me what it means to protect someone, what it means to live a virtuous life. And all of it was for nothing.

"Now." Lum Carro bends over me, his thin wispy hair blowing in the wind. "We're going back to that stage, and you're going to fulfill your destiny. But first, a lesson on what happens when you disobey me." He raises his spear and spins it in an arc. I brace for the blow, but it never lands.

The spear is cleaved in two by a steel sword, and the iron tip falls harmlessly to the ground.

Lum Carro blinks in confusion. "What the—"

A dark figure barrels into Lum Carro, throwing him to the ground. "Get up, Bexis!" Xaleo screams. "Fight!"

By now, he's attracted the attention of the sentinels and weaves between them. Lum Carro gasps on the ground next to me. My fingers grasp the severed spear tip, and I drive it into his chest with all my strength.

His face turns white as his eyes pop open. Blood coats his brown teeth as he grimaces in pain. "You evil witch!" he chokes. Red bubbles form on his lips. "This isn't over."

"For you, it is." I twist the spear, and his eyes go cold.

I collapse on the ground, tears streaming down my face. My entire body is a mass of welts and bruises. Lum Carro stares sightlessly at the crimson stars, his weathered face twisted in an expression of hate and indignation. After all these years, I finally find closure in the rapture of bloody steel. Even in death, he mocks me.

Xaleo crouches by my side, his icy blue eyes full of concern. "Come on. We have to go."

"You came." It's a strange thing to say, but my mind is so frazzled, my body so exhausted, I can hardly keep my eyes open.

"Alright," Xaleo says. "Hang tight." I'm dimly aware of being lifted over Xaleo's shoulder, but when I close my eyes, all I can see is my father's sightless gaze locked on me, his bloody scowl seared into my memory forevermore.

CHAPTER 22

My head is a torrent of pain.

I open my eyes with a groan, then blink through a haze of confusion.

"Good. You're awake." Xaleo peers down at me, his shaggy black hair falling over his face, blue eyes blazing like icy beacons, calling me back from the darkness. "I was afraid you were going to sleep straight through the night."

Night? When Juzu and I entered the lighthouse it was nearly dawn. I'm lying on a hard mattress on the floor of a rundown apartment. The walls are bare, the windows boarded with planks and nails, and there's no furniture. But a furnace in the corner holds a small fire, radiating soft waves of heat. I sit up on my elbows, wincing from the aches that cover my body. "Where are we?"

"You're safe." Xaleo crouches beside me. He's wearing gray trousers and a heavy black cloak over a brown tunic. "We're in an apartment in Red Tree."

Red Tree? Somehow, we made it halfway across town. "How did we get here?" I try to sit up, but hiss as pain lances through my shoulder. Memories surface of Lum Carro's assault—the way he sneered as he smacked me with his spear. I should be grateful the bastard didn't stick me with the pointy end, but he did enough damage as it is. My shin throbs, and my face is a swollen mess. No wonder Xaleo is looking at me like that.

Embarrassment bubbles in my belly. I'm a complete wreck—bruised and battered and barely able to sit up—while Xaleo had to carry me like a helpless child. Meanwhile, he battles sentinels and comes away looking like some kind of dark god—the firelight catching on the sharpness of his jaw, the cut of his tunic accentuating his warrior's build. And he's not even trying.

"Here." He offers me a small pouch full of yellow powder.

"*Yras?*" The sight of the stuff makes my stomach lurch. "How did you get this?"

He shrugs. "Stole it from the Sanctum."

I'd laugh if it didn't hurt to move. "That night you visited me?"

He hands me a canteen. "Take it."

As I wash the bitterness down with ice-cold water, Xaleo sits beside the mattress. "You're lucky I found you."

"That happens a lot." I grimace from the taste of the *yras*. Some of it has gotten stuck in my teeth. I stick my finger in my mouth to scrape it out. "If I didn't know better, I'd think you were stalking me."

"How could I resist?" Xaleo grins, his tone casual.

I freeze, my finger still in my mouth. Heat rushes into my cheeks, and I drop my hand, averting my eyes as I wipe spit on my tunic. *Well. That was embarrassing.*

Xaleo pretends not to notice. "Bexis, what happened to you in there? Where is the Aevem?"

I killed my father. That's what happened. Shame curls in my chest. I killed both of my parents—how many people can say that? Lum Carro deserved it, sure, but at some point, I might have to accept that *I'm* the problem. Maybe he was right about me.

Monster.

I shiver, shoving the thought away—deep down where it cannot hurt me. Because that's not the only thing that happened down there. The grotesque black heart. Vogul's shimmering nedozul blade. And Juzu upon the pulpit, his wolsai breathing plumes of silver fire...

He's still back there.

The realization is akin to jumping in an icy lake. My fatigue fades as sober clarity settles into my bones. "I have to go back."

"To the Shadow Realm?" Xaleo shakes his head. "Look at yourself. You're lucky to be alive."

"I don't have a choice." I swing my legs over the side of the mattress. A wave of dizziness washes over me. I place my hands on the bed and squeeze my eyes shut, willing it to pass quickly. The *yras* is already starting to work, sending prickly sensations through my back and shin, but it will be a few hours before the stiffness goes away.

"You're still healing," Xaleo says. "If you push it, you're going to get yourself killed. And what good will that do?"

I ignore him and assess myself. My jaw is puffed up. My shin has a lump the size of an apple. My pockets are empty, and Xaleo has taken off my belt. Anxiety rushes through me. "Where is my—"

"Your knives are here." He pats a bundle that contains my pack and holds out my tone pipe. The cold reflective surface shimmers in the dim light of the furnace. "But slow down for a second. I can't help unless you tell me what's going on—"

I snatch the pipe from his hand. "Vogul has Juzu." The words are difficult to say, as if speaking them makes it more real. Urru's prophecy comes back to me.

The Aevem's light will falter.

My breath catches in my throat. "He could have run, but instead, he saved me. And I left him there." My eyes burn and the room blurs as reality begins to sink in. If Juzu is still alive, there's no way I can get to him. Vogul has hundreds of acolytes from the Faceless Coven, along with an army of well-trained sentinels. And what do I have? A tone pipe and tears.

Xaleo rubs my back as horrible sobs ratchet through me. "I know this is hard. But start from the beginning. What happened after you left the White Keep?"

I tell him about the Shadow Realm and Lum Carro's deception. About Vogul's speech to the Faceless Coven, and their goal to resur-

rect the shaji king. I tell him about the bleeding heart and Juzu's sacrifice. Xaleo listens with his arm around me, his face stoic and calm.
The more I speak these horrible things into reality, the more solid he
becomes. He doesn't wilt or react with fear or anger. He is a rock for
me to lean into, a pillar of strength. By the time I finish, the tears have
dried, and my despair gives way to a steely resolve.

"You were right," I say. "Vogul left the nedozul behind because she
wanted us to open the gate and meet them in the Shadow Realm. This
whole time we've been playing into her hands."

Xaleo brings his knuckles to his lips, his eyes brooding. "I knew
Vogul was evil. But this is much worse than I feared." He rises to his
feet and paces the room. "Did Olaik tell you about the War of the
Dragon and the Serpent?"

"Yes." I wrap my arms around my knees, missing his warmth and
proximity. "King Rhazaran led his armies of shaji through the gate
and enslaved mankind."

"If Vogul summons Rhazaran, there will be another war. The only
reason we were able to push them back last time is because we had
armies of resonance trappers, but the world today is weak. The kingdoms are divided, and there are only a few Khatori left. If Rhazaran
returns, he'll cut through us like we're nothing. It will be the end of
the world as we know it."

I shake my head. The creatures in the Shadow Realm were dark and
insidious. Any world ruled by monsters like that would be a writhing
hellscape. "We need to get Juzu back," I say again. "We have to save him."

"We don't even know if he's alive," Xaleo points out. "Besides, you
said it yourself. He came back to save you. It would dishonor his
sacrifice to throw yourself at Vogul. You're the missing piece. Without
you, their whole plan falls apart."

"Easy for you to say." I stand, my hands clenched into fists. "You've
had me lying to him from the start. You're probably thrilled he's out of
the picture so he never finds out who you are."

Xaleo holds up his palms. "I just don't want you to throw your life
away for nothing."

"Well, you can't keep me here." I show him my beastmark. The black symbol tingles. "I still have the sigil. It's only a matter of time before the phantom finds me and takes me back. While we're sitting here doing nothing, they could be stabbing Juzu with nedozul." I shout. "You might not trust him, but I do. He's my friend. I won't abandon him."

Xaleo's eyes blaze like two blue moons, but his face is stone. "I'm not saying we should abandon him. But have you considered that Vogul might use Juzu as bait to lure you in? That rushing to save him is exactly what she wants you to do?"

I growl in frustration. It kills me that he's right. "So I'm supposed to do nothing?"

"Just think for a minute!" His voice rises. He points at me. "Calm your heart and use your head. The fate of the world depends on how we choose to proceed. This is bigger than Juzu, and it's bigger than your grief."

I hitch a breath. Xaleo's cloak is wet on his right shoulder. "You're bleeding."

He shakes his head and peers between the boards on the window. "It's nothing."

"It's not nothing." I sit back on the mattress, and take a deep breath. "Let me see."

Xaleo purses his lips. "Are you a medic now?"

My tone softens. A calmness washes over me. "I get it. You're a big tough warrior. But if you bleed out, you're not going to be any help either." I pat the spot next to me. "So get over here."

Xaleo sighs and plops next to me.

I probe his shoulder. The fabric of his cloak has been sliced through and it's slick with blood. "You're going to have to take this off." I indicate his cloak. He gives me a sidelong glance and grunts. His face twists into a grimace as he pulls the cloak and tunic over his head, revealing his naked torso.

Blood rushes to my cheeks. His skin is pale, his lean body thickly corded with muscle. Black tattoos cover every inch of his chest, shoulders, and abdomen in a dizzying array of foreign script and geometric patterns that spiral and weave across his flesh.

It feels far too warm in this room, but that must be the *yras*. I focus my attention on his shoulder wound. It's a clean cut that's lacerated his upper deltoid, but it's not deep. Blood drips down his bicep. "When did this happen?" I ask.

"In the Keep," Xaleo huffs. "A lucky strike. Bastard attacked from behind."

So he's mortal after all. After seeing him fight, I wasn't sure that he could bleed like the rest of us. "This is going to need stitches," I whisper.

Xaleo rummages through his bag and pulls out a kit. He hands me a needle and a roll of twine. "Have you done it before?"

In answer, I use gauze to staunch the bleeding, then loop the twine through the needle and get to work. Xaleo stares at the bare wall. He doesn't grimace, but his face grows a bit pale. His bare skin radiates heat, and the space between us crackles. Every time our skin makes contact, a ripple of excitement passes through me.

When I finish, Xaleo inspects my work, and with an appreciative nod, he puts his soiled shirt back on. "Thanks."

The moment of calm has given me clarity. I touch my cheek, remembering what Juzu said at the temple as he cut my bonds. "We have to find Shytar."

Xaleo raises an eyebrow. "And who is Shytar?"

"The Toymaker," I say. "She's a Dreamspeaker, a friend. She can help us."

"Alright." Xaleo rubs his chin but doesn't appear convinced. "Where is she?"

I bite my bottom lip. "The last time we visited Shytar, Juzu led me through a maze in the slums of the Hollow, but her workshop is powered by some strange kind of magic. It moves around, and I don't know how to find it on my own."

"Okay, great." Xaleo scoffs. He returns to the window, gazing out at the street. "Another terrible plan."

"Will you shut up?" I rest the back of my head against the wall.

Despair is a weight in my gut. This is hopeless. Even if we find Shytar, then what? Juzu is stronger than I'll ever be. If he can't stop the phantom and the coven, what am I supposed to do? All of this seems to revolve around me, and none of it makes any sense.

I tuck my hair behind my ears and take a steadying breath. "Why me?"

Xaleo continues looking out the window. "What?"

"Why does Vogul need *me* to bring back Rhazaran? Why can't she use Juzu? Or you? Or anyone else?"

"I don't know." Xaleo turns to face me. "I wish I had a better answer for you."

"There's nothing exceptional about me. I'm not strong. I'm not courageous or good or kind." Vogul's words from the pulpit echo in my head. *A worthless rat. A coward. She is nothing.* Her assessment stings, but only because it's true. "Why are you always protecting me?" I ask. "If I'm the last piece that Vogul needs, why not kill me?"

"Now you're being stupid."

"Am I?" I purse my lips. "Because it seems logical to me. If Vogul can't summon Rhazaran without me, why am I still alive?"

Xaleo crosses his arms. "We're not talking about this."

"What aren't you telling me?" I press. "Why are you so intent on keeping me safe when everything would be better if I were dead?"

Xaleo growls, frustrated. "You *are* special."

"How?"

"You just are."

I blink. "Is that all you got?"

"I can't explain it," Xaleo says. "But there's goodness in you. I knew it from the moment I first saw you—you were giving cake to the orphans. The way you risk your life for your friends. The way you say you don't trust anyone, and yet you're willing to die for Juzu even though you only met him a few days ago. I see it in the way you move, the way you speak, the way you smile—" He cuts off abruptly, his cheeks growing red. "I'm not going to let you die."

Blood rushes to my cheeks. I wasn't aware that Xaleo was looking at my smiles. "You're an idiot."

Xaleo turns away again. "Are you hungry? There's a bakery across the street."

I cock my head, an idea blooming in my mind. "Do they have cake?"

Xaleo shrugs. "Probably."

"Brilliant!" I stand, a smile spreading on my lips. "I know what we have to do."

He quirks an eyebrow. "Eat cake?"

"Yes," I say. "That's how we find Shytar."

CHAPTER 23

IT'S THE DEAD OF NIGHT.

The red moon cuts the black sky like a scythe, staining the snow deep crimson. Despite the heavy chill, the warmth of several loaves of sweetbread bleeds through the cloth sack and seeps into my back.

We stopped at Red Tree Market to stock up on the Rovers' favorite treats—cinnamon cake and chocolate zucchini scones and sourdough muffins—then packed everything into three massive sacks that Xaleo and I are hauling down the street like a pair of oxen.

I admit, we may have gone overboard, but Mo is my last hope of finding Shytar and convincing her to help me save Juzu. An extra scone or two might mean the difference between life and death. I pray to all the Saints that Mo will still be in the area.

The smell is intoxicating, and it takes all of my willpower not to stick my head in the sack like it's a feedbag and gorge myself. But Xaleo is with me, and I feel self-conscious around him, which is stupid. He's a brute and a killer with nice eyes, who for some reason likes it when I smile, and that makes me feel weird and squirmy inside.

"Are you sure this is a good idea?" Xaleo hefts his bag of cakes over his shoulder, and although I feel a little silly walking down the street with sacks of confectionaries, Xaleo somehow makes it look dignified. He has that way about him. "Involving the little ones could put them in danger."

"We're not going to put them in danger. Shytar's workshop roams around the city like a stray goat," I explain. "There's a trick to finding it when you need it. Mo can tell us how."

"How does a workshop roam around the city?"

I shrug. "When Juzu brought me there, he led me around in circles for an hour. It was like we had to get lost before we could find where we were going. When we got there, we found her in a trashcan, and the workshop was underground."

Xaleo snorts. "That sounds made up."

"I know. But that's been my life ever since I met Juzu. Crazy stuff keeps happening. It's like I've stepped into some kind of weird dream where nothing makes sense."

"You really care about him," Xaleo says as we cross the street, our boots crunching in the snow.

After everything we've been through, I can't deny it. "Yeah, I do."

He scratches his ear. "Why? You only met him a few days ago."

I pause, breathing a cloud of red into the air. When we sat together in the monastery garden, Xaleo shared his story with me. He's saved my life twice since then, and he's proven to be someone I can depend on. Now he wants to know more about me, and the words stick in my throat. Shame has kept me from telling anyone about my past, but now Lum Carro is dead, and the truth is, I don't know how to feel about it.

"Sorry," Xaleo says, sensing my discomfort. "I didn't mean to pry."

"I had an accident when I was a child," I say. "I was too young to remember what happened. All I know is my mother died and my father never forgave me. He made me feel like a monster. Unlovable. A piece of human garbage."

"That's horrible." Xaleo stares at the ground. "Nobody deserves that."

I continue. "Juzu was different. He didn't lie to me. He treated me like I was someone who mattered. He made me feel like I was worth something."

"Maybe I was wrong about him." Xaleo presses his lips into a line.

"It's not your fault," I say. "What happened to you was awful too."

He sighs. "I can't imagine having a father like that."

"What were your parents like?" I ask.

"My memories of them are scattered." He runs a hand across his mouth, taking a moment to compose his thoughts. "My father was a blacksmith. He always smelled like smoke and oil. My mum used to take my sister and me to the river on sunny days."

I try to picture Xaleo as a child holding his mother's hand and eating sandwiches by the water. It's difficult to reconcile that image with the man before me. But Xaleo is human, which means he was innocent and young once. Just like me. "That sounds nice."

"Those memories should make me happy..." His throat tightens as he swallows.

My heart breaks for him. I hated my father, but I can't imagine what it would be like to have a wonderful loving family and see them slaughtered before my eyes. "I'm sorry you lost them."

He wrinkles his nose and averts his gaze. "Are we almost there?"

"Just up ahead." I tuck a strand of hair behind my ear. I'm still not sure what to make of him, but one thing is certain: Xaleo is not an unfeeling brute. He was wounded as a child, and he's spent his whole life since trying to heal in the only way he knows how. I can't help but feel a sense of kinship with him. We're both alone. We're both struggling with horrible situations. And we were both born under the same moon. I've never met anyone whose experience was closer to mine.

The Ujjarum temple stands on the corner—a dilapidated pagoda of black and crimson. The roof is half-collapsed, the railings splintered and covered in ice. There are no footprints on the sidewalk, no movement in the shadows. I take the steps two at a time, and Xaleo follows. But he pauses as we enter the atrium, his blue eyes blazing.

I turn to face him, scanning the room. There's nothing here but dust and ice. The filigree backboard is frozen over, and the crimson rose altar stands against the far wall like an ancient plinth. "Is there a problem?" I ask.

Xaleo glares around the room as if expecting the shadows to leap out and attack him. "Can't you feel that?"

The hairs on the back of my neck raise. "Feel what?"

"There's an energy about this place." His gaze fixes on the crimson rose altar, and he takes a tentative step forward. "A power I've never felt before."

I frown. "I've walked through here dozens of times, and I never noticed anything."

"You must not have been paying attention. This place is alive with resonance. Like a fuse about to explode."

I roll my eyes. "Now you're just being a dick. Come on, let's go see if Mo's out back—"

"Wait." Xaleo unslings the sack of confectionaries, places it on the floor, and approaches the dais. "This place is old."

"That's a brilliant deduction." I gesture to the dust and the filth. "What gave it away?"

"No," he huffs. "I mean *really* old. Like, thousands of years."

Thousands? "How can you tell?"

"This writing here," he points along the base of the dais. "Is Kolej script. Which means this is probably one of the first Ujjarum temples..." He presses his fingers into the dais, and something clicks. Thin resonance lines bloom to life along the crimson rose, and the stone begins to shift. I stare, my eyes wide, as the dais turns, and a pedestal rises from the ground, bearing a decorative metal box fused into the stone. Xaleo raises an eyebrow. "Still think it's nothing?"

"That doesn't prove anything," I say, though a flicker of unease creeps into my chest. How many times have I sauntered straight through here without looking around? "What is it, anyway?"

He bends closer as he wipes away years of cold dust, inspecting the dais for other hidden secrets. "I don't know. But the energy that I felt, it's coming from inside."

A tremor of uncertainty runs through me. The air feels heavier now, charged, as if the box is watching us. A ridiculous thought. But still. I inch toward the exit that leads to the courtyard. "Maybe we should leave it alone."

His fingers trace along the edges of the box, stopping at two slim slots on the top. "Look here. We need some kind of key to open it."

"Xaleo," I say, my unease spilling into frustration, "we don't have time for this."

He gives me a quizzical look, then reaches toward me. I retreat a step, but he takes my hand. His touch is gentle, his eyes calm and serious. "You have to feel this."

My mouth is dry. And I don't resist as he pulls me toward the dais and places my palm firmly on the box, then glances at me expectantly. "Anything?"

His touch is warm, but the metal is ice cold. I shake my head, my heart thumping loudly in my chest. "I don't know what I'm supposed to be feeling."

"Close your eyes," he insists. "Focus on the box."

I sigh and do as he says. The metal is so cold my fingers go numb. I have to resist the impulse to tear my hand away and jam it in my armpit for warmth. I open my mouth to tell him to stop wasting time, but a wave of sensation makes me pause.

Beneath my palm, it's like I can feel strands of gold and black dancing around the box like swirling flames. Something within calls me, drawing me in, imploring me to dig deeper, to come closer. *Resonance.* Xaleo is right. There's power here.

"You feel it?" Xaleo asks.

"Yes." The sensation is ominous and dark, like an oppressive shadow that looms over our heads. I open my eyes. "What does it mean?"

"Shall we try to open it?"

I bite my bottom lip, still not convinced that's a good idea. "You said we needed a pair of keys."

He scoffs. "And I thought you were a thief." With one finger, he taps the lid. "Let's try infusing it with resonance—"

Blue radiance grows in his palm. Sparks shoot from the box, and bright light fizzles across the room as Xaleo soars through the air in a puff of smoke, smashing into the far wall. My heart leaps into my throat.

I rush to his side. "Are you alright?"

"Bleeding stars." He groans and brushes me off. His hair stands on end, and scorch marks line his cheeks.

"What is it?" I ask. "What happened?"

"I saw something," he whispers. "A stone face. And I heard a voice, but I couldn't understand the words. Whatever is inside of that box does not want to be taken. You were right. We shouldn't be in here."

A shiver runs down my spine as I help him up. "Come on. Forget it. Let's see if Mo can help us."

A noise echoes from the courtyard. Something moves outside. Xaleo's body tenses. Images of the phantom rise in my mind. The creature is still out there hunting us. Blood rages through my veins. At least Xaleo's with me.

"I heard it too." I draw my knife.

Xaleo brings a finger to his lips and motions toward the stairwell that leads to the courtyard. We gather our things and leave the temple, stepping outside. It's quiet. Too quiet.

A shadow moves on the other side of the garden. Xaleo stiffens, but I put my hand on his shoulder. "Calm down. It's just the Rovers."

He licks his lips. "Call out to them."

I sheath my knife and place the bag of food on the ground. "Mo?" My voice carries through the darkness.

Nothing.

"I don't like this," Xaleo grumbles. "This whole place feels haunted."

"Put your sword away," I say. "I've never brought someone with me before, and you're not exactly exuding friendliness."

He blinks. Then slides his sword into its sheath. "Happy?"

"Overjoyed." I place my hands on my hips. "Mo, I need your help."

Still nothing. The seconds tick by, and anxiety sinks in my belly. What if we imagined their presence? What if they saw Xaleo with his bloodstained tunic and armor and bolted? What if we wasted all this time while Juzu is imprisoned, being tortured? I don't have time to spend on fruitless endeavors. But if I can't find Shytar, I'll have to come up with a new plan.

"Who's the knuckle-dragger?" Mo's voice calls out from the shadows. Hope ignites in my heart. *She's here!*

"Knuckle-dragger?" Xaleo crosses his arms. "That's unkind."

Relief floods through me like a cold river. "Don't worry," I call out. "He's a friend."

"Tell him to flap his arms like a goose!" Mo shouts. I raise an eyebrow at Xaleo.

"She's joking, right?" He grunts. "I'm not doing that."

I stifle a laugh. "They want to know you're not dangerous."

"And making a fool of myself proves that?"

"Just do it," I say, "or they won't come out."

Xaleo bristles. But he tucks his arms and extends his elbows in an approximation of a goose. He even embellishes and struts around in a circle. His cheeks grow red.

Giggles rise from the shadows across the courtyard. Mo comes out, a smirk plastered to her mouse-like face. She doesn't take her fierce blue eyes off Xaleo as she approaches. "Hez, coppe. Total cringe."

Xaleo purses his lips. "What language is she speaking?"

It takes all my willpower not to embrace her. "I'm so happy to see you."

She quirks an eyebrow. "You look terrible, Bex. Still haven't had a bath, I see."

"I'm sorry I haven't been around, but I brought some food."

Mo notes the three sacks of confectionaries, then sniffs. "I have news. We spotted the Aevem being taken to the White Keep." Mo rubs her nose with her sleeve. "He didn't disappear after all."

My heart leaps. "But he's still alive?"

"Was an hour ago. Didn't look too good though. Beat up and stuff, kinda like you."

Xaleo taps his fingers absently on the pommel of the sword at his hip. "So they took him to the White Keep. That's good to know."

Mo puts two fingers into her mouth and whistles. A young boy comes out. He shuffles forward, his eyes steady on Xaleo, then takes the bags, slings all three over his shoulder, and wobbles under the weight back into the shadows.

"Big haul." Mo watches him go. "Got another job for us?"

"Yes," I say. "We need your help."

Mo tears her eyes from the boy and scans me up and down. "Sure, coppe. What you need?"

"Can you tell me how to find the Toymaker?"

Mo cocks her head in surprise, then glares at Xaleo. "Maybe."

Her aloofness confuses me. "Shytar is my friend," I explain. "We need her help."

"If she's your friend, why can't you find her yourself?"

"I don't know how the magic works. The last time I was there, another friend showed me the way. But he's in trouble."

Mo gives Xaleo another suspicious look, then sighs. "I trust you, Bex. But I don't trust the knuckle-dragger. I can't bring him to the Toymaker."

"It's alright." Xaleo uncrosses his arms. Mo watches as he reaches into his cloak pocket and takes out a pouch. He tosses it on the ground at her feet.

She frowns and picks it up. "What's this?"

"Open it," Xaleo says.

Mo unfastens the string and peers inside. Her face turns white. "Gold?"

Xaleo squats on his heels and speaks to Mo at eye level. "My name is Xaleo. I'm here to protect Bexis from the monsters that want to hurt her. But I won't let them touch her. If you bring us to the Toymaker, you can have that whole bag. Get your Rovers off the streets. Buy a place. Eat like kings for the rest of your lives. Do whatever you like with it. But Bexis and I need to find the Toymaker. Will you help us?"

I can't hide my smile as Mo's expression shifts from suspicion to awe. She glances from Xaleo to me, as if seeking validation that this is real.

I nod. "He's telling the truth. I can't go into details right now—the less you know the better—but we need to get to Shytar. It's urgent."

Mo begins to pocket the pouch of coins, but Xaleo clicks his tongue and holds out his hand. "You think I'm an idiot? You can have the gold *after* you tell us how to get to Shytar."

Mo sucks her teeth and reluctantly hands the gold back to him. "I'll do one better, coppe. I'll take you there."

"You don't have to do that," I say. "Just tell us—"

"I thought you said it was urgent," Mo snaps. "The Toymaker is close. I can take you there right now."

My heart leaps. "How close?"

She grins. "Follow me."

CHAPTER 24

GRAVEYARDS GIVE ME THE CREEPS.

Especially at night, with mist rolling in from the coast and the crimson moon glancing over my shoulder. Ever since I was a child, I've had nightmares of dead hands punching through the frozen ground and hunting for the flesh of the living. I'm not a child anymore. Still, shivers run down my spine as Mo guides us to the old cemetery—a snowy hill adorned with rows of headstones and a granite crypt in the center—surrounded by a wrought iron fence.

We stay off the main road, where a pair of sentinels stand guard at the front gate, and instead, take the long way around, circling to the rear.

Mo stands at the fence's edge, her hands grasping the rails. "This is it."

Fog has broken out over the snow, shrouding the gravestones and ceramic plinths. Anxiety wrestles through my guts. *There's nothing to be afraid of*, I scold myself. *Just dead things.*

"Are you sure about this?" Xaleo frowns through the metal bars. Maybe he doesn't like graveyards either. "I thought it was supposed to be difficult to find."

Mo cranes her neck, peering up at him. "Not if you know where to look, dragger."

Trust is in short supply these days, but it will soon be morning, and who knows what Vogul is doing to Juzu in the White Keep? I steel myself. "Show us the way."

"Great." Mo beams. "Gimme a boost, coppe."

Xaleo and I hoist her up, and she scurries over the barrier like a squirrel. I climb hand over hand and pull my legs over when I reach the top, grimacing as pain flares in my shoulder and shin, but the *yras* has taken away most of the bite. Still, I suppress a groan as I drop to the ground.

"Are you alright?" Xaleo asks.

"Fine," I say. "Stop fooling around and get over here."

He gazes up at the fence and shrugs. A thin line of blue resonance forms around his wrists. He dissolves into smoke, slips through the grate, and re-forms next to me.

"Rezzy!" Mo gasps, her eyes wide. "Pretty slick for a dragger."

"Thank you, Mo." Xaleo dusts imaginary lint off his shoulder. "That almost sounded like a compliment."

I roll my eyes. "Now you're just showing off."

"Come on." Mo takes my hand and leads me toward the crypt, a boxy granite structure with four columns and an intricate stained glass door. She climbs the three stone steps and looks around.

"Where's the workshop?" Xaleo asks, exasperated. "There's nothing here."

"Calm down." Mo takes Xaleo by the arm and forces him to sit on the steps. "Get that bag of gold ready."

"I don't understand." I rest my hands on my hips. "Last time we had to wake Shytar up in a trash can. Maybe she's hidden somewhere."

Xaleo makes a show of looking to his right at the empty graveyard, then swinging his gaze to the left, scrutinizing more empty graveyard. He folds his arms over his knees. "Maybe she's in one of these graves. Should we start digging and see what we find?"

Mo giggles. But I don't find it funny. Uncertainty washes over me.

Maybe Xaleo is right, and this is a waste of time. If Juzu is in the White Keep, that's where we should be.

"Here she comes." Mo points down the row of headstones, where a huddled form waddles up the stone path. The form stops when it sees us. Shytar stares at me with her large brown eyes. She wears a slew of jackets and sweaters and coats—polka dots, stripes, some brightly-colored, and others dark and threadbare—along with several pairs of pants. "Square?" Her voice is high and tenuous. "That you?"

"Yes." I gasp, relief flooding through me.

Shytar gazes at Xaleo and frowns. But then she notices Mo and a smile breaks over her lips. "Hello, Sunshine. I didn't see you there."

Mo runs to Shytar and hugs her legs. "They said they needed to find you. At first, I told 'em to hike, but they said it was urgent."

"I'm sure it is." Shytar embraces the young girl. "It's okay, honey. Why don't you come into my shop and pick out something? You can have anything you like."

"Okay!" Mo takes Shytar's hand and blinks up at me.

"I'm sorry to drop in on you like this," I say, "but it really is urgent. The shaji—"

"Not here." Shytar gestures to the crypt. "Come inside, and we can talk." She climbs the steps and rubs the bald oblong head of the gargoyle to her left.

Just like before in the alley, the stone foundation of the crypt magically maneuvers out of the way, as if being excavated by ten invisible men at impossible speed, revealing the triangular green and brown door.

Shytar narrows her eyes at Xaleo. "You're not going to be trouble, are you?"

He holds up his palms. "I can wait outside if you like. Although, I'd rather not."

"He's rezzy dragger," Mo says. "But real slick."

"Oh." Shytar ruffles Mo's hair. "Well, in that case, I guess he better come inside."

Xaleo purses his lips as Shytar opens the door and whispers in my ear. "Do you understand what she's saying?"

"About half," I admit. "I think she likes you."

The workshop appears the same as last time—a large, cavernous chamber with rows of workbenches and toys scattered over the perimeter—masks and rocking horses, dollhouses and puppets, and piles of refuse in the corner. The room smells of paint, oil, and wood.

Shytar removes her jackets, revealing the same sleeveless tank top and spiraling black tattoos that cover her arms and neck. She guides Mo to a small pile of toys in the corner. "Okay, pick something for the little ones while I see what all the fuss is about."

Xaleo scans the workshop, his lips pressed into a line. "What is this place?"

"She makes toys for orphans," I explain. "They're protective talismans of some kind."

"Hmm." Xaleo nods approvingly as he examines a pink dollhouse with small wooden unicorns prancing on the ramparts. "I like it. There's a warmth here, a goodness that emanates from this place."

"I'm glad you noticed." Shytar crosses her arms and leans against a workbench. A half-painted wooden dragon sits beside her, illuminated by a yellow hand-lamp. There's a tin can full of water holding an assortment of small paintbrushes and pools of paint on a metal pallet. "Where is Juzu?"

I grit my teeth, then tell her everything that's happened since the last time we saw each other. When I finish, Shytar's face is tight and her expression sour. "The Faceless Coven."

"You've heard of them?" I ask.

Shytar fiddles absently with a paintbrush, swirling it through the water can. "They've been around for a long time, but I've always thought they were more like fanatics than real zealots."

Xaleo frowns, turning his attention from a cerulean rocking horse. "You didn't think they were dangerous?"

"It's one thing to *say* they want to bring back the demon lord Rhazaran and sit around in little prayer circles with their lips painted black—it's quite another thing to actually do it." Shytar rests her elbows on the workbench and presses her knuckles into her lips.

"When you came out of the Aoz spouting about the Khamonji Flame, I should have put it together, but I didn't want to believe it."

I narrow my eyes. The room suddenly feels much colder. "But you said that you'd never heard of the Khamonji Flame."

"Yeah. Alright. I lied." She slumps onto a rickety stool and drags her palms down her cheeks. "After two thousand years, I fooled myself into thinking this is how it would stay."

The words hang heavily in the room. Xaleo quirks an eyebrow at me. I shake my head. "Shytar, what are you talking about? Two thousand years?"

She rubs the back of her neck, as if embarrassed. Her eyes gleam like polished glass. "I'm one of the immortals. I was alive when the shaji invaded the world. And if what you say is true, the Khamonji Flame is the only hope of preventing them coming once again."

"You can't be serious…" The words hit me like a hammer. My fingers curl instinctively around the edges of the workbench, seeking something solid to hold onto as my mind spins. I knew there was something different about her, but this is beyond anything I could have imagined. "Even if that's true," I say. "How can you be so sure we need the Flame?"

Shytar sighs, holding up her palms. "I was the one who forged it. Alright?"

"Wait a minute." Xaleo runs his fingers through his dark hair, then plants his hands on his hips. "You want us to believe that you're the one who forged the Khamonji Flame two thousand years ago?"

"Yes, that is what I just said." Shytar clicks her tongue. "You're both rather dense about this."

"Ridiculous." Xaleo scoffs, pacing the room. "This is a waste of time. What are we even doing here?"

"What would convince you, slick?" Shytar stands upright, and despite the fact that Xaleo is a foot taller than her, she looms over him. A strange energy emanates from her skin as her tattoos begin to move, twirling and dancing across her flesh. Her eyes glow with brilliant iridescent light, and the room darkens. The rhythm that pulses through the room feels unlike any resonance trapping I've witnessed.

Whatever this is, it's something different, something ancient and formidable. Shytar purses her lips as the energy fades.

"Okay." Xaleo holds his ground, but a sheen of sweat breaks out on his brow. "Fine. Maybe you're not lying."

"Not this time," Shytar says. She looks at me, guilt plain on her face. "I'm sorry I didn't tell you before. I really am. But it's better if people think I'm just a person."

My jaw hangs open. I can't look at her the same way. A moment ago, she was a strange witch who slept in trashcans and made toys underground. Now she's an immortal wizard who forged the most powerful weapon the world has ever seen.

A surge of hope runs through me. "Forget the Flame. With your powers, you can help us!"

Shytar hoists herself onto a table and frowns. "I can't help you fight the shaji."

"Why not?"

"There are blood pacts. Immortal agreements that prohibit me from interfering directly."

I cock my head, confusion wafting over me. "Screw the blood pact. We need to save Juzu and stop Vogul from summoning Rhazaran."

"You don't understand," she says. "It's impossible. The only way to stop them is to use the Flame." Shytar crosses her arms. "But that weapon was made for Entaru. No one else can wield it."

"Urru said the Flame was mine to wield," I say. "I saw it in the Aoz. She said I needed to unite the blood of the Saints."

"You have no idea what you're talking about." Shytar absently picks up a half-finished doll and begins stuffing it with cotton. "Do you know what they call the last person who used the sword?"

I bite my lip. "The lost Saint?"

"The Betrayer. The Cursed. Demon Spawn. Entaru saved all of mankind, and you all worship her underlings and call them Saints, but none of *them* were willing to do what needed to be done. Entaru stopped the Immortal Dark. She's the reason we've lived in peace for the past two thousand years. She was the strongest, bravest, most

honorable woman I've ever known, and her memory is a sacrilege."
She tosses the doll on the bench and picks up another.

I bite my bottom lip. "You knew her?"

"I loved her!" Shytar stands up straight, her fists clenched. "Like
she was my own daughter. She came to me for help, and instead I gave
her the key to her demise."

I soften my tone. "What happened to her?"

Shytar presses her fingers into her forehead. "I was there when
Rhazaran breached the gate and the Immortal Dark spilled into the
world. I was there when the kingdoms of men fell and the shaji took
root. It was a hellscape of horror. Shaji roamed the countryside, and
the dead never stayed in the ground. When Entaru asked me to make
a weapon, I never intended for *her* to wield it."

"But she used it to save the world," I say. "Even if she's not remembered for it, she still did it. That has to count for something."

Shytar gives me a pitying look. "The Flame of Khamonji can only
be used at a terrible cost. It will bind to your soul, corrupt your
internal resonance, and turn you into something not unlike the
Immortal Dark itself. You'll be a monster—a demon—and mankind
will hate you for it. They'll fear you, hunt you, kill you." She shakes
her head. "No. It's best to leave it be."

"Leave it be?" Xaleo narrows his eyes as he places his palms on the
workbench. "We should let the Immortal Dark take the world? What
about Juzu? What about the millions of people that will die?"

Shytar arranges the dolls in a row, averting her eyes. "I understand
that sounds monstrous to you. But when you've been alive as long as I
have, you realize that time is a river that never ends, and the cycle will
shift again and again. The names will change, and the faces will be
different, but the hearts will beat to the same harmonies as always.
You and everyone in this world are going to die whether the
Immortal Dark comes or it doesn't. Perhaps you don't need to fight.
Perhaps we can just let the world turn and find some contentment in
that."

I step around the bench and take Shytar's hands in mine. I force
her to look me in the eye, to see the conviction in my heart. "I'm not

willing to let the world burn. I'll do whatever it takes. Please, tell me how to find the Flame."

Her expression tightens. "If you try to bond to the sword, and it refuses you, you will die. If—against all odds—you should succeed, your fate will be worse than death. More horrible than you can imagine. I cannot be responsible for your damnation. I'm immortal. I'd have to live with it for all eternity."

I shiver. "I understand what's at stake. But you're not responsible for my choices. If I'm willing to take the risk, then who are you to stop me?"

"You're just a child." Shytar lets her eyes trail from mine to the ground. "Brave and stupid. But you're right. It's not my decision to make."

"Then you'll help us?" Xaleo asks.

Shytar's shoulders hunch as she removes her hands from my grasp. "Not many people know the old history. Hezha, Orran, and Ujjek were commanders in the Shadow Rebellion. Along with Entaru, the four of them were the first Khatori. They formed a union, a bond that was fortified with resonance and harmony. Stronger than any I'd ever witnessed. It was with the power of that harmony that I was able to forge the Flame all those years ago. To summon the weapon again, the union must be remade. The blood of the Saints must be reunited."

"The Saints are dead." Xaleo's voice is edged, but it's lost its bite.

Shytar ignores him. "Before she died, Entaru preserved the blood of the Saints in the blood relics, totems that bear the bond of Entaru's greatest commanders. For Hezha, a topaz ring, a silver feather for Orran, and Ujjek's music box."

I sit back, letting Shytar's words sink in. "So we gather the relics, and the Flame will reveal itself. But how are we supposed to find them?"

Shytar shakes her head, letting her palms fall to her sides. "Unfortunately, I can't help you with that."

I frown. A topaz ring, a silver feather, and a music box. Three small items that could fit in the palm of my hand. "They could be anywhere." My stomach drops. "We'll never find them in time."

"Not anywhere," Xaleo says, his voice firm. "In fact, I think I know where two of them are."

My mouth falls open. "A moment ago, you didn't know they existed. How could you know where they are?"

He paces the room, his fingers tracing his jaw. "Grandmaster Olaik wears a topaz ring and guards it like treasure. And we found the metal box in the Ujjarum temple where we went to see Mo. That has to be Ujjek's music box."

He's right. I could kick myself for not seeing it too. During our meeting in the monastery, Olaik played with his ring like a nervous child, and the metal box had two keyholes—one for the feather and one for the ring. "Okay," I say, a glimmer of confidence blooming in my chest. "That makes sense."

"But I don't know where to find the feather." Xaleo pauses, his brow furrowed. "That might be a problem."

"No." The answer hits me like a thunderclap. "High Radiant Siras was wearing one around her neck," I say, recalling the gleam of the silver feather pendant on her chest. "That's it. It must be."

Shytar circles around the bench, her presence grounding as she look us each in the eye. "Bring the feather and the ring to the Ujjarum shrine. Once the relics are united, the sword will reveal itself to you. Or it won't. Regardless, you'll know." She exhales deeply. "Are you absolutely certain this is what you want? You're damning yourself either way. There is no winning."

"Yes." Conviction burns in my chest, steady and unrelenting. "Either I'll get the Flame and use it to stop the coven, or it will reject me, and I'll be dead. Either way, we'll prevent them from summoning Rhazaran."

Shytar's brown eyes glisten in the dim light. "You're just like her, you know? Entaru's spirit is alive within you."

"I'm no saint." I wipe my nose with my sleeve, feeling suddenly awkward. We have some semblance of a plan—crazy as it might be. There's no more time to waste. I touch Xaleo's elbow. "We should go."

"Wait!" Mo runs over, her frizzy hair bouncing with each step. She throws her hands on her hips and glowers at Xaleo. "What about me?"

"I haven't forgotten our deal." He reaches into his pocket and hands her the pouch of gold. "I'm sorry I doubted you."

Mo wrinkles her nose. "Thanks, knuckle-dragger—" She takes the bag of coins and places it in her pocket with reverence. Then she glances at me. "What's your move?"

I sigh. "The Hezhani Monastery first. Olaik will be amenable. He knows his history. It will be harder to get into the Sanctum to see Siras."

"I can help." Mo smacks her lips. "Rovers aren't rezzy but we're plenty slick."

I put my hand on Mo's head. "Thank you for your help, but this is too dangerous. Go back to your Rovers. Take care of them. If things get bad in the city, get them out however you can."

Mo frowns and presses a Kolej doll into my hands. "You're not going to die, are you?"

"Of course not." I smile weakly. The doll is a strange thing with an off-putting skeletal smile that grins up at me. I understand the gesture and put the doll into my pocket.

Mo doesn't appear convinced. She throws her arms around my waist and presses her face against my stomach. "Thank you," she says, her voice muffled and thick. "For everything."

My eyes burn as I return the girl's embrace. I can't think about the end. Not yet. Not until Juzu is safe.

I gently extricate myself from Mo's grip, only to be embraced by Shytar, who squeezes me tight. When she pulls away, her eyes search deep into mine.

"Good luck, Bexis," she whispers. "Juzu would be proud of you."

"Thanks."

As I join Xaleo by the stairs leading back up to the graveyard, my resolve hardens over my fear. Our task seems all but impossible—gather the blood relics to obtain a cursed sword and use it to stop an ancient cabal from summoning a demon king. Seems too absurd to be real. But there's too much at stake to give in to doubt.

"To the Hezhani Monastery?" Xaleo asks, his voice calm, but edged with tension.

I nod, gripping my tone pipe in my fist. "Let's give Olaik a visit."

CHAPTER 25

Sentinels. Dozens of them.

Xaleo and I huddle in the bushes across from the Hezhani Monastery. The night is dark, the roads covered in crimson ice, and my breath comes out in plumes of wicked vapor. The temperature has plummeted, and the cold slips into the sleeves of my jacket like icy fingers. Outside the monastery, a full contingent of armed soldiers man the front gates and patrol the walls.

"Why are there so many of them?" I ask. The last time Juzu and I were here, a few sentinels watched the entrance, but this is different.

Xaleo peers between the branches of a spruce tree. "Olaik would never allow them to have such a strong presence here. Which means Phekru has taken the monastery by force, just like he took the Sanctum. But there's something else too…"

"Something else?"

He shifts, causing snow to fall from the trees and strike his shoulder. "Vogul is here. I can feel her."

Bleeding stars. A shiver runs down my spine. "Just our luck. You think they're after the topaz ring?"

"Not necessarily. Olaik controls the deadliest fighting force in the city. She could be here to talk to him."

"Or threaten him."

Xaleo nods, his expression dark. "If we go inside now, there's a chance she'll see us. We'll be forced to attack."

"She won't see us unless you do something stupid." I put a hand on his shoulder. "I know this is hard for you. You have every right to want Vogul dead, but we can't fight her without the Flame. This job is espionage. Not assassination. If we attack her, we'll both die."

"Yeah. I understand the objective."

"Promise me you won't do anything stupid."

His eyes narrow as he purses his lips. "You have my word, Bexis. I'll follow your lead."

"Good." I turn my attention back to the monastery. "Now, how do we get inside? The guards are going to be a problem. Even with shadows to hide us, there's too many of them."

He gestures to the coast on the left side of the walls. "There's a tunnel by the sea that will lead us to the basement under Hezha's Hall."

"See? You're already proving yourself useful." I take out my tone pipe. "Let's go."

He rests his hand on my wrist, pulling me back. "They have phasers."

"No worries there." I reach into my pocket and take out the silver pearl. The small iridescent stone shimmers in the dim light. "We have this."

"A Vadan pearl." His jaw drops. "How did you find that?"

"Juzu gave it to me." I put the pearl back in my pocket. "So long as I have it, I can trap without being detected by the phasers, but you can't. So don't—"

"Do anything stupid." Xaleo rolls his eyes. "You already said that."

"So long as you understand."

I use the tone pipe. Resonance purrs through my veins. I veil myself in a shadow cloak, then give one to Xaleo, just like Juzu taught me. Once we're both hidden from view, we exit our hiding place in the grove and circle the monastery, heading toward the sea.

Saltwater tinges the frigid air as waves hit the rocky beach. The

Shadow Sea is a black mass that stretches into the sky, and the crimson moon descends into the north. Only the tips of the monastery buildings are visible from the beach. Xaleo gestures silently to a sewer pipe dug into the hill.

I wrinkle my nose but don't protest as we slip into the tunnel. The smell of waste and filth makes bile rise in the back of my throat. The bottom layer is frozen and slippery, but liquid muck gushes over my boots as we slosh through the dark.

"How far?" I cover my nose and breathe through the collar of my jacket.

"In two hundred yards, we'll find a ladder to your right," Xaleo whispers. "It leads to the cellar of Hezha's Hall."

"Something beneath the water brushes against my leg, and I have to bite my lip to keep from calling out. "Where will we find Olaik?"

"This late at night, he's usually in his office. But with the sentinels banging on the front door, I doubt he's curled up by the fire with his books."

"So how do we find him?"

Xaleo is close enough I can feel him shrug. "The mess hall? The training grounds? We'll have to stay vigilant."

"That's not much of a plan."

"Sometimes you have to improvise. We're here." He takes my wrist and guides me to the ladder. The wood is cracked, and the cold sends a shiver up my arm. I take a deep breath. Once we enter the monastery, we're in enemy territory. Every minute matters, and every decision could mean the difference between life and death.

"It's alright," Xaleo says. "You're not alone. I'm right here with you."

"Thanks," I say with a sarcastic bite. "That's comforting."

I climb the ladder and throw open the latch door. The cellar isn't much lighter than the tunnel. We enter a stone room lined with shelves filled with jars of canned goods—beans, peas, pickles, and cabbage. Sacks of grain and flour and rice are stacked along the far wall.

Xaleo scrapes his dirty boots on the stone ground. "We don't want to leave prints."

"You know this place better than me." I gesture to the stairwell leading up to the next floor. "Lead the way."

Together, we climb the stairs and enter a dark hall. Shouts and screams echo in the distance. Xaleo's body stiffens, but he gestures for me to follow. We dash down a corridor, take a left, and then another left. Xaleo freezes.

"What is it?" I whisper.

"There's someone on the ground." He creeps forward and falls to his knees.

A blond woman in yellow robes lies in the middle of the hall in a pool of blood. I recognize her as the woman Xaleo sparred with during his initiation ceremony. Sister Fadi.

My heart seizes. For the past three months, Xaleo lived with these people in the Hezhani Monastery, trained with them, shared bread, and made friends. He was accepted as an initiate, and now history is repeating itself. It's callous of me, but the mission comes first. All that matters now is getting the topaz ring from Olaik.

I place a hand on Xaleo's shoulder. "You should go back."

"I'm fine." His jaw clenches. With one last look at his friend, dead on the floor, he rises to his feet and brushes my hand from his shoulder.

Shouts echo down the hall.

Xaleo tenses. "Come on."

As we enter the mess hall, my blood runs cold. A hundred bodies lie on the floor. The tables are crooked, remnants of meals scattered and forgotten. The stage where Xaleo fought is covered with the dead, their vacant eyes staring into nothing.

My mouth opens in horror, a sick dread twisting my stomach. The smell of blood fills the air with cloying copper. This wasn't a battle; it was a slaughter. Not a single sentinel lies among the fallen.

Xaleo's eyes have grown cold as he takes in the carnage. For a moment, he just stands there, unmoving as his breathing intensifies. His hands clench, then open, fingers shaking with fury. "No… No, this can't be happening. Not again."

My instinct is to avert my gaze, but death is everywhere. There is no escaping it. Vogul did this. She single-handedly killed every monk in the mess hall. Devoted warriors who had spent their lives disciplining their minds and bodies, snuffed out like candles at the whim of this monster.

I want to tell Xaleo that I'm sorry. That I feel his pain. That we will make Vogul pay for her crimes and that everything is going to be okay, but I can't. Not now. "We have to go," I say instead, hating how cold it makes me feel. But every minute matters. "Don't do anything stupid."

He blinks, snapping out of his thoughts. He wipes his forehead with the back of his hand, then scans the room once more. "Olaik isn't here." His voice is a frigid monotone, unfeeling and mechanical. "I think I know where he'll be."

He leads the way up the stairs to the balcony and across the terrace. We scurry through a hall to a set of stairs. I hear a scream from below that turns my blood to ice. Xaleo places a hand on the small of my back.

"This is the training ground. We'll have a view from above."

I allow him to guide me up the steps and into the rafters. We settle on the beams and gaze down at a vast chamber with hardwood floors and bare white walls.

Olaik kneels within, facing a small stone altar. He burns incense and wafts it in the air. "I knew you would come," he says, "but I admit, I thought I had more time." He's about thirty paces from my position in the rafters, yet his voice carries easily through the atrium.

"Your monks are prodigious warriors." Vogul strolls across the chamber, her stilettos clicking with every step. Six royal sentinels follow several paces behind her, decked out in full black plate armor and regalia. Vogul herself is wearing armor for battle—gold pauldrons and a black surcoat inlaid with scarlet thread in the image of a dragon. She stops several paces away and curls her black lips into a smile. "But they died like cattle."

Olaik bows his head. "You will pay for your crimes, Vogul. In this life or the next."

"I look forward to it." Her emerald eyes blaze behind dark lashes. "You know why I'm here?"

"I do." Olaik takes a stick of incense and places it in the trough by his knees. Coils of lotus smoke spiral into the air. "And I'm afraid I must deny your request. I will not help you."

Xaleo tenses at my side. A pang of anxiety wrestles through me. If Vogul attacks, will he be able to control himself, or will he do something stupid after all? I knew Vogul was dangerous, but the sight of the mess hall brings new clarity to her cruelty as well as her power. If Xaleo confronts her now, he'll die.

Vogul rests her hands on her hips. "You know, I've always detested the Orrethics. They're pompous, arrogant swine. They think they own the world. But the Hezhani are different. Subtle. Stoic." She crosses the room, standing beside Olaik by the dais. "I admire you. You've accomplished so much with so little. It would be a shame to wipe it all out for nothing."

"You've already killed everyone I love," Olaik murmurs. "What else can you take from me?"

"You must know that this can only end in two ways. Either you help me or you die. Does your life mean nothing to you?"

The Grandmaster shifts and then slowly rises to his feet. He rests his hands on his knees as he raises himself to his full height. "A life without love isn't a life."

Vogul purses her lips. "Tell me where the blood is kept, and I'll let you start over, build a new flock, train new disciples. There is no reason your trees must burn and your temple must be razed to the ground. Tell me about the blood relic, and I'll let you live."

Olaik smiles and spreads his arms wide. "I am the blood of Hezha. My line has been unbroken for two thousand years. Her heart beats in my chest."

Vogul growls. "If you do not give me what I want, Coppejj and all who live here will burn. Fire will consume the harbors, its waters stained with oil. The ships will be destroyed, and the streets littered with bodies. Women, Olaik, and children too. Do not test me."

Olaik bows his head, turning his gaze back to his candles. "If you seek the blood of Hezha to raise the ilk of Rhazaran, you must reap the blood from my corpse."

"Perhaps you're right," Vogul says. "The Lord would enjoy hearing about your death."

Olaik's eyes burn with vehemence, cold pits of disciplined fury. He brings his hands together, and the topaz ring glistens from the index finger of his right hand. "And you must know my vows are broken in the name of self-defense. If you seek my blood, I will fight you with everything I have. I will hold nothing back."

My breath catches in my throat. Olaik is the greatest warrior in the world. But even he can't fight resonance with steel. Xaleo places a hand on my shoulder, an affirmation that he will hold to our agreement. No matter what happens. My heart attacks my sternum like a raging bull trying to escape a cage.

Vogul laughs, a sound that sends the hairs on the back of my neck standing on end. She holds out her hands in a placating gesture. "I didn't want it to come to this. Remember that."

Olaik holds his cane up to the candlelight and pulls it apart. A long silver blade shimmers through the shadows. He sinks into a fighting stance.

Xaleo's hand grips mine. The gesture takes me by surprise, but his gaze is locked on Olaik. I squeeze his hand. *I'm here. You're not alone.*

Vogul nods to the royal sentinels. They brandish halberds and press the attack. Olaik moves like water falling from a high eave through a grainy mist on a cold morning. He ducks the first strike and slashes. His sword cleaves straight through armor, and the first royal sentinel drops as his arm falls on the floor. Blood sprays in all directions, but Olaik does not pause. Another blow is already on its way.

Five sentinels step onto the killing floor, and Olaik weaves between them, his mouth in a tight line, his movements a blur. Gone is the old doddering man with bad knees and a sore back. Another swipe and another fountain of blood erupts on the floor. The sentinels advance, their faces expressionless. They strike with deadly precision, but compared to Olaik, it's like they move through molasses. Olaik spins through them, dicing them to pieces.

One by one, the sentinels hit the floor, until Olaik and Vogul are the last ones standing. The whole contest lasted ten seconds. Six corpses lie on the floor.

A thrill of hope shoots through me. Maybe Olaik can pull this off. Maybe he can defeat Vogul all on his own.

"Impressive." Vogul extends her hand. A snake of red resonance darts across the room and wraps around his throat. Olaik drops his sword and struggles to free his airway.

Vogul clasps her hands behind her back and strolls around the choking man. "You have trained your whole life in martial arts. But *my* arts are dark and furious. Your swordplay means nothing to me."

Olaik's face turns blue. His eyes widen with fear as understanding washes over him. He cannot fight her. No one can.

The impulse to act is so strong I nearly jump from the rafters, but there's nothing I can do. If Vogul finds us, we'll be dead too. It takes every ounce of discipline to remain in place. Xaleo's grip is so tight, I can't feel my fingers. I watch in suspended horror, powerless, as Vogul's stilettos echo in the chamber. She unsheathes a steel dagger and rams it into Olaik's belly.

I inhale sharply, as if the steel punctured my own flesh. My eyes burn, but I force myself to bear witness as Olaik lets out a soft moan. The tendrils of red dissolve, and the grandmaster crumples to the ground in a bloody heap.

Vogul wipes her blade clean with a piece of cloth, then tosses it on the ground. "In the new world, there will be no use for temples to false prophets or holy books full of lies." She bends low to place a kiss on his cheek. "It's going to be glorious. It's too bad you won't be around to see it."

She smirks and spins on her heels, calling out to the sentinels keeping watch outside the room. "Burn it all down! Make sure none of it survives."

Soldiers enter as Vogul takes her leave. They use torches to light the murals on fire, the ravenous flames catching quickly, consuming the painted walls. Black smoke billows toward the ceiling, thick and choking.

Olaik lies forgotten on the floor as he slowly bleeds out. The
sentinels leave him behind as they rampage through the rest of his
home.

As soon as the soldiers are gone, Xaleo leaps from the rafters and
crashes to the ground. I let the shadows fall around me and use a bit
of rope to rappel down. Smoke burns my eyes. Heat sears my lungs.
Xaleo is already at the grandmaster's side.

Olaik sees me approach, and his mouth opens. Blood drips from
his lips. "You came back," he says.

"I'm sorry." My eyes sting. The weight of helplessness crushes me.
"I wanted to help but—"

"His wound is deep." Xaleo applies pressure to Olaik's stomach.
His hands are covered in blood. "We need to get him to the
Sanctum—"

"No, Xal." Olaik's eyes never leave mine. "My time is done."

Xaleo puts a hand on the grandmaster's shoulder. "You have to let
us try."

Olaik shakes his head. He brings his trembling hands together and
pulls off the topaz ring. With shaky breaths, he places it into Xaleo's
palm. He struggles to get the words out. "Keep this... safe for me."

"I will." Xaleo bows his head, his voice cracking with emotion.
"Thank you. For taking me in. For giving me a place."

Olaik touches Xaleo's cheek. His voice is a ghostly whisper, barely
audible over the crackling flames. "If you wish to honor me," he says.
"Find peace through... forgiveness."

"Forgiveness?" Xaleo's voice rises into near hysteria. "You want me
to *forgive* her?"

"Not just her." Olaik's lips tremble, and his eyes go dark. His head
slumps against the floor.

Xaleo's hands shake as he turns his gaze to me. His eyes are pools
of pain so deep it takes my breath away. "I can't," he whispers. "I can't."

The flames continue to rise and smoke billows in torrents. I can
barely breathe. "Xaleo," I shout over the roar. "We have to go. We need
the feather!"

His eyes are blue furnaces that cut through the smoke. He presses the ring into my palm without meeting my gaze. "I'm not going with you."

"Of course you are." I shove the ring in my pocket and reach for his hand, but he pulls away from me. I recoil, hurt. "You said you wouldn't do anything stupid."

"I'm sorry." He stands rigid, quivering with fury. His eyes are blue tempests. "I need to go. I need to..."

"No." My voice breaks. Panic claws at my chest. "I can't do this alone. Please, come with me."

"I'm going to make her suffer." He steps away from me, resonance crackling across his arms. "She cannot keep getting away with this."

"You're not thinking clearly," I insist. "We need the Flame. It's the only way to fight her."

"I'm sorry." As he turns away from me, blue lines of resonance gush from his palms, and he dissolves in smoke, leaving me alone in the suffocating heat.

"Xaleo!" I scream, despair tearing at my throat. "Come back!"

But it's too late.

He's gone.

CHAPTER 26

I CUT THROUGH THE HOLLOW ON MY WAY TO THE SANCTUM.

Heavy snow tumbles from swollen black clouds. A layer of mist snakes across the mottled roads as strong winds tear through the alleys and streets. Fear is a palpable thing, an undercurrent that flows like a river through my veins. If Vogul knew Olaik had the blood of Ujjek, then she might know about Siras too, which means she could be heading for the Sanctum right now. Siras is in danger, and there's no backup plan. If I can't get the pendant, all is lost. If Xaleo had stayed, we could put our heads together and come up with a contingency plan, but now I'm on my own.

Anger bubbles in my chest. I can't believe he left me. I thought he was someone I could rely on. But the truth is, I don't know him at all.

The Sanctum rises to my right, a behemoth of black stone, its silhouette barely visible in the driving sleet. The campus stretches the span of three city blocks, a giant structure that resembles an old fortress. It has spires and buttresses and crenelated parapets with arched stained glass windows. Under normal circumstances, the windows would glow with varicolored light from within, but tonight they're all dark. Sentinels man the main entrances like black steel gargoyles, halberds and scimitars in hand, which indicates the Sanctum is not as abandoned as it appears.

A crack of lightning cuts through the black sky, punctuated by a crash of thunder that explodes across the city. I clench my jaw. Normally, I'd try to scale the walls, find a way onto the roof, and enter the Sanctum from one of the upper floors, safe from prying eyes, but the weather makes that impossible. The walls are sheets of ice, and without the proper gear, I wouldn't make it ten feet without falling. There's only one other way I can think of to get inside—the same way Juzu and I escaped.

I make my way toward the courtyard—the same spot where I first saw Xaleo playing his flute under the statue of Orran. Had that only been a few days ago? A blue streetlight shines in the courtyard, illuminating the downpour in flakes of blue. A figure stands alone beneath the light. I pull up short, my heart racing. *Shytar?*

The Dreamspeaker cries out, her face turned to the sky. Her amalgamated coat drips with ice and rain as she wraps her arms around herself and sobs. My instinct is to run to her, to get her out of the cold, and wrap her in a blanket. But something about this situation sends a tremor through my belly.

Why would Shytar be standing here in the rain all by herself? The woman who lives in a mobile workshop and hides in trashcans has suddenly thrown caution to the wind and openly exposed herself to the elements—for what purpose? I clench my hands into fists. No. That is not Shytar, which can only mean one thing.

The phantom has come for me.

Fear traces icy fingers up my spine. I hunch low and hide beneath a plinth in the stone wall that lines the walkway. It gives me some respite from the weather as I try to gather myself.

"Bexis..." Shytar moans. It's a pitiful mournful sound, a sound that breaks my heart. She is silhouetted by a blue streetlight. The statue of Orran stands above her. Part of me understands that this is a trap, but another part of me isn't sure. What if it *is* Shytar? What if she remembered something about the blood relics and she's trying to find me before I make a terrible mistake?

Stay focused, I think. *Just move on.*

"Bexis, please," Shytar moans. "Help me! I was wrong. I need you."

"No," I whisper. My heart throbs. "You sick bastard." The topaz ring radiates heat in my jacket pocket. I hold it in a clasped fist, feeling a soft pulse of warmth that emanates through my body, urging me onward, fortifying my strength and will to persevere.

I circumvent the courtyard at a distance and leave the phantom behind as I approach the Sanctum with a pit in my stomach. The demon does not follow or give any indication that it has spotted me in the gale of the storm. The entrance to the tunnel is hidden behind a pair of yew bushes on the eastern side of the building. I slip into the hole and find myself in a pitch-black tunnel with stone walls and a low ceiling. It's cramped, but I'm glad to be free of the wind and snow. The silence within is deafening after the roar of the storm.

Frigid water drips from my cloak and collects in puddles on the floor. The cloak itself weighs too much, so I shrug it off and leave it in a sopping pile at the foot of the tunnel. It will only slow me down from here, and the water will be impossible to hide with resonance. I need to be nimble and light on my feet.

As I feel my way through the dark, anxiety mounts in my spine. I have no idea if these tunnels are branched, if there's a network like the system in the White Keep, or if it's a straight shot to the Sanctum prayer chamber.

I can't see a damned thing. I miss Juzu's colorful moths and his umbrella light. Thinking of him sends a pang of worry through my chest. It's been hours now since the coven took him to the White Keep. An eternity. And they could be torturing him at this very moment.

Hold on, Juzu. I'm coming.

A sound makes my blood run cold. I will my heart to beat more softly as I strain my ears in the darkness.

Singing. It's faint at first but grows louder as I draw closer to the prayer chamber. This isn't a single voice but several that coalesce into a discordant harmony that sets my teeth on edge. It's unlike any choir I've heard before, creating an ululating discordant hum that makes my bones ache until I want to squirm out of my skin. It reminds me, vaguely, of the sensation produced by the phaser. But where the phaser's trill is sharp and piercing, this is dull and achy.

The trap door is located in the back of the room, behind the dais. The door is cracked slightly, and I can make out the pews lit up with candles. Black-robed figures sit in every available seat, and a line of luminaries extends down the central aisle. Sentinels herd them, like sheep, toward the dais, which I can't see from this position. The discordant singing seeps into my bones, creating a veil of disharmony that raises the hair on the back of my arms.

I blow into my tone pipe. Resonance crackles beneath my skin, and I wait for a trill of disharmony to snare me in place, but nothing happens. I breathe a sigh of relief, willing the shadows to bend at my fingertips as I slide the trap door open and creep around the dais. As the stage comes into view, I freeze, my legs locking into place. I have to hold my hands over my mouth to keep from crying out.

The pulpit is covered in corpses.

Most are luminaries, their white and silver robes stained red and their mouths twisted in expressions of horror. Three old women stand before the pile of bodies, their skin sallow and covered in sores, black robes over atrophied frames. But it's their faces that make my blood run like icy sludge through my veins.

They have no eyes or noses, no cheeks or ears. Their heads are like smooth oblong marble, featureless except for toothless gaping mouths that emit that terrible discordant singing. Stringy black hair falls over their slender shoulders as they hold hands on the dais and sing a wordless, toneless song.

I watch in horror as an acolyte of the coven, wearing a dragon-embroidered robe, stands at the pulpit brandishing a knife. "Bring up the next libation," he croaks.

A sentinel guides the next luminary in line up the steps to the dais. The young man does not resist. His face is blank; his eyes glazed over. He seems to feel and think nothing as he walks with effortless grace and stands next to the pulpit.

"The Darkness is Immortal," the acolyte rasps.

"Eternal and free," the members in the pews chant back.

"In Rhazaran's name, we ask you to lay your bodies down."

The young luminary takes the knife from the acolyte. "The wolf is our shepherd," he says, his voice a terrible monotone. "Of my own free will, I offer my body and blood."

The faceless women continue to sing, their discordant song rising in pitch and strength. The young luminary raises the knife and plunges the blade deep into his own belly. A sheet of red falls over his white robes, and he falls to his knees, a smile on his lips.

Bleeding stars. I don't know what I expected. I have no love for Orrethics, but this is more hideous and evil than anything I could have dreamed. If I don't do something, all of these people are going to die. But what can I do? If I reveal myself now, the sentinels will capture me, and I'll be stabbed with nedozul and used to summon the Immortal Dark.

As much as it pains me, I have to accept the only way I can help anyone is by getting the Flame, and to do that, I must find Siras and retrieve the silver feather pendant.

Applying every ounce of my willpower, I inch along the back wall, making sure to keep my distance from the nearest coven members. They are enraptured by the display on the dais. I slip unseen through the wide double doors and into the Sanctum hallways. My hands shake, and my knees tremble. The discordant song fills me with a wrongness that shakes me to my core; every step I put between myself and the prayer chamber helps. But now I'm faced with another dilemma.

The High Radiant could be anywhere in the Sanctum. The campus is massive, spanning several city blocks, and I can't blindly search the entire complex. But what other choice do I have? A pit of despair opens in my chest. I need to hurry. Every second I dally, people are dying. But I can't run around like a fool. I need to be smart. *Think Bexis!*

A flicker of shadow blooms across my vision. A small orb of darkness coalesces several feet from my face and pulses with soft black light. I blink—it resembles the orb I saw in the Aoz. Hope blooms in my chest. "Urru?" I whisper. "Is that you?"

In answer, the ball floats down the hall. Resonance hums through my bones as I follow. Juzu's words echo in the back of my head. Urru is tethered to me, but she is not bound by me. Perhaps she knows where to find Siras. It's a better plan than simply knocking on doors. Urru leads me down a hall and up a flight of stairs, until I reach a door locked by chains.

"Is this it?" I ask. "Siras is behind this door?"

The ball of shadow bobs up and down, then dissolves into nothing. "Wait!" I hiss, but it's too late. I'm alone again. I try to temper my disappointment. Juzu said it takes a lot of energy for wolsai to take physical form. Urru must have seen my situation and done everything she could to help. Now, it's up to me.

The chains on the door are bound by a massive steel padlock. I will the shadows around me into a small funnel, bending gossamer strands of silver resonance and pushing them into the keyhole. The device clicks as it unlatches. I pull off the padlock, remove the chains, and open the door.

Siras sits on the floor in one corner of the unembellished stone room, her wrists bound by chains and shackled to iron buttresses in the wall. Instead of her traditional vestments, the High Radiant wears simple clothes: a gray tunic and dark trousers. Her face is smeared with dirt, and her lip is swollen and bleeding. She squints into the darkness, looking straight through me.

I let my shadows fall, and she blinks in surprise. "Bexis. Is that you?"

"Yes." I close the door behind me. "Are you alright?"

"Fine." Siras laughs, a hopeless enervated sound. "If you're here, that means Juzu can't be far. Please tell me he has a plan."

I work on the shackles at her wrist, willing shadow into the lock. The metal repulses the resonance—I can't unlock it. "What the stars is this?"

"It's no use," Siras says. "It's disharmonic steel. Where is Juzu?"

I drop the chains and swallow a lump in my throat. "He was taken."

Siras frowns. "Taken?"

I squat on my haunches to look the High Radiant in the eyes. "They're keeping him at the White Keep."

"So it's over?" Her lips tremble as her shoulders slump. "The world is ending."

"Not yet," I say, hoping I sound more confident than I feel. "I'm going to take the Flame of Khamonji."

Siras's expression moves from one of quiet skepticism to one of disbelief. "That's a myth. The Flame isn't real."

"Listen." I take a breath. "I don't have time to explain everything. Master Olaik is dead. Before he died, he gave me this." I hold up the topaz ring. The gemstone flashes with a burst of brilliant yellow light. The warmth seeps through my palm and settles in my bones.

Siras leans forward, transfixed. The yellow light reflects in the black of her eyes. "You're serious?"

"I don't know why, but I'm the only one who can take the Flame and put a stop to this. I need your help. You have the blood of Orran."

She leans her head against the wall and scoffs. "I've always been a believer, you know? You can't become High Radiant of the Orrethic Church without having faith. But I never thought it would come to this." She reaches into the front of her tunic and pulls out the silver feather pendant.

I reach out my hand. "Every minute we waste, people are dying in the prayer chamber. Some kind of faceless demon witches are slaughtering your people."

"The Eyeless of Nhammock." Siras nods, her gaze never leaving the silver pendant. She licks her lips. "Their songs lure the innocent into trances of death. I can hear them singing in my head."

My breath hitches. "What are they?"

"They are generals of the shaji armies, servants of the Immortal Dark."

"But how are they here?" I ask. "I thought they needed Rhazaran before the shaji could come through the gate?"

"I don't know what's happening," she admits. "I've wondered why everyone in the Sanctum fell prey to the song of the Eyeless except me." She shudders. "I'm afraid if I give you this pendant, I'll become like them. That I'll lose myself to the songs."

I freeze. The last thing I want is for Siras to end up like the luminaries in the prayer chamber. "Then don't. Keep it. If I can break these chains, we can get you away from the Eyeless. Then you can give it to me later."

"No." Siras shakes her head, her grip on the feather tightening. Her eyes glisten with raw fear. Her breathing quickens. "These chains will not break. And every second that passes more people are dying." She holds out the pendant, her face pale and resolute. "If there's even a chance that it will help you stop this, you have to take it."

The silver feather shimmers in the darkness. A war rages through my chest. I need the pendant and I need to get to the Ujjarum temple as quickly as possible. But I can't leave Siras here either. My hands shake. "Are you sure?" The conviction I had only a moment ago now seems weak and sputtering. "I can't guarantee that this will work."

"Juzu believed in you." Siras takes my hand and presses the pendant into my palm. "I believe in you too."

The pendant radiates silver light that seeps into my skin and surges through my veins. It's similar to the warmth of the ring, but different too. The combination of energy fills me with an electric glow, a power that mingles with my resonance and brings fresh energy to my limbs and muscles. "Thank you." My voice cracks. "I promise I'll do everything I can."

"I know—" Siras blinks, confusion settling across her face.

"What's wrong?" My heart thumps in my throat. "Is it the Eyeless?"

"I can hear…" Siras squeezes her eyes shut and claps her hands over her ears. "You need to go. Now."

I rise to my feet and head to the door, but I pause with my hand on the knob. This feels wrong. How can I just leave the High Radiant in this prison to be consumed and controlled by demons? What kind of person have I become? I turn from the door, intending to try the chains one last time.

But the sight that greets me takes my breath away. Siras stares at me with solid black eyes, her head cocked sideways, chest heaving. Her teeth glisten, bared in a feral snarl.

My heart races. I take a tentative step forward. "Siras?"

She shrieks—a sound so raw and animalistic it sets my teeth on edge. Before I can react, she lurches forward and crawls toward me on all fours. The chains grow taut as she hurls herself against them, snapping her jaws like a rabid wolf.

I stumble back, too terrified to think as I wrench open the door and squeeze through, slamming it shut with all the strength I can muster. Siras thrashes on the other side, her screams a blend of agony and rage that echoes down the corridor.

I stagger backward, my hands shaking as tears stream down my cheeks. "I'm sorry," I whisper, the words catching in my throat. "Bleeding stars, I'm so sorry."

Each step feels like a betrayal, but I force myself to keep moving. Away from the door. Away from Siras. But the High Radiant's howls intensify, clawing at my heart as I slip into the shadows and head for the Ujjarum temple.

CHAPTER 27

Do not stop.

I tear through the snowy alleys of Red Tree Market, veering toward the Slags, back to the Ujjarum temple. The storm surges. Wind rips through the streets in a deafening roar. Without my heavy jacket, the cold bites into my flesh. My fingers ache. My legs go stiff.

But I cannot stop.

Siras's screams echo in my head like a specter that chases me through the night, driving me forward despite the exhaustion that threatens to overwhelm me at any moment. The pounding on the door, the horrific animalistic shrieks. She sacrificed everything to give me the feather—a fleeting chance to get the Flame—and I don't even know if it'll work. Fear is a ravenous leech in my heart; dread sinks like a stone into the bottoms of my feet.

Olaik is dead. Juzu captured. Siras possessed. Ajjan is on a ship bound south. Shytar has given me all the help she can, and the Saints only know what's happened to Xaleo. I am alone. The realization forces me to push through the stitch in my side, the searing agony of my lungs as they heave in ragged gulps of gelid air.

Just keep going. That's all I can do now.

Thunder splits the sky, and a flash of lightning forks through the clouds, illuminating the dilapidated streets of the Slags. Somehow, I've run all the way here without stopping, as if the ghosts of everything I've lost will catch me if I dare to slow down. The shops and windows are boarded up. Nobody's out in this storm.

I jog across the street. The Ujjarum temple comes into view—the crimson pagoda emerging from the dark like an apparition. Relief washes through me. I expected resistance: a battalion of sentinels, members of the faceless coven. Perhaps Vogul doesn't know as much as we'd feared.

I begin to slow as I approach the temple, fatigue and exhaustion creeping into my bones. Snow continues to fall in swirls over my head, cloaking everything in a veil of white darkness. My heart rages. Blood crashes through my ears. I stop, placing my hands on my knees, and try to find my breath.

Something isn't right. The temple looms ahead, silent and still. Dark shapes dance before me, rippling through the snow as a prickle of awareness crawls across my skin. I can feel it—a presence within the storm, a conscious malevolent sneer that watches from the shadows.

Waiting. Hunting.

Maybe I am not as alone as I thought.

Fear trickles like ice down my spine. I begin to back away, but the beastmark erupts in a fountain of pain. I hiss and clutch my forearm as white heat sears through my bones. It's like an invisible branding iron is being pressed against my flesh. A strange tingling rises on the back of my neck, an awareness of resonance that bleeds into my subconscious.

A blood-curdling shriek cuts through the storm, propelling me into action.

I run—sprinting into the dark, across the street, clutching my forearm against the pain. Footsteps crash behind me. Wind howls at my back and pummels my face with ice. My arms pump. Legs scream. The temple atrium is *so* close, and yet—so far away.

The beast roars, practically breathing down my neck. I'm not going to make it. I have to fight. My heart lurches as I whirl, knife extended, bracing for talons to strike.

But I stand in the road, alone, as the night swirls around me.

Bleeding stars. Did I imagine it?

I use my tone pipe to trap resonance. A fire sparks in my chest, and the cold is pushed back. Warmth spreads to my extremities. My vibrational awareness expands into the night, beyond the snow and the storm.

There.

A cloud forms before me, cutting off my access to the temple; a swirling mass of dark mist mixed with torrents of wind and snow spirals into a violent vortex. I raise my hands to my face, squinting through the ice.

The beast has grown since the last time we met. Its eyes are pits of fire the size of my head. It has a vulpine face with a muzzle of vicious black fangs. Its body is long and sinuous, with a deadly barbed tail and spines extending from its back. Gruesome horns curl out of its head, and its bat-like skeleton wings spread twenty feet in each direction.

I take an involuntary step back, doubt and fear mingling in my mind—am I really going to fight this thing? If Juzu and Xaleo couldn't defeat it, what chance do I have? I need to get into the temple. To get the Flame. I need more time.

"Daughter of Shadow." The beast lowers its head and lets its jaw hang open; viscous saliva drips onto the ground, steaming in the cold. The voice doesn't come from its mouth but arises from my mind as if it's already inside me. "This has gone on long enough."

I can hardly think. Blood thunders through my head.

"I can taste your fear." The beast takes a step forward, black talons digging into the snow. "You don't want to die."

I swallow, forcing myself to speak. "You can't kill me," I shout above the wind. "You need me."

The voice laughs. "For now. But your usefulness has its limits."

Every instinct I have tells me to run. To throw my knife with all my strength and flee. To abandon this ill-conceived plan and save myself. But somewhere inside me, conviction burns with a strength that settles deep in my naval and anchors me in place. I have the Kolej doll. It saved me once, perhaps it will do so again.

The phantom takes another lumbering step forward. "Everyone has abandoned you. You have nothing left. So why continue to fight your destiny? Come with me, and I can make the pain go away."

I raise my knife. "If you could take me, you would have already done it." My words are greeted by a crescendo of intense pain from the beastmark that threatens to knock me to my knees. Blood pours down my wrist as the flesh blisters. I let out a groan, yet stand fast, my shoulders squared, rooted to the road.

The phantom cackles and spreads its skeleton wings. The wind whirls around us. "Don't you understand? I am the Immortal Dark. I am the reason the world turns. You cannot stand against me."

Rhazaran. The realization takes my breath away. Of course, the phantom is not just any shaji, but a proxy for the Lord himself. But still, something keeps him at bay. He cannot do what he needs to do without the nedozul. I still have leverage, which means I have a chance.

I take a deep breath, rallying my resonance and feeling the inexorable hum course through my veins. "If you want me, come and get me."

The phantom lunges, shooting black coils of resonance across the street. The vibration slams into me. The pain is immense. Pulsing white lights flicker across my vision. I taste blood on my tongue. A presence has taken residence in my mind, trying to break in, to taint the harmony and consume my soul.

I take out the small Kolej doll that Mo gave me. The strange cotton skeleton glows with a brightness that emanates over me like a shield, but Rhazaran's energy remains a penetrating force against my mind.

"You are not a child of light, Bexis," Rhazaran shouts in my head. "A piece of the Immortal Dark flows in your blood like black ochre that feeds the essence of your soul. Release your pitiful resonance and kneel."

I ignore the pain that rages through my body and focus all of my energy on maintaining the resonance—absorbing the energy from the doll and supporting the shield around me. I cling to the memory of Juzu saving me in the Shadow Realm. Of Ajjan holding me tight. Of Xaleo's touch upon my skin and Mo's smirk as she wraps her arms around my waist. But my strength begins to wane—my muscles burn and my bones ache. The weight of despair settles on my shoulders. I cannot withstand this fury. And Rhazaran knows it.

The shadows writhe as the shield of light begins to splinter. The cotton doll turns to ash in my hands, its strange toothy smile withering into dust. And then, finally, the shield evaporates too.

I lie on my back, chest heaving. The phantom towers above me, its spine arched, wings spread. "Close your eyes, Bexis. It's almost over."

And I know that he's right. There's nothing I can do. He has won.

The phantom reaches toward me with a barbed talon. A bubble of energy has formed between us and my consciousness starts to flicker. Shadows cloud my vision and the world falls away. The wind ceases. The roar of thunder dissolves into an icy silence.

I feel no pain, no cold or any discomfort at all. I am surrounded by black—a darkness so thick it coils around me like smoke, invading every inch of my body, bringing with it a sense of deep calm. And in this silence, everything is still.

"You are mine," Rhazaran whispers in my head. "You will bleed."

"You will suffer!"

"You will…"

"You…"

"WILL NOT HAVE HER!"

The darkness erupts in a fountain of gold and silver, a compound resonance that hums through the black space and rushes into my lungs, catapulting me back into the world. I gasp as the wind rushes through my ears and the snow hits my face. Resonance howls through my veins. Gold and silver weave into intricate gossamer filigree across my skin, forming a protective barrier around me.

The phantom recoils, snarling and spitting. "How?"

In answer, the silver and gold light extend from my raised palms and coalesce into the shapes of two radiant figures that rise before me.

The golden glow forms around a woman with yellow hair, clad in glimmering battle armor. She clutches a burning spear in her hands, casting an aura of fire that reflects off her skin like sunbeams. The silver resonance crackles around a man draped in flowing white robes, his long white hair cascading like silk down his back. He brandishes a deadly curved saber that glows with selenic power as the air around him sizzles.

My jaw drops. The blood relics thrum in my pockets, each giving off a faint aura of color that wraps around me. The aura fills me with warmth that surges to my extremities. The beastmark tingles and the pain fades. *The Saints,* I think. *Hezha and Orran.*

As if reading my thoughts, Hezha bows her head. Her eyes are like two burning suns, her skin glowing in the dark. Orran raises his sword, his gaze piercing through the dark with the power of brilliant moonshine.

"Go to the altar." Orran's voice booms like thunder. "Take the Flame and finish this!"

Hezha turns to face Rhazaran. "We'll buy you as much time as we can."

"Impossible!" Rhazaran shrieks. The beast leaps into the air, teeth bared. In response, Hezha and Orran rush forward to meet him, flying into the sky as gold and silver explode around them and power ripples across the ground. I watch, stunned, as the Saints soar into the sky and battle the demon, pushing Rhazaran backward, and creating an opening for me to flee into the temple.

I've been given a second chance. One shot to make this right. With renewed vigor, I crawl to my hands and knees and break into a run. I take the temple steps two at a time, crashing into the atrium and dashing toward the altar on the far wall.

As the blood relics come into proximity with the crimson rose shrine, the resonance lights up like a beacon. An explosion of radiance shoots outward in a concentric circle. The other relics harmonize, merging their vibrations into a breathtaking confluence of energy.

The steel music box glows like it's on fire as I place the topaz ring and the silver feather into their respective slots. The colors weave,

divide, break, and combine in my third eye. It's a symphony—a rain-
bow. A crescendo of perfect pure vibration that creates a fissure of
power.

I stumble backward as the altar twists. And the floors rotate.

And the world melts away.

CHAPTER 28

AN OCEAN OF WHITE ASTERS STRETCHES AROUND ME. NO HILLS. NO mountains. Only an endless horizon of black sky mottled with swirling pink constellations. A billion stars wink down at me as I lift a hand to my cheek, blinking hard to clear my vision.

"Bleeding stars." My voice trails off, echoed by ghostly whispers. It feels like I've had too much of Shytar's fungus tea. A breeze cuts across the field, sending thousands of asters rippling like waves. A chill trickles down my spine, and I sense a strange vibration in the air, similar to the one I felt in the Shadow Realm—only here it feels different, open and vast.

Where is the Flame? What am I supposed to do here? There's so much pressure resting on me, it feels wrong to be sitting in this peaceful meadow when Hezha and Orran are out there fighting Rhazaran. When Juzu is being held by Vogul, and Xaleo... The Saints know. I don't have time to waste. But which way do I go?

The air prickles with electricity as the sky shifts, bleeding into a frantic collage of color. My knees hit the ground as the field tilts beneath me. The whole world seems to move, but I remain anchored in place. When everything settles, a pyramid stands before me. I gaze up in awe, a chalk-white snake of fear coiling in my gut.

The structure is similar to the ziggurat from the Shadow Realm, but there are subtle differences. This pyramid is built of granite slabs, with a ring of broad black columns framing the entrance, its pinnacle adorned with golden stars that glimmer against the sky. A grand stone staircase leads up to a wraparound veranda that seems to glow with a garish spectral light. It's larger even than the White Keep and more imposing than the Sanctum.

The Flame must be inside. Whatever future awaits me, it starts or ends here.

I rise to my feet, arms out to steady myself, and dare the world to start spinning again. But all remains still. The only movement is a thin layer of blue mist that creeps through the flowers. I place one foot in front of the other, picking up momentum as I go. Slowly, I cross the field of asters, and step up to the staircase. The air seems to thicken as an ancient hum rises from the stone itself.

A flash of light breaks through the sky, splitting the dark horizon. A moon of blue shadow, like a cobalt star, flickers into being above me.

I hitch a breath. "Is that—?"

"Bexis." The voice is a susurration that raises the hairs on the back of my neck.

My heart pounds. "Who's there?"

From the shadow of the archway, a serpent emerges, uncoiling itself with eerie grace and slithering across the temple balcony. I step back, my heart stuttering as the creature approaches, its sinuous body easily a hundred feet long, covered with black-and-silver iridescent scales. Blue ophidian eyes pin me in place. Its forked tongue flicks through the air, tasting me, measuring my mettle. I force myself to square my shoulders and hold my ground.

"Good." The serpent erupts in a fountain of pale light before dissolving into shadow. A gust of smoke spirals outward and slams into me. I throw up my arms, shielding my eyes.

When the smoke clears, a girl stands before me—she's probably only a year or two older than me. Black hair falls down her back and frames a face with soft round cheeks and a pointed chin. She wears a black dress, cut with gold trim—a style I've never seen before that laces up the side and leaves one shoulder bare. Her eyes are almond-shaped, the color of shale.

"Urru?" I ask, incredulous. The last time I saw her, she was a child. "You grew quickly."

"I didn't grow, Bexis." She smiles, a knowing glint in her eyes. Though she appears as a young woman, her gaze carries ancient wisdom, a reverence that makes me stand taller. "I'm a wolsai, remember? I can take any form I like."

"Then why did you take this one?"

"Because I remember who I am. Or at least, who I used to be." She holds out the fabric of her dress. "This is what I was wearing on the day I was banished to Nhammock."

So many questions flood my mind; it's hard to pick one. "You used to be a human?"

"I used to be." Urru places her hands on her hips. "But I'm not anymore."

"How can that be? I thought you were a wolsai."

"As it turns out, wolsai is more a state of being than it is a state of matter."

I scratch my chin. "I don't know what that means."

"It means things are different in Nhammock. The rules that apply to us in the mortal world don't matter there." Urru comes closer, takes my hand. "But spirit-realm physics isn't why you're here. Come." Together we begin to climb the stone stairs, making our way toward the temple entrance. My heart thumps harder with each step.

Urru chews her bottom lip. "I'm sorry," she says softly. "For all of this. For the pain you've endured in your life. The trials that you've faced over the past few days. I know what the world is asking of you better than most, and I understand how unfair it is. No one has any right to ask you to bear this burden, and yet they ask it anyway."

I exhale deeply, still trying to wrap my head around all of this. "It's not your fault—"

"It *is* my fault, actually." Urru's eyes flash. Her jaw tightens. "You didn't ask for any of this, but I did. I chose you. I'm here because I need you to take the Flame. I'm the reason all of this happened to you."

Her words send a chill through me. "What are you talking about?" I pull my hand from hers, tentative, uncertain.

"You have to understand." We pause halfway up the steps. She clasps her hands and sighs, her gaze drifting toward the sky. "Two thousand years ago, the world was a much different place. Rhazaran was the supreme emperor. He held the world with an iron fist. The stars bled every night, and humans lived in chains. That is the world I was born into." Urru's shale eyes turn to me. The sadness there is deep. Penetrating. "Most people thought the shaji were gods, and humankind was being punished for generations of avarice and hubris. There was no way to fight back. The Darkness is Immortal—it cannot die. The fate of humankind was written in stone."

I frown, trying to piece together the implications of what she's saying. "You were alive two thousand years ago?"

"I was," Urru confirms. "I was a slave. But that changed when I discovered my soul was bound to a spirit, and that I was destined to be much more." A wistful smile touches her lips, but her eyes remain clouded with sorrow. "I found others like me, and we pushed back. Resonance gave us the ability to fight. But we still had a problem."

Unease grows in my shoulders. "You couldn't kill him."

"That's the thing with immortals." Urru wrinkles her nose. "So, I visited an old friend—"

I hold up a hand, cutting her off. The realization washes over me like a storm. "You went to Shytar," I say, barely believing the words as they fall from my lips, "and had her forge you a weapon to banish the shaji into the Shadow Realm."

Urru nods.

My mouth runs dry. "You're Entaru, the lost Saint."

"Yes, and no." Urru purses her lips. "I'm not her anymore. But I used to be."

All the pieces fall into place. "That's why your sigil is on my arm. That's why everyone calls me Daughter of Shadow."

"Yes." Urru laces her fingers by her chest, her expression grim.

"Rhazaran wants you because you carry the Flame—the only weapon that can harm him. He can never be whole until the Flame is destroyed and he reclaims that piece of him that was cut away when I defeated him all those years ago." Her voice hardens as she speaks, a fire igniting behind her eyes. "That is why you must use it against him before it's too late."

A hollow laugh escapes my throat. "Entaru..." My voice falters. "So I was right. I'm not special. I'm just unlucky. Why didn't you tell me this before?"

"It took a while for my memories to settle." She sighs, a mix of regret and understanding in her gaze. "You can still call me Urru, by the way. It's what my mother called me."

"Urru," I repeat. "I never imagined..."

She takes my hand once again, her touch warm and grounding. "This burden should not be yours, Bexis. But here you are. And now you must decide."

The temple towers over us, its shadow a jagged wound against the dim sky, its presence looming like an ancient kraken. I swallow. "What will happen to me?"

We start up the steps again, moving slowly. "There are three possibilities," Urru explains. "If you take the test and do not pass, you will die. The Flame will die with you, and the Immortal Dark will return. If you take the test and pass, the Flame will bond to you, and you alone may use it to banish Rhazaran once again into the Shadow Realm. The cost will be high. You will lose everything you hold dear." Urru's voice breaks, but she clears her throat and continues.

"The third option is to go back now and live for as long as you can before the world ends. Rhazaran will return. The gates will reopen, and the shaji armies will flood into the world of the living. The kingdoms of mankind will fall before the storm. There will be no stopping them this time. The wolsai are weak, and mankind is weaker."

"Three terrible options." My voice wavers, my throat thick with the weight of this decision. I cannot run from this, neither can I hide or skirt my responsibilities. There's only one option that makes any sense. "If I can save my friends... I'll take the test."

Urru regards me with a mix of admiration and concern. "You are remarkable, Bexis. One of the strongest people I've ever known—and I grew up with the Saints."

A bitter laugh escapes my lips. "I don't feel strong."

"Even after hearing everything, you still want to take the Flame. You still want to save the world."

"Honestly? I don't care much about the world."

"Oh?" Urru cocks her head. "Then why risk everything?"

I stare at my feet, my breath catching in my throat.

"It's important to know before you take the test." Urru touches my elbow. "You can tell me."

I take a beat to collect my thoughts. "For the longest time, I felt like the world hated me, and I hated it right back. I'd been lied to and hurt. And I just wanted to be left alone. But something changed when I met Juzu. He was the first person in years that I could actually trust. Even when he lied, he did it to protect me. And I'm grateful for other people in my life." I shrug. "I'm doing this for them."

"Good. That's very good."

I let my gaze linger on the pyramid. "Tell me what I have to do."

Urru guides me to the granite columns. "You must enter and see what the Flame wishes you to see. Whatever it asks you to do, Bexis, you *must* do it. There can be no hesitation. There can be no bartering. The only way to bind to the Flame is to face this test with steel in your veins, and to know that you are worthy."

"What kind of test?" I ask. "I don't understand."

"That is for you to see. Alone." Urru clasps my cheeks in her palms and kisses my forehead. "I want you to know I am proud of the person you have become. I could have chosen anyone that day, but I chose you, and perhaps the old gods smile upon us."

"Alright." I pull away from her, forcing an empty smile onto my lips. "No pressure. The fate of all humankind depends on my successfully contracting a horrible curse that will corrupt my soul and turn me into a monster. What could go wrong?"

"I know." Urru smirks sadly, her gaze dropping for a moment.

"And no one will thank you for it either. If all goes according to plan, they won't even remember your name."

"Wonderful." I shake my hands, trying to steady my nerves. The air feels heavier now, as if the temple itself is holding its breath, waiting to swallow me whole and suck me into the belly of oblivion. Once I go inside, there's no turning back. "Thank you, Urru," I say, the words coming out flat. "I know you think you've cursed me, but I've always wanted to die in an imaginary temple. Now, I finally get the chance."

She lets out a soft humorless laugh, then places her palm on my shoulder. "Luck, Bexis."

I take a deep breath, my chest tightening as I step forward. The shadows rise to meet me, curling around my body like living tendrils as they pull me into the inky depths of the temple.

CHAPTER 29

I ENTER A BLACK CORRIDOR, MY HEART HAMMERING AGAINST MY ribcage. This is it. Either the sword accepts me, or I die. Failure is not an option. Too many people are counting on me. I wipe my palms on my trousers and try to steady my breathing.

This place is like a maze. It's so dark I can't see my boots. Using my fingers, I probe the stone walls and inch down the hall, mindful of each step. When I come to an intersection, I take a right turn, and then another. With effort, I push the fear from my mind, resolve settling in my gut like steel. If what Urru said is true, this has been my destiny from the day I was born.

After the next right turn, there's a light in the dark—a flickering orange glow that fills me with hope and terror. I'm close to my goal, yet the stench of death is like a noxious cloud that hangs in the air. Every step brings me closer to the end—or a new beginning that's too terrible to fathom. It's one thing to accept death as a concept. Everyone dies; I understand that. It is the one certainty in life that only the immortals can escape. But as I draw closer to my destination, the realization hits me once again.

I don't want to die. I don't want to be damned to the eternal swirls of Nhammock for two thousand years. I don't want to leave Juzu and

Xaleo and Ajjan forever. It feels like cosmic cruelty to finally have something worth living for only to have it all wrenched away.

But it doesn't matter what I want. All that matters is finding a way to defeat Rhazaran and stop Vogul from opening the shaji gate.

I take a deep breath and step into the orange glow, entering a small square room with a raised platform in the middle and two large plinths along the wall. Black tapers surround the central altar—a granite slab that serves as a table.

A statue stands at the opposite end of the room. It's a carving of a woman, her long hair cascading down her chest all the way to the floor. She wears a dress, and ripples of stone mimic the folds in her fabric. It looks so real. My knees tremble as I step closer to the altar, uncertainty squirming through me. What now?

"Welcome." The statue moves, making me jump. The woman's head shifts, leaving ghostly trails in her wake. The stone eyes pin me in place. "To the Chamber of Reckoning."

My breath catches. My instinct is to flee, but my legs lock. "Who are you?"

"Call me, Olvai." The statue blinks down at me and leaves her place on the wall, her movements somehow graceful and disjointed at the same time, jerking from position to position while simultaneously gliding across the room.

"We are the guardians of the Flame." Olvai gestures to the walls at my right and left.

Two other statues emerge, stepping through the solid stone as if it were a curtain. I blink, trying to make sense of what I'm seeing. The stone people cross their arms, peering down at me. Their faces are smooth and emotionless, but I can feel the weight of their judgment upon me.

Olvai brings her hands out to her sides. "Our job is to make sure you are worthy of carrying the most dangerous weapon ever created. So tell us, Bexis. Why are you here?"

Is this the test? Will my life, and ultimately everyone else's, depend on how I answer this simple question? I take a moment to choose my words with care. "I'm here to pass your test."

Olvai hums. "But why?"

I bite my bottom lip. "To save the people I care about. To fight the forces that seek to enslave humanity. To push the Immortal Dark back into the Shadow Realm."

The guardians mutter to themselves in a language I cannot understand. Olvai raises a hand for silence. "And what makes you worthy to bear the Flame of Khamonji?"

The question catches me off guard. What do the guardians want to hear—that I'm destined for this, that the last bearer or the Flame chose me for this purpose? I suspect false confidence would be met with skepticism. Juzu would tell me to be honest.

"I'm not worthy," I admit. "The truth is... if it were up to me, I wouldn't even be here. The only reason I came is to save my friends. And I'm willing to do anything to protect them."

Olvai hums once again, the baritone rumble vibrating against the walls. "Step up to the altar, Bexis."

I take three steps and stand before the stone slab. It appears more like a table than an altar. Olvai shifts and jerks until she stands on the other side, facing me. Her stone features are impossible to read—her cheeks stoic and unmoving, her eyes blank. She places her hands on the table, causing it to shift. I force myself to remain still as the stone mottles black and red, and melts away. Orange flames lick upward as the altar bursts into fire. The flames dance inches from my face, and yet I feel no heat. From the depths of the roaring fire, a pulpit rises, and upon it sits a sword.

The blade is black as pitch, curved, about three feet long, and three inches thick. The handle is wrapped in black silk, with a handguard of brilliant steel. Jewels stud the pommel. Silver, black, red, and gold. The sword vibrates, bending the air around it.

"Behold the object of your desire, Bexis," Olvai says. "The Flame of Khamonji. Forged by Shytar in the mountains of Xajara. Breaker of the Immortal Dark."

A wave of awe and dread washes over me. This is the weapon that defeated Rhazaran two thousand years ago and ended the season of shadow. This is the weapon that damned Entaru to Nhammock for two thousand years and warped her soul into something no longer human. I shudder at the thought; this isn't just a weapon—it's a vessel of untold suffering.

Voices rise in the back of my mind. Softly at first, and then growing in pitch and intensity. I hear men screaming in pain, women shrieking, and children crying. Goosebumps break out on my arms as terror courses through my veins. The power of this weapon is mind-numbing. Inconceivable. Horrific.

And yet, this is what I must wield. This is how I can save Juzu, Xaleo, Siras, Zhira, and all the rest of the people of Coppejj. This is how I defeat Rhazaran and stop Vogul. My hand trembles as I reach for the hilt.

"Not yet." Olvai's voice rumbles through the chamber. "First, you must prove that you are worthy."

"What?" I ask, annoyed. I thought I'd already passed the test. "Tell me what to do, and I'll do it."

Olvai clasps her hands again, and the sword vanishes in a cloud of smoke. The room flickers in a flash of light, and suddenly there are two stone tables in the room. I blink down at Xaleo, lying prone on the table, his eyes closed. Juzu lies next to him.

"Juzu!" My heart flutters with hope as I brush my fingers along his cheek. His flesh is warm. But his eyes do not open. "Wake up," I say. "Please, wake up." He breathes in a steady rhythm but doesn't stir.

I frown, then move to Xaleo, placing my hand on his shoulder and gently shaking. His eyes flutter, like someone caught in a dream.

I turn back to Olvai, my shoulders squared. "What have you done to them?"

"Your friends have too much power over you." The stone woman stares at me. "These bonds are dangerous. They expose you to manipulation and can be used to leverage you away from your duties. To wield the Flame, you must prove, beyond a doubt, that you are pure."

I take Juzu's hand in mine and squeeze. "Please, help them," I stammer. "Wake them up."

"They will not wake. Now that they have entered the chamber, they will stay here forever, unless you pass this test. There is only one way for them to leave this place."

I glance up at her. "Why did you bring them here?"

"The wielder of the Flame must be willing to sacrifice everything. She must be willing to do the hardest thing imaginable, to endure the greatest pain that any human can face. But she must also be unwavering in her convictions. That is how you prove your worth. That is how you take the Flame and escape this chamber."

I shake my head. "I don't understand. What do you want me to do?"

Olvai extracts a wicked serrated knife. She holds it out to me.

Her meaning sinks in and black terror creeps up my spine. "I can't kill them," I stammer. "I won't!"

Olvai extends the knife. "You must choose. Death is the cost of living. If you cannot do what must be done, your world is doomed."

"Take me instead," I shout. "Take my home, money, respect, my city, anything. Take anything else!"

"You cannot bargain. You must act with certainty in your heart. That is the only path to the Flame. Do what needs to be done, or you will stay here for eternity." She glances at Juzu and Xaleo. "Nobody said this would be easy."

My hand shakes as I take the knife. Urru said I needed to do whatever the guardians told me, but this is not what I had in mind. I stand next to Juzu's altar. His face is relaxed, his wild gray hair spread upon the stone. He appears peaceful and calm. How can I do this? How can I kill the man who taught me what it means to be accepted? The man who taught me to trust again? Juzu came back for me. He loves me, lied for me. How can I be the one to end his life?

Then there's Xaleo, who has saved me more times than I can count. Yes, he abandoned me in the monastery, but he's also endured so much loss and suffering and has sacrificed everything to keep me alive. Am I going to repay all of that by slaughtering him on an altar like a fowl? This cannot be what the Flame demands of me. It simply can't be.

"Choose," Olvai commands. "Time is short."

A sob leaves my lips. Tears stream freely down my cheeks. What alternative do I have? If I don't do it, they're both dead anyway. If I don't do it, the Flame will remain in this chamber until the end of time. The Immortal Dark will pour into the world, and the shaji armies will rise. Millions of people will die.

"Measure the cost of one life against the weight of an entire world," the stone woman says. "No one is worth the return of Rhazaran."

"These two mean more to me than all the rest combined." I grip the knife so tightly my knuckles turn white. "The world would be empty and meaningless without them."

"For you, maybe." Olvai nods. "But if you take the Flame, you cannot stay with them. You will be damned. You will become a ghost. Happily ever after does not exist for you, Bexis. You know this."

She's right. I've always known it. But now, I cannot make myself act. I try to steel myself, but my breathing is harsh, and my chest convulses with sobs. I hold the knife to Juzu's throat, but the blade quivers. The vibration is all wrong. Horrible. Discomfort settles in my bones, and I know with iron certainty that I cannot do it.

That I should not do it. This is not the way.

I remove the knife from Juzu's throat. "I refuse."

Olvai hums disapprovingly. "Your perspective is too small, Bexis. Think about the ramifications. Try to step outside yourself."

I shake my head. "There is a clear line between right and wrong. Juzu taught me that. If the Flame will not allow me to save my friends, I'll find another way."

"You will never leave this chamber, and neither will they." Olvai raises her hands as if to snatch the knife from my grasp, but I leap backward. "Stupid child," the guardian snarls. "You will be the death of us all!"

I dodge as another guardian reaches for me, then press myself into the far wall. The tunnel that brought me here is gone. There is no escape. The guardians close in around me.

Death is the cost of living.

An idea blooms in the back of my mind—a terrible, brilliant idea.

They cannot hold me here, not if I choose to leave on my own terms. I hold the knife before me and, before I can change my mind, slam the blade deep into my sternum. Pain erupts like wildfire, splitting bone and sinew as the steel finds my heart. My vision fractures, the edges burning black.

Somehow, this is better. This is right.

The world dissolves, fading into a sweet silence that falls around me like stars.

CHAPTER 30

PLEASE, BEXIS.

Come back to me—I know you can. Just open your eyes.

Xaleo's voice cuts through the distant roll of thunder like a siren, calling me back from the black waters of the Shadow Sea.

I awaken beside the rose altar in the Ujjarum temple. Panic surges as my fingers scrabble at my sternum, expecting to find a blade embedded in the flesh—but there's nothing. No wound. No blood. I roll onto my side, coughing and sputtering as cool air rushes into my lungs. I drink it in, phantom pain lancing through my chest with each breath.

"Bexis!" Xaleo gathers me in his arms, brushing hair from my face, rocking softly back and forth. "You did it. Thank the Saints. I thought you were dead."

I revel in the warmth of his touch—strong and sturdy and real. I choke on tears that drip down my throat. "I didn't. I couldn't—"

"You're okay now." He wipes my cheeks. "You're alive. That means the Flame accepted you."

His confidence shatters me into a million pieces. I push myself away from him, the warmth of his touch suddenly unbearable. "I didn't pass the test. I failed."

"What?" Xaleo stiffens. His eyes narrow. "How do you know?"

Because you're still alive. I bite my bottom lip. How do I explain it to him? "The guardians of the Flame told me to do something terrible. Something I couldn't do." I touch the space where the blade punctured my sternum. The ghostly pain makes me wince. "They tried to keep me there, but I escaped—"

"Bexis, you're not making any sense." He grips my shoulder, a firmness in his touch. "You're not dead. That means you succeeded."

He has a point. Why *am* I alive? I shouldn't be here. A crash of thunder brings me back to reality. Panic jolts through me. "The phantom," I say. "Where is it?"

Xaleo glances at the entrance of the pagoda. "Was it here?"

I crawl to my knees and try to rise, but a wave of dizziness forces me to stay low. I grit my teeth. "Yes. It attacked me right outside."

"You were alone when I got here."

Orran and Hezha must have pushed Rhazaran back. If I can't use the Flame, perhaps the Saints will be the answer to defeating the Immortal Dark. I crawl to the crimson rose dais and stand, using the altar for balance. The shrine flashes with a brilliant white light, and the blood relics glow with the strength of the sun. The harmony reaches deep within me and begins to ease the pain.

Xaleo stands at my side. "The Flame," he whispers, his eyes growing wide.

Hope blooms in my chest. Perhaps I passed the test after all. Somehow, stabbing myself was the right thing to do? The light is blinding; I can't make out what lies upon the shrine, but the vibrations thrum through my veins. A crescendo builds, filling every part of me, and then, suddenly, the light fades. On the shrine, where the blood relics should be, there is a small pile of ash.

"No..." I run my fingers through it, despair coiling around my throat. The blood relics are gone and, with them, any hope of fighting Rhazaran.

"I don't get it," Xaleo says, his voice flat. "Where is the Flame?"

"I told you." I sink to the ground with my back to the altar. The depth of my failure settles in my gut. Now Juzu will die. Vogul will summon Rhazaran and open the demon gate. The shaji armies will follow. Siras' sacrifice was for nothing. Olaik died for nothing. Urru chose the wrong girl, and now the Flame is out of reach. The world as we know it is over. "I wasn't strong enough," I say. "I couldn't do it..."

"I don't believe that." But the uncertainty in Xaleo's posture says everything that I'm too afraid to say. The stone guardians tested me. They showed me what was necessary, and I refused. Now the world will suffer the consequences. The fact that I'm still alive to see it all burn is a penance, not a consolation.

"There has to be another way." Xaleo's voice is cold and disbelieving. He rests his hand on the pommel of his sword as he bends to one knee. His blue gaze locks onto me, his jaw tight. "There has to be."

"There isn't." The realization is an iron weight in my stomach. I want to scream. To pull my hair and shout. But I scarcely have the energy to move my head from side to side. None of this is right. None of it is fair. We came so close. Only to come up short in the end.

"We can't give up." Xaleo touches my cheek with gloved fingers. His eyes blaze with icy heat that sets my throat on fire. "So long as we draw breath, we can fight."

I place my palms on his chest. He's so close. "I was ready to die," I say, "but then I didn't want to. And now that I'm alive, I feel glad. Does that make me horrible?"

Xaleo wraps his arms around me, encircling me in warmth. "No. You're here with me. And that's all that matters."

My vision blurs as I bury my face in his chest. "What are we going to do? We can't fight them. We can't save Juzu—"

"Hey!" Xaleo places his hands on my shoulders and gazes deep into my eyes. "We still have each other, and we'll figure it out. I'm not leaving you again. I'm not going to let anything happen to you."

His face is only inches from mine. I want to melt into him and disappear, to give him all of my fear. And in that moment, I realize he would take it.

"Where did you go?" I ask.

"I lost myself for a minute. But I never should have left you." He cups my cheeks in his hands, his touch solid and warm. His eyes are shimmering pools that pierce through me. "I see you, Bexis," he whispers. I feel his breath on my cheeks, heat pulsing from his body. "You are radiance surrounded by shadow. A light that cuts through the dark and somehow lives within it, unscathed."

"Unscathed?" I echo, the word catching in my throat as the room swims. His presence is intoxicating. Too much and not enough all at once. "I'm not what you think."

"No," he says, his voice barely above a whisper. "You're more."

His gaze lingers for a heartbeat—uncertain, searching—and then the distance between us closes. He touches his lips to mine, tentative at first—a question posed. And the answer sparks between us, a soft purr that crescendos into a wildfire.

His arms are around me. I press my body into him, my fingers raking through his hair. I'm sinking and floating. Soaring and unraveling all at once. My heart is a war drum. My lungs desperate for air. And I cannot get enough.

But he pulls away, and it's like someone has doused out the sun. I gasp, breathless. Lightheaded and greedy. I want more. To kiss him again. To never stop. To forget all of the horror around us and live within this fleeting moment of goodness as the world burns to ash.

"You see?" His chest heaves as he tucks a strand of hair behind my ear, his touch gentle, reverent. "There's still something worth fighting for."

My heart begins to settle. Maybe he's right. Maybe there's still hope. I open my mouth to respond, but the air shudders with electricity as thunder booms, rattling the crumbling roof of the pagoda.

"Such a touching moment." Vogul's voice cuts through the chamber like a scythe.

In an instant, all the warmth in my body drains, replaced with a cold so sharp it drags across my chest like talons. I jump up, spinning to face the door, knife drawn.

Xaleo steps in front of me, his shoulders squared, resonance already crackling over his arms.

"Sorry to interrupt." Vogul stands in the doorway, her black lips curled into a sinister smile. In her hand, she brandishes a silver piece of metal. *My tone pipe.*

Instinctively, I reach into my pocket. Empty. My stomach drops.

Vogul places the pipe in her pocket and grins. "You were sprawled on the floor, all alone. So vulnerable. So weak." Her eyes are fierce emeralds lined with black. "The blood has been spent," she says, stepping into the room. "The relics are destroyed. The Flame is no more and, with it, any chance of banishing the Immortal Dark." She laughs. "I should thank you, Bexis. You've sealed the fate of the world."

I grit my teeth, my pulse racing. "We don't need the Flame to kill you." I hold up my dagger. "Or your coven."

She smirks and strolls into the chamber, her stilettos clacking with each step. "Even if you kill me, it would accomplish nothing. Rhazaran's return is all but assured now."

"Don't come any closer." Xaleo draws his sword. The steel rings as it flashes in the dim light. His courage bolsters my own. My grip tightens on the knife. We'll have to attack as one. Together. It's the only chance we've got.

Vogul pauses, her eyes gleaming with predatory amusement. "Don't play with me, boy. You may have Bexis fooled, but I know what you really are."

Xaleo's body tenses, uncertainty clouding his features.

"Don't listen to her," I snap, stepping to his side.

"Oh yes." Vogul grins. "Did you really think I wouldn't notice you were skulking around the Hezhani temple, playing noble vigilante and killing my soldiers?"

"It doesn't matter," Xaleo says, advancing in measured steps. Blue resonance flickers around him, dancing the length of his blade. "I'm going to make you pay for everything you've done."

"You are a shadow. An insubstantial nuisance." Vogul gestures to me. "At least Bexis had the spine to face me head-on. But you? You're a coward. You've waited years for your moment, and you still can't do it, can you?" She holds her hands out to the sides, raising her chin to expose her chest and throat. "Go on then, Xaleo. Strike me down."

My heart pounds against my ribs, a warning bell in my ears. This reeks of a trap. But Xaleo is already pressing forward. "Wait!" I shout, but it's too late.

He lunges. His sword swings through the air in a blur of steel and light. Vogul sidesteps effortlessly and counters with a vicious elbow in the ribs. The force sends him hurtling across the room, crashing into the wall. The pagoda groans in protest as chunks of the ceiling fall to the ground and shatter like glass.

"Xaleo!" I rush to his side, falling to my knees. My hands tremble as I press them against his shoulders. He doesn't move. Blood trickles from his forehead, tracing a crimson path down his temple. My heart clenches.

"Don't worry," Vogul says with the nonchalance of someone who has better things to do. "He'll survive. Probably."

I rise to my feet, my knife extended before me. Sweat drips down my neck. What in Hezha's fire am I going to do now?

"All alone." Vogul cackles. "Again. And without this pipe, you're little more than an ill-tempered teenager."

She's right, but I continue standing between her and Xaleo, uncertainty washing over me in waves. I can't fight. But I can't give up either.

Vogul stands ten paces away, a cruel smile on her lips. "Aren't you curious what we've done to your beloved Aevem?"

My breath hitches, cold fury bubbling in my heart. "You monster."

"Yes, that's right." She sneers, relishing my anger. "He's a screamer. And he *loves* you. That's going to be his downfall."

"Stop—"

"And before this is done, I'll come for the others too. Ajjan, Zhira, Shytar…" She tilts her head. "And of course, little Mo and her Rovers. I'll enjoy listening to them howl."

My hands clench so tight, my fingernails dig into my palms. This woman—this *beast*—is the reason for all the pain I've endured the past few days. A creature that would threaten innocent children. Anger and fury and hurt coalesce into a rhythm that beats in my heart, a harmony that I've never experienced before.

Every time I've used the tone pipe and caught resonance, the feeling has been like catching a flame within my chest, but this is different—it's a blazing inferno that radiates to my hands and feet. When I touch it, resonance roars like a hungry animal. The vibration tears through me, spilling forth like a fountain. Red light crackles across my skin.

"Bexis," Xaleo mutters, stirring on the ground. "Don't!"

But I barely hear him. The energy speaks without words. I must move, attack, and destroy this wicked witch once and for all.

"Very good. I knew the darkness was in you." Vogul reaches for her resonance, and I sense it bloom inside her like a crimson orchid. "But do you have the guts to use it?"

The knife trembles in my hands, vibrating with raw power. Black and red resonance coils up my arms, bleeding into the blade, ensconcing the steel in a malevolent glow. My breath hitches. No more hesitation.

I charge.

Vogul moves like lightning, drawing her blade in a single fluid motion. Steel meets steel with a spark of red light. She counters with a lateral slash. I duck, feeling the deadly whoosh of air as her blade sails just above my head. I try to strike again, but she kicks me in the gut, sending me sprawling across the stone floor.

I scramble to my feet, numb to the pain. Resonance crashes through my veins.

"Fascinating," Vogul muses, spinning her sword. "But it's still not enough to save your friends."

My knife feels alive. Hungry. This new harmony is like a river of unbridled fury. All the hate, anguish, and despair I've carried spills out of me in a violent torrent. I attack again, this time feinting with my knife as I ram my knee into her stomach and pull her hair, throwing Vogul onto the ground.

Her body smacks the stone with a satisfying crunch. I scream. It's a sonic relief of agony. Causing her pain only feeds the storm inside me. Her blood belongs on the floor. It belongs on my hands. I want to make her shiver with the horror of it. I want to make her hurt and beg.

I pounce.

Vogul recovers before I make the killing blow. She rolls and slashes, repelling my blow and sending my momentum crashing into the wall. My shoulder explodes with fresh pain.

"Enough of this." Vogul approaches, no longer smiling. Blood trickles down her chin. Her chest heaves as she raises her hands. A net of red tendrils streaks toward me.

I gather my resonance and push against it. The two vibrations collide with a deafening crack. A wave of power slams into me as the chamber fills with dust and shards of stone. Tiles rain down, cutting my arms and stinging my face. My knees buckle as the knife starts to slip from my grasp.

"Xaleo!" I shout, my strength fading fast. "Finish her!"

Vogul starts to laugh, a sound that's incongruous with the surroundings. The resonance between us fades, and she brandishes a jagged piece of green glass. The triumph in her eyes chills me to the bone. "You still don't get it, do you?"

My heart hammers. The red resonance screams in my chest, urging me onward. The knife pulses with renewed vigor.

KILL

KILL

I clench my teeth and rally for a final push. A surge of raw hatred consumes me, driving me across the room with a guttural cry. I leap into the air, my dagger aimed directly at Vogul's throat.

But my blade is intercepted by another. Xaleo stands between us, his sword barring my path. The resonance within me falters, recoiling in confusion.

"What are you doing?" I hiss. "Get out of my way."

"No." Xaleo's eyes are glassy and expressionless. His face is a blank mask. Haunted shadows dance across his skin as his eyes turn from icy blue to a blazing red. He groans in agony and drops his sword.

I catch him as he falls, ignoring Vogul's cackling laughter as it fills the chamber. The torrid fury that fueled my resonance fades to horror. "What's happening?" I shout. "Please—"

"No!" Xaleo pushes me away. Green light emanates from deep

within his ribcage, a luminance that's so bright it burns through his flesh and his cloak, filling the chamber with a ghoulish glow. I crawl backward on my hands and knees, my throat burning.

"Yes." Vogul wipes blood from her chin as she stands beside him. "Xaleo was the first tether," she says, "that allowed me to find Lord Rhazaran in the Shadow Realm."

"No," I whisper. This isn't possible. It can't be real.

Vogul laughs. "Behold—"

A billow of shadow envelops Xaleo. His skin turns black, and mist shoots from his spine. His eyes turn into pits of pure fire, and his face elongates into a vulpine snout. Claws sprout from his fingers as skeleton wings burst from his back in a spray of black viscera. The phantom shrieks at the ceiling, saliva dripping from black fangs into a pool on the floor.

Cold numbness fills my soul. Xaleo is the phantom. He's the proxy for Rhazaran that has haunted my every step. This whole time it was right in front of me, and I didn't see it.

The fight bleeds out of me. I collapse onto the stone ground, despair a dead weight in my heart. The red fury has been replaced with blinding hopelessness.

"Xaleo…" Tears burn my eyes. I can still feel his lips on mine, and the current of passion that erupted between us. That was real. It was visceral and solid. *He didn't know*, I tell myself. I have to believe that. He doesn't know who he is right now.

Vogul grins. "You have lost. The Flame is destroyed. You will be the final sacrifice, and Rhazaran will bind with the missing piece that Entaru stole from him two thousand years ago. The Immortal Dark has finally returned."

What happens next could be a dream. Dimly, I'm aware of the sentinels pouring into the chamber, their boots echoing in my ears. Iron hands seize my wrists, yanking me to my knees. But I don't resist. I'm barely even here.

Then Phekru emerges by Vogul's side, resplendent in black plate armor, his scarred face twisted in a rictus of triumph.

"Take the girl to see the Eyeless," Vogul commands. "There can be no mistakes this time. I will make the final preparations for the summoning."

The captain of the guard takes me by the arm, personally hauling me to my feet. I stumble forward like a marionette, my body no longer my own. As we leave the temple, I take one last look behind me.

The phantom arches its spined back, raising its head to the sky. Its bellow splits the night, a sonorous roar that leaves me gasping for breath as my heart shatters all over again.

CHAPTER 31

NUMB.

That's the only way to describe how I feel, though it's not entirely accurate. I'm aware of the shackles around my wrists, how they chafe against my skin. I sense the icy wind, the remnants from the storm slashing at my cheeks, and the tears frozen in salty streams that make my face stiff. I can't keep my shoulders from slouching as Phekru and a squadron of sentinels march me back through the Hollow toward the White Keep.

I feel all of this, and it means nothing. My internal world has come to a standstill, a wasteland of darkness from which I shall never recover. All this time, Xaleo was the creature hunting me. The pieces fall into place. Every time the phantom attacked me, Xaleo was there shortly after. The tragedy of this revelation has cut me to my bones. The true horror of nedozul is plain as night, Urru's prophecy seared into my mind.

The Bard's heart will burn.

I knew nedozul could be used to control someone's will, but with Xaleo, it must have replaced memories. His whole recollection of the events before and after his parents' murder was wrong. Was there really a girl named Ceirsa who had lived in his village, or was it all an elaborate lie they'd implanted in his head?

Only one thing is certain—it was Xaleo and not his friend who was placed on a post and stabbed with nedozul. The wound must have healed over the years, or been concealed with dark magic. Xaleo was the first tether. The greatest tragedy is that he doesn't even know it. All these years he was hunting Vogul, but she's always had him in the palm of her hand. No matter what we do, she's three steps ahead of us.

It leaves me enervated and hopeless. If they could implant memories into his mind, was anything about him real? Do I know him at all? I still feel his lips on mine, his arms around me, those blazing blue eyes filling me with hope and warmth. Yes, it was real. More real than anything I've ever felt. I bite my bottom lip, struggling to keep the tears from falling.

"You shouldn't feel bad." The captain slides next to me. He carries an active phaser on a chain tied to his belt. I spot the White Keep against the smoggy skyline. The storm seems to be dissipating. Phekru rests his hand on the pommel of his great sword. He's wearing a tight military surcoat with flashy silver buttons. "No one can resist Kandra Vogul. I learned that the hard way too. But once you stop fighting, things get better." He chuckles. "Besides, you gave her more fight than the Aevem. And that's saying something."

A spark of emotion rumbles through the stillness of my mind. "Is he still alive?"

"Sure, if you call that living." He shrugs. "It doesn't matter. Life and death don't mean as much as they used to. The shaji horde is coming, and Rhazaran will take his place as the One God."

"And that makes you happy?" I still can't comprehend how anyone could want this to happen. "Why?"

Phekru grins. "The Saints were never gods. They were men and women. They betrayed the person who saved them. Then they got greedy. This world has been Godless for two thousand years. And you wonder why everything has gone to stars." He hacks a ball of phlegm and spits it on the ground. "We had a decent run at it, but mortals aren't meant to rule themselves. We're inferior beings."

"And what do you get out of it?" I ask, unable to contain it. "You think Lord Rhazaran will reward you?"

Phekru's eyes sparkle with mirth. "The Khatori have been the gate-keepers of resonance. But magic is for everyone. With the return of the Immortal Dark, the gateway will be open, and your kind will fade into the pages of history. A new order will rise. A liberated world where miracles happen every day for common people"—he gestures to his men—"like us."

"You're damning us all because you're jealous?"

The captain sighs as we cross the courtyard and make for the entrance of the Sanctum. "When I was five years old, I was brought to live at the Hezhani Monastery. By the time I was thirteen, I was accepted into the military. The training we endured there was hell." He runs a finger down the length of the scar that covers his face. "We would camp without food or water, and our commanders would force us to train harder, march with blindfolds in rain and sleet with bare feet and shields smashed into our faces."

The hallways inside are empty, but I can hear the strange singing. A pool of dread opens in my belly, but Phekru doesn't seem to notice.

"But when I fought my first real battle," he continues, "I learned they did all those things to prepare us for something that no hell could prepare us for. You can simulate marching, starving, fatigue, discomfort, and hopelessness. But the test comes when the man who guards your flank, who shares your bread and your fire, who laughs at your bad jokes and dreams of home and peace"—Phekru's voice grows heavy and grave—"when he gets his head caved in by a barbarian mace. When you're peeling fragments of skull from your eyelids. That's when you learn what life is."

I start resisting as we come to the rosewood doors of the prayer chamber. "What does that have to do with anything?"

Phekru grins. "The Immortal Dark means no more war. It means a world in which there are no squabbles. No battles or killing. No insurrections, coups, or betrayals, and no need for warriors. No greedy lords taking the clipped coppers from old crones on their deathbeds. No kings or queens or armies of men to rape and burn and pillage. There is order and peace."

"You truly think the world will be better off run by demons?" My stomach churns. I don't understand how anyone could believe this. "But why?"

"Have you met people?" Phekru barks as he shoves the doors open and hauls me inside. "At least the shaji don't pretend they're anything but what they are. Humans are liars. You should know this as well as anyone by now."

The prayer chamber is as I saw it before, but the pews are empty, and there's a pile of corpses by the pulpit. The faceless women are still standing there, no eyes or noses, only long black mouths, their skin sallow and ghostly, like melting candle wax.

"Please," I beg. "Don't do this."

"As if I had a choice." We walk down the central aisle. "After the fiasco in the Shadow Realm, we're doing things differently this time. You understand." He shoves me toward the base of the pulpit. "These are the Eyeless. They've been waiting for you."

The women turn their featureless faces toward me. Although they have no eyes to see, their mouths are gaping holes that observe me with cold serenity. A shiver runs down my spine.

"What are they?" I ask.

"They are the Blessed," Phekru says, "kissed by the Lord and given eternal life."

The Eyeless are almost seven feet tall and have long droopy ears. They hold hands, open their black mouths, and begin to sing. The sound that comes out is deeply discordant. I can feel it in my heart. The dissonance creates a disharmonic field that makes the walls tremble.

The nearest Eyeless steps forward. "Bring the girl forth." Her voice is a susurration, like leaves blowing in an autumn wind. Phekru and the sentinels lift me. I thrash and fight, but it's no use. One girl cannot resist five armed soldiers. They place me on the dais so I'm lying on my back, then tie my ankles and wrists with leather straps.

"No," I sob. Fear is a living beast in my mind, a creature that stalks and runs through me. I don't want to die. It's one thing to sacrifice my life for my friends, my city, or the world, but it is quite another to die alone, gazing into the demonic wrinkled faces of the Eyeless.

The Eyeless draw nearer. Each step is unnaturally smooth and graceful. They smell like dead algae. One holds up a shard of nedozul.

"This will bind you forevermore to Lord Rhazaran," Phekru says, answering the question in my eyes. "With this cut, we will imbibe your soul into the service of the Immortal Dark."

An image of the black heart fills my mind. The sickening pulse of black ochre and the stench of decaying flesh. My stomach lurches as bile rises in my throat. Sensation comes back to me, the numbness giving way to cold penetrating fear. I toss my head from side to side, struggling against the straps that bind me, my wrists burning where the leather bites into my skin.

"Relax." Phekru's voice is harsh and stoic. He brandishes a knife. The blade winks in the torchlight. My breathing grows ragged as he leans over me, taking hold of the neckline of my tunic.

"Stop!" I gasp. "Please—"

"Hush." With a slow, deliberate motion, he drags the knife down the center of my chest. The fabric gives way with a soft rip, exposing my sternum to the air. My skin prickles as he inspects his work. With a soft nod, he sheaths the blade and steps back.

One of the Eyeless floats around the dais, making her way from my feet to stand at my side. She raises the jagged green shard of glowing steel—already activated—pulsing faintly in her hand, each throb matching the discordant rhythm of the chant still filling the chamber. She speaks a prayer in a guttural, broken language, her voice thick with malice. Spittle dribbles from her lipless mouth as the discordant song crescendos, worming its way into my head.

The Eyeless holds the blade with two hands and raises it high above her head, the deadly point directed straight at my chest.

"No," I choke, my body trembling with fear. I stop resisting now. All I can do is watch. "Hezha's fire—"

Then she drives the dagger down.

The force of the blow is like being hit with a cannon. It punctures my sternum, cracking bone and sinking deep into my lungs. Pain is a scarlet river in my mind. I scream until my throat is raw. Until I taste blood. White heat flares up, and I feel the glass cauterizing and binding to my flesh, preventing internal bleeding from killing me.

The Eyeless twists the handle, causing the blade to snap. She looms over me, her horrible black mouth twisted in a grin. The sentience there—the pure frozen mirth—sends a tremor through my soul. I can't breathe as darkness seeps into my vision. Blood bubbles from the wound, spraying outward in every direction. The Eyeless's smooth face is speckled red as it continues to sing. The nedozul is cold, so damn cold that soon my torso is numb. Veins of black spread like spider webs up to my throat, reaching my shoulders, sending a sick tingling into my hands and arms.

THUMP THUMP

I am not alone in my head. My heartbeat aligns with that of the Dark.

I see a vision beyond vision, the third eye opening in the chasm of my soul. The black heart gushing viscera into the streets, filling the gutters with toxic sludge. Xaleo screaming in agony upon a dais much like this with the Eyeless before him. Juzu alone in a tower covered in filth, terrified and broken. A man of white stone before a pulpit of bones, his skeleton wings spread over a blue moon and a silver chalice filled with blood.

Where the moons meet the sea and the stars bleed into dusk, the Aevem's light will falter, and the Bard's heart will burn. That will be your final test.

THUMP THUMP

I scream and thrash, but it does no good.

Phekru stands pale-faced at my side, his eyes wide with bewilderment or horror or perhaps even ecstasy. "Yes," he breathes, his voice shaking. "You are beautiful."

The Eyeless places a sickly white hand on my neck. It feels like a dead fish dragging across my flesh, wet, cold, and rotting. My breath catches as it leans closer, its malformed mouth hovering inches from my face. The horror is surpassed only by the sheer blinding pain as the nedozul throbs violently in my chest.

Behind me, the doors to the prayer chamber crash open, the sound tearing through the room like thunder. An arrow whistles just over my face, taking the Eyeless clean in the throat. Black blood gushes over my bare chest, cold as seawater. I press my lips together, my surprise giving way to revulsion as a second bolt hits her face, flinging her away from me like a broken doll.

Chaos erupts. I gasp, chest heaving as a flurry of arrows and missiles slice through the air, each one finding its mark with deadly precision. Men scream. The Eyeless shriek as they die. Phekru barks orders, trying to rally a counterattack, but it's pointless—they've already lost.

From my position on the dais, it's difficult to see the newcomers by the door. But Phekru raises his arms in surrender, his lips turning into a frown.

"Drop your weapon!" A familiar voice cuts through the prayer chamber. I crane my neck, but I can't see her face behind her mask. She points a crossbow at Phekru, daring him to move.

He shakes his head, disbelieving. "Saints be damned, Councillor, I didn't think you had it in you—"

"Look on the bright side, captain," Zhira interrupts, her voice cold and deadly. "You won't make that mistake again."

The crossbow twangs.

A bolt hammers Phekru in the chest, puncturing the steel armor and throwing him against the wall. The captain of the sentinels cries out, his fingers scrabbling at the shaft as blood bubbles around the wound. He curses, then collapses on the floor.

Dead.

CHAPTER 32

ZHIRA REMOVES HER MASK AS SHE EMERGES FROM THE SHADOWS. HER black hair is tied in a ponytail that sways as she walks. She wears black armor with leather pauldrons and studded trousers. Her raven eyes are wide with terror as she approaches the altar.

"Nice of you to drop by." I grit my teeth against a surge of pain that radiates from the nedozul, shooting from my sternum to the tips of my toes. Yet—seeing the leader of the Blackbones is such a welcome sight, I almost forget my agony.

"Hezha's fire." Zhira gasps as she sees my chest. "What have they done to you?"

Reluctantly, I follow her gaze, craning my neck to inspect the wound. The handle of the dagger has been broken off, lying some-where on the ground. My flesh has been sealed, and only a small protuberance of glass is visible—a jagged nub that pulses with green light, sending waves of sickness through my belly. The skin around the wound is inflamed, and black veins spiderweb up my neck and shoulders.

I rest my head on the dais, closing my eyes as whispers and ghostly sibilations echo through my head. I pull at my restraints. "Alright, enough gawking," I rasp. "Get me out of here."

Zhira nods to one of her henchmen—a broad-shouldered beast of a man—who takes out a pair of pliers and cuts the straps. Once my hands are free, I groan and roll onto my side, wiping the Eyeless's blood from my face. Then I probe the glass with my fingers. It's cold to the touch, like a blade of ice sticking out of my skin. I shudder as a wave of horror pierces through me. I want it out. With all my heart, I want it out of me. Despair is a lead weight in my chest, crushing and squeezing and breaking me to pieces.

Get it out.

"I came as soon as I could." Zhira helps me into a seated position. She eyes the nedozul with a frown creasing the lines on her face. "Only a moment too late."

"I'm glad you're here." I force steadiness into my voice, projecting a tenuous calm that feels like it could snap at any moment. Despair wells inside me. It's over. The coven has won. I scratch at my sternum, digging my fingers into the tender flesh, trying to ignore the sharp flare of pain that blooms with each movement.

GET IT OUT.

But there's nothing I can do. Talking about something—anything —is the only way to keep the horror from overwhelming me. The throbbing light begins to dim, but I still hear the heartbeat in my head. I lick my lips. "I thought you were going to stay low."

"I was low," Zhira says, stepping around the altar and standing in front of me. "But when we heard the Aevem was taken to the Keep, I feared the worst." She bends closer, her face just inches from mine; the intensity of her gaze burns through the haze of pain that hangs over me like a shroud. Then, unexpectedly, she takes my shoulders in her hands.

The gesture takes me by surprise—in all the time I've known her, Zhira has never touched anyone except to maim, but here she stands —a pillar of strength, offering comfort and support. "You haven't taken the Bones yet," she continues, "but make no mistake, Bexis. You're one of us now. That means we're here for you. No matter what. Until the very end."

I laugh, a humorless, pitiful sound that sends tremors of pain through my neck. The taste of blood stains every breath I take. I gesture to my chest. "It's too late."

"We'll see about that." Zhira straightens. "How do we take this thing out?"

"We can't." The words leave my lips, gravid and final. Saying it aloud makes it real, and my desperation gives way to serene acceptance. The end has finally come. There is no escape—no more running, no hiding, and no fighting. "You have to kill me," I say. "That's the only way to stop them."

"That's not happening." Zhira snorts as she places her hands on her hips—obstinate and ready to dig in her heels. "So how about we come up with another plan."

"You don't understand." My hands start to tremble, and cold sweat breaks out over my back. "It's over. Now Vogul will use me as a vessel to bring Rhazaran into the mortal world."

"It's not over until we stop fighting." Zhira crosses her arms. "Is that what you're telling me? Are you giving up? Because I don't accept that."

I've never seen that fire in her eyes before. That protectiveness. It occurs to me for the first time that she cares about me. Beneath the veneer of distrust and cavalier cruelty, she really cares. Why did I never notice it until now?

I open my mouth. Close it again. Shake my head. "I don't know..."

"Well, I do." Zhira gives my hand a reassuring squeeze. It's an oddly intimate gesture from the leader of the Blackbones. "They may have all the cards. But we have a few of our own. Let's get you out of here. We can keep you hidden. Perhaps if they can't find you, they won't be able—"

"No. Hiding was never an option, but now it's truly over. The only way to stop them is to kill me."

"I told you"—Zhira exhales, frustrated, her eyes imploring—"that is not happening."

"Please, Zhira." I swing my legs over the dais. The room is full of so much death. There's a pile of corpses by the pulpit. The bodies of the dead sentinels are fresher, and their blood is pooling all over the ground. "If I'm not already bound to Rhazaran, I will be soon. He has what he needs to come into the world."

A wet wheeze cracks the air. Zhira stiffens, reaching for her knife.

But it's only Phekru, lying on the ground with a bolt protruding from his ribs. I frown. The captain of the guard is still alive. Blood bubbles on his lips and he clutches his wound with a grimace, struggling into a seated position against the wall.

"Stubborn bastard." Zhira wrinkles her nose in disgust. "You have something to say?"

Every breath is a gut-wrenching wheeze. The captain is clearly in agony. But still, he grins, flashing bloodstained teeth. "Even death won't protect you now." He coughs weakly. "It's finished."

"How?" Zhira eyes me up and down, her brow furrowed. "Do you feel any different?"

I touch the nedozul and shake my head. This whole time, I thought the moment the nedozul pierced into me, I would immediately turn into some kind of zombie. I hear voices in my head, but they're only whispers. Maybe Zhira is right. Maybe I can fight one last time.

I stand from the altar, woozy and unsteady. Every movement causes pain, but I manage to kneel by Phekru's side, forcing myself to look him in the eye. He reeks of death. Even despite his actions against me, his pain gives me no pleasure. "Tell me how it works," I say. "If you help me, we can find you a medic. If any of the luminaries are still alive—"

"Like stars we will." Zhira spits. "Let him bleed."

I hold up my hand for silence, then turn my gaze back to Phekru. "Please—"

"I am a soldier. My passing was never meant to be easy," Phekru says, gasping. "It'll all be over soon anyway."

Zhira strolls over, her lips pursed. "We could also make things a lot worse." She grabs hold of the bolt.

"Bleeding stars!" Phekru spasms as he grits his teeth, his cheeks puffing as he exhales. "What do you want to know?"

"The nedozul," I say, doing my best to stay calm. "The summoning. What is Vogul's plan?"

Phekru grimaces. "We were supposed to bring you to the keep. That's where the summoning will happen."

"Alright." At least we know where they're all gathered. "And where is Juzu?"

Phekru's breath turns into a death rattle. "The Aevem will be there. And so will your little friend."

Xaleo. My heart beats faster, and the nedozul pulses with green light. "And there's no way to stop it?"

Phekru laughs, prompting a film of blood to ooze down his chin. "No. There's no way to stop it. You already belong to him. You will serve him for eternity—"

Zhira kicks Phekru in the chest, driving the bolt sideways into his flesh. His neck tenses in pain, but he dies with a smile on his red lips.

I stare at his body, motionless on the floor, and a weight sinks into my chest. He deserved this. Saints, he deserved worse. But no matter how much death surrounds me, I cannot allow myself to become numb to it. Phekru was a person. He believed the Darkness would save him. And instead, it took root in his mind and consumed him. Now he's dead, and who will mourn him?

"I've always hated that man." Zhira helps me to my feet. I wobble for a moment, lightheaded. "Come with us," she urges. "If they want you, they can pry you from our cold dead fingers. Without Phekru, the sentinels are spineless goons."

"It won't work," I say, steadying myself on the stone wall as exhaustion threatens to overtake me. The nedozul has opened a channel that I cannot escape from. I feel it. I can feel *him.* "Phekru was wrong about a lot. But not about this."

"So what are you going to do?"

"I'm bound to the Immortal Dark. I can feel it in my blood. I can feel Xaleo. And the Magistrate too—even though he's dead." I close my eyes, sensing, rather than seeing, shades of scarlet and blue that form into rough shapes. One is larger than the rest, a pit of darkness, like a black moon that pulls light and energy into it.

"There are others too," I say. "Other people bound by the nedozul, feeding into Rhazaran." I open my eyes, and a strange sense of certainty settles into my heart. "It's too late for me, but there's still a chance to save Juzu."

Zhira cocks her head. "Bexis, don't tell me I saved your life so you can get yourself killed. If you go to the White Keep, you're not coming back."

The concern in her voice washes over me. "This is the moment. The history of our entire world hinges on the decisions we make right now. I don't know how to stop this, but Juzu might. He's the last Aevem in the north, and he's our last hope."

"Bexis—"

"I'm already dead, Zhira. Can't you see that?"

She growls in frustration. "What's the plan, then? We march you to the keep with your head held high and ask them to please stop what they're doing?"

I sit on the dais and gather my wits. "I have to kill Xaleo—The phantom. It's the only way out of this."

Zhira sucks her teeth, as if she can barely believe what I'm saying. "I won't pretend to know exactly how all this works, but isn't that what you've been trying to do this whole time?"

"Yes, we've been trying to fight the phantom. But it's only invincible when it's the phantom. When it's Xaleo..." I remember the wounds on his shoulder after our encounter in the Shadow Realm. Was this what the guardians were trying to tell me—that I need to be willing to let my friends die because that might be the only way to save them? I sigh, uncertainty swirling in my belly.

Even if given the opportunity—if I could somehow outmatch his skill with a blade—could I really do it? Could I hurt him? Could I kill him? The thought fills me with dread, but I don't have a choice. Like it or not, this is the only way. "Xaleo bleeds like the rest of us."

"That's comforting, but how are you going to make sure you're facing Xaleo and not the monster?"

"Look." Frustration swells in my chest. "I didn't say it's a good plan."

"No, you didn't." Zhira sits beside me. "Because it's a terrible plan." She's right. But it's better than nothing. "I'm not asking you to come with me." I take a knife from one of the dead sentinels and slip it into my belt.

Zhira whistles. "You still don't get it, kid."

"What?"

"You are not alone anymore." She places a hand on my shoulder. "And you're not going to be alone ever again. I promise you that."

I furrow my brow. "What are you saying?"

"If you're going up to the keep, you'll need an escort." Zhira bends at the waist and removes a helm from one of the sentinels. She places it on her head and winks, then leans forward and takes the now dun phaser from Phekru's belt. "And it just so happens, now that Phekru is dead, I have the most powerful army in the city."

I raise my eyebrows. "I thought you said it was a bad plan."

"It is. But it's marginally less terrible with the Blackbones at your back. Besides, you're right. This is the seminal moment of our time, and I'll be damned if I'm not there to see the world end."

There's a commotion at the door, and Ajjan pokes his head inside. His ponytail rests over his right shoulder. "We're going to have to move soon," he says. "There's a patrol outside." He catches my eye and his lips curl into a smile. "Hi, Bexis."

"Ajjan?" I can't believe my eyes. He should be on a ship to Shezhi right now. I limp across the room and wrap my arms around him. The nedozul aches, but I don't care. "What are you doing here?" I whisper.

Ajjan squeezes me tightly. "Your friends are with you, Bexis."

My eyes sting, and the world blurs as he releases me and holds my shoulders. "I can't tell you how good it is to see you," I say.

He grins. "So what's this about a suicidal mission that will lead us to certain death and possibly damnation?"

Zhira places her hands on her hips. "The Blackbones are going to war." The soldiers in the room raise their weapons in salute.

Ajjan whistles softly, then drapes an arm around my shoulders. "We Blackbones are gangsters for a reason. Bones to barrel, we've got no good sense."

CHAPTER 33

THE WIND HOWLS AS THE BLACKBONES LEAD ME ACROSS THE ROYAL grounds to the White Keep. Zhira, Ajjan, and four others have taken armor from the dead sentinels to disguise themselves. I'd feel better if we had more men, but it's too great a risk to have Blackbones hunting sentinels for their armor, and besides, we're low on time. The moment someone discovers Phekru's body, we lose the element of surprise.

Four sentinels stand guard at the entrance. They spot our arrival and hail us in. My heart slams against my sternum as we draw near. This is a risk. Zhira has one of the most recognizable faces in the city. However, she knows all the protocols and hand signals. She's been a councillor for long enough to know the ins and outs of the White Keep. She keeps her head down as we approach.

"Don't worry." Ajjan marches at my side up the steps to the main entrance. "Just keep scowling."

I purse my lips and hold my tongue. The binds dig into my wrists, so I don't have to pretend to be displeased with this arrangement. Ajjan jostles me into position as we come to the top step and stand beneath the grand marble archway.

"You're late." One of the sentinels steps forward. He has a purple scar on his chin. "Where is Phekru?"

"Captain caught wind of a disturbance in Red Tree." Ajjan stands at attention, his grip tight on my wrist. "He'll be along."

"Alright." The sentinel scans me up and down like a prized pig. I give him my most unpleasant glare, but that only makes him lick his lips. "Is she tamed?"

"Oh yes." Zhira holds up a phaser. Dread spikes through my gut; it's such a horrible invention, so much wrongness contained in such a small package. But it's not active, thank the Saints, but even if it was, I still have the Vadan pearl in my front pocket. The guard wouldn't be able to tell the difference, but a trapper would know for sure.

"Good." The sentinel stands before me and touches my cheek. I try to pull away, but the Blackbones hold me fast. "So pretty," he says. "You're going to put on a show for us tonight, aren't you?"

I feel Ajjan stiffen at my side and pray he has the discipline to stay in character.

"I guess we'll see," I say.

He sneers, tracing his fingers down my cheek to my neckline, making my skin crawl in disgust. His eyes fall to my chest, where the nedozul glows. "It's a pity to carve up such a beautiful creature."

"We don't have time for this," Zhira snaps. I find myself impressed. For a woman with no formal military training, Zhira can put a lot of steel in her voice.

Every head turns toward her.

The sentinel blinks in surprise. "Soldier?"

"You said it yourself, we're late," Ajjan responds, taking charge. "Unless you want me to explain to the captain that we were detained at the gate because you wanted to put your hands on the prisoner—"

The sentinel scowls and steps back. "Bring her to the roof."

"The roof?" Ajjan cranes his neck to the sky. "Not inside?"

"That's right. I guess the priestess wants a good view of the moons when it happens." The sentinel ushers us forward and gestures to the steps that lead to the parapets. "We'll be behind you."

The stairs are slick with sleet, and the whole keep is frosted with a sheet of ice, making it appear as if the whole castle is embossed in crystal. Ajjan holds my arm steady as I climb, unable to support myself with my arms bound. "I shouldn't have let him touch you," he whispers. "I'm sorry."

"You did exactly what you were supposed to do." I would have liked to bury my dagger in that fool's belly too, but doing so would have accomplished nothing.

"Stop talking," Zhira snaps. "They could be listening."

We hike up the walls in silence, which gives me time to reflect on what a horrible plan this is. We're walking into a den of snakes with little hope of leaving. Each step brings us closer to certain death. The nedozul pulses with green light in a steady beat that matches my heart. Sibilant whispers echo in my head, incoherent voices muttering in languages I've never heard.

As we ascend to the highest section of the keep, the northern sky opens up to us. It's almost dawn, and the horizon bleeds scarlet. The black storm clouds that dumped so much snow and ice on the city have scattered into watercolor striations of cobalt and pink.

Two crescent moons loom in the sky like a pair of scythes—one red and bloody and the other clean silver steel. Between them rests a third moon. It looks like a cut of sapphire against the dark sky, a round orb of luminance that shines upon us with unwavering strength.

"What in the stars is that?" Ajjan asks.

I nearly stop in my tracks, but the guards push me from behind. I can't take my eyes off the blue moon, small compared to the others but twice as bright. It cuts straight through the clouds like a beacon from a distant shore. Despite its brightness, it doesn't illuminate the clouds around it. It's like a ghost, a specter that looms above us—watching, waiting.

"The shadow moon," I say. The hairs on the back of my neck prickle. The doorway between Nhammock—the realm of wolsai and spirits—and the world of man has not been opened in seventeen years. Why now?

All over the world, babies born within these moments will be bonded with wolsai—a new infusion of resonance trappers. Is this part of Vogul's ceremony, or are the wolsai trying to help? It's a bit late for that.

The nedozul pierces my lungs with every breath, throbbing with a sick glee that makes my stomach lurch. The taste of blood lingers on my tongue, metallic and sharp.

Zhira gives me a firm glare. "Maybe stop staring at the sky and focus on the task at hand."

I blink, shifting my awareness to the rooftop. Moonlight illuminates a stage and pulpit where a crowd of coven members are standing in a concentric circle. Numerous posts are raised, with corpses dangling from the iron. Coven warlocks work on them with metal instruments, collecting blood in bowls of pewter. The phantom isn't here. My stomach drops. The plan hinges on the small chance I can reach Xaleo, but if he's not here, what hope do we have?

Vogul stands behind the pulpit. She's ditched her battle regalia and wears a tight-fitted dress of black and red. Her hair, braided with silver jewels and rubies, cascades down her back. She wears a shawl of black silk with red brocaded dragons stitched across the side. Her eyes are painted black, making her emerald green irises burn from across the rooftop.

"Good," Vogul says. "She's been bound." The coven members turn, and their eyes fall on me. "Bring her to me."

Zhira stiffens at my side. "Hezha's bloody tits," she hisses. "This really was a bad plan. What are you going to do now?"

I take a steadying breath. No matter what happens, Zhira and her men will be here, but I've convinced her not to act unless I give them a sign. No use having them die for nothing, and I have no idea how this is going to go.

"Stay in character and improvise." I try to reassure her, but my hands tremble as she shoves me forward. I stumble through the crowd, drawing closer to the bodies. The stench of blood and death makes my stomach churn.

The disguised Blackbones bring me to the pulpit. Ajjan gives my bound wrist a reassuring squeeze before leaving me with Vogul and taking up position behind the pulpit.

Vogul looms before me, her black lips curled into a wicked smile. "Do you like what we've done with the place?" she asks, gesturing to the bodies hanging from posts.

I force myself to look at them, to witness the wanton cruelty and monstrous horror of the Faceless Coven. I swallow a lump in my throat. "Those are the council members."

"Most of them, anyway." Vogul stands at my side, gazing up at the dying and the dead with reverence. "I gave them a chance to save themselves, but now their lifeblood will be harnessed in the summoning. Every death, every drop of blood, will be used."

"You people are sick," I stammer. "You already won. Why do all of this—" The nedozul shifts, causing a lance of pain to shoot up my spine. A wave of nausea ripples through me, and I have to bite my tongue to keep from crying out.

Vogul laughs, her eyes brimming with delight as her attention falls on my chest. She extends a hand and touches the mended flesh, her fingers brushing against the tiny bit of glass that yet protrudes from the skin. "How does it feel to bear the soul of a God?"

I wince as a man's scream is cut short by a knife. A pit of dread sinks into my bowels. "I don't feel much different."

"You don't even realize how lucky you are." Vogul wrinkles her nose. "But as usual, the Lord's graces are wasted on those too terrified and stupid to appreciate them." She leans close, her aldehyde perfume wafting over me like a noxious cloud as she presses her lips to my ear. "It will be over very soon."

My nostrils flare, and my stomach twists in revulsion.

"Oh, you poor baby." Vogul tucks a strand of hair behind my ear. The intimate gesture makes my intestines curl. "There was never a future for you that wasn't fraught with shadow. You were born to bleed, to suffer, and to sacrifice."

She gestures to the sky, where the shadow moon pulses to the same rhythm as the nedozul. "You see the results of our work. Every ounce of pain, every soul collected, all of it is channeled through the nedozul. We've summoned the gateway to Nhammock. Risen for the last time. Look upon it, Bexis. Today, the world of humankind falls, and the shadow moon breaks." She directs her attention behind the pulpit. "It's time to begin. Bring him out."

A figure emerges from the crowd. My heart nearly stops. Lum Carro lumbers forward, his scarred face twisted in a gleeful grin as he drags Juzu onto the stage. Blood thunders through my ears and my fists clench. I drove a spear through his heart. How is that pitiful excuse for a man still alive?

"You thought your father was dead?" Vogul laughs. "Oh, no. The Lord has taken a special interest in him."

Lum Carro grunts as he drops Juzu at my feet. The Aevem slumps like a sack of rocks.

"Juzu!" I say, my eyes burning. I drop to my knees, wishing my hands weren't bound so I could touch him and let him know I'm here. The Aevem's eyes, once electric and fierce, are dark and colorless. His waistcoat is torn. Blood stains his shirt, coats his frazzled gray hair, and streams down his cheeks. He's so frail, so weak and damaged that it breaks my heart. "Can you hear me?"

His dark eyes blink, as if he's fighting his way through a fog. "Bex-is," he stammers. "Is that you?"

"It's me," I say. "I'm here."

He's wearing a phaser across his neck that bursts with red light. My heart plummets. He's caught in a disharmonic snare. My vision blurs. It's too much for me to stand. "I should never have left you. I thought if I had the Flame—"

"As touching as this is." Vogul snaps her fingers. Sentinels haul Juzu to the back of the stage, and two others drag me forward.

The members of the coven have gathered in a circle around us. They wear black robes, their hoods pulled low. From the corner of my eye, I notice Zhira beside Juzu, hauling him to his feet, and I catch it— the sleight of hand that only a master thief could manage. Zhira switches the dull phaser for the one around Juzu's neck. It's so slight as to be almost imperceptible. Zhira slips away, bringing the active phaser with her.

Vogul raises her hands to the shadow moon. "Behold the bridge to Nhammock and the sacred unity of Darkness." Vogul approaches

Juzu, resting a hand on his shoulder. "We can watch together, Juzu. Witness the depth of your failure." She smirks. "You had a second chance, but you still couldn't protect her."

"No," Juzu whispers. He struggles to rise to his feet, but sentinels hold him down. "Please—"

"Even with all of your false honesty and the sniveling dogma of your Virtue, you failed. Every ounce of pain will fill the Immortal Dark with power, channeled through your ward. So I need you to feel it, Juzu. Watch now, as the Daughter of Shadow is crowned in blood."

My jaw clenches as a shadow blooms in the sky, blotting out the stars in a smog of darkness that coalesces like a meteor and crashes into the rooftop with enough force to break stone. Rubble, ice, and dust fly into the air as the coven members scramble backward and sentinels shout in alarm.

The phantom rises before us, thirty feet tall, skeleton wings spread, larger and fiercer than ever before. Red eyes burn with the heat of a wildfire. The beast arches its back and turns its face to the sky as it bellows thunder into the night. Inky tentacles wriggle through the stone as the rooftop quivers.

"Xaleo!" I shout, but my voice is swallowed by the howling wind. I stand alone on the stage as the monstrous figure towers over me. Fear is a tempest in my heart, making my hands shake, but I force myself to stand tall. It's impossible to reconcile that this colossal beast and the dark-haired boy who kissed me in the Ujjarum temple are one and the same. "I know you're still in there." My voice is a trembling whisper now. "I need you to remember."

The creature's maw hangs open, saliva dripping from its fangs. A voice blooms in my head. "The boy is dead."

"Liar!" I scream, the word tearing from my throat as the nedozul in my chest flares to life. Rhazaran's weight presses down on me, a suffocating presence clawing at the edges of my mind. But beyond the darkness, there is Xaleo—a flicker of light struggling against an ocean of black.

"Please," I stammer, inching toward the beast despite every instinct screaming for me to run. "You said you would fight until the end. You promised you would never leave me."

In response, the phantom rears back, its maw widening as green light erupts from its throat, forming a concentrated beam that streaks toward me. My body reacts, muscles tensing to leap away, but the nedozul stirs, sending a pulse down my spine—freezing me in place. Light bursts from my sternum, answering the phantom's blast with one of my own. The two energies merge in a bridge of dark harmony. A thousand heartbeats thunder through my skull—pulling, stretching, and warping reality itself. Flashes of color explode across my vision.

A voice rises like a siren, echoing in my mind. "Daughter of Shadow," the creature purrs. "Why don't you come inside?"

CHAPTER 34

I STAND ON A PLATFORM OF STONE, SURROUNDED BY ROWS OF DOORWAYS that stretch endlessly in every direction. Above me, the sky is a canvas of swirling galactic dust—hues of violet, gold, and silver blending in chaotic harmony. Millions of stars wink down at me from a sky of infinite obsidian.

I'm back in the Aoz, the world within my mind. I blink, trying to adjust to the sudden shift—only moments ago I was caught in the skeletal embrace of the phantom, surrounded by a horde of soldiers, fighting for my life. But now, everything is quiet. Warm air floods into my lungs. I rise to my feet, limbs trembling with fear. Why did Rhazaran bring me here, of all places?

"There you are, my darling."

A man emerges before me, as if stepping between invisible curtains. His skin gleams like marbled pitch, diamond eyes locking onto mine. I take a step backward, my breath catching in my throat.

The face that peers back at me is unsettling—vaguely human, but wrong. His nose is too small, his mouth too large, with ghostly white lips that sit too low on his jaw. A crown of black vines encircles his bald head, and he wears a black cotton suit over broad shoulders. He holds a metal staff and wears a belt at his waist with a dagger in a sheath. His expression is bemused, but not unkind.

"I have to admit. I thought you'd put up more of a fight."

I blink, trying to gather my bearings. "Who are you?"

He gives me an unnerving grin, his wide mouth stretching across his face. "I am God."

Dread squirms in my belly. "You're the shaji king. Rhazaran."

His expression doesn't falter. He gives a slow, mocking bow, then claps his hands. "Very good."

Every muscle in my body tightens, bracing for an attack. But he remains still. His posture is relaxed, almost bored. I thought Rhazaran would be a demon—a monster of fire and shadow. I was not expecting an ugly old man.

"Why are we here?" I ask.

"Ah." He gestures to the doors that line the platform, surrounding us. "This place is you. It's everything that you've ever known. All your memories, thoughts, fears and hopes and dreams. And it's all mine now."

I reach instinctively for my knife, but I have nothing. My tone pipe is gone too. The only weapon within sight is the dagger on his belt. If I can get close enough...

Rhazaran laughs. "We're far past the point of fighting, Bexis. Come, I want to show you something."

I bite my bottom lip. So long as he thinks I'm harmless, that works to my advantage. I just need to bide my time.

He swings his staff in an arc over his head. The platform rumbles, and the sky blurs into an incomprehensible stream of light and color. The doors disappear and the platform itself vanishes. My stomach flips as the world revolves around me.

When my feet land on solid ground, we stand upon a road surrounded by barren wasteland. Bones scatter the empty field, along with the charred remains of smoking buildings and dead trees. A sprawling fortress rises from a hill, a mass of black stone and spiraling steeples that reach hundreds of feet into the air. Crimson stars litter the night sky, and fires burn in the distance, filling the air with rancid ash that coats my lungs.

"The Shadow Realm," I say.

"No." Rhazaran spreads his arms. "This is Coppejj two thousand years ago, during what your historians call the season of shadow."

I clench my hands into fists. "It's horrible."

"Yes, it is. I hadn't had a chance yet to rebuild properly. You humans are an obstinate species, as truculent and fierce as you are stupid. The last time I came here, I thought to bend humanity to my will, to rule over them. The wolsai punished me for my weakness." Rhazaran smiles. "I won't make that mistake again. Your world is going to fall, Bexis. For the crime of banishing me into the Shadow Realms, I will lay waste to everything humans have built, and I will snuff out every last one of you."

Rhazaran waves his staff again, and we come to a fork in the road. Beyond it lies a field of bodies that stretches into the horizon. Hundreds of thousands of corpses, skeletons, limbs. Men, women, children, the old, the young, the rich and derelict. All dead. Piled into mountains, scattered like seeds on the wind.

"But why?" My chest constricts, the horror nearly overwhelming. But I still have my wits. I'm right next to him now; the dagger is just out of reach. A little closer and I can end this with a single stroke. I lick my lips, working moisture into my mouth. "We're no longer any threat to you."

Rhazaran nods. "Mortals never grasp the big picture. Your lives are ephemeral things, and you think that makes them precious. But in truth, it makes them cheap. What I offer mankind is simple. An end to suffering, disease, hatred, and violence. What I offer is darkness, yes, and silence. Don't you see? Isn't that better than the horrors you inflict upon each other? You of all people should recognize this."

He turns, gesturing to the field of death and exposing his knife. I take a breath, then strike, lunging toward him and tearing the dagger free. In one fluid motion, I drive the blade into his chest with all my strength. The dagger sinks into his flesh up to the hilt. My heart pumps, blood raging through my ears.

Rhazaran blinks, confused for a moment, then—far from being stunned—tilts his head back and laughs. "You cannot kill me, child. I am without beginning or end." He pulls the blade from his flesh and slips it back into his belt. There is no blood. No wound. I take a step back as he turns to face me, diamond eyes narrowed. "You, however, are a candle facing a hurricane. You've spent your entire feeble life hoping the world would change, that you would find a place, and that people would come to your side. But look around you, Bexis. At the end of things, you are alone. The Aevem failed you. Your friends are too weak to protect you. Nothing has changed."

The beastmark aches, and I fall to my knees, the true hopelessness of my situation crushing me. At this moment, it all makes sense. I can see the shape of my life. Born into a world that did not love me. Told I was a monster from the moment I was old enough to understand speech. Kept in isolation, a murderer who deserved all the hate and pain and vitriol that life threw my way. That's who I am. And that's what the world does to people. Why would anyone suffer so much to preserve it?

A world of betrayal. A world of lies. A world of pain and brutality where innocent people suffer for no reason. Where the kind are tortured by the tides of time and the cruel are rewarded with power and riches. Maybe Phekru was right. Maybe it's better if it's all gone.

Rhazaran seems to sense my uncertainty. "Yes," he says. "The world of mankind is fraught with horrors beyond anything even I can conjure. They lie and rape and murder and pillage and steal and torture. It is beyond darkness. You know this is true. Look what they've done to you." His hand touches my cheek. "How they lied to you. How they hurt you. They don't deserve your sacrifice, Bexis. They don't deserve your life, your soul. Give it to me, and together, we can right all the wrongs that have been done to you."

Something about his tone prickles my skin. He would not be asking if he could take what he wanted. He needs something from me, otherwise we wouldn't be here, which means I can still fight. "I'll never join you."

Rhazaran smiles. "What if I told you that we can get justice for your mother? Revenge for Lum Carro's crimes and the lies that he seeded into your mind."

This gives me pause. *Lies?* There were countless untruths that Lum Carro told. He concealed that he's a resonance trapper, that he worshipped a demon. But Rhazaran's words seem to hint at something else, something deeper hiding in plain sight. My mind races, flipping through memories as a pool of dread deepens in my belly. I should know better than to trust the shaji king, but his words have already sunk their hooks into me. "What lies?"

Rhazaran smirks, his eyes sparkling with a mixture of amusement and exasperation, then he raises his staff. The air around us thickens as tendrils of shadow twist and coalesce into a steel door, its frame lined with bolts, chains dangling from the edges like iron vines. "Your life is not what you think," he says, gesturing within. "It would be easier if I showed you."

I frown, my gaze lingering on the door. In this place, doors lead to memories—some repressed, others forgotten to time. It's likely whatever he wants to show me is a lie, some trick to taint my resonance or turn my emotions against me. My rational mind knows this, and yet... and yet, there's a tingling deep in my stomach, a tremor of certainty— or perhaps it's only a fool's hope—that there's something here, something that could finally explain Lum Carro's cruelty and the horrors I endured as a child. If there's even a chance...

I clench my hands into fists, steadying against the current of doubt. I don't trust Rhazaran—not at all. But I need to see what's on the other side of this door.

"Okay," I say, resolve settling like cold cement in my gut. "Show me."

"You won't be disappointed." Rhazaran's long bony fingers graze the steel handle, and the chains clatter to the ground with a metallic clank. He hesitates for a brief moment, his diamond eyes glimmering with strange mirth. "Prepare yourself," he whispers. "This will not be easy to see."

My heart flutters, anticipation mounting. With a slight push, he swings the door open, and a blinding light floods out, swallowing the shadows. I squint against its harshness, my pulse quickening as the air crackles. My stomach squirms, and anxiety thrums through my skin, each nerve screaming a warning. I press it down, willing my heart to harden. Without another thought, I step through the threshold.

* * *

A gust of icy wind ruffles my hair. I inhale sharply, surprised at the sudden change of scenery. Rows of gray houses extend to my right, their roofs slanted, windows lit with lanterns and candles. To my left, the Shadow Sea sprawls under a stormy sky, scarlet clouds gathering over black waves.

Hezha's fire. I know this place—the eastern outskirts of the city, a housing district for fishermen and factory workers called the Barrel. This is where I grew up, before my father and I moved to the Slags. The houses are old but sturdy, untouched by the rot and ruin that seep into the slums on the other side of town.

"Do you remember?" Rhazaran's voice sends prickles across my skin. He stands beside me like a ghost. His face is stoic, his eyes harrowing pits of black.

"Yes." I swallow a lump in my throat as my gaze drifts to the house across the street. It's unremarkable—a squat two-story structure with gray siding and a brick foundation. The windows flicker with orange warmth. I know it—but recognition feels distant, fogged over, as if I'm peeling back layers of memory and discovering a film of rot beneath them.

It's my old home. It burned down years ago, but I've never returned here, never even considered it—and yet here it stands, disturbingly familiar, haunting and cold. The storm has picked up, and the wind howls. Snow drives down the street with a vengeance.

"Why have you brought me here?" I ask.

"Because this is the night when your destiny found you," Rhazaran replies, his voice smooth as ice. "And it would be a shame to fade into nothing without understanding the tragedy that is your life." He extends his palm, gesturing across the street. "Shall we go inside?"

My heart stutters. The reality of what I'm about to see freezes my limbs. Dread and shame and horror mix in a suffocating weight that presses against my chest, making it hard to breathe. My mother is inside that house. The woman I murdered. How am I supposed to face that?

"I don't know if I can," I say, my voice wavering in the wind.

"Didn't the Aevem teach you the importance of truth?" Rhazaran clicks his tongue. "You can run from it, you can hide, but truth will follow you, and if you ignore it, you'll be crushed beneath the weight." He takes my wrist, his touch dead and cold against my skin. A shiver creeps up my spine, my stomach twisting in revulsion. "Don't worry, Bexis." His eyes dance with amusement. "I'll be right beside you."

I grit my teeth, wishing with all my heart that Juzu were here with me now, his warmth and confidence giving me strength—or Xaleo with his unshakable calm. Stars, I'd take Ajjan or even Zhira in this moment—anyone but this twisted demon. But the answers are there—the truth behind what happened, why everything turned out the way it did. I have no choice but to carry on.

"Fine," I force out. "Just do it."

Rhazaran waves his staff, and the air thickens once again. Our surroundings shift, and suddenly we're inside my old house.

The smell hits me first—rosemary and chicken broth mingling with musty wood and the smoky scent of candle wax. A fire crackles softly in the hearth. My breath catches as I take in the kitchen—a snug square room with a wooden table separating it from a small living area with a window that overlooks the street. Everything is familiar and yet impossibly distant, like looking through a distorted mirror, watching a life that used to be mine but now belongs to someone else. And yet, I know with iron certainty, that I am home.

A woman stands at the kitchen counter, her back to me. Black hair falls over her shoulders, her form solid and familiar. She's dressed simply—a white tunic, brown trousers, and thick wool socks. She hums as she stirs a stew pot with an easy rhythm. Her voice is beautiful, mesmerizing—the lullaby tugging at something deep inside me. My heart begins to ache, and my eyes threaten to spill over. *Mother.*

I inch closer, barely daring to breathe. Each step feels like a mile. How many times have I yearned to see her? How many nights have I lain awake, tormented by her absence, wishing I could touch her, could tell her how sorry I am, how I wish things had turned out differently? And now she's here. Standing before me like nothing happened. All the unspoken words burn on the tip of my tongue, but I cannot speak.

As she turns, I catch sight of her face. Blue eyes. Skin smooth and radiant as she dips a spoon into the pot, then brings it to her lips and blows.

"Addy?" I breathe, confusion crashing over me. She looks the same as she did in Juzu's healing memories. "I don't understand."

But Juzu's sister doesn't turn or react to me. This is a memory, I remind myself, not something that I can affect. She tastes the stew and smiles.

"Dhaima," she calls out. "Are you hungry?"

"Yes!"

My attention shifts to the living area, where a dark-haired girl plays in the corner of the room, surrounded by a pile of toys. She holds a doll to her chest and giggles.

"No." I shake my head, stepping back. "This memory isn't right. There's something wrong."

"And yet, you know it's true." Rhazaran appears at my side, his presence cold and unsettling. He quirks an eyebrow. "This is your house. That is your mother. And that little girl over there? That is you."

"But..." My voice falters, words slipping like sand through my fingers. How can I not recognize my own mother? I saw Addy and Dhaima in Juzu's memories and never made the connection. I walk around the room, my heart racing, as Addy places bowls and spoons on the kitchen table, her movements rote and calm.

"Why do I feel like I'm seeing a stranger?" I ask.

"Trauma," Rhazaran explains, his voice a low murmur. "The human mind is a fragile thing. And Lum Carro certainly did his best to deepen those wounds. I'm surprised the memory isn't more damaged."

Dhaima hops into the kitchen, skittering at Addy's feet.

As if on cue, a knock sounds from the front door.

Addy wipes her hands on a dish towel and answers the door. I stand by the foyer, ready to peer into the eyes of Lum Carro, but a different, familiar man stands in the hall.

Juzu is younger, handsome. He doesn't have spectacles, and his hair is longer, falling in dark locks around his shoulders. I shake my head. *This is a lie. None of this is real.* And yet—I know, without knowing how—that this is the truth.

"Juzu!" Addy beams, stepping aside to let him enter. "Come in."

"I hope you don't mind." Juzu takes off his hat as he strolls into the room. "I was in the neighborhood, and I—"

"Uncle Ju!" Dhaima rushes across the room and wraps her arms around Juzu's legs.

"Hello, little one!" He picks her up. "You're getting bigger every day, aren't you?"

"Like you!" she proclaims, cackling as he spins her around.

"That's right," Juzu agrees, his silver eyes crinkling at the corners as he gazes at his niece with fondness.

Addy wipes the table with a washcloth and huffs. "Will you stay for dinner? I've got stew."

"It smells wonderful." Juzu smiles and sets Dhaima down on the edge of the table, her legs swinging in the air. "But I can't stay. I just wanted to see how you were doing. If you've had any more incidents."

"Yes, actually." Addy turns her back to the stove and places her hands on her hips. "It was the strangest thing. We were playing with her toys, and the whole room went dark. Her eyes turned bright violet. It stayed like that for two, maybe three seconds, and then it was gone."

"Nothing to worry about." Juzu touches Dhaima's nose playfully. The girl giggles. "It means she's growing up. She will be drawn into harmony for a time before she learns her way. Strange things may happen around her."

Addy takes Juzu by the arm. "We're lucky to have you. I can't imagine going through this alone."

"And you'll never have to." Juzu takes his hat from the post. "I have to run, but I'll be back tomorrow morning." He puts a hand on Dhaima's head. "Come to me if you need anything. Anything at all."

Addy gives Juzu a hug. "I love you."

"I love you too." He turns to Dhaima, now preoccupied with a doll on the table, and squeezes her little hand and kisses her cheek. "See you later, little flower."

I turn to Rhazaran as Juzu leaves the room. "If this is my memory, and you're right—that means, I'm Dhaima. Addy is my mother. Juzu is my uncle. But then who is Lum Carro? What happened here?"

Rhazaran crosses his arms, a menacing smirk spreading across his lips. "All is about to be revealed—"

The window shatters. Glass tinkles to the wooden floor like droplets of rain. Time slows as the air thickens.

Addy screams and clutches Dhaima to her chest. The young girl's eyes are wide with terror. A shadow slips through the window, a miasma of black vapor, like a cloud of smoke that spills into the room and begins to coalesce into the shape of a man—tall, menacing, and unmistakable. My blood turns to ice.

Lum Carro. He looks exactly the same, old and gray, his skin sallow and leathery and lined with weathered scars. His gray beard hangs over his chest. His eyes are dark and brimming with malevolent intent that seems to drain the warmth from the room. My chest tightens as desperation claws at me. I need to stop this—I need to save them—but I cannot change what has already happened. I watch in horror, helpless, as Lum Carro draws nearer, his movements slow and deliberate, savoring each moment.

Addy pushes Dhaima behind her and stands tall, her limbs shaking with fear. "W-who are you?"

Without a word, Lum Carro's smile widens into a wicked grin. He says nothing. Just reaches to his belt and pulls out a long shimmering knife.

"No!" Addy's scream pierces the silence, raw and horrible. "Please don't—"

Lum Carro lunges, grabbing her wrist and forcing her down. She hits the floor with a sickening thud. I wince as her face twists in pain. She fights, struggling beneath his weight, every inch of her body resisting. But Lum Carro is relentless. He pins her down, his strength unyielding. Dhaima weeps in the corner of the room, shrieking in terror.

Blood surges through my ears. A high whine screaming through my head. I stand across the room, numb, as the realization hits me.

Lum Carro is not my father. He's not even related to me. And I didn't kill my mother.

He did.

I launch myself at him, but my arms swing clean through him, as if I'm made of nothing but vapor. "No!" I scream. "Get off her!" But it's only a memory. I can't do anything to change it.

The man I called my father sneers down at Addy and strikes her on the side of the head with the blunt side of his knife. My mother stills. Blood pools on the floor.

Lum Carro rises to his feet, turning his attention to the child. Dhaima sobs hysterically, snot and spit running down her face. He approaches, his eyes alight with cruelty I cannot bear to witness. A fire ignites in my chest. It swells and expands with every heartbeat until the fury sears through me, consuming every part of my being. I tremble, powerless to act but alive with a hatred so raw and blinding I can barely keep from screaming.

"There we are." Lum Carro holds her tenderly as she squirms and battles, then presses her head into the crook of his shoulder. Dhaima goes limp in his arms and the apartment falls into silence.

"You are one lucky little girl." Lum Carro's voice is a deathly rasp as he touches her cheek, an evil grin on his face. "I'm going to take good care of you, Bexis. That's your name now. Bexis." A wave of despair washes over me. This twisted monster took everything from me. My home, my family, my whole world. Even my name.

He strides across the kitchen, extracts a bottle of liquor from the cupboard, and takes a deep pull, the brown liquid sloshing as it dribbles down his chin. Then he pours the rest over the wooden table. A match flickers to life in his fingers. I watch, numb, as he tosses it on the table and sets the house ablaze. Flames erupt instantly, a ravenous inferno that consumes everything in its path.

Lum Carro takes a coarse wool blanket from his jacket and wraps it around Dhaima, bundling her up and tucking her beneath his arm as he approaches the broken window. In one fluid motion, he jumps—the cold wind slicing past them as they descend into the shadows below.

I scream silently as the flames engulf the room. "That's enough," I say to Rhazaran. "Take me out of here."

"As you wish." Rhazaran snaps his fingers, and the room bleeds away. We stand again in the barren field of smoke and fire.

Silence crashes around me. My chest heaves as wanton anger bubbles from deep within. "My whole life is a lie." The words fall from my mouth like ash. "I never killed anyone."

"No," Rhazaran confirms. "Lum Carro wanted you to believe that you did."

"Why?" I ask, tears streaming down my face. "Why did he do it?"

"He's a zealot," Rhazaran explains. "He knew you were born under the shadow moon, and he knew you were related to the last Khatori in the north. He believed that made you special."

"He poisoned me." The depth of his treachery sinks into me like a toxic cloud. "By convincing me I was a monster. It corrupted my internal resonance. That's why I had such a difficult time trapping. It's why Urru never fully awakened."

A strange feeling settles into my gut. A hum that I instantly recognize as a kind of harmony. It's dark, and it vibrates within me, but it's not discordant like the energy of the phaser. This is true harmony, and yet it's insidious, menacing, and dangerous.

"Revenge," Rhazaran says, his lips pursed. "That's what you're feeling. And that is what I have to offer. Join me, and we'll put an end to Lum Carro. We'll put an end to Kandra Vogul. I can feel your hatred for them burning in your soul, Bexis. I know you want to cause them pain. You want to make them suffer. I can give this to you."

The resonance of revenge opens inside me. It rings through every cell of my soul, every inch of my essence. Yes. It feels right. It's like a path has opened before my feet and all I have to do is put one foot in front of the other.

"Embrace it," Rhazaran says. "All you have to do is let me in, and I will do the rest."

"And your followers?" I clench my jaw. Resonance swirls around my arms, encircling my fists. "I want them dead."

"Yes!" Rhazaran laughs. "You may do whatever you wish to them." He steps closer, a maniacal grin on his face. "You can have it all. Justice. Revenge. The power to ensure no one ever hurts you again. At my side, you will be immortal. You will become the Darkness, a river without end."

The resonance congeals into a solid pit in my heart, a roaring ball of infernal power. "Tell me what I have to do."

Rhazaran draws closer to me. "Let me in."

The resonance picks up steam as Rhazaran speaks. It vibrates through me, filling me with a deep dark violet. It crackles across my skin. There is power here—so much power. Yes, this is what I've always wanted. No more running. No more hiding. I'll be untouchable. I'll belong to something greater than myself.

"No, Bexis!" Urru's voice is a distant whisper against the harrowing vibration that tears through me. *"There is another way!"*

Rhazaran bends forward so his lips touch my ear. "LET. ME. IN."

"You can still save them!" Urru screams, louder this time. *"You can still fight!"*

The darkness surrounds me. It absorbs my soul. There is no light. No moon. No stars. I feel no fear. No love. No loss. No pain. There is only darkness, unyielding and focused. A burning rhythm of infinite black pulses through me, cold fire blazing through my flesh. Then, abruptly, everything stands still, suspended in eerie silence.

"Bexis, you need to stop this." The voice echoes through the void, a siren call that brings me back to my senses.

The fire within wanes. I open my mouth, barely daring to believe it. "Xaleo?"

He stands before me like a seraph, blue eyes blazing, his crooked smile melting the hate that's coiled around my heart. "I'm here," he whispers. "I'm with you."

"Is it really you?" I nearly weep, relief and hope merging into a wave of powerful emotion.

"Yes." He takes my hands, his touch soft and firm.

My heart throbs. "How?"

"We're connected through the nedozul," he explains, his voice strained and urgent. He gestures to Rhazaran, frozen on the desolate road, his diamond eyes shimmering. "He's manipulating you, driving you toward vengeance so he can consume your soul."

My heart races as understanding dawns. "This is what he did to you." My voice trembles. "He stoked your need for vengeance against Vogul and used it to turn you into the phantom."

He nods. "I know it's hard. But you have to fight him."

"How?" My vision blurs.

"Let it go." He lifts his palm to my cheek, his touch sending sparks of warmth through my spine. "You cannot change the past by destroying the future. I chose vengeance, and look what I became."

"No—" I shake my head. "No, they don't deserve my forgiveness. They deserve fire."

"It's not about what they deserve. Forgiveness is for you, not for them." Xaleo's grip weakens as he begins to fade away.

"No." Panic surges through me as I reach for him, sobs rattling through me. "Please don't go. Please, don't leave me here."

"Promise me," he insists, his voice firm but fading. "You will not turn."

Tears stream down my face. Every fiber of my being wants fire, pain, vengeance… but Xaleo's touch is a ghost upon my skin, and I know he's right. Still, I have to force the words from my lips. "I promise."

He slips away. Time whips back into motion. The resonance tears at my soul, shooting through my veins with a force that takes my breath away.

"That's it," Rhazaran croons. "Let me in."

This time, I fight, resisting the flood of power. But it's overwhelming. Ghostly fingers claw at my eyes, my mouth, my throat—ripping, tearing, trying to climb within.

I scream. "NO!"

And then I see it—a tiny flame, blooming like a burning rose against an infinite black horizon. It grows and rages into a billowing inferno, forming into a fire, and then a blade. I reach out, swimming in this sea of darkness. My hand clasps the hilt and light streaks through me.

"What are you doing?" Rhazaran steps back. For the first time in our meeting, uncertainty lines his features. His lips twist. "You're making a mistake, Bexis. Let me in! LET ME—"

The Flame of Khamonji fires gossamer strands of light into the air, hot as the sun. They blast through the stone ground and crack through the foundations of the road, slicing through the bleeding stars.

"No!" Rhazaran shrieks. "Stop this at once!"

The power is a wave of white fire that erupts from me like a volcano. The vibration of vengeance withers and is replaced by the steady blazing force that has no name. The light is so bright it's blinding. I scream from the force of it. Rhazaran howls in fury. The world between worlds takes me, and I plummet into the cosmic abyss, my soul hurtling through the fabric of space-time as I catapult back into my body.

CHAPTER 35

WIND HOWLS THROUGH MY HAIR AS THE WORLD CRASHES INTO ME LIKE an avalanche. Pain pulses through my veins, sudden and seizing. My chest heaves as gelid air sweeps into my lungs.

The phantom towers above, skeleton wings draped around us like a cage, its hulking horns silhouetted by the three moons and bathed in the molten glow of dawn. Energy between us ripples and wanes, forming a bridge. The beast's lips peel back, and its crimson eyes narrow, blinking slowly as it realizes something is amiss.

Bexis! a voice screams in my head. *What are you doing?*

I grit my teeth as raw power surges through me. The bridge between us flickers and brightens, shifting from green to pure radiant silver, the light igniting in the phantom's eyes. The beast recoils, letting out a strangled howl of pain as it struggles to escape.

I stand firm as the light whips around me in a tight vortex. Time slows as my awareness expands. I can feel every frantic heartbeat, taste the fear bubbling from the watching crowd of the Faceless Coven, their eyes wide with a mix of ecstasy and terror.

The sentinels are frozen, uncomprehending horror pricking at their necks, weapons gripped with white knuckles. Vogul and Lum Carro remain at the pulpit. Their postures indicate confusion, as though uncertain if they should interfere. I locate Zhira and Ajjan standing with Juzu at the back of the stage, the three of them waiting for some sign that I am still myself, daring to believe I can pull this off.

As I shift my weight, the phantom rears its head, its muscles taut. Saliva dribbles in long strings to the icy ground, as the beast prepares to snap its jaws around my neck, a death blow meant to break my body in half and leave me in a steaming bloody heap.

Fear works its way through the base of my spine, all the way to my neck. I've escaped from the Aoz. Somehow, I've brought myself back to the real world, but I'm still no match for this creature, and if I don't do something quickly, I'm going to die.

"It's here," Urru's voice whispers in my head. A small silver ball unfurls in my chest—a winter orchid blooming in the frost. The depths of infinity open within me. Urru's voice comes again, a steadying hand against the tempest within me. "All you have to do is take it."

I close my eyes and give in.

Time warps once more. Everything happens simultaneously. Vogul opens her mouth to scream. Zhira drives a blade into the belly of the nearest sentinel. Light crackles across Juzu's palms, and Ajjan gives the signal for the Blackbones to strike. The coven fall over themselves to leap backward, but Blackbone swords are already upon them. The phantom's eyes open in wild fury as it lunges for my throat, fangs bared.

I twist to the side, narrowly avoiding the jaws of death, then flex my muscles, ripping apart my bonds. I extend my right hand, tapping into the power within me. Light explodes from my skin—an eruption of violet and black radiance blazing around me like a living bonfire. From the flames, a sword takes shape, the iron hilt cool against the raging heat of my palm. The long black blade pulses with shadowfire—a storm born of flesh and steel. The Khamonji Flame.

This is not possible, a voice in my head cries. *Kill her!*

KILL HER!

The phantom lunges again, swiping with its deadly talons. I leap backward and slash a diagonal arc that slices through the phantom's wrist. The talon lops off and falls to the ground as black viscera and smoke spill into the air. The phantom's flesh sizzles as the beast howls and retreats, its wings curling in pain. Resonance tears through me, obliterating my base emotions. Fear does not exist. Doubt has no place in my mind. The phantom flaps its wings, rising into the air, then diving at me with the full force of its weight.

But the Flame has a mind of its own. I roll out of the way and slash once more. The blade lengthens mid-swing and cuts through the phantom's abdomen. Black blood spills onto the frozen rooftop, staining the snow in dark rivulets. The beast topples and collapses in a writhing heap. The sword speaks through me.

Burn it. Burn it all away. And I know what I have to do. There can be no hesitation. I swing the blade before me, crackling like a violet inferno. The resonance flows through me like a river, awakening every nerve, every fiber of my being, as it pours into my foe.

The phantom shrieks and pulls back from the light, but it's too late. The Flame envelopes the beast. Its wings ignite in black flames that lick the night air. Red resonance swipes at me from the side. The Flame sucks it up like a magnet, but the diversion forces me to tear my eyes from the phantom.

Vogul stands to my left with Juzu in her grasp and a knife to his throat. "Stop this now, or the Aevem dies!"

My heart races, caught between the need to vanquish the phantom and the urgency to protect Juzu. What's left of Lord Rhazaran's proxy screams in agony. I lower the Flame, turning to face Vogul.

Juzu's eyes are wide with fear. Silver light spills down his cheeks. "Bexis, finish this! Don't—"

"Shut up," Vogul hisses. She stares at me, her emerald eyes glistening. "You want revenge, don't you? You want to kill me? Well, I'm right here."

"This is beyond me now," I whisper.

I have no concept of where the eternal power ends or if it has swallowed me whole. Light flares as the phantom continues to scream, and I tighten my grip on the blade. "It doesn't matter what you do. There's no going back now."

"You are mistaken." Vogul's voice rises above the din, sharp and commanding. "Kill her," she shouts, the desperation in her tone contrasting with the malice in her eyes. "In the name of your Lord, kill her!"

Members of the coven move to obey Vogul's command. Sentinels surround me. But they're tentative, afraid. They see the power crackling across the black blade, and they know any attack they make is futile. Yet still, they press forward.

The sword in my hand is so light, it may as well be a feather. "If you want to live, you will lay down your weapons," I call out to them. "If you attack, you will die."

But my words have no effect. They are bound by darkness to obey. Twenty soldiers trained by Olaik at the Hezhani Monastery attack with spears and scimitars. I've never trained, and I have little combat experience, but the Flame hungers for action. It has seen wars and battles far more dire than this. The resonance picks up, and I match the tune with a soft hum, aligning myself with the Flame.

I let the harmony within guide my movements. I cut them down as quickly as they come. Their attacks are clumsy and slow, like bumbling children. The Flame melts steel and cuts through bone. There is no clash of swords, no thump of steel on steel. There is only death and fire as the bodies drop around me.

Vogul raises her hands into the air, using the respite to gather her resonance. The red power crackles over the Aevem's skin, sizzling and smoking. Juzu arches his back and screams. His hands tighten into fists, his jaw clenching as his hair catches fire and his skin turns black.

"Stop this!" I shout. "Hurting Juzu won't save you."

"You think you've won, but you haven't," Vogul says. "There will be others. This is not the end." She bares her teeth, her emerald eyes ablaze as red resonance crackles at her fingertips. She throws Juzu to the ground as the resonance spills over her and spins into a vortex of power. "Now watch as your beloved Aevem dies screaming—"

A blade punches through Vogul's abdomen from behind. Blood sprays onto the snow, painting Juzu's cheeks red. Vogul blinks in surprise.

Ajjan releases the hilt of the sword, and it clatters to the ground. Blood dribbles down Vogul's belly, pooling in the snow like a carmine rose, vivid against the cold white. She folds her hands over the wound, as if she can staunch the river of blood, then opens her mouth in shock, her lips twisting in a rictus of pain.

"No..." she whispers, her voice a fragile thread as she sways, her emerald eyes dimming. "This isn't right."

Through sheer will, she takes a step toward me, but she falters and sinks to her knees. A horrible moan escapes her lips—an animalistic howl filled with desperation and anger. The fury in her gaze defies the inexorable creep of death.

Driven by primal hatred, she digs her fingers into the snow, and starts to pull herself toward me, dragging her body with a fierce determination. I take a step backward, horror crawling up my spine.

"You cannot kill me!" Vogul heaves the words out. A trail of blood extends behind her. "I will make you pay..." She reaches for my throat, her hands trembling, slick with red. But her strength finally runs out. Her head drops, and she goes still.

I exhale sharply, scarcely daring to believe my eyes. The witch who branded me with Entaru's sigil, killed Xaleo's family, murdered Master Olaik, burned the Hezhani Monastery, and slaughtered fifty innocent monks is dead.

Ajjan wipes his forehead, smearing blood on his face. "She certainly had a flair for the dramatic. I'll give her that."

I ignore him and rush to Juzu's side, falling to my knees. He's still alive, but he's in bad shape. His skin is scorched black in patches around his cheeks. Blood and pus seep from open wounds on his neck and chest.

"Juzu!" I cry, uncertain of what to do. "Talk to me."

He gasps at my touch, then seems to relax when he sees me. A soft smile spreads over his lips. "Don't look at me like that," he says. "I'm fine."

My heart aches. "Liar."

He chuckles as his eyes scan the rooftop. The last of the sentinels have been defeated, and the remnants of the Faceless Coven have surrendered. Zhira and her Blackbones have won the night.

"You did it." His voice is so fragile it breaks my heart. "You passed the test. You defeated the coven."

"It's not over yet," I say, "but we're getting you out of here. We can bring you to the luminaries, and they'll fix you up."

"That would be lovely." Juzu rests his head in the snow. "Maybe Siras will finally let me smoke in peace."

I rest a hand on his shoulder, my heart wrenching. I don't know if any of the luminaries have survived. I don't know if Siras will ever be the same. "I'll have a talk with her."

"Uh, Bexis," Ajjan shouts. "I hate to break it to you, but that thing isn't dead yet." He gestures to the phantom, still twitching in the snow.

I nod and have Ajjan switch places with me. It kills me to leave Juzu in his current condition, but I have one last thing to do. "Stay with him," I tell Ajjan. "Help him."

"Of course," Ajjan says. "Go."

The Flame crackles to life once more as I approach the phantom. My boots crunch in the snow; an icy silence has settled over the whole rooftop. The beast is so large it takes up half the roof. Its body is mangled, wings crushed beneath its bulk, spines broken, horns splintered.

"This isn't over," Rhazaran whispers in my head. The connection between us has weakened. *"The Flame will kill you. You'll wither in Nhammock for thousands of years."* The voice cackles. *"And I will still return."*

"It doesn't matter what happens to me." I grip the Flame with both hands as I circle the hulking beast. "Your plan failed. You must return to the Shadow Realm."

The phantom spits black blood into the air. It's weak, dying. *"If you kill me, Xaleo dies too."*

"I don't believe you." The Flame begs for fire. I feel its deep yearning to expunge this foul demon back into the depths from which it came, and yet I know with unfaltering certainty that Xaleo is alive. And that he can be saved.

Silver light flows from the nedozul in my chest into the blade. Warmth spreads down my limbs and through my fingertips, and the black blade erupts in shadowfire.

"You have to let me go." Xaleo's voice echoes in the back of my mind. *"Let me go."*

My heart hardens into steel. "Never."

I jam the blade into the phantom's chest, as close to the nedozul as I dare. Light floods through the beast, illuminating its body from the inside out, burning away the inky blackness as the shadows wend and wither. The tether between me and Rhazaran snaps. Dimly, I can feel the beastmark tingling, but it's a gentle sensation, like drawing a feather across flesh.

As I close my eyes, my internal world balloons into a vast cavern of light. The darkness has been pushed away, and for one breathless moment, I think I'm too late.

But no. Xaleo is with me, though his pulse is faint. I dive deeper and discover a small flicker of blue among the ocean of white. The Flame opens a path, and a bubble forms around me.

Xaleo floats alone, his arms crossed over his stomach, his shaggy black hair suspended in weightlessness. Tendrils of shadow encircle him, like the gossamer strands of a spider's web. As I reach for the tendrils, pain lances into my forearm. I try to ignore it, but the sensation intensifies until it fills me from head to toe. I howl in frustration. I'm so close, but I still can't reach him.

"You've nearly done it." Urru's voice punctures the white. She stands beside me, wearing a white dress that contrasts with her dark skin. Her hair is tied in a bun behind her head.

"I need to save him," I say. "I can't let him die."

Urru frowns. "No, you can't, but the consequences for you will be terrible."

I have come too far to question myself now. There's no going back. "Just tell me what I have to do."

She circles Xaleo, who floats in the air. "Use the Flame to remove Rhazaran from the nedozul in Xaleo's chest and store it in your own."

"Then we banish him to the Shadow Realm," I say. "Just like you did two thousand years ago."

"Yes, but it's not that easy." Urru's expression darkens and her eyes cloud with unmistakable grief. "Once you cut it out, a piece of Rhazaran will be freed. The only way to keep him contained is to hold him yourself. You must be the host, keeping him safely within the Flame."

Realization sweeps through me with rising terror. "It's not the Flame that will corrupt me. It's *him*. Rhazaran."

"The Immortal Dark," Urru agrees. "A piece of him will live within you for the rest of your life. The Flame is a prison that allows you to hold evil. But the process will destroy you."

A tremor of doubt runs through me, but it passes quickly. There was never any other choice, never a moment that it could end any other way. I accepted this when I faced the guardians, and I accept it now as the only way to save Xaleo.

The Flame coalesces into my hand. I step to Xaleo's side and touch the blade to his sternum. The nedozul beneath his flesh begins to throb with terrible black energy. Rhazaran's soul recoils from the Flame, but I can sense the power reaching for me like invisible tentacles.

My hands tremble as a black mist bleeds out of the nedozul in Xaleo's chest and into the glass in my own. I crash backward, thrown into the ground with incredible force. Pain ratchets through my body, and the Flame dissolves with a suddenness that takes my breath away.

When I open my eyes, I'm back on the rooftop, and the cloud of shadow fades into the night.

I hoist myself on my hands and knees, surrounded by corpses and blood. The pain in my chest is palpable; the nedozul feels like it's on fire, but I force myself to face the smoking remains of the creature that hunted me. Amid the ruined and scattered carapace, Xaleo lies on the ground, his lean body curled in a fetal position, his face concealed behind his hands. I crawl to him. Every movement is excruciating, but the pain is a mere hindrance as I lift Xaleo and cradle his head in my lap. He's so cold. I stroke his shaggy black hair, a gesture as fragile as my hope.

"Wake up," I whisper. "Please, just wake up." It's a command. A plea. But he refuses to obey. His skin is pale, his face still. The silence is suffocating. I place a shaky hand over his heart. Nothing.

"No…" Despair hits me like a hammer to the chest. My face burns. I cannot breathe. "Open your damn eyes, you idiot!"

He stirs. Hope ignites in my heart.

"Xaleo!"

His eyes flicker open. Bright and blue. He looks at me as if through a fog, blinking slowly. "Bexis?"

I choke on a sob, tears spilling down my cheeks as relief and exhaustion threaten to overtake me. My hands tremble as I trace his jawline, barely able to contain the storm inside me. I press my lips to his forehead. He tastes of sweat and ash, but I don't care. "You were wrong," I whisper. "I didn't have to let you go."

His eyes shimmer with wonder and disbelief. "How did you do this?"

"It was you." He's so solid. So tangible and real. I can feel his heartbeat again, steady beneath my touch. "You brought me back."

He struggles to sit up, and reluctantly, I let him go, propping him up with my palms. His breath is ragged, but there's strength in his movements.

"It's over." Juzu's voice is weak, but he grins nonetheless, his eyes like beacons of silver piercing the night. Zhira and Ajjan stand beside him, both coated in blood. The moons shine from above and the fingers of dawn brighten the horizon.

Juzu glances around at the carnage and nods softly. "Bexis has saved us all."

CHAPTER 36

I SIT ON A BED IN THE VISITOR SUITES OF THE WHITE KEEP WITH MY legs crossed, spinning the tone pipe between my fingers and watching the metal siding as it reflects light from the yellow lanterns on the wall. Someone spotted it among the rubble on the rooftop, sitting in the snow as if it wanted to be found.

It's funny, before any of this—before I met Juzu or Xaleo or Shytar or uttered the name Kandra Vogul—this tone pipe was the only thing tying me to the outside world. It was the only thing that gave me any value to anyone. If Lum Carro hadn't given me this pipe, my whole life would have been different. Just thinking the name sends a pang of dread through my gut. His body was never found amid the carnage. I lost track of him during the battle, and he must have escaped, which means he's still out there somewhere, biding his time, plotting his next move.

The truths Rhazaran exposed have shaken me to my core. It's not an easy thing to accept—that your entire life is a lie, that everything you believed to be true was actually a malicious scheme to corrupt your soul. But it's also a blessing.

That phase of my life is over. The girl who lived in the shadows— the one who didn't belong anywhere and didn't trust anyone—she died in the Shadow Realm when Juzu came back for me. My history is an indelible part of me, but it's also in the past, and it can only touch me if I allow it. It's the future that concerns me now, but in light of everything that's happened, and the terrible consequences that have been promised to me, I don't know what's going to happen. And maybe that's okay.

I sigh, placing the tone pipe on the nightstand. Juzu has been in the infirmary for two days. The luminaries say he needs rest, but that he'll make a full recovery. Getting him back has been the biggest relief in all of this. After everything he's done for me, saving the world would be hollow if Juzu wasn't a part of it.

Zhira moved quickly to secure her position as Magistrate, and after her heroics on the rooftop plus Vogul's brutal execution of any rival councilmembers, no one raised any objections. The government of Coppejj will recover, and thankfully, most of the population was never aware of how much danger they were in. It will take some time for everything to settle, but life will go on.

What does that mean for me? Any minute now, I expect some terrible power to run through me. Urru promised that taking the Flame would result in a fate worse than death. Shytar all but said I would need to banish myself into the abyss of Nhammock to protect those I love. But so far, I don't feel any different. The jagged shard of nedozul has pierced my chest, but for two days now, it's been quiescent, causing no pain—like it's been a part of me for my entire life. The questions swirl. How much longer do I have? When will I begin to lose myself to the tides of darkness? And do I have the energy to find happiness and contentment before that happens?

There's a soft knock at the door. I swing my legs over the bed. "Come in."

Xaleo enters, resplendent in a fitted black tunic that accentuates his broad shoulders and muscular physique. My heart flutters as he smirks, leaning against the jamb, his icy blue eyes taking in the room: crimson curtains trimmed in gold, an ornate rug, and satin yellow sheets on the bed with big fluffy pillows.

"You look comfy," he says, bemused.

"Yes, very." I stretch my arms overhead and yawn dramatically. "Where do they have you?"

"I'm not staying in the Keep." His gaze drifts to the chandeliers. "This is a bit much for me."

I nod, but unease stirs inside me. Xaleo has been distant since the ordeal on the rooftop, giving me more space than I expected. I'm not sure what to make of it—part of me bristles at the sudden coldness, but another part understands. The past five years of his life have been a lie. He needs time to sort through it, and I get that, but I hope he comes around before it's too late.

"I didn't ask to be pampered like this," I say, a touch defensively. "Zhira insisted. She's even holding a banquet in my honor."

"Oh, I heard." Xaleo enters the room, his eyes sweeping over the floral tapestry that hangs from the wall. "It should be quite the party."

"Wanna ditch?" I press my palms into the mattress, swinging my legs back and forth like a mischievous child. But beneath the playful act there's a thread of hope. "We can get some cinnamon bread and go to the pier. Watch the moonrise."

"Not a chance." He sits beside me, his shoulder rubbing against mine. The scent of lavender soap lingers in the air. "Zhira's right. You deserve to be pampered. You did save the whole world after all."

"Right." I purse my lips. I'm not sure how I feel about that. It's nice to be appreciated, but the prospect of standing in front of a crowd of hundreds of people is mortifying.

"Besides," Xaleo says, a grin tugging at the corners of his lips, "I saw the banquet hall. They have mountains of cinnamon cake. Mo was in there, and I swear she was drooling on the floor."

I smile despite myself. "Mo is here?"

"All the Rovers." He chuckles. "Wait till you see them. Mo has gone on a spending spree since I gave her that bag of gold. Her whole gang is decked out in silk trousers, fur-lined boots, and fancy wool jackets. Mo is wearing a silver tiara and babbling street slang at anyone who will listen. The service staff have no idea what to do with her."

I laugh, and some of the uneasiness bleeds away. "Okay. I guess that's worth sticking around for."

Xaleo shifts his weight, his expression turning a shade more serious. "I wanted to show you something." From his pocket, he pulls out a flat stone with a jagged edge.

My breath hitches in my throat. "Is that...?"

Xaleo nods, then smoothly lifts his shirt, revealing an inflamed scarlet scar in the middle of his tattooed chest—three inches long and an inch thick.

I gasp. *That wasn't there before.* I saw him with his shirt off when I stitched his shoulder. His chest was smooth, unmarred. "What happened?"

"I know," he says. "It's ugly. The entry wound had healed over completely, the glass buried so deep I didn't know it was there. But it reopened when the nedozul fell out a few hours after you saved me."

"Does it hurt?"

"Not anymore." He smiles. "It might be the first time the curse has ever been reversed."

He lowers his shirt, then places the stone in my hands. My impulse is to recoil, but there's a strange beauty to it—iridescent black and pearl with stripes of pink and red and orange that crisscross over the surface like molten veins.

"You literally did the impossible," Xaleo whispers.

My cheeks flush. "I don't know about that."

"Modesty doesn't suit you." His tone grows serious. "You saved my life. You saved Juzu's life. You saved hundreds of thousands of innocent people in Coppejj, and millions of others all over the continent. Vogul and Rhazaran gave you everything they had, and you overcame them. What will it take for you to accept that you're pretty damn amazing?"

"I didn't do it alone," I say. "Juzu helped. And Shytar. Mo, Ajjan, and Zhira. I couldn't have done it without any of them." I pause, resting my hand on his, hopeful, my touch posing a question that I'm afraid to learn the answer to. "And you."

He hesitates—one beat, then two. After an eternity, he laces his fingers with mine.

Warmth radiates through my chest. Yes, this is what I want. This is what I've been missing. I rest my head on his shoulder, resisting the urge to melt into him right here.

"Bexis," Xaleo says, his tone regretful... sad.

No. Don't you dare—

He unlaces his fingers and retracts his hand. His absence is a cold space that circles around my heart.

"Why?" I ask, my cheeks burning.

"I feel like the biggest fool in the world," he admits.

"Xaleo—" I touch his cheek, urging him to meet my gaze. His blue eyes shimmer in the lantern light. "What's wrong?" I press. "Talk to me."

He averts his eyes and stands, putting more distance between us as he paces the room. "I thought I was fighting them. I thought I was protecting you."

"You were—"

"No." His voice trembles with raw emotion. "I was the creature that tried to kill you. I still don't know how many of my memories about my past are real. I don't even know how many people I've killed." He holds his hands before him as if they're stained with blood. "Hundreds? Thousands? I'm a monster, Bexis."

"You are *not*." It physically hurts me to hear him say these things. "It was Rhazaran, using you through the nedozul—"

"I dream about them." His arms fall to his sides. "I see their faces and hear the screams. I taste blood, feel flesh between my teeth." He shivers and rakes a hand through his shaggy dark hair. "I'm grateful that you saved me, but I don't know where to go from here."

I rise to my feet and stand before him, shoulders squared. I place my hand over my chest. "I know how you feel."

His blue gaze catches mine, and a hint of recognition ignites there. But he shakes his head, the weight of despair heavy in his voice. "You deserve the world. Not a beast."

I purse my lips and pull the neck of my tunic down, showing him where the nedozul has changed from a sickly green to a deep obsidian black. Dark lines extend through my flesh, webbing up my neck and across my shoulders.

Xaleo exhales sharply. "Why does it look like that?"

"I have him," I say. "Lord Rhazaran is within me now. The Flame has him trapped where he can't hurt anyone ever again."

"That's why mine fell out." Xaleo places his hand on his chest as his face contorts in anguish. "You shouldn't have done that. You should have let me die and let Rhazaran die with me."

"It doesn't work like that." I cup his cheeks in my hands. The need to connect is almost overwhelming. "I learned something up on that rooftop. The man I thought was my father was a liar. He murdered my family when I was a child, and he kidnapped me, changed my name, and fed me a stream of lies about my past. He made me believe that I killed my mother—that I was the monster." I stare directly into his icy blue eyes. "You're the only person in this world who understands a fraction of what that's like."

He opens his mouth, closes it, then wraps his arms around me, pulling me close. "I'm so sorry."

I settle into the nook of his embrace, feeling his heart beating against mine. "I don't know what's going to happen to me now. Shytar said it could take some time for the Dark to corrupt me. Weeks, months, even years. But it's just a matter of time." I rest my head on Xaleo's chest, inhaling his warmth. "You say I deserve the world," I whisper. "All I want is you."

Xaleo's pulse quickens. "Bexis—"

"And when the time comes, you have to make sure I don't hurt people. Make sure I don't become the demon that destroys the world." I lick my lips. My eyes burn. "Promise me you'll do that."

"You make a compelling argument." Xaleo takes a deep breath. "Alright. You win."

"So you're not leaving?"

He shakes his head squeezing me tighter. "No, I'm not going anywhere."

"Good." A smile spreads on my lips. So much is still wrong, but at least this one thing is right. And it feels incredible.

"Bexis!" A girl's voice pipes up from the door, making me jump. Mo stands in the doorway. I barely recognize her. She's wearing a gold robe and a silver tiara. Her hair has been washed and brushed, and her face is clean. Her rosy cheeks glow, practically radiating health. She crosses her arms. "Nice room, coppe. And you *finally* took a bath!"

"Mo," I say, pulling away slightly from Xaleo. "What are you doing up here?"

"Magistrate sent me. Says no one is allowed to eat anything until you get to the banquet hall." Mo sticks out her chin. "Which is a real stupid rule."

"When has that ever stopped you before?" I chide her. "Don't tell me you've gone soft now."

Mo gives me a mischievous grin and extracts a cinnamon cake from her pocket, which she pops into her mouth. She beams and talks with her mouth full, spilling crumbs all over the floor. "What the Magistrate don't know won't hurt her!"

"Damn straight," Xaleo agrees, a grin plastered to his face.

"Come on." I rest my hand on her shoulder. "I'll head down with you, and we can steal some more."

Mo smacks her lips happily. "The High Radiant wants you to see the Aevem first."

I perk up at this. "Juzu is awake?"

She nods. "Been asking for you."

"Alright." A pit sinks into my stomach. I've been trying to see Juzu for days, but I still have no idea what I'm going to say to him.

"I'll go with Mo to the banquet hall, and you can meet us down there when you're done." Xaleo squeezes my hand. "And you better not ditch."

"I wouldn't dream of it."

Mo takes Xaleo by the arm and pulls him into the hall. "Come on, dragger, with rezzy we can steal a whole chicken!"

* * *

Juzu has a private room in the royal chambers, which has been crawling with guards. One of Zhira's first acts as Magistrate was to overhaul the city watch and replace all the officers and captains with her own Blackbone sergeants. They patrol the halls in force, wary of any sign of disloyalty in the White Keep. Nobody knows how far Vogul's influence had spread—how many of the followers believed in the cause versus simply being compelled by fear into treachery.

I'm grateful for the security, but it all seems a bit much. Vogul is dead. Without her and the Faceless Coven, there is no coup, no movement.

As I approach Juzu's room, Siras greets me at the door. The High Radiant wears a simple white cassock. Her black hair is combed and falling to her shoulders. Her cheeks have a healthy glow, but there are still bags under her eyes.

"Siras!" Relief floods through me. The last time I saw her, the Eyeless had driven her into a raving madness. She was throwing herself at an iron door like a wild bull.

She smiles and embraces me in a tight hug. "I was wondering when I'd get to see you."

"I'm so sorry," I stammer. "When I left you in the Sanctum, I didn't think I'd see you again."

"Me either." She pulls away but keeps her hands on my shoulders. "Honestly, I thought I was a goner. But I woke up, and the darkness had vanished, and I knew you'd succeeded." She traces a finger between her breasts where the feather pendant used to sit. "I'm so proud of you, Bexis."

"I couldn't have done it without you."

She smiles knowingly, then gestures to the door. "You're here to see the Aevem."

I nod. "How is he?"

"Smoking." Siras wrinkles her nose. "What else is new?"

I stifle a laugh. "That's gotta be a good sign though, right?"

"Why don't you see for yourself?" She opens the door and ushers me inside. The herbal scent of jalpe smoke hits me in the face as soon as I enter a plush royal bedchamber.

Juzu lies in bed, propped up by cushy red pillows. The table next to him carries a platter of fruits and cakes. He holds a goblet of wine in one hand, his pipe in the other. His legs are crossed, and he wears fuzzy pink slippers on his feet, his black fedora tilted at an angle on his head.

He beams as I enter the room. "Ah, there you are!"

I can't help but grin. "Here I was worried that you might die, and you've been in here drinking and smoking and having the time of your life."

"I can't complain!" He smacks his lips. "I feel like a plate of waffles smeared with syrup and raspberry jam." He sits up and places his wine cup on the table. "Thanks to you."

I step farther into the room, waving my arms to dispel thick clouds of smoke. No wonder Siras is annoyed. "Everybody's saying that lately. Like I saved the world all on my own."

He quirks an eyebrow, a teasing glint in the glowing silver of his eyes. "Didn't you?"

"No." I let out a frustrated sigh. "You guided me, protected me, believed in me. If it wasn't for you, we would all be dead. It should be you that they're honoring tonight."

"Thank the Saints it's not." He chuckles. "You're wrong, by the way. All I did was stand beside you, and I'm honored to have done it."

"You did a lot more than that—"

"Stop being ridiculous. Do you think Entaru defeated Rhazaran all on her own? Of course not. Her friends stood beside her and together they prevailed, just like you. You rose up when victory seemed impossible. You didn't give up on your friends. That's why you get a banquet and I get to smoke in my room without a certain High Radiant saying a word about it."

"Still, it feels wrong to be celebrating."

Juzu raises his pipe. "You have to celebrate when you can. Laugh while you can. Love while you can. Because we never know what tomorrow will bring."

He's right about that. My thoughts drift to Xaleo, to the moment we shared in my room. There's a lot to be grateful for. "So," I say, holding my arms to the side, "what happens now? When do we start Aevem training?"

Juzu takes a deep drag from his pipe. His brow furrows as he exhales a plume of yellow smoke. "I regret to inform you that your time as my ward has come to an end."

"What?" My stomach drops. "But why?"

"Because," he explains, his voice soft and comforting, "you're not destined to become an Aevem."

I touch the nedozul in my chest. "Because of the Immortal Dark?"

"No, it has nothing to do with that."

"Then why? Did I do something wrong?"

"Of course not." Juzu takes off his hat and places it on the bed, then swings his legs over the side so he faces me directly. "You're the descendant of Entaru. For two thousand years, the Khatori have trained Olezhi, Yawji, and Aevem. But the fourth order is the Shukon, the Shadow Dancers. I think it's time they returned, and I can't think of a better person than you to start it up again."

I pause, letting his words sink in. "But I'm not a Khatori. I barely know how to use resonance."

"Not yet. But you will. Besides, the shadow moon was in the sky for two entire days. There will soon be thousands of new trappers. Kids that will be hungry to learn from you, the Savior."

The Savior. "Do I even have time?" I ask. "Before the Flame kills me?"

"We can't predict what the world will bring to us. All we can do is live in the moment, plan for an ideal future, and hope that we're around to see it. The alternative is madness, and I'm not going to let that happen to you." He gives me a knowing smile.

I'm grateful for his words. For the past three days, all I could think about was the curse, and what would happen in the future. But now, Juzu has given me a mission, something to occupy my mind.

"I can't do it on my own," I say. "I don't know where to begin."

"You're not my ward, but I'm still here for you every step of the way." Juzu reaches to the nightstand and pours himself a fresh goblet of wine, then pours one for me. "It will be a wonderful puzzle!"

This sounds better than anything else I have planned, but a weight still lingers in my chest, something I can't ignore any longer. I shift on my feet, my hands restless at my sides. "There's something else I need to talk to you about."

"Anything." He takes a sip from his wine cup, his gaze steady, and gestures for me to continue.

I open my mouth, but the words stick. My stomach tightens, a flutter of nerves that makes it hard to breathe. This is stupid. It's Juzu. I have nothing to be nervous about, and yet—the weight of this revelation presses on my chest. I don't know how he's going to react. "Rhazaran... showed me things on the rooftop," I begin. "Things about my past."

Juzu doesn't say anything. He simply waits for me to continue.

I can tell from his expression that he doesn't know. Doesn't even suspect the truth. But how do I tell him something like this? I bite my bottom lip. "Lum Carro wasn't my father," I continue. "He wasn't even related to me. I was kidnapped as a child. My family was murdered."

Juzu blinks, his eyes lined with restrained horror. "Oh, Bexis..."

"There's more—" I take a deep breath. There's nothing to say but to say it. "Bexis isn't my name." I pause, hoping the meaning will sink in.

"I don't..." His brows furrow as he studies me, the silence extending between us. Slowly, his expression shifts from compassion to one of quiet skepticism. He places his pipe on the nightstand beside the bed, giving me his full attention. "What is your name?"

Suddenly, it's difficult to breathe. My eyes burn, and my throat tightens. "You really don't know?"

He exhales through his nose, his lips tightening as he shakes his head softly from side to side. "No," he whispers. "No, it can't be..."

A lump forms in my throat. My limbs are frozen, and all I can do is stand here in the middle of the room, exposed and vulnerable, my heart aching.

"What..." Juzu's eyes shimmer, his voice dropping so low I can barely hear him. "What is your name?"

In situations like this, words are useless things. I cannot speak, and even if I could, there is no way to convey the storm of emotions that swirl in my chest. So instead, I cross the room, picking up speed, and throw my arms around the man who plucked me from the shadows and brought me into the light. My guide. My teacher. My family.

"Dhaima?" Juzu embraces me, his voice hoarse and trembling. His body shakes with suppressed sobs. "Is it really you?"

"Yes." I press my cheek into his chest, feeling the steady beat of his heart. Strong, steadfast, and real. "I'm here."

"Oh, Saints," he breathes, shivering with silent tears. "Your mother would be so damn proud of you. *I'm* so proud of you."

No one has ever uttered words like this to me. They sink in slowly, taking root deep within my heart, a warmth that tingles under my skin—strange and unfamiliar, yet intoxicating. A validation I never knew I needed. My whole life, I'd thought I belonged on my own. I thought I had no family, no friends, and nothing to live for. But that was never true.

Despite the darkness that lives on the surface of all things, a sliver of light has always shone through just out of reach.

All I had to do was find it.

EPILOGUE

THE JOB IS SIMPLE. ENTER THE BLACK CRYPT UNARMED AND ALONE, locate the grave marked with a yellow ribbon, and dig up one of the bones. Apparently, this is the prize that will mark me forevermore as a member of the biggest crime syndicate in the world.

"And remember," Ajjan says as he walks me through the abandoned graveyard. "Don't let the skeletons touch you."

"Skeletons?" I frown, but my curiosity piques. This ritual has always been shrouded in mystery. Members aren't allowed to talk about it, and no one has told me anything beyond the bare essentials. "Nobody said anything about skeletons."

Ajjan rolls his eyes. "Where do you think bones come from, Bexis?"

"I had assumed that someone put them there for me to dig up—not that I was defiling an actual grave."

"I'm not allowed to say anything else." He stuffs his hands in his pockets as we approach the crypt—a square granite structure with tall columns that support a triangular roof. A layer of fine mist has settled around the rows of graves. Our boots squeal in the snow that fell through the night.

I scoff, my breath fogging in the moonlight. "Real helpful, Ajjan, thanks."

He pauses, glancing at me from the corner of his eye, then reaches into his pocket and takes out a silver flask. He uncorks it and takes a swig, then hands it to me. "For luck."

The gesture isn't exactly novel, and yet my reaction takes me off guard. My impulse has always been to say no—to keep my wits sharp, cold, and clear—but something seems different now. As much as I try to shrug it off, there's a weight to this moment. I'm about to throw my lot in with the Blackbones, to be ensconced in a community where I will always have a place. Not too shabby for a little orphan girl who grew up alone in the Slags, always looking out for herself, always on the outside looking in.

I swallow hard, the reality sinking in. I will never be on the outside again. Surely, such an occasion warrants a break from tradition.

"Screw it," I say, snatching the flask from his hand.

"Look at you." He raises his eyebrows, a grin spreading on his lips. "All grown up."

"Shut up." Hard liquor hits my throat and burns like starfire, but I force myself to swallow. I cough as the vapors sear into my lungs, making my eyes water. "Ugh. Hezha's fire, what is this?"

"It's actually called Hezha's Fire. Local brew."

I grimace. "Well, it's disgusting."

"It grows on you." Ajjan pockets the flask as we reach the base of the crypt. "Are you sure you want to do this? Once you go in, there's no going back."

"Yeah, I'm sure." A wave of apprehension ripples through me as I stop in front of the arched wooden doorway. This is stupid. After everything I've gone through over the past few weeks, entering this crypt is a trifle, and yet... anxiety flutters in my belly like a swarm of moths. "Alright," I say, steeling myself with a deep breath. "Give it to me."

"Suit yourself." Ajjan passes me a burlap sack to collect the bones, along with a small spade to dig them up. Then he takes a step back, leaving me alone before the crypt. "But I still think it's a mistake."

I hesitate before going in, a question hanging on the tip of my tongue. My friend gazes back at me, the moonlight hitting his face, mist swirling at his boots. He risked everything to help me, and I owe him my life. It's one thing for a trapper to face danger, armed with power and magic, but Ajjan had none of those things. He had nothing to gain, and everything to lose.

"Why did you stay?" I ask, resisting the urge to look at my feet.

His smile fades, just slightly. "What do you mean?"

"You had one foot out the door. Everything was lined up perfectly. You could be on the other side of the world right now, eating your weight in coconuts. But instead, you decided to stay. Why?"

He rubs the back of his neck, shifting his weight from side to side. "It's embarrassing, really."

"Come on," I press. "Tell me."

"Well." He licks his lips. "I realized that Emceni wouldn't be the same without you. And I guess I have some unfinished business in Coppejj."

I tuck a strand of hair behind my ear, a soft warmth bubbling in my belly. "You stayed because I needed you. Because you're my friend."

"No." He stares at the ground and kicks the snow. "I stayed because you're my family."

A wave of nameless emotion works through my chest. I have so much to live for. It pains me to think that I won't be around long enough to see them all grow old. I force the emotion down, grin, and punch Ajjan in the arm.

"Hey!" He rubs his shoulder. "Damn, girl, you punch like a walrus."

"I love you too." I plant a kiss on his cheek. "Now if you'll excuse me, I have some bones to dig up. Any advice?"

"Yeah. Don't let the skeletons—"

"—touch me. Yeah, I got it. Whatever that means." I climb the stone stoop. The magnitude of what I'm about to do rests easily on my shoulders now. Zhira has wanted me to join the Blackbones for more than five years, and today I finally do it. It's a clear demarcation—the old Bexis would cringe at the mere thought of committing to other people, but now, I can see the value in it.

It's good to have someone at your back when things get hairy, especially if that someone is a bloody criminal who doesn't mind getting their hands dirty. In fact, those are the best types of friends to have.

The arched door opens with a squeal, and I turn back before plunging into the crypt. "Ajjan," I say. "I'm glad you came back. I can't imagine this place without you."

"You've gone mushy on me." He takes another drag from his flask. "Go violate an open grave, and then let's go get drunk…"

He trails off as his gaze lifts upward to the sky.

"Ajjan?" I ask, following his eyes. "What—"

Light explodes across the heavens, blinding and brilliant. I sidle back up to Ajjan. Together, in silence, we watch a star streak across the night, trailing white fire in its wake. The ground rumbles beneath our feet. The trees sway as a strong wind whips the mist into a vortex.

"Bloody Saints," Ajjan mutters under his breath. "What's happening now?"

"I don't know," I whisper, my heart racing. The nedozul in my sternum begins to tingle, as fear blossoms in my heart like a winter rose. The star arcs southward, roaring and radiating a gold nimbus of flame that sets the sky ablaze.

"Whatever it is," Ajjan says, draping his arm across my shoulders and pulling me close. "It's beautiful."

Yes, it is beautiful. And terrible. But that's the nature of power and darkness. One cannot exist without the other.

I pry the flask from Ajjan's fingers, lifting it to my lips. This time, I don't balk as the whisky burns down my throat. This time, it feels good.

"What's that thing you said in the Sanctum?" I ask, my voice raw. "The reason that we're Blackbones."

"Bones to barrel," he whispers, "we've got no good sense."

"That's right." I turn away from the star, focusing my attention on the crypt and the job at hand. "And thank the Saints for that."

* * *

Dear, Reader

Words cannot express how grateful I am to you— this story would not exist without you. Immortal Dark is the culmination of nearly two years of my life. It carries no small portion of my heart, and having you here at the end means everything to me.

Every page you've turned, every moment you've spent with Bexis, Juzu, and Xaleo, has been part of a shared adventure that I will always cherish. Writing stories would mean nothing without you to breathe meaning into them. I hope you were able to connect and find yourself within these pages.

If you enjoyed the story, it would mean the world to me if you would take a moment to leave a rating or review on Amazon and Goodreads. Every review is a testament to our shared experience, a gift from you to me that I will always hold dear. And as an indie author every little bit helps!

Thank you so very much.
  With love, from the bottom of my heart.
  - Shermon

STAY CONNECTED

Hey there!

If you enjoyed Immortal Dark and want to keep up with my writing journey, I'd love to hear from you!

Use this QR Code to find my linktree.

From here, you can sign up for my newsletter to get the latest updates on new releases, promotions and bookish content. You can also check out my website, amazon page, and goodreads, or follow me on Instagram and TikTok for additional content.

Don't be afraid to pop in and say hello!
    I look forward to hearing from you :)

More books by Shermon Kodi

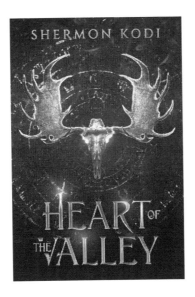

The Valley must feed, and Serena is next.

Raised to hold a lone vigil over a realm of spirits, Serena is the only one who can stop the Ghostorms and maintain the magic barrier that keeps the dark forces at bay. Though she knows it's her duty, she's terrified to leave the safety of her temple and the priests who trained her.

When her only friend is cut with a cursed blade, Serena has no choice but to face her fears.

She must journey through the Valley of Souls and embrace her destiny before it's too late. If she fails, the agents of evil will finally be freed from their prison, unleashing a new age of darkness upon the world.

Find Heart of the Valley on Amazon

MORE BOOKS BY SHERMON KODI

* * *

More Books by Shermon Kodi

The Rhor demands blood.

The demon lives in Tola's head, corrupting her thoughts and driving her mad. She is the ruler of the most powerful empire the world has ever seen, but she is a prisoner in her own mind. When she succumbs to madness, the Rhor will pass to her baby brother— the only person she truly cares for.

Tola will stop at nothing to prevent this from happening, but her sanity is crumbling. How much longer can she hold on? Is there a way to stop the Rhor for good, or will the cycle of possession consume her brother, as it consumed her father, and now consumes her?

Find Songs of the Rhor on Amazon

* * *

About the Author

* * *

Shermon Kodi is a legally blind YA fantasy author who finds inspiration in the quiet knolls of Chittenden County, Vermont, where the long snowy winters drive one to pair wool socks with moccasin slippers and curl up by the furnace with a pot of chamomile tea and a book about monsters in dark places doing dark things. Through his writing, Shermon seeks to explore the resilience of the human spirit, the tenacity of good people faced with hard times, and the relationships that light us up, make our hearts smile, and carry us through life's storms.

When he's not writing, Shermon spends most of his time thinking about writing.

He knows this is a problem—although, he contends, it's a good kind of problem to have. Occasionally, he'll break from his routines and really let go—sleep in till 7 AM, drink tea instead of coffee, read in the mornings, or plug in the '07 Strat and reminisce about the days when he dreamed of being a rockstar instead of an author.

He'll be the first to tell you: "No regrets!"

Life is funny like that.

END